Polly Parrett Pet-Sitter Cozy Mysteries Collection

Books 1-5

LIZ DODWELL

Liz Dodwell

Polly Parrett Pet-Sitter Cozy Mysteries Collection (Books 1-5)
Copyright © 2017 by Liz Dodwell
www.lizdodwell.com

ISBN 978-1-939860-28-6

Published by Mix Books, LLC

Table of Contents

FREE SHORT STORY OFFER

Join the in-crowd to be the first to know about new releases, specials and giveaways, and as a bonus receive a free short story.

Sign up to the Liz Dodwell newsletter here.

Doggone Christmas

A Polly Parrett Pet-Sitter Cozy Murder Mystery
Book 1

LIZ DODWELL

One

ALL I WANT FOR CRISTMAS IS TO BE A BUTIFUL PRINCESS.

"Well, that didn't work out," I thought ruefully as I looked at the childish note. "How old was I when I wrote that? Six, maybe?"

I glanced at myself in the dusty old mirror propped against a pile of boxes. I'd never been a pretty child but braces had taken care of the crooked teeth and color-in-a-bottle gave highlights to my otherwise mouse brown hair, but there was nothing I could do about my one green eye and one brown. Oh, I'd tried colored contacts but they were so uncomfortable and it seemed rather like stuffing your bra with socks: they had to come out eventually, so what was the point? Now, at 27, I was resigned to the fact that I was passably attractive, sometimes sexy but never beautiful.

I was in the attic of my mother's home, the family home in Maine where my two brothers and I grew up outside a small town with the improbable name of Mallowapple. Two years ago my parents had split up, leaving Mom angry and embittered. Seb and Keene, my brothers, and I had been trying since then to persuade Mom to get out of the rambling old farmhouse that she couldn't possibly maintain, and she'd finally agreed. That's why I was in the attic, freezing my you know what off on a really cold November day – just after

13

Thanksgiving - and making a start on clearing out thirty years of keepsakes while waiting for the realtor to arrive.

There was a sudden burst of high-pitched yaps mingled with a throatier bark. At the same time my mother's voice came from below, "Polly, he's here!"

"Coming!" I climbed down the attic steps then raced down to the first floor reaching the front door just as the man hit the bell, which caused the dogs to increase their volume and excitement.

"Enough!" I clapped my hands and gave 'the look' as three heads turned to me. Angel, a pitbull / Rhodesian ridgeback mix, Vinny, a miniature poodle and Coco, a toy poodle.

"Back!" I pointed to an old blanket on the floor and the trio obediently moved to it.

"Stay!" Then I opened the door.

The man standing there was nothing less than gorgeous. Close-cropped wavy brown hair, ice-cool gray eyes etched with laugh lines, and the most sensuous lips; he had a rugged air about him yet was dressed in a dark bespoke suit that had been tailored to complement his athletic frame, and a crisp white shirt, open at the neck.

Way to make an impression, Polly, I thought, feeling conscious of my dusty attic attire, no make-up and hair pulled into a severe pony tail. Still, I did my best to put on a brave face and smiled brightly at Mr 'Hottie.'

Unfortunately my dogs, though very obliging with the commands, 'Enough' and 'Back,' had never quite got the grasp of 'Stay,' and as the realtor reached out his hand to introduce himself, my mutts hurled themselves joyously at the stranger, knocking him to his back while they drooled and slobbered a welcome. The attaché case he'd been carrying flew from his grasp, the top popped open as it landed and the contents were strewn across the front porch.

"Leave it," I shrieked. "Off, off!"

The dogs totally ignored me and continued their ministrations on Mr. Hottie, who actually wasn't looking quite so hot right now as he struggled to regain his footing. I grabbed Vinny and Coco, one under each arm and, herding Angel, managed to shove them back in the house and close the door.

Thoroughly embarrassed, I turned my attention to the scattered papers, snatching them up and stuffing them back into the attache case, which I then held out to the realtor who was brushing dog hair from his expensive suit. I wondered if I should mention the streak of slobber down his left pants' leg but decided it might be better to just apologize.

"I'm so terribly sorry. They're not usually quite that boisterous. They must really like you."

He glared fixedly at me and, to give him his due, didn't flinch at my odd-colored eyes as most people did. Of course, he might still be in shock so I pressed gamely on. "You must be from the real estate company."

"And you must be Mrs. Parrett," he practically snarled.

"No, that's my mother, Edwina. I'm Polly Parrett."

When he remained silent I babbled on, "Um, well, come on in. You won't have to worry about the dogs any more. Now that they've met you they'll settle right down."

Still he said nothing, just raised his eyes a little, so I opened the door and led him inside.

Angel, Vinny and Coco were relaxing on various items of furniture and, as promised, paid no more attention to us, though Mr. Hottie glanced a little furtively at them. At that moment my mother wheeled herself in. Much to my relief she was in her best greeting visitor mode. "Hello. I'm Edwina, how nice to meet you."

This time, Mr. Hottie did show momentary surprise. *He didn't know she was invalided and in a wheelchair.* Taking her hand gently he responded, "The pleasure's all mine. I'm Tyler Breslin, Breslin Realty Associates."

"Oh, we were expecting a Mr. Woodford, not the owner."

"He's one of my associates. I usually only handle the upscale clients (*What a snot! Upscale? What were we? Worthless?*) but he had a family emergency and I didn't want to leave you in the lurch."

"How very kind of you. We're honored."

Honored? My mother never spoke like this. She was acting as if Breslin was practically royalty.

"Why don't we get down to business?" I piped up before the syrup got any thicker.

"Yes. My daughter is an excellent business woman. She has her own company, you know. She operates a pet-sitting service."

Breslin turned to me. "And I can tell you're uniquely qualified for that." The acid was positively dripping.

I gave my sweetest smile, deciding not to rise to the bait, mostly because I couldn't think of anything suitably snappy to say. "So Tyler, how should we proceed?"

Was that a slight twitch at the corner of his mouth? My God, perhaps the man could smile after all.

"Why don't you give me a little background information, then I'll take a look around the house."

So I explained that we wanted to find something small and manageable for Mom and hoped to get enough out of the old house to give her a decent nest egg. "We figured we should get the house professionally painted and cleaned but didn't know if we ought to replace carpeting as well. Everything is terribly dated and my brothers and I plan to help with the costs but funds are limited."

"You're on the right track but let me quickly check something here." Tyler got up from the chair in which he'd been sitting and stepped to the corner of the room. Bending over, he pulled up a corner of the worn old rug. "As I suspected, there are genuine hardwood floors under here."

The floors weren't the only thing he exposed. His butt looked like a shag rug with all the dog hair he'd picked up from the chair, though it was still possible to tell it was a sexy tight ass.

"Is that good?" my mother asked. *Of course a tight ass is…. Oh! She was talking to Tyler.*

"It's great. For a relatively small amount of money you can get the floors refinished and you'll immediately increase your home's value and appeal. Hardwood floors are really in demand right now."

Mom looked pleased and I was glad to see her in a good mood for once. While she waited for us downstairs I took Tyler on a tour of the old homestead – six bedrooms, three bathrooms, a peek into the attic, then down to the huge kitchen, old-fashioned morning room and the basement.

"You can see why Mom can't go on living here alone."

"I assumed you lived here as well."

"No, I need to be closer to my clients, so I have a small place in town. When Dad was still here we'd talked about him and Mom one day retiring to Florida and I would take over the house to create a pet boarding center. There are more than 10 acres here as well, you know, and a huge horse barn with several other outbuildings. Of course, they're all in need of some work now but I just can't afford it."

Sighing, I ushered Tyler back into the living room where Mom had set up a pot of tea with a few cookies and the bottle of sweet cream sherry that she always kept for special occasions. *Oh, no!* That bottle hadn't been used since before Dad left, it must have turned to vinegar by now. And I was sure Mr. Hottie was more of a martini man.

"Do sit down, Tyler, and have a cup of tea," Mom gestured to the hairy chair. "Or perhaps you'd care to take a little sip of sherry?"

Tyler didn't miss a beat. "Sherry would be delightful, Mrs. Parrett." Graciously he accepted the glass; I took mine with extreme trepidation. Together we toasted to a successful sale, then we sipped. The stuff was absolutely ghastly. I gagged, Mom simply didn't know better and Mr. Hottie smiled warmly at Mom and said, "Delicious."

While we sipped we discussed terms. Tyler urged that we not over-improve the property because we risked not getting the money back in a sale. He told us he would work up some comps and get back to us with a suggested sale price in a couple of days, then he stood to leave. The dogs sensed something was up and came to say goodbye. Surprisingly, Tyler accommodated them by scratching their ears and three tails wagged happily.

"Thank you," I said as I walked him to the door, "for being so nice to my mother and drinking that awful sherry."

"Your mother is a lovely lady who's had a really rough time. I enjoyed meeting her." His smile this time crinkled those laugh lines round his eyes. *Mr Hottie just went way back up in my estimation.*

Two

In the few minutes it had taken for me to see Tyler out, Mom had reverted to bitter mode.

"It's not fair that I'm being forced out of my home, especially with the holidays coming. If my disability money wasn't so paltry I could fix the place up. Your father should do something. It's his fault anyway that this is happening."

Oh, Lord.

My mother had given riding lessons and been a fairly successful competitor in show jumping until a fall left her paralyzed below the waist. It also left her angry and depressed. Unable to ever ride again she couldn't bear to keep her beloved horses or continue with her business. Dad was a trooper and took over the household chores along with the extra care Mom's condition required. Then the lousy economy caught up and he was laid off from the accounting company where he'd worked for years. He struggled to make ends meet by working as a private consultant but, with the loss of health care insurance Mom's incessant quibbling and ungrateful attitude became too much. He took off with the pharmacist who regularly filled Mom's prescriptions. Though I was hurt and angry at his abandonment at first, having taken over the role of caregiver I had come to sympathize. And to give Dad his due, the pharmacist wasn't some 20-something but a mature and intelligent woman.

Liz Dodwell

"Mom, we've been through this before. Dad signed the house over to you and it has a lot of equity. With the proceeds from the sale you should be able to live comfortably for the rest of your life." *And maybe my life will be a little easier. I won't have to spend an hour a day driving out here.*

"But it's our family home. There are so many memories." *She had a point there.* Then she started to cry.

I hated to leave her like this but I had a dog-walk to get to. Fortunately, at that moment one of my cats appeared and jumped on her lap. Cappy (short for Cappuccino because he had a strip of white hair above his mouth that looked like a milk mustache) resided with my mother. Actually, I had six cats but my little house in town was already maxed-out with pets so Lief, Ollie and Cappy stayed with Mom. So far it had been a perfect arrangement. My mother loved the cats' company and they had the run of the whole house. I was concerned how things would work when Mom moved though, and realized I hadn't mentioned that to Tyler. I'd have to give him a call.

Taking advantage of Cappy's distraction I hastily departed. I'd be back in the morning anyway, to help Mom get dressed. Five days a week she had an aide who came in to bathe her and get her ready for the day. The rest of the time it was mostly up to me, and tomorrow the aide was off. Seb lived 1,000 miles away; Keene's home was a two-hour drive from here but he and his wife tried to visit every other weekend and would stay overnight.

On the way to my house to drop off the dogs before my scheduled walk I dialed Tyler's number. It went straight to voicemail and I was annoyed to find myself a little disappointed that Mr Hottie himself hadn't answered. I left a message that we'd need a place where three cats would be OK then set aside all thoughts of real estate and got back to business.

Three

I'd enjoyed the dog walk. I don't do a lot of hands-on work these days but one of my team of six was on vacation this week so I was filling in.

Back in my home office (OK, it's the kitchen table) the time sheets were staring at me. I hated paperwork. One of these days I'd be able to afford an assistant to take care of such things; for now I just had to suck it up. I glanced at the clock. I should be able to finish by about seven, then I could reward myself with some of the pistachio gelato that was calling me from the freezer. Five minutes into my calculations the phone rang. I didn't recognize the number so I answered in my peppy work voice, "Pets and People, Too. This is Polly, can I help a pet or a person today?"

"Um, actually, I'm calling to help you." *Tyler!*

"Oh, hello. Is this the realtor?" *The realtor?* Why didn't I just say the man's name? Why was I a blithering idiot all of a sudden?

"Yes, it's Tyler." Emphasis on his name. "Is this a bad time?"

Get a grip, Polly. I took a calming breath. "Not at all. You saved me from a mountain of paperwork. At least, temporarily."

He laughed – I liked the sound.

"Polly, I got your message and I've found a couple of properties that might be of interest. Also, I've been running some figures that I'd like to go over with you. Do you think you might have a couple of hours tomorrow?"

"I have a really full calendar for the rest of the week. Let me look....."

"Great." He interrupted. "Then let's talk over dinner tonight. I'll pick you up at seven."

"Uh, um, well, I'm not sure...." Mr Hottie was asking me on a date?

"That's not a problem, is it? Strictly business, of course."

"Of course," I said coolly and gave him my address.

Annoyed at caving so easily to Tyler's imperious assumption that I'd be readily available when it suited him, I consoled myself with the fact that at least I'd get a decent dinner – and I'd make him pay! *Dinner! Oh, my god. Where would he take me?*

Tyler Breslin, CEO of Breslin Realty Associates did not strike me as a burger and beer type of guy and with my seriously limited finances that's about all I was familiar with. Hell, nearly all my clothes were 'pet' clothes – scruffy and comfortable gear that could handle dog drool or parrot poo. I didn't have a thing to wear amongst the country club set if we went somewhere swanky. For that matter, I was still in my dirty old dungarees and sweat shirt from Mom's attic and, beginning to panic, I realized I only had about an hour to get ready! And the house was a wreck!

I raced for the shower, shedding clothes on the way. Exactly fifty minutes later I was washed, coiffed and dressed in my only decent pair of black skinny jeans with a panther-print Lanvin top that I'd picked up for $100 in a consignment store a year before. For that price I figured it was a steal, though I really hesitated to shell out so much money. The fact that it was a charity store to benefit abused animals tipped the decision in favor of buying. If Tyler was really dressed up I figured I could tell him I assumed our 'business' dinner would be casual and suggest somewhere middle-of-the-road that would suit us both.

Just then the dogs' ears' pricked up. *Can't the man be fashionably late?*

I grabbed the papers off the table along with the clothes I'd strewn on the floor and hid them in the kitchen cupboards. Fortunately that was no problem as I only had a few cans of food and a couple of cracked coffee cups. As I stepped into my shoes there was a knock on the door.

"Just a minute," I yelled over the dog's barking.

I'd opted for three-inch heels. I'm only five two and Tyler must be at least six two so I felt I needed an advantage. Maybe it wasn't such a good idea, though. My life was spent running around in sneakers and the sudden thrust into the stratosphere had me a little wobbly. I tottered to the door.

Tyler stood there in old Levis, boots and a down jacket. As the dogs rushed out he was ready for them and got down on one knee to scruff their necks. From that vantage point his gaze moved from my feet, slowly up my body 'til he was looking directly into my eyes when he grinned mischievously.

"You might want to reconsider those shoes. There's a chance of snow tonight….. You look really great, by the way."

27

I didn't know whether to be annoyed or flattered so I just pirouetted on my stilettos intending to flounce away and let him see how good I looked in tight jeans. Only I'd forgotten everything I ever learned at my childhood ballet classes and my graceful pirouette became a klutzy lurch as my heel caught on the doormat and down I went. The dogs, of course, loved this new game and this time I was the one to be slobbered over.

"Are you OK?" I swear he was trying not to laugh.

Pink with embarrassment I shoved Angel away, "Of course I'm fine." *Like I do this all the time?*

Tyler leaned down, took hold of me under the arms and lifted me to my feet as if I weighed no more than a mouse. *Wow, he must really work out.* Then he picked something off the floor and held it out to me.

"My heel. It broke off. Now I'll have to wear flats."

"It's probably safer that way." And this time, there was no doubt he was laughing.

Four

Dinner was in a small Indian restaurant that had recently opened up in town. The aroma of warm spices was wonderful and the décor a sumptuous mix of dark woods, rich reds and golds. There were no chairs. Instead, the tables were low and flanked with even lower benches or surrounded with cushions. I was just thinking it was lucky I wasn't in three-inch heels when we were instructed to leave our shoes in a cubby near the entrance. *OK, then.*

Only a handful of tables were occupied and we were seated in a quiet corner where the lights were low. I figured that was good because I looked better in soft lighting but not so good if we needed to read Tyler's paperwork.

"Are you familiar with Indian cuisine?"

"Yes, well, no." My first instinct was to appear to Tyler as worldly and sophisticated, then in almost the same instant I remembered a date when I was just 16. My soon-to-be-ex boyfriend took me to a Mexican restaurant. Without realizing it I ordered the hottest thing on the menu and, with my girlish figure in mind, declined the rice that was normally served with it. I sweated like a horse and it took me an hour to choke down my meal. By the time I was done my hair was limp, my mascara unknowingly had run from my watery eyes and my dress was sticking damply to my back. There went that romance.

Tyler was looking a little puzzled at my response. "Why don't I order for both of us?"

"Good idea," I said.

"Do you like beer?"

Obviously my looks didn't shriek "Champagne."

"Yes."

"Then we'll both have Kingfisher beer and a pot of your fennel tea," he instructed the server. "We'll start with lamb kabobs and the cucumber, tomato and cilantro salad. For the main dish we'll have chicken biryani – medium heat. And please take your time. We don't want to be rushed."

Turning to me. "I hope you enjoy this. I spent six weeks traveling through India after college and I really came to love the food."

"It must be wonderful to travel. I've hardly been out of Mallowapple and I never went to college either." Since my attempt at dressing like someone that I'm not hadn't worked I figured it was better that I just be me. No point in pretending to be worldly or well-educated when I wasn't.

"College isn't all it's cracked up to be. Do you know how many highly educated people there are who can't find work in their field? I bet there are college grads who'd be glad to work for you right now."

"As a matter fact, there already is one." And next thing I knew I was telling Tyler how I'd always wanted to work with animals but hated school, so the idea of years of college just never appealed. I started as a dog walker, then people began to ask if I could help with other errands while they were at work or on vacation. Soon it was more than I could handle alone so I hired another person as an independent contractor. Now I had six contractors, all licensed, bonded and insured and operated a busy pet care and concierge service.

"What's next?"

"Eventually the pet boarding facility I mentioned to you before. Business is great but I've still got a lot of saving to do before I can afford a property."

"Well, I hope you'll come to me when you're ready."

I smiled wryly.

By the time our food arrived I'd learned that Tyler had taken over the family business when his dad took early retirement. He'd successfully expanded into commercial real estate and had more than 20 agents in his office. I wondered why he was bothering with our sale when he could easily hand it off to one of those other agents.

When I'd asked what he did for down time he'd looked puzzled. "Hobbies, sports, you know," I'd persisted.

"There's no time for play," was his response, and there I'd left it, thinking that explained his invitation to combine business with the necessary function of eating.

The meal was marvelous. Fragrant, moist and just spicy enough. While we ate Tyler told me he thought we could market the house for $300,000 to $350,000.

"That's terrific!"

"Before you get too excited, let me explain a couple of things. A house that large is actually harder to sell. You have more than 4000 square feet. Most people who are looking for something that size can afford a home that's new or completely modernized. And the outbuildings could be a plus – or not. They're not in bad shape but they do need some work and, again, a lot of people simply don't want to do that."

My elation was swiftly plummeting. "What do you suggest?"

"Stick with the original plan. Clean, paint and refinish the hardwood floors. That's still going to cost you about $15,000 but I can recommend people to do the work. On the other hand, if your mother would be happy in a condo then there are some newer properties, well under $100,000 and wheelchair accessible, that I can show you."

"OK, but what if the house doesn't sell?"

"It will sell. I'm giving you the worst-case scenario in the interests of full disclosure."

After that I felt rather deflated and Tyler obviously had no interest in me other than as a business prospect. *Why did I care? I hadn't even liked him at first.* But I did care. I was finding myself drawn more and more to him and I didn't like thinking of myself as the unrequited lover.

My mood picked up when we got dessert though. Something called Kulfi ice cream; amazingly light and sweet with my favorite pistachios and a hint of rose water. Yum!

Five

We were the last to leave the restaurant even though it was only nine. As we stepped outside, we realized why. Snow was falling heavily and it wouldn't be long before the roads were covered.

Tyler drove a Subaru Outback. It was turbocharged, all-wheel-drive and a smart choice for the sometimes rugged terrain where we lived and the bad weather we sometimes endured. We were parked a couple of blocks away in a covered area.

"I'll get the car and pick you up here," Tyler offered.

"No need. I can walk with you." *After all, I **was** wearing boots.*

As we neared the parking lot we heard raised voices coming from a nearby alley. Then very distinctly someone said, "Control that dog or I'll shoot him!"

That was enough for me. Without thinking I bolted round the corner yelling, "Don't shoot. Don't shoot."

Startled faces turned my way. A cop, legs wide with his gun in a two-fisted hold pointed toward an old man who had his arms round a large dog that was growling warningly at the cop.

The cop recovered first. "Get back, lady. This is police business."

I planted myself between the policeman and the dog. "Don't shoot. I can help."

"Lower that weapon!" It was Tyler, who'd followed me into the alley. His voice was so commanding that the officer looked confused. In a calmer tone Tyler continued, "I suggest you call for back-up and let's all behave reasonably about this."

"I don't know who the hell you think you are but you're interfering in a police matter." Waving his weapon at Tyler he ordered him to move over so that we were all bunched together. Then he did use his radio to call for help.

Behind me the old man was sobbing while still hugging his dog. He looked in his 70s though my guess was a hard life on the streets had aged him and he was probably closer to 60. And his dog was a she; a pitbull, more stocky than my Angel and not young, either. I hunkered down. "What happened?"

"He wants to take Elaine from me." *Elaine? Wonder who she was named after.* "She's all I've got. We've never been apart," and, in fits and starts, part of the story came out.

He'd rescued Elaine as a pup. Some kids had tied cans to her tail and were throwing fire crackers at her. Another pup was dead nearby with burns and cuts over its body. Rooster – that's the name he gave – chased the kids off. When he turned back to the pup, instead of trying to run off she came to him, cans and all dragging behind her. That kind of bond is not something that's ever shaken and, since then, Rooster and Elaine had wandered the country together, Rooster looking for work where he could, sometimes eating at soup kitchens and sneaking a few bites out to his friend. At night, sleeping wherever they could lay down together.

Apparently, the police officer, who looked like he'd be in his mid to late twenties and, I thought, was overly officious, had seen Rooster with Elaine checking dumpsters. He'd demanded Rooster's ID and address as well as Elaine's proof of ownership and rabies vaccination. When Rooster produced his identification and Elaine's vaccination record, the young cop told him he was still going to arrest him for vagrancy because he had no permanent address and Elaine would have to go to the pound. Rooster pleaded to be allowed to go on his way with his dog but the cop grabbed him to put him in handcuffs, at which point Elaine growled and the cop threatened to shoot her. Enter Tyler and myself.

At that moment the animal control vehicle pulled into the street. Tyler was standing in stony silence, his expression dark.

Rooster began to sob again. "Don't let them take her....please," he pleaded.

"I'm going to do everything I can to help," I promised him.

Five minutes later a heated argument was in force and I was at the center of it.

"Nobody has to go to jail and the dog doesn't have to go to the pound. How many times do I need to tell you, they can come home with me?"

"Lady, the old guy resisted arrest. He's going to jail and we're not leaving a dangerous dog on the streets."

"She's not dangerous," Rooster yelled and to prove it Elaine yawned, a dog's way of saying, "OK, time to lower the intensity level."

"There, you see," I shrieked, "How is that dangerous? Elaine is the sweetest thing ever." At which moment there was a loud blast on a horn.

"Who the hell is Elaine? Nobody told me another woman was involved."

We all turned. In our ire we hadn't even noticed that a second cruiser had arrived with the Animal Control vehicle. The man who spoke obviously had a few years' experience on the other cops and a good few pounds. *Maybe it was true about cops and doughnuts.*

"Rooney, explain!"

The first officer began to speak. When I tried to inject a few words the older cop glared at me. "Miss…?"

"Uh, Polly Parrett, and as I was saying…"

"You won't be saying anything unless you want to be arrested for obstruction. You'll get your turn later."

My jaw dropped. Then it dropped further when he turned to Tyler. "And what's your part in this, Breslin?" *They know each other?*

"We just happened on the scene, Sheriff," and briefly Tyler summed up the situation.

"Is that about right, Rooney?"

"Uh, yes sir, but ….."

"No buts. Here's what's going to happen. You're all coming down to the station to file a report. The dog is going to Animal Control."

"Noooo," wailed Rooster. "Run, Elaine. Go, go away." But the dog just cocked her head and looked confused.

"Rooster!" I said. "I promise I'll get her out and take care of her. She won't survive on the streets in this weather without you. It's better you let them take her for now."

"You promise you'll keep her safe?"

"I promise."

And with tears streaming down his face, Rooster lifted Elaine into the Animal Control van, whispering to her to be good, but as the van drove away we all heard Elaine's desperate howls.

Rooster was bundled into the back of a squad car while Tyler and I were instructed to follow them to the station. Once I was settled in the seat of the Subaru my righteous anger overcame me again. "I can't believe that Rooney was actually going to shoot Elaine."

Tyler hit the brakes and we skidded across the snow-slicked street almost hitting a fire hydrant 'til we ground to a stop against the curb.

"*You* can't believe he would shoot a *dog*? You nearly got shot yourself. What kind of a damn fool stunt was that to put yourself between a cop with an armed pistol – a nervous, inexperienced cop at that – and a snarling pitbull. Of all the stupid, dangerous ideas...... It's a damn good thing I called Sheriff Wisniewski."

"You called him?" I gasped. "Then you're responsible for Rooster and Elaine being split up."

"I'm responsible for preventing a bad situation from getting worse and maybe even for saving Rooster's and Elaine's lives."

Tyler's mood was beyond black by now and my own fury was redirected from Rooney to him.

"Saving their lives," I scoffed. "What are you? God?"

"Do you honestly think either of them could have survived outside tonight? Neither dog nor man are exactly young, and the temperature is going to drop into the teens."

"There are shelters!" I shot back.

"The shelters won't accept dogs and Rooster won't go if he can't take Elaine."

"Well, they could have come home with me."

Tyler sighed heavily and seemed to exhale his rage for he looked at me almost sadly. "You know it was already too late for that. And let's not get into the fact that you'd be taking in a total stranger, a vagrant you know nothing about, and a potentially dangerous animal."

My own anger had not yet deflated. "I'm not an idiot and I'm a good judge of character. Rooster is just a sad, old man who's been abandoned and ignored by cold-hearted people like you and Elaine is a sweet, loyal girl. They deserve better than this."

Tyler's lips tightened into a thin line and his jaw muscles clenched but he didn't respond. Instead, he rammed the car into gear and we fishtailed back onto the street and continued our way to the police station.

It took a couple of hours to give our statements and I wasn't allowed to see Rooster again. I wanted to reassure him about Elaine but was told I'd have to wait 'til the next day.

I was still mad as hell.

"Look young lady, I know you won't believe this right now, but I do sympathize. Thing is, I'd rather put a man behind bars for the night than be scraping up his dead body in the morning."

We were standing at the front entrance when Sheriff Wisniewski made this statement.

"My advice is to get home, get some rest and you'll see things differently in the morning."

Home? Rats! How was I going to get home?

"Do you have a number for a taxi?"

Wisniewski guffawed. "There aren't any taxis on a night like this."

"Well, what about a ride home in a squad car?"

He just looked at me.

"I'm taking you home." *Tyler!*

"I'd rather lie on a bed of nails and eat glass," I said in my best haughty dowager voice. To which Tyler responded by grabbing my elbow, dragging me out to the car and shoving me into the passenger's seat.

"Put your seat belt on," he hissed. "This is going to be a rough ride."

And it was. The road at times was completely hidden beneath the snow, which was rapidly freezing. A drive that normally took 20 minutes lasted well over an hour and it was only because of Tyler's skill at the wheel that we made it safely. Not that I would ever admit that.

Neither of us spoke the whole time. Not even when Tyler deposited me at my house then sped away, racing the wheels, the moment I closed the car door. And in that same moment I realized I'd left all the real estate paperwork in the file on the back seat.

Drat!

Six

Inside my head The Chipmunks were singing 'Pretty Woman.' It was really annoying and I couldn't get them to shut up. Then I opened my eyes. *Oh, right – the alarm.*

I'd set it early; I was on a mission today. I wanted to be at the county shelter when they opened at nine to spring Elaine from her prison and I had to stop on the way to check on Laurel and Hardy, a chatty pair of cockatiels whose pet parents were sunning themselves down in Florida.

My head felt like a bowling ball - I'd slept badly because I was so wired. As soon as I'd got in last night I'd called my mother to make sure she was OK. Thankfully the power was still on and she said everything was fine. I was keeping my fingers crossed that her aide would make it out there this morning.

With some difficulty I extricated myself from the bed. Ditto and the girls, Amber and Taz, my cats, didn't budge. Vinny and Coco looked up to see what the disturbance was then grunted and put their heads back down. Angel had her own bed – I rather envied her.

After a quick shower I dressed and headed outside to assess the situation. In the dark I could see that my van was iced-stuck to the driveway and the roads looked slippery as wet soap. In Maine we're used to rough weather and I figured with a little kitty litter I could rock the van out of the ice but I was concerned about the roads. The van is great for pets but not the most practical vehicle in this type of weather.

Mallowapple is a small town with a small budget so there was only one old snow plow to clear the streets; not that it would do much good with packed ice anyway. The pound was more than a 10 mile drive from my home but at least Laurel and Hardy were on the way.

By nine o'clock I'd made it to the shelter. I'd rushed to take care of my pets; the kitty litter had worked on the van; the cockatiels were in good shape and I'd crept along the roads at a max 20 miles an hour. I was feeling better about things as I reached to open the front door. Locked!

I checked my phone. It was just after nine so I began banging on the door 'til a harried-looking guy opened it.

"We're not open."

"It's after nine and I've come to pick up a dog."

"There's no-one here to help you. I'm just the overnight caretaker and my replacement should have been here an hour ago."

"Then I'll wait," I said, pushing past him.

"Suit yourself," he shrugged.

For the next hour I flicked through year-old copies of magazines that told me how to cook perfect pies, gave me pro tips for demolition and explained how I could sex up my love life. I was getting in to that last one when I heard, "Polly! What are you doing here on a day like this?"

Looking up I saw Dave Cartright behind the counter. We'd been at Mallowapple Junior High together; I used to help him with English grammar. He wasn't the brightest of the 'Mallowapples' but he was a sweet guy.

"Dave, I'm so glad it's you working today." And I told him Elaine's story.

As I finished speaking, he pulled out a file. When he looked inside his face creased into a deep frown.

"Polly, the dog was admitted as a dangerous animal. She can't be released. In fact, she's scheduled to be euthanized at noon."

"What! There's a mistake. Look again, please."

Dave shook his head. "I'm sorry, Polly."

"Wait. Who labeled her as dangerous?"

"Ummm. It's signed by Officer Rooney."

That scum!

"Dave, do you have the number for the county sheriff's office?"

Sheriff Wisniewski wasn't expected in 'til the afternoon. No amount of pleading with the desk sergeant could elicit a home number or any clue as to the sheriff's current whereabouts, nor was he listed in any phone directories. I was sick to my stomach with fear for Elaine. I figured the Sheriff was the only one with the authority to save her now and the last person who might be able to help me find him was also the last person I wanted to talk to – Tyler. For Elaine's sake I bit my tongue and dialed the phone.

"Hello, Polly." His voice was cold but at least he'd answered.

"They're going to kill Elaine," I blurted out and then promptly burst into tears.

Another agonizing hour passed with me pacing in the waiting room. After gulping out the story to Tyler he'd tersely told me would find the Sheriff, then hung up without further ceremony. Not another soul had entered the shelter; not surprising considering the weather and just fine by me - I didn't particularly want anyone to see me in my current state of angst.

"Polly!" Dave was back at the counter. "The Sheriff called." His face lit up. "He's rescinding the order to euthanize."

For a moment my heart stopped; I couldn't quite comprehend what I was hearing and then I burst into tears again – but this time, they were tears of relief. And of course, at that precise moment Tyler walked into the room. *Oh, God. He'll think I'm a weak crybaby. And I must look like hell.* I bawled even louder. Tyler looked astonished and Dave mutely held out a box of tissues. I grabbed a fistful and honked loudly into them. When I looked up I saw that Rooster was right behind Tyler. He was staring at me with an expression of utter fear and I realized he must think I was crying of grief.

"Rooster!" I sniffled. "It's OK, Elaine is safe."

"I'll go get her," Dave announced and while Rooster paced anxiously, I plopped weakly into a chair and Tyler stood stiffly to the side. None of us spoke.

A few minutes passed before we heard the scuffling sound of paws. Rooster stopped in his tracks and we all looked towards the door. As it opened, there stood Elaine. Man and dog gazed at each other for a split second and then all joy erupted. Elaine launched herself at Rooster. He went to his knees and held her to him, which wasn't easy because she was wriggling so much.

In my elation I forgot I was mad with Tyler. "How did you find the Sheriff?"

"He and my dad are both active in the VFW (Veterans of Foreign Wars)," he answered coolly. "I knew they had a board meeting this morning so I called down there."

"But what about Rooster? Did they just let him go?"

"He's out on bail."

"Bail? How could he get bail.....?" My voice faded away as realization dawned. "YOU paid his bail."

"Damn right he did." It was Rooster, standing with his hand on Elaine's head as she leaned against him.

Suddenly, I was starting to feel all warm and fuzzy toward Tyler again. "But what happens now? Where ....."

"Why don't we get out of here?" Tyler interrupted brusquely. "I still have a job to do and I need to get Rooster settled."

"Where are we going?" I asked.

"Tyler's letting us stay with him for a while," chimed in Rooster. "Fact is, if he hadn't offered us a place I'd still be in jail and my old girl would be stuck here." Turning to Tyler he continued, "And I'm going to find a way to pay you back, son. I've never taken charity in my life and I don't mean to start now."

Astonished, I looked at Tyler who was fidgeting uncomfortably. Damn, the man looked cute when he was embarrassed.

"And I'm grateful to you, young lady." Rooster turned to me. "Without you it might have been all over for Elaine. I'm really proud to know you." Now I was the one squirming with discomfort as I shook the hand he held out.

"Um, you're quite welcome," I mumbled. Then, more assertively, "And I'm coming with you. I want to hear everything that happened. In fact, why don't you and Elaine ride with me, Rooster? Then you can tell me your story." *And Tyler can't drive away leaving me behind.*

So off we went. Along the way I found out that Tyler had been at the jail with Rooster's bail when I phoned in panic. Tyler, he told me, didn't miss a beat. "He just took charge. Made some phone calls, made sure the right paperwork was done, then brought me over to the pound." *Hmm. Tyler's definitely decisive. I like that in a man.*

"He's also going to introduce me to his daddy and some others at the VFW. I'm a vet, too, you know - Vietnam. He says they can help people like me, but I'd be glad if they could just help me find a job."

"What sort of things can you do?"

"Well, in the air force I worked on the flight line. I'd been planning to go to college to study mechanical engineering when the war started. A lot of guys went on to college to avoid being drafted but I didn't think that was right, so I volunteered. Then a couple of years in, I got injured in a mortar attack. I was lucky, I just lost a bit of my jaw but they were able to rebuild it. Anyway, that was the end of the war for me. "

Rooster went on to tell me that his name was actually Washington Roosevelt. "I don't know what my parents were thinking, but at school the kids started calling me Rooster, and the name stuck." I also found out he married his high school sweetheart but started having flashbacks and, after a while, his young bride couldn't handle it and left. "I don't blame her," he said. "I could get pretty scary and apparently I struck out a couple of times and hurt her. I don't remember any of it but then I kept missing work at the local garage and they let me go. I was in my twenties and I didn't want to be a burden to my parents, so I hit the road."

"But that means you've been on the road for nearly forty years!"

"It hasn't been all bad. I'd get work here and there, stay in shelters, met some really good people along the way but then I got beaten up by a gang of teenagers and after that I couldn't use my left arm properly and I'll tell you, I was thinking it was time to end it all. That's when Elaine and I found each other. She needed me and I guess I needed her."

I was so appalled I simply didn't know what to say but by then we were pulling into Tyler's driveway. I'd rather expected him to be in the town center in a stylish condo. Instead, we were on the outskirts of Mallowapple and the home before us was a rustic-looking ranch with a wide front porch. I knew the area; I had clients nearby and all the homes were on five to 10 acre lots. Behind the house it was fenced and I wondered if Tyler had a dog. My question was immediately answered when a big brown dog came bouncing out of the house. He had huge, floppy ears, a somewhat crinkly face and the longest legs you can imagine.

Excitedly the dog greeted us all, including Elaine who sat placidly accepting his ministrations.

"His name's Frank," Tyler offered, "after an uncle he reminds us of. We think he's a great dane / bloodhound mix."

We?

I looked back toward the house. Standing in the open doorway a woman waved. A *young* woman. From this distance I couldn't really tell what she looked like but I was sure she must be pretty. How could I have been so stupid? It never occurred to me that Tyler was married.

"Let's go on in," said Tyler

"Actually, I think I'd better head back. I, uh, should check on my team and make sure there were no problems with the weather and stuff." I scuttled toward my car. "'Bye Rooster. I'll catch up with you later."

"Polly, wait!" It was Tyler. "Let me get that file for you so you can look it over with your mother."

I raised a hand in acknowledgement – I wasn't sure I could trust my voice – and got in the van. A few moments later Tyler returned with the papers. I wound the window down and took them, willing my hand not to shake and keeping my gaze averted.

"Are you OK? You don't look too good."

"I'm just cold." And to prove it, I cranked the heater as high as it would go.

"Let me drive you back home. In fact I'll drive your car and have Suzette follow in my car." *Suzette! Of course she'd also have a pretty name.*

"No! I'm all right." Then I made the mistake of looking directly at Tyler. The expression of genuine concern on his face was the final straw. I simply couldn't help myself and I burst into tears – again! Fumbling for the stick shift I managed to put it in reverse so I could back out onto the road.

"Polly. Polly! Stop! What's wrong?"

I could only shake my head as I came close to knocking down the mailbox, but I managed to turn the van and fishtail away, leaving Tyler standing alone in the driveway.

Seven

Someone had pulled little wooly socks over my teeth in the night. At least, that's what it felt like. Talk about dry mouth. I'd made it back from Tyler's, checked with all my sitters to be sure everything was OK, taken care of my own 'zoo,' then poured myself a supersized glass of the only booze I had in the house – a bottle of homemade blackberry brandy, a gift from a client. It was sweet and syrupy and I'd cut it with root beer. Looking at the bottle this morning I saw I'd consumed more than half of it. No wonder my stomach was doing back flips, and the sugar rush it had given me kept me awake for most of the night. Serve me right for acting like an idiot over a guy I hardly knew.

I guzzled down about a gallon of water while the dogs took care of business in the back yard, and prayed none of my sitters would cancel out today. I had a really great crew but things sometimes happen. You know how it is.

Ditto was rubbing around my legs to remind me I had important things to do, like getting his breakfast.

"You'll have to wait a bit, buddy. I need a shower first."

I dragged my carcass to the bathroom, turned the water on hot and let it beat down over me. Of course, that's when the phone rang. I considered ignoring it but it could be a pet emergency. Swearing under my breath I turned off the water, wrapped a towel around me and raced to grab the thing before it stopped.

"Yes, this is Polly."

"Polly, it's Tyler." *What the hell?* It wasn't even seven yet.

"Is something wrong?" It couldn't be good if he was calling this early.

"Rooster's been arrested."

The shock silenced me. Had I heard right? That didn't make sense.

"Polly! Polly, are you there?"

"Did you say Rooster was arrested?"

"The police turned up late last night. They had an arrest warrant for murder."

I simply didn't know what to say. Finally I managed to blurt out, "Murder. But who was killed?"

"A body was found in one of the dumpsters where we found Rooster. As far as I know it hasn't been identified."

"This is insane. Where's Rooster now? Why didn't you call me when this happened?" "When was the body found?" I knew I was babbling but I couldn't seem to stop. Then another thought hit me. "What about Elaine?"

"Elaine is still at my house; she's fine. I did call you, three times, and you have three messages on your voicemail that you obviously haven't checked yet." *Oops, there I go with my big mouth again.* "The body was found late yesterday afternoon, when the trash was being picked up. And Rooster is being held at the sheriff's department until a vehicle can get through to take him to county jail."

"What can we do?" Indignation was beginning to rise in me. "We can't let him be railroaded like this."

"Polly," Tyler's voice was weary, "I've been up all night, I'm still at the station and there's nothing else I can do right now. I'm going home to get some sleep and then I'll be able to think more clearly."

"You can't just abandon Rooster like that."

I heard a sharp intake of breath. "Do you *never* stop? Where were *you* all night? Tucked up in bed and fast asleep, I suppose. And is it at all conceivable that you could believe Rooster just might be guilty? Keep in mind we really don't know him, and he *was* hanging round the dumpster where the body was found."

No, it wasn't conceivable that Rooster was a cold-blooded killer but I bit back the sharp retort I was about to make as I heard my mother's voice in my head, *Once spoken, can't be mended.* Tyler didn't deserve my sharp tongue. Without him Elaine would be dead and it's true, he was there for Rooster last night while I was crying in my blackberry brandy.

"Tyler, I'm sorry. This has been such a shock I'm not thinking clearly. Look, I have a few visits to make this morning. Could we meet later and perhaps between us we can work something out? And let me know if you need help with Elaine. I can go and walk her or even keep her with me."

"We can get together at my office, if that's OK with you? I've already left a message for my attorney so I should have something from him by then. And don't worry about Elaine, my sister will look after her."

53

Sister?

"Uh, that would be Suzette, is it?"

"Sure. She was disappointed you didn't stay yesterday. She wanted to meet you."

"Oh, well, another time." Suddenly, I was feeling a whole lot better.

Eight

We were in the conference room at Tyler's realty office. On the speakerphone Tyler's attorney was talking. "I've contacted Zill Granger and he's agreed to talk with Rooster, but don't assume that means he'll take the case."

"Who's Zill Granger?" I wanted to know.

"He's the best criminal defense attorney in these parts; I only do corporate. Granger will take a look at the evidence and then contact you later. And, Tyler, you do know Granger is pretty expensive?"

"Let me worry about that."

I gave Tyler a grateful look. He was turning out to be a real prince.

"OK. Just wanted to give you a heads-up. I can also tell you that Rooster will be moved this afternoon at two and Granger will meet with him at county."

"Any word on the murder victim?"

"As I'm not the attorney of record the authorities wouldn't give me anything more. You'll have to wait on Granger."

The lack of information was really frustrating me. "When will we be able to see Rooster?"

"Again, I don't know. My advice is to let Granger do what he does best and then you'll be able to make better-informed decisions."

"Right, thanks Fred." Tyler was bringing the conversation to a close. "I appreciate you getting on this so quickly. And send me your bill personally, not to the company."

"It's on me. Your family has done me enough favors over the years and this was nothing much."

With that, we hung up.

Vinny was sitting in my lap while I absent-mindedly scratched his head. Whenever I could I brought the dogs with me and it hadn't occurred to me until I got to Tyler's office that it might not be a good idea. It was too cold to leave them in the van but Tyler had no problem with me bringing them in. In fact, he said he sometimes brought his own dog to work. He'd even lifted Coco up and was now cradling her like a baby, which she absolutely loves.

"Look," I said, "you shouldn't have to foot the bill for a lawyer. I don't have much but I can chip in something." It would have to be an advance on my credit card but I didn't mention that.

Tyler's mouth raised in a crooked smile. "Let's just see how it goes. Meanwhile, I have a business to run and there's nothing else we can do for Rooster right now."

I can take a hint when I have to, and I really needed to get out and check on my mother. The aide hadn't been able to make it out there this morning so mom had to get dressed as best she could. By now she'd probably be in a really foul mood. With luck the dogs would cheer her up. It's hard to be mad when three lovable mutts act like they missed you more than anything in the world.

The drive took longer than usual with the roads still really slick. I took the opportunity to check in with all my crew and was relieved to hear no problems. By the time I pulled up to the house it was nearly two and I was starving. I hadn't felt well enough to eat breakfast and had skipped lunch, too.

The dogs leapt from the van in joyous abandon and bounded through the snow drifts. It would do them good to run around for a while so I steeled myself to deal with my mother and stepped into the house.

Mom was at the window with Cappy on her lap, and she was laughing! I'd practically forgotten that sound; it had been so long since I'd heard it.

"Mom?"

"Come and look. Vinny and Coco are being stealth dogs."

Puzzled, I looked outside and realized what she found so funny. Angel was looking for the two white poodles, but they'd figured out all they had to do was stay still, cloaked in the snow, and she couldn't see them. In fact, if Mom hadn't pointed out the two pairs of eyes peeking through the drifts I would never had known they were there. I laughed with her and it felt good for once to be sharing a happy moment. And before long I found myself telling her about Rooster and Elaine, and Tyler's part in the affair and even about my confused feelings for him.

"Tyler is a nice young man. I knew it the first time I saw him. And he's right about this Rooster character; you really don't know him at all. Remember, a man has been murdered."

"Mom, I'm telling you, Rooster is a good guy. Anyone who can love a dog the way he loves Elaine couldn't be a killer."

"Polly, even some of the worst criminals have loving relationships with pets. I'm not saying Rooster is a criminal, but I am asking you to keep an open mind. You've done all you can for now so, please, let the police and the attorney handle things."

There was no way I was going to let the police bungle things up and I was about to say so, but the look of concern on my mother's face made me swallow the words and I meekly agreed, while keeping my fingers crossed behind my back. My mother knows me well, though, and she sighed deeply and said, "Well, at least promise you'll be very careful."

Grinning, I kissed her on the cheek and for the next hour took care of a few chores around the house, while the dogs came in and settled themselves round the wood stove in the kitchen. When I was ready to leave I found Mom again at the window.

"I'll be off now."

She turned and gave a wistful smile. "I was remembering how much I loved Christmas here when you and the boys were little. We'd have lights around the porch and in the trees outside, and your dad would climb up on the roof and stamp around while I jingled bells in the living room, and…."

"…and we were quite, quite sure it was Santa."

"It was lovely, wasn't it? To gather pine cones and branches and wrap them in big, red bows to decorate the house. I'll miss all that when I have to leave here."

"But we haven't celebrated Christmas here in years."

Mom sighed. "It still always meant so much to look at the mantle over the fireplace and remember the stockings hanging there. And in my mind I can see you, when you were five, sitting by the rocking chair as you unwrapped that stuffed toy rabbit with the red hat and blue bow tie."

"Mr. Beanie," I said. *And I still had him.* "But I so wanted a real bunny."

"Well, I think you've made up for it since then."

I smiled. "Yes, I have."

Nine

Mom's words stayed with me as I drove away later. The farmhouse had been a wonderland of merriment for many Christmases. As a small child I'd been awestruck by the miracle of presents under the tree. In later years it was the gathering of our happy family wrapped in love for each other that seemed miraculous. By the time I was twenty – and Mom was in a wheelchair - it was a miracle if we could spend Christmas day together without Mom's self-pitying absorption dragging us all down to a level of petty bickering.

I made up my mind that I would persuade my brothers to help me bring the magic back home for one last Christmas. We had nearly three weeks to get things together and all the old decorations were still up in the attic. Maybe it would help lift Mom's spirits.

Feeling pretty festive myself, I hummed along to the seasonal tunes playing on the radio as I drove. There was one quick stop I needed to make – my nemesis, Pookie Pie. Pookie was a large, fluffy gray feline of indeterminate origin and sociopathic tendencies. His owner, Bob, doted on him and believed him to be the sweetest creature in all the world. If that was the case, then Pookie used up all his sweetness on his loving pet-parent and saved his ugly, sourpuss self for the rest of us.

Once a week, Bob, a retired librarian, took a day-trip out of town to visit his ailing sister. Truth to tell, Pookie didn't need a visit, but it made the over-anxious Bob happier to know his beloved was being checked on. I didn't think I should inflict 'his nastiness' on any of my crew, so I always took care of Pookie myself.

I trotted up to the front door, key in hand, unlocked it and pushed it inward. A one-inch gap opened before the door came to a jarring stop. *What the…?*

Tentatively I pushed a little harder. Nothing. I put my eye to the gap and swore. *Pookie!*

Bob had an antique hall stand just inside the doorway. It had drawers in it. One of the drawers was open and blocking the doorway. Sitting in the open drawer was Pookie.

Honestly, I swear the bloody cat knows when I'm coming. How he got the drawer open I had no idea. The stand was mahogany and the drawer was heavy. I just had to figure how to get it closed.

It was freezing cold so I jumped back in the van for a while and turned on the heat. The dogs merely wagged their tails at me while I wondered if I could get my hand far enough through the crack in the door to ease the drawer closed, finger over finger. Nothing else was coming to me so I figured I'd give it a try.

Back at the door I peeked in again. Pookie was still sitting there. "Shoo! Sssst! Yip!" I made a variety of noises and banged on the door to get him to move. He weighed more than twenty pounds, for cripe's sake. He casually lifted a paw and began washing it.

"You…….!" *Relax Polly. He's just a cat.*

Forcing my left hand through the gap I got two fingers under the drawer and attempted to lift and close it a little. Have you ever tried lifting thirty pounds with two fingers? I made about a quarter-inch headway when there was sharp sting in my forefinger. With a gasp I yanked my hand out. That little so and so had clawed me! Sucking the blood and nursing my wounded dignity at being bested by a cat, I trotted back to the van to look for an adhesive bandage.

Now what?

I hated to admit defeat and call Bob. Not that I wanted Pookie on my roster but I didn't want to let Bob down, either; his visits to his sister were really important to him. With a sigh I headed back to the door and banged and yelled again, to no avail. I broke a twig off a bush and tried to shove it through the door to poke him. The twig snapped, Pookie looked me right in the eye, yawned and curled up in the drawer, his back to me.

"Aaaaaargh!" I screamed aloud.

"Step back slowly, turn around and keep your hands where I can see them."

The voice scared the bejeezus out of me, so of course I jumped around with arms in a defensive position, only to see Officer Rooney before me, legs apart and hand on his holstered gun.

"Holy cow, what are you doing?" My heart was racing.

"I'm the one who should be asking that question."

"I come every week to take care of Bob's, Mr. Stanton's, cat. Why are you here? Has something happened to Bob?" A sense of alarm was beginning to set in.

Rooney ignored my questions. "Looks to me as if you were trying to break in. All that banging and shouting."

Moron. "If I was trying to break in would I make a lot of noise?" I grit my teeth, took a calming breath and spoke slowly. "Look, I'm a pet-sitter. I take care of pets. Here are the house keys." I held them up. "The door is stuck because the cat opened a drawer and I was yelling to get him to move."

Rooney's face showed disbelief and I had to admit, even to myself that sounded pretty strange. Thankfully, Bob chose that moment to pull into the driveway. Ignoring Rooney, he came straight to me. "Pookie?"

"Everything's fine, Bob. Pookie's up to his tricks; he's blocked me from getting in."

Bob laughed out loud when he heard the story. "That's my Pookums. I should have let you know there's a kitchen door key hidden in the back." *If only.*

Officer Pinhead was dismissed, though not before he got in a last word about disturbing the peace, and Bob and I went into the house. Pookie immediately morphed into a sweet, lovable creature while Bob explained he'd tried to call to tell me he'd be home early. "It kept going straight to your voicemail. You didn't need to come, Polly. I'm sorry." I pulled out my cell and looked at it. The battery was dead. *Oh, well.*

Ten

Back in my car I plugged in the phone and saw there was a message from Tyler. Granger was taking the case. *Yes!*

Of course, I called Tyler back straight away. Turned out Granger not only felt he could help Rooster, he was taking the case pro bono. He'd looked into Roosters background and was impressed with his service and disgusted that he'd pretty much been abandoned afterwards.

"Granger is an ex JAG lawyer."

"JAG. What's that?"

"Judge Advocate General's Corps. It's the legal branch of the military," Tyler explained, "so he has a soft spot for veterans."

"That's terrific. When can we visit Rooster?"

I heard Tyler take a deep breath. "We can't." Shocked, I waited for more. "Only family members are allowed."

"That's bull. Rooster doesn't have any family. Can't we just say we're his niece and nephew or something?"

"It wouldn't work. There's a vetting process, which takes weeks anyway. Look, I'm as bummed as you about this. Why don't we get together and I'll fill you in on everything? There's something else I want to talk to you about as well." *Like, maybe, I'm crazy about you?* "Are you home?"

"On the way."

"I'm only a few minutes from your place. I'll meet you there."

Not again. Here I was in grungy old dog-walking duds, without a scrap of make-up on. I sighed. I was never going to make a good impression on the man.

By the time I got home Tyler was already there. As we stepped inside I glanced around and breathed an inward sigh of relief – it didn't look so bad after all. As long as he didn't go in the bathroom where I had freshly washed bras and panties hanging over the shower rod it would be OK.

"Do you mind if I use your bathroom?"

Oh no! "Um, if you can wait just a couple minutes, I'm pretty desperate myself." *And that's no lie.* Not waiting for a response I dashed in the room and slammed the door shut. Snatching the undies down I looked wildly around for a hiding place. The medicine cabinet was the only thing with a door and it was too small. I'd have to stuff everything behind the towels on the shelf.

Reasonably satisfied my intimates were out of sight, I fluffed my hair, groaned at the bags under my eyes and casually exited.

While Tyler did his thing I cleared some space at the dining table, which doubled as my desk, and did my best to find a pose that said sexy, yet confident but was probably more desperate and pathetic. None of that mattered anyway when Tyler came out holding my best pink bra on his finger. "I needed a towel........uh..." He couldn't say any more because he was obviously trying really hard not to laugh. With delicate precision I removed the garment from his hand, headed into the bedroom and threw it down, stuffing my hand into my mouth and giving a silent scream. That done, I plastered a smile on my face, went back to the table and resumed my pseudo-sexy pose. "So what did you want to talk about?"

Immediately, Tyler became serious.

"Elaine isn't doing so well. She won't eat and I'm worried about her. She's really pining for Rooster."

"Damn, we should have expected that. Is she at least drinking water?"

"She just lays around and shows no interest in anything. Suzette even cooked chicken for her but she didn't give it a look."

"OK, let's not panic. Here's what to do. We need an item of clothing or something with Rooster's scent on it that we can give her. Without alarming Rooster, let's find out what her favorite food is. I assume we can still talk to him on the phone?" Tyler nodded. "It may be she's never liked chicken."

"A dog that doesn't like chicken!"

"You'd be surprised. Three of my cats won't touch it; they only want cheap commercial cat food."

Tyler looked skeptical.

"How many kids do you know who would eat spinach and fish rather than a Happy Meal?"

The light bulb went on. "Oh, yeah," Tyler said.

Soon we had a plan of action. Tyler would ask the lawyer to bring us a used shirt from Rooster so Elaine could have something imprinted with his scent. Meanwhile, we'd offer hot dogs – that always worked with my gang. For good measure, I'd give her some fluids. I always kept an emergency

IV bag on hand, with a boost of B vitamins. "When do you want to do this?"

"Now would be good."

We agreed to ride together then Tyler would bring me home later. Snow was falling again and his Subaru would handle it better than my van.

We entered his house through the kitchen door and were met by the aroma of fresh baked bread. A slender young woman was chopping vegetables at a butcher block counter. Her hands moved with speed and precision and when she saw us she wiped them down the front of a cute, vintage-style striped apron. She smiled and stepped toward me, hands out in welcome. "You're Polly. Oh, I'm so delighted to meet you at last."

I really felt she meant it, and before I knew what was happening she put her arms around me and gave me a sisterly hug.

"Tyler talks so much about you." *He does?* I wasn't sure if that was good or bad, but I willingly allowed myself to be drawn into the warmth of Suzette's personality.

"I expect you're here for Elaine." She gestured toward the corner where Elaine lay on the floor, showing no interest in us whatsoever. "We got her a big, plush doggy bed but she won't use it."

"She's spent most of her life sleeping on the ground. Eventually she'll try the bed and then I bet she won't want to get out." I hoped I knew what I was talking about. "Anyway, let me see what I can do with her."

I went to her and crooned over her for a while. She gave me a look and the slightest flick of her tail, which I took as a good sign. Perhaps she remembered me. She was definitely a little dehydrated, though, so I hooked up the IV and allowed the fluids to do their work. "Let's try her with some hot dog."

Suzette handed me a bag. "They're all beef."

I broke off a piece and waved it under Elaine's nose, then touched it to her lips. She instinctively licked her mouth so I offered the piece to her. She nosed it a little and licked it, then lay her head down again with a sigh.

"Oh, I thought she was going to eat it." Suzette was disappointed while, Frank, Tyler's mutt, looked expectantly at me, so I tossed the piece to him.

"Don't feel too bad," I said to Suzette, "she showed some interest and that's encouraging. I don't suppose you have any peanut butter, do you?"

Tyler, who'd been standing back reached into a cupboard and brought out a jar. "Here."

"Keep it for later. It might stress her if we try and force anything else on her right now. Give her a couple of hours then put a little on her nose. She'll automatically lick it off and, with luck, it will spark her appetite."

"You can do that after dinner. You're staying to have spaghetti with us." *I love spaghetti.*

I mumbled all the usual things about not wanting to be a bother, while my taste buds were screaming, 'Shut up, you idiot.' Thankfully, Suzette was insistent, and I spent a truly pleasant evening with brother and sister. They were obviously very close.

"When he heard the snow storm was heading our way, Tyler insisted I come and stay with him. He seems to think I'm not capable of looking after myself." She smiled fondly at him.

"Hey, that's what big brothers are supposed to do."

"The good thing is," Suzette explained with an innocent look on her face, "then I get to meet the women he likes."

I felt my cheeks begin to burn and Tyler hurriedly changed the subject by telling me that Suzette also worked for the family business, handling the finances and other paperwork.

"Most of the time I'm able to work from home," she said. "In fact, as long as I have my laptop and cell phone I'm good to go anywhere."

Suzette wanted to know about my business. I had plenty of funny stories to tell and we shared a good few laughs before the meal was over.

I managed to get Elaine to lick a couple of blobs of peanut butter from her nose, but she would not be persuaded to eat anything else. At the end of the evening, though, she stood up and began to whine, then pace around in an agitated manner.

"What's wrong?" Suzette was alarmed.

"Probably the IV fluids are making her want to pee," I said. "I'll put her on a lead and take her out."

"I'll do it." Tyler stood. "I need to let Frank out as well."

"I'm quite impressed that Elaine would ask to go out," Suzette said. "I wouldn't have thought she'd be house-trained."

"More likely it's imprinted on her to go in the outdoors. She just wants to do things the way she's always done them." *And she is a really good girl.*

By the time Tyler drove me back there was another inch of snow on the ground: soft vanilla cream on top of hot chocolate popped into my mind. Mallowapple residents took the holidays seriously and many houses were alive with strands of colored lights, chubby snowmen in the front yards and a good few Santas hanging out of chimneys. It was enough to make any cynic feel optimistic. If you're a Christmas lover, like me, you can believe that wishes *will* come true. So, silently, I made a wish that Rooster and Elaine would be together again by Christmas day.

Tyler insisted on walking me to the door. I'd like to think it's because I inspired his gentlemanly spirit, but I suspect it's because he was afraid I'd fall and hurt myself and then he'd be stuck with me for a while. Anyway, at the door he let go my arm and I cursed myself for not hanging mistletoe from the lintel. So I was surprised and excited when he leaned toward me – *he's going to kiss me!* – and gave me a chaste kiss on the cheek. *Rats!*

Eleven

The next morning was business as usual. One of my crew had slipped on ice and hurt her elbow. She was on the way to get it X-rayed; meanwhile, I'd have to pick up her visits.

I was out the door at 7.30. At 12.30, weary and very hungry – there had been no time for breakfast – I found a parking spot near Bennie's Diner and trudged inside. The diner was an institution, famous for its Mallowapple meatloaf. As far as I knew, there was actually no apple in the meatloaf, nor was there a Bennie. In fact, no-one knew who Bennie was. The current proprietress of the establishment was Nita, a middle-aged, motherly type who knew more about town gossip than the women who hung out at the Combing Attractions hair salon.

Bennie's always did a steady business but I got lucky and scored an empty window booth. The diner was only a few doors from the Indian restaurant where Tyler and I had eaten on the night we met Rooster, which meant it was also close to where the body had been found.

Nita herself came to get my order.

"Well, hi, hon. How ya doing? I hear you got yourself mixed up in a murder. What happened?"

There's nothing subtle about Nita's insatiable desire for scandal. I tried to deflect her interest.

"I'm really in a rush, Nita. Can I get my order in and then maybe we can chat if I have time?"

"I already ordered the meatloaf for you, and Cindy's bringing coffee. We'll have a few minutes before your meal comes out."

Wow, the woman has this down to a fine art. I caved and gave her a very abbreviated version of events, by which time the food arrived and I stuffed my mouth so I couldn't talk any more. Nita slid from the booth, then paused.

"You know, the guy was in here just before it happened.

I practically spit the food out. "Sit back down," I spluttered. "You mean the victim?"

"Don Hardwicke? Yeah."

"How do you know his name?"

"That new officer; Rooney. He's a strange one, he is. Acts like he's Wyatt Earp or something. He was in here, too, that night."

My head was spinning. "Back up, Nita, and start from the beginning."

She slid back into the booth and I learned that Rooney had a thing for Cindy, the waitress, who couldn't stand him. *Smart girl.* Trying to impress her, he'd given her his version of the incident, in which he single-handedly captured a dangerous criminal, *the lying scumbag,* and had let slip Hardwicke's name.

"Did he say anything else about the victim?"

"No, but I chatted with the man a bit myself." *Of course you did, bless you.* "He was a nice young man. Said he was a giftware and décor salesman. He was just passing through Mallowapple but the roads were so bad he decided it would be safer to stay the night. Do you believe it? He thought he'd be safe and he ends up dead. Poor man."

"Did you tell the sheriff this?"

"Course I did. Not about the name, though. I didn't know that 'til after I spoke to the sheriff."

"Was there anything else that happened? Anything unusual?"

"Now that you mention it, he left all of a sudden. Hadn't even finished his dinner; just threw money on the table and hurried out. I wouldn't have noticed 'cept Cindy was saying good riddance that Rooney was out the door.... "

"Whoa, whoa! Rooney was here, too?"

"That's right. He just picked up a coffee to go. I dealt with him myself so he wouldn't have a chance to bother her and was watching him walk out the door and that's when Hardwicke got up and left."

"Did they notice each other – Rooney and Hardwicke?"

"I couldn't say, hon."

"Well, what time was it?"

"I don't know exactly, but it must have been about twenty minutes before the hullaballoo in the alley."

I asked Cindy a few questions, hoping she might have more to add, but that was that.

I needed to share this with Tyler, so I gave Nita a big hug. "Don't ever change anything about yourself." Startled, she laughed, "Why ever would I?"

Back in my van I hit speed dial. *OK, so I have Tyler on speed dial; it's no big deal.*

"I was just about to call you," he answered.

Without waiting to hear why, I blurted out my news.

"Hmm, that's pretty interesting." That wasn't exactly the level of excitement I was hoping to hear.

"This opens up a whole lot of questions"

"I get that," he said, "but before we discuss it, let me tell you why I was going to call."

Oh, right. I forgot he had news as well.

"Zill Granger stopped by with a sweater and jeans from Rooster, so I'm on the way home with them now. Elaine drank a little water this morning but still wouldn't eat, so let's hope this does the trick.

"Granger also arranged for Rooster to call at three this afternoon. Can you be available?"

It was already nearly two and I had a date with Mutz von Kuckenschutz, a young and energetic german shepherd who required an hour-long walk.

"No problem; we can do a three-way call," Tyler said. "I'll call you as soon as I have Rooster on the line."

"Works for me," I replied.

"Think about what you want to ask or say. Rooster is only allowed 15 minutes and we don't want to waste the time."

A little before the appointed hour, as I was settling Mutz back in his house, my phone rang. Expecting Rooster to be on the line I answered with a cheerful "Hey, Rooster."

"Polly, it's only me." *Tyler.* "I want to give you some good news quickly – Elaine ate some chicken. Your idea worked, Polly. She got Rooster's scent from the clothes and her tail started wagging immediately. Now we don't have to pretend everything's alright."

"That's wonderful. I'm so relieved."

"Me, too. Now hang up; Rooster should be calling any moment."

Twelve

When the phone rang again a few minutes later, it was with a genuinely happy voice that I answered. Rooster, naturally, wanted to know all about Elaine, and Tyler and I gladly told him all was well.

"She's a sweetheart," I said. "You've nothing to worry about."

"How do you like Zill Granger?" Tyler switched gears, conscious of the clock.

"He's a fine man. I don't know how I'm ever going to repay you all for your help but I promise I'll find a way."

We mumbled things like, 'no need' and 'glad to,' then asked a few questions in hopes Rooster might remember something helpful, but there was nothing new. He'd never heard of Donald Hardwicke, never been in Mallowapple before, hadn't seen or heard anything unusual. "Except when Elaine growled," he added.

"What do you mean?" Tyler and I asked simultaneously.

"She doesn't have a mean bone in her body, but she growled at the officer."

"He was being aggressive toward you, so I wouldn't think that's so odd," I said.

"That's not it. She started growling before he ever said a word or pulled his gun. It's just not like her.

"Look, they're telling me I've got to go. Hug Elaine for me and tell her I love her." He started to choke up. "And thank you both, again. Thank you, thank....."

Rooster's voice cut off and for a moment there was silence.

"Polly! Are you still there?"

"I'm here. I'm just not sure what to say. This is all so wrong."

"Don't lose faith. Granger says all the evidence is circumstantial. There's nothing to tie Rooster to the body; no prints, no DNA."

I sighed. "That's only what I expected, but it doesn't get Rooster his freedom yet."

Thirteen

For the next few days things hummed along much as usual. My one sitter was still out. I was able to spread her visits amongst the rest of my crew except for Tiddles, who needed three visits a day, five days a week.

You might guess how Tiddles got her name. She was a lovely long-haired dachshund, and a puppy mill rescue. They're notoriously hard to house train, but whenever Tiddles got excited or upset, well, she just couldn't contain herself.

Tiddles and her pet parents were fairly new clients and, frankly, I was having a harder time training them than their dog. Try getting two boisterous young boys to come through the door slowly and calmly and ignore their pup for a while. The mother wasn't much better. She would talk to the pooch in a high-pitched baby voice – not that there's anything wrong with that, I do it all the time – but it also triggered Tiddles tiddles. The good news was they loved their little pup and were committed to giving her a happy life.

The roads had all been cleared and I was making my regular visits out to see Mom. She was still in a nostalgic mood, and I'd spoken to my brothers who both agreed it would be a great idea to plan one last family Christmas at the old home.

Suzette had got into the habit of phoning each day to give me updates on Elaine. I was realizing that was indicative of her thoughtful, generous nature. She was still at Tyler's and had issued a standing invitation to come over any time, but I'd just been too busy.

During one call she had a request. Tyler was driving to Bangor on business the next day, and Suzette wanted to go with him and do some Christmas shopping. Frank would be fine on his own, he could let himself out through the doggy door, but she wasn't comfortable leaving Elaine. Would I take her?

Of course, I was delighted. I had a full schedule, but Elaine could ride along for the day with me.

So the following morning, Tyler and Suzette dropped Elaine off at my house on their way out of town. Tyler was wearing the suit he'd worn when he first came to Mom's house - sans dog hair - and this time with a light gray shirt and skinny tie in a cornflower blue paisley pattern. He looked so sizzling hot he practically melted the ice off the doorstep.

We made arrangements for the pair to collect Elaine when they got back, said our goodbyes and I watched as Tyler pulled away, wishing I could be the kind of arresting beauty who probably caught his eye.

I'd already walked Angel, Vinny and Coco so I bundled Elaine into the van and off we went. My dogs are not allowed in the front seat but I made an exception for Elaine and let her sit beside me, thinking she might not like the van because driving was a pretty new experience for her. I needn't have worried. She sat up, gazing with some apparent interest at the passing scenery. Whenever I made a stop, she waited placidly for me.

By mid-morning, I figured I'd better give her a quick walk. We stopped in the town center, where there was a small park. I'd put Elaine into a harness that would be more secure than a collar. As if she understood that, she'd licked my hand and wagged her tail.

So, there we were ambling around, Elaine sniffing the grass and me thinking she must be just about the sweetest dog in the world. She finally found a spot that suited her 'business' and I was just reaching for a doggy bag when she belied my earlier thought with a low, insistent growl.

"You'd better be planning to pick that up."

By now I knew that voice – Rooney. Wordlessly, I turned while pulling my hand from my pocket with one of the pink, paw-print-branded baggies that I used for pick-up duty.

Putting on the kind of syrupy voice that really irritates people, I held up the bag. "Perhaps you'd like to do the honors."

Rooney's eyes narrowed and he stepped toward me, at which point sweet Elaine morphed into mean dog. She stood stiffly, head forward and ears back, her muzzle wrinkled to expose her teeth, a deep snarl in her throat. It halted Rooney in his tracks immediately.

"That's it. I'm calling this in and getting animal rescue to come and pick that beast up."

For a few beats I stopped breathing, then a flood of anger surged in me. I reached for my phone and started scrolling through the contacts.

"What are you doing?"

"I'm calling Sheriff Wisniewski to report you for threatening me, then I'm calling Zill Granger, my attorney."

Whether Rooney was more afraid of the sheriff or the lawyer I don't know, but my ploy had him backing off faster than a scalded cat.

"Hold up a minute. Let's not be hasty." He held his hands palms forward in a submissive gesture.

"Hasty," I retorted, "it's not *me* being hasty."

"OK, maybe I jumped the gun." *There's a truism for you.* "But I'm an officer of the law and it's my job to keep the town safe and you can't deny she was aggressive to me."

"And you can't deny you were threatening towards me about scooping poop. Besides, you're the only one Elaine's ever growled at." *Which shows really good taste.* I didn't add that last bit, of course.

"Maybe I'll let it go this time."

"This time? Are you saying there'll be a next time? Are you stalking me, Rooney?"

I must have hit a nerve, the man visibly paled.

"Don't be absurd. I'm an officer…"

"Of the law. Yeah, yeah, so I heard." I was on a roll now and ready to give him a real tongue-lashing, but in an effort to save some dignity he actually pretended to get a call over the radio. It was laughable. We both knew that he knew that I knew the call wasn't real (did you get that?), but I decided it was wiser to go along with the hoax and just get rid of him.

"You'd better go where you're needed, Rooney."

He had to throw a few last words at me as he stalked off. "I won't forget this, Miss pet-sitter." And he wasn't saying it in an endearing sort of way.

Even though I had no undies hanging in the bathroom, I was relieved when Tyler and Suzette declined my offer to come in when they arrived to collect Elaine. Frankly, I was embarrassed for Suzette to see what a sloppy housekeeper I was, when she could have been the next Martha Stewart.

"I do have some news for you, though," I said, to which Suzette immediately suggested I come with them.

"Thanks, but I have to deal with payroll tonight or I won't have anyone working for me." Then to Tyler I said, "Call me later if you have time."

I gave Elaine a great big hug, said my goodbyes and girded my loins for paperwork.

A big glass of wine was at my side; my reward for completing my fiscal duties. I was about to take a sip when Tyler phoned. I launched into an account of my confrontation with Rooney. In the telling, some of my agitation came back but I didn't realize it until Tyler interrupted.

"Calm down, Polly. Take a deep breath and another sip of wine."

"How do you know I'm drinking wine?"

"I saw a bottle on the table when you brought Elaine to the door."

I laughed. "OK, Sherlock, now tell me who killed Donald Hardwicke."

"That I can't do, yet, but I can tell you his wife is in town."

"Really?"

"My dad told me. You remember he and the sheriff are pals: they had a card game last night and Wisniewski said the wife is at the C'mon Inn with her father. They had to identify the body and apparently are staying a few more days."

"Hmmm. I wonder if they'd talk to us."

"I'm not sure how it would help," Tyler said. "I suppose it's worth a try, though."

So we agreed to meet at the inn the following morning, then I went back to my thoughts and my wine.

Fourteen

The text read, 'Can't make it, can you go it alone?' I was already at the door of the C'mon Inn when Tyler's message came through. Having never conducted an interview in a murder investigation before I was a little unnerved at being in sole charge, but I certainly wasn't going to let Tyler know that. I replied, 'No problem.'

Hattie Pan was the proprietress of the inn, a tall, angular woman, brittle as old bones. Her late husband had been the jovial side of the partnership, but despite her lack of congeniality she ran a clean and charming establishment and had a steady business. She also had a pair of Siamese named Chatty and Kathy, with whom I was on speaking terms as their caregiver when Hattie visited her family in Ohio once a year.

"Hi, Hattie." I leaned casually against the reception desk as Hattie responded to the dinging of the bell.

"Oh, it's you," spoken with a nasal twang while looking down said nose.

"I'm looking for Mrs. Hardwicke. Can you give me her room number?"

"And just why would you want to see her, Polly Parrett? She doesn't have any pets with her."

"How are *your* little darlings, by the way?"

In an instant her demeanor softened and she began to prattle on about Chatty typing on the computer keyboard and

Kathy balancing on the curtain rod. I oohed and awwwed in the right places until she wound down. Then I gave her my spiel.

"You know it was me who interrupted the scene in the alley where Donald Hardwicke was found? Well, I just want to give my condolences to his family and see if I can answer any questions that might help them find some closure." I cringed as I said the lie. Though if they could tell me anything that would help me find the real killer, then I *would* be bringing closure, wouldn't I?

Hattie's lips tightened into a thin line. *Well, a thinner line.* Then she exhaled loudly. "Perhaps I could call up to the room."

A few minutes later, a fifty-something man stepped into the lounge where I was waiting.

"Miss Parrett?"

"Yes," I held out my hand, "thank you for seeing me, and I'm so terribly sorry about your son-in-law."

"Actually, I really don't know why you're here."

I took a deep breath. "I was there when Rooster – that's Mr. Roosevelt – was arrested. Since then, I've come to know him and I don't believe he murdered Donald. I was hoping to talk to you and your daughter and perhaps find some clue to the real killer."

Uh oh. He was looking apoplectic.

"You have some nerve. The police seem pretty certain they have the killer, but you want to drag Mary and me through the muck to save him!"

This wasn't going at all well. I soldiered on, though.

"Don't you want to be sure the real murderer is brought to justice?"

Before he could answer, another voice was heard. "I do." The speaker had a look of someone whose joy had been ripped from her, yet she held herself erect and was holding on to sanity – just. "I'm Mary Hardwicke, this is my father, Ray Gethings." She patted his arm and directed her attention at him. "It's alright, Pop. It will help if I talk about it." Turning back to me, with a lopsided smile that didn't meet her eyes she said, "Shall we sit?"

We settled ourselves around a small coffee table and I found myself telling her how I came to be in the alley, what had happened and then describing Rooster and his life.

"So you see, he's just not the kind of man who would take another life."

"You're not convincing me," Ray said. "A Vietnam vet with PTSD who's admittedly been violent in the past. Sounds like exactly the right person is behind bars."

"Pop," Mary cautioned, "he sounds like the kind of person Donny would want to help.

"Polly, thank you for telling us all this. Ask me anything you want. I'll help in any way to see justice done."

For fifteen minutes I asked every question I could think of and was disheartened with the answers. Neither Mary nor her father knew of any connection between Don and anyone in Mallowapple. They'd never heard of Mallowapple before this and Mary was sure her husband had not planned on staying here. And, no, they could think of no-one who might wish Don harm.

"He is….was…a wonderful husband and father. We have two beautiful little girls, ordinary jobs, belong to the PTA. Donny is a Rotary Club member and we like to barbeque hot dogs and hamburgers."

I was getting desperate for something of use. "Is there anything unusual that happened to him? Ever?"

Mary put her head back on the seat and raised her eyes to the ceiling. A long moment later she looked at me. "There was an incident when he was in his teens, though I don't see how it could possibly relate to this."

I widened my eyes expectantly.

"Donny and two of his friends were hunting. There was an accident and one of the kids got shot and died. Only it wasn't an accident."

"Wha… what!" Ray stiffened.

Mary gave him a guilty look. "I'm sorry, Pop. I promised I would never tell anyone, but I guess that doesn't matter anymore. Please, keep quiet 'til I get it all out."

"Go on, Mary," I said.

"They were on private land, owned by the family of the boy who was killed. They were after wild turkey but they saw a deer. The other two boys – not Donny – fired and it went down. They started arguing over who had bagged it, when suddenly, the one boy simply raised his rifle at the other and pulled the trigger.

"Donny said he was completely stunned. He was going to run for help when the other kid threatened to kill him as well unless he swore to everyone that it had been an accident. When Donny began to object, the kid said he'd just have to kill Donny's family.

"There was a big fuss, of course, and plenty of suspicion, but Donny was too terrified to tell the truth. He was only fifteen, you know. Then, a year or so later, the bad kid's family moved away."

"Do you know where?"

Mary shook her head.

"Did you know this boy?"

"No. My home was in New Hampshire. I met Donny at a sales conference in Boston and didn't move to upstate New York 'til after we married."

It was a terrible tale, but I wasn't at all sure it helped.

Ray stood, signaling an end to the conversation. Thanking them both and promising to keep in touch with any news we turned to part.

"Oh, one more thing," I said. "What was the boy's name? The one who shot his friend, that is?"

"It was John Sulkey."

I shook my head. It didn't mean a thing.

Fifteen

In the middle of the night I awoke and sat bolt upright. I'd been dreaming that a multi-tentacled creature had been chasing me, only it had Tyler's head and was wearing a cornflower blue paisley tie. I didn't know whether to run away or stop and say, 'Take me, I'm yours.' Apparently the sleeping me decided it was best to give up on the whole sequence and so here I was, wide awake and fidgety.

Sighing, I extricated myself from the bed between a host of furry bodies. Vinny half-opened one eye and Taz complained because I had to move her a teensy weensy bit. Other than that, the whole gang slept on.

My mind wouldn't settle down, so I decided I may as well put it to good use. Opening up the laptop I tried to organize my thoughts in print. All I did was end up with a page of rambling ideas and very few hard facts. Looking over the notes the name John Sulkey jumped out at me. Curious to know more about the incident I ran a search, adding in Hardwicke's name, home town and the year the killing happened.

A few articles popped up about a teen accidentally shooting his friend. They didn't tell me more than I already knew and there were no pictures of the kids, presumably because they were underage. For the heck of it I ran a general search for John Sulkey with the town name, and bingo! Up popped a picture of the junior varsity high school football team. Sulkey was listed as the seventh from the left in the back row. I zoomed in on the face. The quality was really grainy and it was a small image to begin with, but as I peered closely I understood what it means to say your blood runs cold.

It took me a few moments to get over the shock. Then, without thinking, I snatched up the phone and hit speed-dial for Tyler.

"Polly?" The voice was groggy. Hell, I hadn't realized it was three thirty in the morning. *Oops.* Then the tone became alarmed. "Polly. Are you OK? I can be right over if you need me." *Well, that was gratifying. He really must care.*

"Polly! Say something!"

"I'm OK, everything's fine. It's more than fine. I think I know what happened to Don Hardwicke."

Sixteen

The coffee maker coughed out the last of the fresh pot. Coffee was one of the few things I always had on hand. Fortunately, everyone took it black, as there was no milk or sugar to go with it.

It was mid-morning. Tyler, Zill Granger and Sheriff Wisniewski sat around the kitchen table. We'd been talking for over an hour. Wisniewski had objected to meeting at my place but Granger had managed to persuade him it was for the best. Now he sat taut, palpable waves of anger coursing from his body.

Tyler had arrived on my doorstep soon after I'd called him. When I opened the door he'd crushed me in a warm embrace. "Don't ever scare me like that again."

I acted innocent. "What do you mean?"

"You can't call me in the early hours of the morning without scaring me. There's a killer out there. I thought you were in danger." *Wow. This was more than gratifying.*

"Sorry," I mumbled.

I'd gone through my notes and my theory with Tyler, who then called the attorney. Granger came right over and I went through everything again. Then Granger contacted the sheriff and I'd repeated my hypothesis for the third time. Wisniewski had confirmed one thing we weren't sure of – the time of death. As far as I was concerned, that pretty much sealed the deal.

"There's still no hard evidence," Wisniewski said.

"But now you have enough to check DNA and fingerprints against another suspect." Granger gave the sheriff a hard look.

"I'm going to take care of that as soon as I get to my office. Fingerprint samples will be on file, but it will take a while for the DNA."

"Is this enough to get Rooster out on bail?" Tyler asked.

"That's for a judge to decide," Granger responded, "but I think there's a good chance."

"What more do we need?" I was probably on my eighth cup of coffee, so I was a little excitable.

"Let me check it off for you again:

We now know Hardwicke's body was most likely in the dumpster at nine, when Tyler and I came upon Rooney playing Robocop with Rooster and Elaine.

Hardwicke left Bennie's Diner suddenly, right after he saw Rooney. That suggests he followed Rooney out.

Elaine growled at Rooney – twice. In fact, she growled both times she saw him and she never growls at anyone. *That* suggests she senses something bad about him.

Officer Anson Rooney is John Sulkey. That's his face in the high school picture. So, not only is he a known killer, the photo puts him in the same school, at the same time, as Don Hardwicke."

"Young lady, a dog growling will not get a conviction. I am going to pull Rooney in for questioning and put him on suspension. If there's a fingerprint match then that's a whole different ballgame." Wisniewski stood. "Thank you for the coffee. Now I'm going to get on with my job."

It wasn't much longer before Granger left. Tyler headed out soon after with a promise to call later. We all had work to get on with. Fortunately, my injured sitter was back on the job and I'd been able to re-arrange my schedule to clear the morning.

As I was setting off on my rounds a call came in from Suzette. "Polly, can I ask a big favor?"

She'd taken Elaine to the vet for a check-up and come outside to find her car wouldn't start.

"I'm waiting for a tow-truck now, but could you come and get Elaine? I don't want to drag her to the repair shop or leave her at the vet's. She'll be happier with you."

"No problem. I'm only a few minutes away. I'll head over now."

I settled Elaine in the front seat as Suzette's car was hooked up. We exchanged a quick hug and she promised that she or Tyler would swing by in the evening.

I enjoyed having my sweet friend with me again and she seemed to enjoy riding around. We only had a couple more stops to make when a call came in. I didn't recognize the number but, when you're in my business, you always answer.

"Pets and People, Too. This is Polly, can I help a pet or a person today?"

"This is Sheriff Wisniewski. Polly, it looks like you're right about Rooney. We matched his fingerprints."

I slapped the dashboard in glee and yelped.

"It's not all good." *Uh, oh.* "Rooney must have got wind something was going on and he's disappeared."

"Disappeared? You mean as in he's run away?"

"I mean we haven't been able to find him. He ditched his squad car, he's not responding to calls and he's not at his apartment. There's a BOLO out on him but I need you to be careful."

"What do you mean by careful?" I squeaked. "Am I in danger?"

Wisniewski tried to reassure me. "I'm only saying you should take sensible precautions. Keep your eyes peeled and keep your doors locked."

That didn't sound very reassuring.

"Have you told Tyler?"

"I left a message for him. Apparently, he's with clients."

"OK, sheriff. Thanks, I guess."

"If you see or hear anything, you call right away."

With that he hung up and I was left feeling nervous and unsure. There wasn't much I could do, though, except finish my visits and get home.

It was a relief when I pulled into my driveway, though not when I saw my automatic light wasn't on. Six o'clock hadn't come yet, but the sun had set long before and it was really dark. I felt horribly vulnerable. *Why didn't I carry a gun?*

Of course, I had no idea how to use one. Perhaps I should rectify that.

Telling myself to stop being such a wuss, I got out of the van and went round to open the door for Elaine. With key in hand we approached the door when Elaine stopped in her tracks. She stiffened and started to growl. *Oh, hell.* I knew what that meant. Rooney was here.

I hesitated, not knowing whether to run back to the van or rush for the door. But Elaine didn't hesitate at all. She charged forward as Rooney stepped from the bushes, raising his pistol at her. The only things I had were the keys and the dog leash. I flung the keys at Rooney's head and caught him right in the eye. Instinctively, he reached upward and the gun discharged harmlessly in the air.

Now Elaine had him by the leg. He turned the gun back to her and I cracked the leash at his hand like a whip. Unbelievably, it jerked the gun from his grip. I was beginning to feel like a regular Indiana Jones.

With his free leg, Rooney kicked savagely at Elaine's head. Without so much as a whimper she went down. Enraged, I hurled myself at him and we both fell to the ground. I clawed and bit but he was bigger and a lot stronger than me, and maybe just as desperate. My arms were pinned behind me and a knee to my stomach knocked the wind out of me – hard. I gagged and struggled for breath as he flipped me over so I was eating dirt. With his weight on me, I couldn't move or breathe. Then I felt something round my neck. Even as I was already losing consciousness, I realized it was the leash.

Thoughts of my mother, my dogs, my cats and Elaine flashed through my brain and I tried even harder to fight but my efforts became weaker and weaker. Suddenly I was bathed in a white light. *So this is it. This is what dying is like.*

Seventeen

Eww. Tyler needed breath mints if he was going to keep kissing me. I reached out to push his face away. *When did he start growing facial hair?*

I opened my eyes. Angel was looking right at me and my head hurt like hell. Come to think of it, my whole body hurt. "She's awake," I heard someone say.

"Thank God." That was Tyler's voice. He moved into my vision. "You're safe now. We got him. You'll be OK."

I wondered what he was talking about, then it came to me in a rush. I couldn't help myself; I burst into tears and clung to him tighter than a limpet to a rock. Then I thought of Elaine.

"She's awake but she's been taken to the emergency vet, just in case."

I heard another voice announce the arrival of the ambulance. "Who's hurt?" I asked.

"You. You're going to the hospital to get checked out. That was quite a beating Rooney gave you."

"I don't understand what happened."

"I know. I'll explain everything later. Right now I'm going to let the EMTs take care of you.

That was pretty much it for me until I woke in a hospital bed with my mother beside me, holding my hand.

"Polly Parrett, you do make life difficult for me," but she smiled as she said it and I smiled back. Or tried to; my jaw didn't want to cooperate.

"You're lucky. It's not broken, but the bone is badly bruised. The doctor says there will be a lot of swelling and a good bit of pain for quite some time."

"It doesn't feel painful now."

"That's the drugs," Mom said. "You also have a couple of broken ribs and a lot of scrapes and bruises and can expect a very sore throat. And there's a terrible bruise around your neck where....." Mom's eyes glossed with tears and her breathing started to get ragged.

"Where Rooney tried to strangle me," I said softly.

Mom nodded and bit her lip. I waited for her to compose herself. Considering the circumstances, I was surprised I was so mellow. Must be another effect of the drugs.

I wanted to know about Elaine, and who was taking care of my own creatures.

"As far as I know, Elaine is fine. I called one of your sitters and they have everything else in hand. They'll take it in turns to stay at your house as long as need be and they'll cover all your own visits, so you're not to worry." *I have a wonderful crew.* "I also called your father and he'll be here today."

"You actually talked to dad?"

"Whatever else I may think, he's still your father and deserves to know what's happened. He said he'll stay as long as you need him and do whatever he can to help. Now, I'm supposed to call the nurse when you wake." She pushed her chair away from the bed.

"Wait a minute. You have to tell me what happened."

"Tyler happened. And that's all I can say right now without falling apart."

I drifted in and out of sleep. At one point when I awoke, Wisniewski was there with a female officer to question me. He was surprisingly considerate and when he was finished I said, "I need you tell me what happened last night." And so he did.

Rooney had deliberately broken the driveway light and hidden at the side of the house, waiting for me to get home. Of course, he'd had no idea that Elaine was with me. The sheriff believed his plan was simply to shoot me. *Rooney seemed to like that modus operandi.*

The white light I'd thought was my pathway to another life, was actually the headlights of Tyler's car. He hadn't got the sheriff's message alerting him to Rooney's escape. Meanwhile, Suzette had asked him to collect Elaine. He'd arrived in time to pull Rooney off me and save the day. When the police arrived, they found Tyler cradling me in his arms, with Rooney out cold.

"If you think you look bad," *I didn't think that. How bad did I look?* "you should see Rooney. Tyler really did a number on him. He must have been one angry man." *That was so sweet.*

Apparently, after Tyler had given me up safely to the EMTs, he'd driven out to collect my mother and bring her to the hospital and had stayed with her, and me, through most of the night. He left in the morning when he had to retrieve Elaine from the emergency vet.

"So she's alright?"

"She had a relatively mild concussion. Nothing that should cause any permanent damage."

This day was getting better and better, but I still didn't know *why* Rooney had killed his old friend. The sheriff explained.

"Once we got Rooney in custody, he let it all out. He seems to think he's justified in everything he did."

"He's wacko."

"I won't argue with that. Anyway, Hardwicke recognized Rooney in the diner. He followed Rooney out and accosted him, saying he'd been quiet long enough and it was time for the truth to be told. Rooney persuaded him to step into the alley where they could talk. You'd think Hardwicke would have known better, but he practically signed his own death warrant right then.

"Rooney had to do something quickly but knew he'd attract attention if he fired his gun. So he picked up a brick and smashed Hardwicke's head, then heaved him into the dumpster, hoping the body wouldn't be found for at least a few days.

"That's when Rooster came along. He had no idea what had happened – though apparently Elaine knew something. Anyway, the last thing Rooney needed was someone opening the dumpster where he'd just hidden the body."

"So he had to come up with an excuse to get Rooster out of the way," I injected.

"Exactly. Luckily for Rooster, you and Breslin showed up."

It was a case of being in the right place at the right time.

Eighteen

I was in hospital for a total of three days. Dad had arrived and spent his time between the hospital room and my place, taking over pet-care duties there. I was really happy to see my parents getting along. Perhaps Mom had finally put her angst behind her.

There was a steady stream of visitors. Both my brothers turned up, my crew members stopped in to reassure me that all was well, Suzette popped in a couple of times and Tyler came to see me. I found myself feeling awkward and shy around him; I didn't know what to say. Happily, Mom filled the gap and showered him with gratitude to the point that *he* appeared awkward and shy.

When I was discharged it was with a lot of painkillers and instructions to take it easy. Not too bad for someone who was nearly killed.

It was decided – not by me – that I would stay with Mom until I was completely healed. That was sort of like the blind leading the blind under the circumstances, but I acquiesced and my four-pawed gang and I made the move. Dad stayed for a few more days, using my house as his base, and ran errands and fussed over both of us. It was nice.

The best thing that happened was Rooster's release. While I was still hospitalized he was freed and joined his beloved Elaine at Tyler's home. I wished I'd been there to see the reunion. On the second day at Mom's Tyler brought them out for a visit. It was very emotional. We all shed a few tears, Rooster most of all, thanking us for caring for a 'worthless stranger' and his old dog.

When things calmed down, Mom and I headed to the kitchen to make tea. Dad had the presence of mind to buy a good bottle of sherry, so we added that to the mix.

"You know what struck me?" Mom said. "Rooster referring to himself as worthless. It's so sad he should feel that way. He's obviously a good person."

"Perhaps we can find a way to help," I said. "I remember Tyler told me the VA had offered to do what they could and I'm sure that hasn't changed. Rooster is a proud man, though. He won't accept anything if he thinks it's charity."

I set a plate of gingerbread cookies and brandy-soaked Christmas cake on Mom's lap and followed her with the tea and sherry as she wheeled her way back to the living room. We were all chatting when the heat came on with its usual squealing and sputtering. Mom gave her usual apology, "It's been that way for years."

"I can probably fix it for you," Rooster said.

Dad immediately told him not to worry about it, but Mom and I looked at each other, then Mom turned to Rooster and asked, "How are you at house painting?"

Nineteen

Christmas Day

It had snowed heavily overnight. I looked through the window and it seemed as if our house had been wrapped in silvery white paper, like a present under the tree. Inside was the gift of warm Christmas colors, a cheerful fire, the scent of cinnamon, nutmeg, and pine from the freshly cut garlands; all mixed with a generous amount of laughter and love.

My brothers had arrived a couple of days earlier. Keene's wife, Megan was with him of course, and Seb had brought a girlfriend. There was no doubt the relationship was serious and I took to Ellie right away.

The guys strung the house with lights of red, blue and green. They'd found the perfect tree, which had been decked with the old ornaments I'd found in the attic. To be clear, I should say the *upper* part of the tree had been decorated. Bright, shiny objects are wonderful, but potentially dangerous toys to kitties and pooches. It looked a bit odd, I suppose, but to us it was still beautiful.

Rooster was with us too, and Elaine, of course. Since Rooster had fixed the heating, he'd started painting and doing other odd jobs for Mom. Rather than drive him back and forth from Tyler's, Mom had suggested he stay in one of the spare rooms. It was working out great. Not only was stuff getting taken care of, it was a real boost to Rooster's sense of self-worth and Mom was enjoying the company.

We'd put presents under the tree for Rooster and his faithful companion. Not surprisingly, Rooster got teary-eyed when he pulled out the aran sweater we'd got for him and read the card packaged with it: 'Friends are the family you choose. Welcome to our family.'

Elaine didn't know what to make of her gift. My dogs have as much fun ripping the paper off the packages as they do with their new toys. So Rooster pulled the paper apart to reveal a big beef-flavored chewie, which Elaine took very gently while her tail waved energetically.

What a perfect Christmas this was. Well, almost. As I looked around the room at Keene and Megan, Seb and Ellie, Mom and Rooster, a wave of loneliness swept over me. Try as I might to put Tyler from my mind, I couldn't help but wish there was something more to our relationship. He'd been invited to join us but declined, saying his family always spent Christmas at their timeshare in Bermuda.

"Polly," Mom called. "Give me a hand in the kitchen while the others set the table."

Dutifully, I headed for the kitchen. Megan and Ellie joined us and we pulled the turkey from the oven, popped the sweet potato casserole under the grill to brown the marshmallows, stirred the homemade cranberry sauce and drizzled a little more olive oil over the roast asparagus. When everything was ready we carried it into the dining room. By the time we were finished the table looked magnificent and the smells had me drooling almost as much as the dogs.

"There's one too many settings," I pointed out.

"I don't think so," Mom said.

"There are seven of us and we have eight settings. I'll clear it."

"No, dear. We're going to need it."

At that very moment the dogs jumped up in unison and dashed to the door as the bell chimed.

"Why don't you get that, Polly?"

Everyone was looking at me as if they knew something I didn't. *I hate that.* Hesitantly, I went to the door.

"Enough!" I said to silence the dogs. "Back!" I pointed to their blanket and obediently they moved back and stood there. "Stay!"

I opened the door and the dogs launched themselves at the man standing there. He might have been able to keep his footing if the porch had been shoveled and salted, but it hadn't. Instead it was slick as an ice-rink. The man's legs went out from under him and down he went, the bag he'd had in hand emptying its contents of prettily packed boxes into the snow.

"Tyler!"

The dogs were happily dishing big wet kisses on his face and plopping wet paws over his Arcteryx jacket.

"Off," I shrieked, "Off," trying to pull Angel away and lift Coco into my arms. Instead, my feet went in all directions and I fell onto my back next to Tyler. Mortified, I turned my face to his. For several seconds we looked at each other, then he burst into laughter. Before I knew it, I was laughing with him.

Together we hauled ourselves up and gathered the gifts.

"What are you doing here? You're supposed to be in Bermuda."

"There was something I really wanted to bring you."

From his pocket he drew a slightly crushed sprig of mistletoe. Holding it up high he pulled me to him with his free arm and kissed me. A real kiss. *Merry Christmas to me.*

You're probably thinking that's the end. Well, it's not. After we'd settled ourselves around the table Mom chinked her glass and announced, "Before we eat, I have something to say.

"More than bringing the Christmas holiday back to this house, you've brought the spirit. I've been reminded of how it feels to be part of a family and of the things you can accomplish together.

"For the past couple of years I've been absorbed in a misery of my own making. That's going to change. I want to get back to work and I want to do something that will benefit others.

"Rooster and I have been talking." We all glanced at him, wondering what was going on.

"He tells me there are lots of homeless vets, with pets, who just want a chance to get back to a normal life. I want to give them that chance. I want to make this home a sort of half-way house for those people. I know it's a huge undertaking, but Rooster has agreed to stay, and between us all I believe we can make this work."

There was a stunned silence.

Seb, Keene and I began to object but Mom raised her hand. "I don't want to hear anything negative. All of you, please, think on it and we can discuss it after the holidays. For now, let's just make this the merriest of Christmases."

"I'll second that," Tyler said, raising his glass. "And I would be proud to help in any way." *He is the greatest guy.*

We all raised our glasses with him and chinked them together. "Merry Christmas," everyone said, and lying in front of the fire Elaine gave us a doggy grin and thumped her tail loudly on the floor.

Go here to get a FREE short story from Liz, and become part of the In Crowd to receive insider news, previews and specials :

http://lizdodwell.com/signup/

The Christmas Kitten

A Polly Parrett Pet-Sitter Cozy Murder Mystery
Book 2

LIZ DODWELL

One

The box was red with Santa faces on it, tied rather sloppily with green ribbon. The van's headlights swept across it, sitting prominently on my front porch, as I pulled into the driveway.

It had been a really long day. Christmas was only a week away and a lot of my clients had left to spend the holidays in other parts of the country, or just to get away from the cold. Florida was particularly popular and, right now, it was appealing to me as the heating on my old van gasped and coughed while it struggled to stay alive. Thankfully, I didn't have to go out again and a long hot bath was calling to me.

The dogs of course heard me coming and there was a cacophony of howls and yips behind the door. My poor mutts had been alone for nearly eight hours and they weren't used to it, so first order of business was to let them out in the yard. Oh, I'm Polly Parrett, by the way, and I own a pet-sitting service, Pets and People, Too, in Mallowapple, Maine.

At this time of year many of my regular customers give me little gifts, but I wondered who would have left a gift at my door. Keys in hand I bent down to pick up the box and recoiled in disgust as my olfactory senses caught a whiff of something decidedly malodorous. *Oh no, not another of Mrs. Weevleduntz's plum puddings!*

Mrs. W. was one of Mallowapple's more eccentric residents, and the proud parent of a one-legged rooster named Lefty, which was odd because he only had his right leg; shouldn't he have been called Righty? Anyway, she'd had a husband once, but he'd walked out claiming he'd had enough of the loud-mouthed, dirty, hen-pecking bird. He was talking about his wife, of course. I didn't think she was that bad, though she wouldn't win any popularity prizes.

For all her oddities, though, Mrs. W. was devoted to Lefty and a host of other damaged and abandoned critters, and I couldn't fault her for that. I could, however, be critical of her cooking skills. It was last Christmas that I'd discovered she had a serious problem with her sense of smell – she didn't have any – when she proudly presented me with a homemade plum pudding. She'd used genuine suet to make it, which must have been completely rancid, and it was all I could do not to barf right there and then. Instead, I put it in the very back of the van and drove to the local dump with all the windows open – it was barely 35 degrees.

Sighing, I figured the box could wait until I'd dealt with the dogs, so I opened the door and Angel, Vinny and Coco tumbled out. Always the boy, Vinny went straight for the bushes to lift his leg fifty times; Angel, my sweet pit bull mix, wanted hugs and kisses, but Coco – sometimes called "the nose" – went straight for the stinky box.

"Oh no, you don't." I tried to scoop her up but she was going wild, whining and clawing, and slipped from my grasp so her paw caught in the bow of the ribbon. Instinctively she tugged, the ribbon came loose catching the edge of the lid and off it flipped. Coco was delighted and stuck her head over the side, her little nub of a tail wagging like crazy (she's a toy

117

poodle). Using considerably more caution I peered inside, dreading the sight of oozing plum pudding.

What the...? This was no boiled pudding. Trying to make itself as small as possible amongst a pile of pee-sodden, stinky tissue paper, was a kitten.

"You poor little thing, you must be frozen." Slowly I reached for the tiny creature and stroked its head with a finger several times before cradling it in my hand. "Let's get you in the house."

The kitten's ears and paws were cold, so I held it close to allow my own body heat to warm it while I set up a bed in a basket with a heating pad and a fleece blanket. Cold is more dangerous to a kitten than hunger, but with no emergency vet in Mallowapple – or anywhere near – I'm always prepared to take care of most situations.

Coco was still dancing around in a fever of excitement. I really wasn't sure of her motivation; did she think this was a wonderful new toy? To be safe, after I wrapped the kitten up I set the basket on the kitchen counter out of reach while I took a few moments to get my jacket off and dash to the bathroom. On the way back I grabbed a jar of powdered kitten formula and a bottle of unflavored Pedialyte. I was guessing the kitten to be around five or six weeks old, so partially weaned, but not knowing how long it had been without food I thought the formula would be the easiest to digest.

Rounding the corner into the kitchen I stopped short in horror. There was one of the dining chairs close to the counter and the silverware drawer pulled open creating steps up to the counter, and there was Coco *on* the counter, her head in the basket. I flung aside the formula and leapt straight forward across the kitchen table. Unfortunately, I'm no Carl Lewis – he was a famous long jumper – and my leap actually landed me *on* the table where my paperwork was stacked, and I slid inevitably to the floor with the papers, and taking the dining chair out in the process. Feverishly I disentangled myself and pulled myself up to the counter to find Coco now curled up in the basket, diligently washing the kitten who she had tucked into her chest. *Well, I'll be a monkey's uncle.*

A short time later I carried the basket to the couch to feed my new charge. I made Coco walk but she jumped up to supervise anyway. Ditto, my fat tuxedo cat, ambled out to see what was going on and was met with a low warning growl from Coco.

"You'd better back off, Chubbs. She's getting very possessive."

With my formula-filled syringe at the ready I picked the kitten up; this time, my finger touched something on its neck. It felt like chain. I pushed the fluff-ball's hair aside; it *was* chain. Gold chain. A gold chain bracelet, in fact. Surely no-one would have put a bracelet round a kitten's neck and left it as a gift for me? The only person I knew who could afford such a thing was my boyfriend, Tyler, and he'd never do anything as stupid as put a kitten in a box and leave it out in the cold.

I undid the clasp and held the bracelet up. It was quite plain; the sort of chain you add charms to. Turning it over I noticed something on the back of the clasp. Letters; it looked like AVO, or maybe AVD. Someone's initials, perhaps?

Coco interrupted my thoughts with a little whine and looked pointedly at me, then at the kitten. "Alright, miss. Let's take care of your new baby. I can tell you, though" I lifted up the little one's tail and took a quick look, "*she* has brought us quite a puzzle."

Two

"This is easily a $500 bracelet." Tyler picked up the piece from among the dregs of our Chinese take-out and fingered it. "Are you sure there's no one who would give it to you?" His voice was light, but did I detect a slight note of jealousy? *Awesome*.

"Are you jealous?"

"Just wondering if I need to keep a closer eye on you."

You know, Tyler Breslin is super-sophisticated, sexy and smart – and let's just say I'm not – yet for some reason he wants to be with me. How lucky can a girl get? I snuggled down so my head fit comfortably against his shoulder as we sat on the couch. "If anyone needs to worry, it's me. I saw how Britney Harris was giving you the eye during the Christmas caroling at the town square last week."

"She was not."

"Was, too, and don't tell me you didn't notice."

"Okay, I did notice," Tyler grinned and lifted my chin so I was looking at his face, "but no woman can take the place of my lady with the alluring eyes."

Oh, wow. You don't know how great that makes me feel because I have a condition – grandly called heterochromia – which means I have different colored eyes. One is green and one is brown. I used to be embarrassed by it but Tyler says it's very sexy, and I'm not about to disagree.

Going back to the bracelet, I took it from Tyler. "I guess I'll drop this off at the Sheriff's office when I take the kitten over to the vet in the morning. Maybe someone has reported it missing."

"The Sheriff is hardly likely to be interested in 'lost and found' when he has a murder case to deal with."

"What murder case?"

Tyler's eyebrows rose in astonishment. "You haven't heard?"

"Obviously not," I said crossly, "or I wouldn't have to ask about it."

"OK, OK." Tyler threw up his hands. "It happened just around the corner from here; there must have been cops and reporters all over the place. I can't believe you didn't see anything."

"Well I wasn't here, was I? Today I was over in Corkeep," that's a neighboring town, "filling in for one of my crew, and with all the extra holiday business I had 21 calls to make. I haven't even had a chance to do any Christmas shopping yet, and on top of that I have an abandoned kitten to deal with." I was beginning to get really irritable.

"Why don't you have another glass of wine?" Tyler's voice was low and soothing, which only ticked me off more.

"Just tell me what happened," I snarled.

He poured the wine anyway, then settled back.

"The dead woman is Nicole Whittier; did you ever meet her?"

I shook my head. "Isn't she the one who bought the old Fickett place on Woodland Lane? The one whose husband you never saw?" Tyler is a real estate broker and gets most of the Mallowapple listings.

"That's her. She claimed he was overseas on a mission. He's an Army Ranger – special ops. At any rate, she had his Power of Attorney and everything was in order, so the sale went through with no problems. She seemed a nice enough woman; I can't imagine why anyone would want to kill her. The police aren't giving out details of how she died but word is that a blow to the head did it."

"Whose word is that?"

"Becky Marchand heard it from Doreen Crocker and told Nita who told me when I stopped in for lunch."

"Ah." That all made perfect sense to me. Becky is best friends with Doreen who is married to Stan Crocker, our local doctor, who occasionally has to attend crime scenes because the nearest coroner is hours away. Doreen would have squeezed Stan for information and immediately ratted to Becky, who would have told her other friend, Nita, who owns Bennie's Diner, and from there Nita would have blabbed to everyone who came in.

"Anyway," Tyler went on, "the even bigger news is that the woman's two daughters are missing - actually, according to Nita, the woman is their stepmother - and nobody knows where the father is right now."

"You mean he killed his wife and took the girls?"

"No, just that his whereabouts are unknown. He could be deployed somewhere, or training... and probably has no idea yet that anything has happened."

"That's awful. Those poor kids. How old are they?"

"Six and ten; Amalie and Sophie."

"Shouldn't there be a search party or something? What if they just ran away?"

"There was a search party," Tyler said. "I was out with them all afternoon but the volunteers were sent home when it got dark."

At this time of year the sun sets by four o' clock, and overnight temperatures can drop below twenty, which didn't bode well for the girls if they were out there. Of course, if they were in the clutches of some blood-crazed murderer that would hardly be any better. I sighed and looked at the little kitten, contentedly curled up with Coco, and wished the two girls had been dumped on my doorstep as well.

Three

"I'm so cold." Amalie's voice was hardly more than a whisper as she hunched in her pink puffer coat; then it turned into a wail. "And I'm hungry!" Her little face scrunched up in misery and her lips quivered as she tried not to cry. "I want to go home. I want my daddy."

Her big sister wrapped her arms around her. Sophie, who was ten going on thirty, had watched out for Amalie since she was a baby, when their mother had died giving birth. She had taken one look at the babe, wrapped in a blanket with a funny knitted hat on her head and making little snorting noises and she'd burst into tears, so overcome was she at the amount of cuteness she was witnessing.

Because Daddy was gone so much, she'd taken it upon herself to be the best big sister Amalie could have. Oh, there had been several live-in nannies, but Sophie understood that none of them could love Amalie as she did, and she monitored everything they did. Then came Nicole. She wasn't a nanny; Daddy had brought her home one day and told the girls she was a special friend. Later, when he told them she was going to be their new mother Sophie had cried and raged that she didn't want another mother. Daddy had said she'd feel differently in time and that, anyway, Amalie deserved a mother, to which Sophie had yelled Amalie didn't need a mother because she had her!

Two months later, Daddy and Nicole were married. That was about a year ago, and now here they were in Mallowapple and everything had gone wrong. Anger and self-pity welled up inside Sophie. She hated Mallowapple and she hated Nicole. But now Nicole was dead and Daddy would probably be angry, and she didn't know what to do.

Amalie's crying brought Sophie back to reality and she rubbed her sister's back. "Just a little bit longer. We'll find somewhere soon, but you have to be brave just a bit more. Please, Ammi?"

A loud sniff told Sophie her sister would try and, holding hands, they trudged on through the snow, with Sophie thinking how much she hated that, too.

Coming from Texas the girls had been filled with excitement to think they'd finally get to experience snow. Well, there hadn't been any – until today. At first it had been fun; they'd rolled in it, tossed handfuls into the air and tried to catch snowflakes on their tongues. But now it was hard work crunching through the crystallized inches, and everywhere Sophie turned things looked the same.

She'd insisted they stay off the roads, out of sight. Their house was close to the edge of town so it hadn't been difficult to slip across the field and through the tree line. At first the trees weren't too dense, then they started to run into low-growing brambles that tore at their clothes and their faces. With luck, they happened on a hiking trail – not that they knew what it was – and they followed it 'til they came into a clearing. Walking round the edge of the clearing they found another trail, only this time it was a deer trail. If they'd gone just a bit further they would have picked up the hiking trail again, and the searchers who came looking for them several hours later might have caught up with them. As it was, they pushed on as best they could until here they were, in a sparsely treed place, cold, frightened and completely lost.

It was only a few minutes later that Sophie noticed it was lighter up ahead. With a firm grip on Ammi's hand she pulled her toward it. As they got closer they realized the lights were a mix of colors.

"Is it a house?" Ammi sounded hopeful. "They probably have hot chocolate. And sugar cookies. Do you think they'll have sugar cookies? I love sugar cookies."

"I don't know." Sophie was afraid to get her hopes up. "We'll have to get closer and see."

And so they kept going, hurrying now, 'til they got close and their mouths dropped open in astonishment.

"Is this Santa's house?" Ammi asked. And, indeed, it was understandable she might think so. There was a large, old house, draped in lights; they hung from the eaves, around the windows and across the roof. A brilliant star sat atop the house with lighted angels trumpeting horns on either side. Wreaths with big red bows hung on the siding and Santa waved from a sleigh above the porch. In front of the house at least a dozen trees glittered brightly and, around them, a toy train chugged, pulling trolleys filled with toys.

As the girls stood there the front door opened, spilling even more light into the dark night. "Down," snapped Sophie, and pulled Ammi to the ground with her. An elderly man stood in the light while a dog stepped past him and walked stiffly down the steps. The door closed and the girls watched the dog wander towards some nearby bushes and sniff around before squatting to pee. It was obvious from her deliberate movements that she was an old dog, but her senses had not yet failed her, for as she turned to head back to the house her nose lifted and she looked directly at the sisters. For a few moments she stayed still, but then she began to move toward them.

"Oh, no." Sophie braced herself to run when, at that moment, the door opened and there stood the man again.

"Elaine, come on!"

The dog paused and looked toward the man, then back at the girls.

"Come on old lady. It's time for bed."

Elaine gave a slight whimper and a wag of her tail as she continued to eye the girls, then reversed her course and headed back inside. As the door closed behind her the lights went suddenly dark and Sophie rolled on to her back. "Phew. That was close."

"But aren't we going inside? I thought we were going to have sugar cookies." Ammi was on the verge of tears again.

"We have to stay hidden, silly. Look, there's something over there," she waved off to the right. "Let's go see." And wearily they dragged themselves away.

Four

"You did good," said Doctor Jim as he examined the kitten.

Beside me, Coco stood on her hind legs and pawed at the table. The doctor looked down. "You and Miss Coco," he corrected himself.

"She looks to be about six weeks old, so it's fine to start her on solid food, but supplement it with the formula for a while yet. She's a little thin, otherwise in pretty good health. We should get her started on deworming treatments, though."

"Whatever you say, doc." "I scratched Coco's head. "See, I told you she'd be OK."

Relieved that the kitten had no serious issues I turned back to the doctor. "I don't suppose you have any idea where she might have come from?"

"None at all," he said cheerfully.

"So she's just another throw-away."

The doctor picked her up and eyeballed her. "She could be a Scottish Straight."

"A what?"

"You've heard of the Scottish Fold cat breed? Their ears fold forward onto their faces and give them a sort of owlish look, but sometimes a kitten is born with normal ears and then they're called Scottish Straights – at least, by some people." He held the kitten towards me. "Look at those big, beautiful round eyes and the chubby cheeks. That's indicative of the breed."

"Is her coloring typical of the breed?"

"No, they come in all colors. But they have a trademark pose; they will sit back and rest their front paws on their belly. Like Buddha."

Huh, go figure.

When we were all done the doc escorted me out to the reception area. "What's the damage?" I asked.

"No charge. You're doing a good thing. Consider it a Christmas gift."

"Thanks, Doctor Jim. And you have a very Merry Christmas yourself."

I gathered up my charges and took them out to the van where Angel and Vinny were waiting. Because my schedule was so crazy I'd decided to take the kitten to my Mom's where there were plenty of people to care for her. The big old farmhouse where I'd grown up had been converted this past year to a halfway house for homeless veterans and their pets. Actually, it was an ongoing process but we now had three rooms in the main house and one of the barns had been turned into a dormer of sorts. There were eight bedrooms upstairs, nothing plush but they were private and there were a couple of shared bathrooms. Downstairs was communal living space with a kitchen and recreational area.

I'd been involved in a murder investigation last year and met Rooster, a Vietnam vet who had been injured in a mortar attack and suffered from PTSD. He was living on the streets and wouldn't go to a shelter because none of them would allow his dog, Elaine, in. That's when Mom had come up with the idea to use the space she had at the old farm to help others in the same situation. Rooster had since become a permanent fixture and occupied one of the rooms in the house.

Anyway, to get back to the story; it was not yet eight. Doctor Jim was always early at the clinic and he never minded if I just stopped in. And I'd already dropped off the bracelet at the police station, which was opened at six sharp, Monday to Friday. Tyler was right, too, no-one was interested in it; the focus was on the missing girls. So my plan was to drive out to *Welcome Home* – that's the name we gave the halfway house – drop off the kitty and my dogs, load up on Mom's good coffee and get my Christmas shopping done while I had a chance.

You're probably wondering why I don't do my shopping on the internet when I'm always so busy. Here's the thing: I love Christmas. Really, it's my favorite time of the year – the food, the caroling, the decorations, the way complete strangers suddenly treat each other like long lost friends with cheery greetings and warm smiles. I just revel in the atmosphere, and that includes finding the right gifts for everyone. It's just so much more personal to go into a shop and pick something up and know instantly it's perfect for someone you love.

It had snowed steadily throughout the night. Mallowapple didn't have the resources to sand or scrape the roads unless really necessary, but people around here knew how to handle the weather. I'd had my snow tires put on a few days ago, when the bad weather was forecast, so the thirty-mile drive to *Welcome Home* would be no problem. There were a few tire tracks along the way but, other than that, the landscape was a pristine white wonderland that sparkled in the early morning sun. It was so lovely I burst into song with a chorus of Joy to The World, at which the dogs looked at me in alarm – um, I don't have much of a singing voice. I didn't care, though, and after a while they decided I wasn't in pain or going spastic, and I just kept on singing.

Pulling into the driveway my spirits soared even higher as I took in the festive scene before me. Several of our residents were already busy, adding toy soldiers along the porch rails of the house and building a crèche where the baby Jesus would lie in the manger. When I was a kid, my parents always made a big deal of the Christmas decorations for me and my brothers, Seb and Keene. But things change, and last Christmas had been the first time in years that the holiday spirit had been found once more at the old homestead. This year, the residents had collectively decided to create a real spectacle and have an open house on Christmas Eve. Notices had been put in local publications and flyers distributed, and we were really hoping for a good turnout.

I waved to everyone as I headed into the house, cat carrier in hand and dogs at my feet.

"Hellooo!" I made straight for the kitchen, drawn by the smell of coffee. Mom was in there, clearing breakfast dishes. She turned her wheelchair as I entered.

"Hi, sweetheart. I just made a fresh pot for you." *She knows me well.*

I probably should tell you, Mom was once a champion show-jumper 'til she had an accident that left her without the use of her legs. She sank into depression and, when my dad couldn't take it any longer and left, she became bitter and angry as well. Thankfully, her involvement in *Welcome Home* changed all that; she's back to being the strong, take-charge woman I always admired. She's even started giving riding lessons, and we now have two rescued horses for that purpose. Honestly, I'm so proud of what's been accomplished this past year. We had a lot of help from the local VFW (Veterans of Foreign Wars), both to get our 501c tax status and to do the physical work necessary to rehab the farm, and we still work closely with them to help our residents find work and permanent housing.

"Hey, Mom." I bent down and kissed her cheek, then put the carrier on her lap. "Here's your littlest resident."

She lifted the kitten out and a voice behind me said, "Oh my gosh, she is so precious."

I looked over my shoulder and smiled at Captain Linda Gutierrez, the only female guest we currently had. "Wanna take on a new job?" I took the kitten from Mom and held her out to Linda. Tentatively she reached out with her left hand. "I, I don't know. What would I need to do?"

Linda had lost her right arm, her right breast, and suffered severe burns in an IED ambush while accompanying Rangers as a nurse in Afghanistan. She'd also suffered terrible depression and guilt because she had been the lone survivor. Four months ago she'd come to us with a big old mutt, after wandering the streets for more than two years. Fiercely independent and private, she probably wouldn't have sought us out if her dog hadn't been sick. With no means to pay for his care she'd swallowed her pride and asked for help. Jocko, the dog, perked up for a while, but he was old and tired and a few weeks ago we dug a final resting place in our pet cemetery and said goodbye. That night, Linda disappeared. We put the word out to find her. It took a while but finally she was seen in a town about 100 miles away, asking for work in a restaurant. We sent Rooster to get her. He's walked in her shoes and was the most likely to be able to bring her back. Only thing is, we didn't know if we could get her to stay. It struck me that the responsibility of once again caring for a living creature might be just the medicine she needed.

"She needs to be fed every few hours," I said, "and litter box, play area and such set up for her. It's best to keep her away from the other cats for a while yet. In a couple of weeks we can gradually begin to introduce them."

For such a tiny thing the kitten had an almost thunderous purr. Linda held her to her cheek then kissed the top of her head, and an edge of her lip turned up in the slightest of smiles. "I don't really know anything about cats, but I guess I could try."

Yes! Mom and I exchanged a fleeting glance of triumph. It was the first positive sign we'd seen from Linda since she'd been back.

"In that case, I'll help you get organized," I picked up the coffee pot, "*after* I get a dose of caffeine."

"We're going to need some hot chocolate, too." I whirled around to make a snappy remark to Rooster about turning into a marshmallow – he's a die-hard coffee drinker – but the words choked in my throat. He stood there, an arm around each of two very bedraggled-looking girls. Instinctively, I realized these must be the missing kids, but I was so taken-aback I was lost for words. Not so my mother.

"Polly, put the kettle on. Girls," she addressed the sisters, "come in where it's warm. I've got some sugar cookies I baked just yesterday."

The smaller child's eyes went wide with delight. She must really like sugar cookies, I was thinking, but she surprised us all by pulling free of Rooster's hold and rushing toward Linda.

"Dopey," she cried out, which struck me as a little rude. "You found him." And I realized she was talking about the kitten, not Linda, as she reached her arms upward.

Five

"You could have knocked me down with a feather when I saw them lying there on the horse bedding." Rooster was recounting to Sheriff Wisniewski how the girls had been found. For a while in the kitchen it had been a madhouse, with everyone asking questions at once until Mom took charge, delegating Rooster to call Wisniewski, and organizing hot baths, clean clothes and a meal for the kids.

"They must have come through the forest. That's almost 10 miles direct from the town. It's a miracle they ended up here. Just a few steps in a different direction and we'd have been looking for frozen bodies this morning." Rooster shook his head in disbelief. "It was Batt Vargus who found 'em. He's on mucking out duty this week and went to get some clean shavings to lay in the stalls and there they were, fast asleep. It's a good thing we keep the barn heated."

Mom had seated the kids at the kitchen table with more hot chocolate. They looked pretty bedraggled with bits of shaving stuck to their clothes and in their hair. Sophie, the older girl, was withdrawn, almost sullen. Ammi, on the other hand, turned out to be quite the little chatterbox and soon their story began to come out.

Amalie had found the kitten and brought it into the house. Knowing her stepmother would not be pleased she took a bracelet of Nicole's and put it around the cat's neck because in her child's mind it would "make the kitty more pretty."

Nicole, as expected, told her to get rid of the kitten. When Ammi cried and begged to be allowed to keep the kitten Nicole had snatched it, saying she'd throw it out with the trash. It was then she noticed her bracelet and became absolutely furious, and slapped Ammi across the cheek. More frightened than hurt, Ammi screamed. "I said she was mean and ugly," she told us, "and I wished she'd never married daddy. Then she was going to hit me again and Sophie told her to leave me alone and pushed her and, and..." the words trailed off and Ammi looked anxiously at her sister who glared back. Moments later Sophie's features softened and she sighed, "It's alright, Ammi. I guess we have to tell the truth; that's what Daddy would want." She squared her shoulders and looked right at the Sheriff. "I killed Nicole," she said.

Six

After a minute or two of stunned silence during which we watched the tough ten-year-old morph into a frightened and lonely little girl who sank to her knees, dissolving into tears, the first to react was Linda. She stepped forward, placing the kitten into Mom's lap then dropping to the floor, putting her one arm around Sophie and pulling her close. Silently, Amalie rushed forward and climbed onto Linda's lap, where she clung while Linda rocked back and forth making soft crooning noises.

The rest of us hovered awkwardly around, unsure what to do, until sweet Elaine, who'd been watching everything from her bed in the corner, padded over to the trio and bent her head to nuzzle the girls. Shamed that a dog was showing more compassion and initiative than we were, we moved as one to surround the children, muttering reassurances.

It was then the officer who'd accompanied Wisniewski walked in. "Uh," he did a double take.

"What is it, Frellick?" Wisniewski spoke curtly.

"This is Ms. Harris from Child Services, Sheriff." And he stepped aside to allow a pug-faced woman entry. *Well, to me she looked a little puggish: solemn eyes, wrinkled brow and squashed nose.*

"I hope you weren't planning on questioning that child without me present, Sheriff Wisniewski?"

"No, ma'am." The Sheriff raised his hands. "But I am going to have to detain her. She just confessed to murder."

"Then you'd better make sure you mirandize her; but I want to speak to both girls first... alone."

Wisniewski sucked in a deep breath. "Frellick," he snapped, "you're with me. Rooster, you too. I want a word with you."

When the front door slammed shut, Mom turned to the social worker. "You can take the girls into the room across the hall. It will be private there."

"I'll come with you," Linda said, keeping a possessive arm around Sophie as Ammi hung on to her leg.

"Just the girls," the woman raised her hand in a blocking motion, then used that same hand to gesture impatiently at the sisters. "Come along." They gazed at her in wide-eyed terror and held even tighter to Linda.

"They've been through terrible trauma," Mom pushed her chair forward, "and they've formed a bond with Linda. I think it best she stay with them."

The two women glared at each other, but I knew my mother's look. I'd been the recipient of it enough times, and I had no doubt who was going to win this eyeballing contest.

Ms. Harris glanced away. *Told ya!* "Very well." And she marched away, Linda ushering the girls behind her and giving Mom a grateful look over her shoulder.

I was running late, and there was really nothing I could do to help Mom. Besides, I had to stop and take care of a bathroom break for a charming Pekingese named Han before

I did my shopping. So I kissed Mom on the cheek, called the dogs and loaded them into the van and off we went.

Seven

Han's "parents," Kathryn and Will Beaudry, both worked from home, so this was not a regular visit. Today they had a meeting to attend that would keep them occupied for five or six hours and they didn't like their precious boy to be alone that long. They lived in a lovely antique Colonial home, which they'd renovated themselves, with access through a security gate. I had the code but couldn't reach the keypad from the van and had to climb out. It was a bit of a nuisance and I was always fearful the gate would start closing before I got back in my vehicle.

I punched in the numbers, the heavy gates began to swing open and I reached quickly for the open van door... too quickly. I slipped on the packed snow, falling forward. Grabbing the door handle I was able to spare myself from ending up on the ground; instead the door slammed closed as I leaned on it and caught my baggy sweater firmly in its grasp. My head bounced off the window and I clung on, slightly dazed, waiting for my fuzzy brain to clear when I heard the click of the lock. *Oh, no.* The dogs, reacting as if this were some new game, were bouncing and barking and one of them had hit the lock. Inside the van I could see my keys hanging from the ignition and my cell phone laying on the console. *Aaargh.*

The squeal of the gates starting to close brought me back to my senses. The gate code was a six-figure number that I kept on my phone, and for the life of me I couldn't remember it now. There might be a way for me to get into the house but I'd have to get through the gates first. With barely another thought I tugged at the bottom of my sweater to pull it over my head but it would only stretch a few inches. So I crouched and wriggled downwards, backing out of the garment and dragging my arms through it so the sleeves were inside out as it dangled from the door, and I was left topless. *Thank goodness I wore a bra today.*

My effort was to no avail. As I straightened up the gates shut with a depressing finality and I was left standing half naked in the freezing cold. I worked my way back into the sweater and forced my mind to consider how to get out of this plight. The dogs were looking expectantly at me, waiting to see where this new game was going.

"Open the door," I squeaked in that high-pitched voice we use for pets and babies. "Come on guys. Jump on the lock again. Good puppies. Yaaay." And to demonstrate I bounced up and down as best I could while attached to the vehicle, and banged on the window. Angel yawned and lay down, Vinny decided it was more fun to wrestle with the quilt that covers the back seat; only Coco continued to watch intently, but didn't move a muscle.

For the heck of it I thought I'd better check the doors, just in case one would open, so I slithered out of the sweater again and went around the van, but no such luck. In frustration I yanked at my errant clothing, willing it to tear away. Who knew that I owned the one piece of knitwear that was stronger than ripstop nylon? At this rate I was going to have to knock on a neighbor's door and expose myself as an idiot as well as a 34B, or I was likely to freeze to death.

To delay doing anything so embarrassing for a while longer I bent down and started to shove my torso once more into the sweater.

"Hello, Polly."

I froze – metaphorically, that is. I knew that voice. Slowly I pushed my head through the neck opening and tried to lean casually against the side of the van to address the speaker. Trouble was, I'd inserted myself facing the gate and could only twist part way round.

"Britney," yes, it was the dreaded temptress, "how nice to see you," I hissed.

She smiled with fake sweetness and stepped from her car across the street. "I noticed as I drove by you seemed to be having some trouble, and I couldn't leave a friend in distress, now could I?" *Friend? My patootie.*

The worst of it was, I really was in a pickle and had no option but to swallow my pride and ask for help.

"I, uh, locked my keys in the van and…"

"…and got yourself all caught up," she smirked. "Not to worry, why don't you just worm your way back out of that, uh, sack thing, and come and sit in my car while I call for help."

I bit back the words I wanted to say and freed myself for the last time as I heard Britney say, "Hi, Tyler." *She was calling my boyfriend?*

I won't bore you with all the details of what happened next. As irritated as I was that Britney would call Tyler, it actually made sense. He had access to my house where there was a spare key for the van. When he arrived on the scene, Britney hugged him and clung to his arm and I got even more pissed because he didn't seem to mind it. And when he laughed at my predicament, that was it. I sucked my lips between my teeth and did my best to spit fire from my eyes.

"Thank you for your assistance, Tyler." I spoke in a formal tone, snatching the jacket he'd brought for me. "There's no need for you to stay any longer." And I turned my back, stepped into the van with as much dignity as I could muster, and drove through the gates at last.

Eight

You can be sure I was very careful getting out of my vehicle when I reached the house, and I opened the door to find Han sitting calmly on a padded hall chair. He fixed me with his inscrutable gaze and waited expectantly for me to approach and acknowledge his greatness.

You know, Pekes were bred in the Chinese Imperial court, maybe as long ago as 200 BC, during the Han Dynesty (now you know where Han got his name). Kathryn once told me a really sweet legend where a lion fell in love with a marmoset – that's a really cute little monkey – but the difference in their sizes made a union impossible. So the lion asked the protector of animals, Ah Chu, to make him as small as the marmoset so they could marry. Ah Chu agreed, but was so impressed by the lion's devotion that he left his heart the original size, and from this unlikely pair the Pekingese – or Lion Dog – was born.

Han certainly lived up to the legend, I thought, as I stroked his silky hair. He was quite fearless; I'd seen him face down much bigger dogs with barely a twitch of a whisker.

"Come on, oh Regal One." I tucked him under my arm and we headed out back. It was slick with ice at the top of the stoop and snow had drifted up to the top step. Still cautious after my recent episode I set Han down so I'd have both hands free to close the door behind me. Only thing was, his little legs went out from under him and he slid head first into the deep snow.

"Oh, jeez. Han!" I fell to my knees, which wasn't too smart because I jarred the heck out of my back, and scrabbled with my hands to dig him out. I managed to get hold of him and haul him to safety, holding him close and crooning, "It's OK, you're OK now."

I heard him snuffling and he struggled to get out of my arms. Could this day get any worse? I'd made a fool of myself in front of Britney Harris, pissed off my boyfriend, and now even Han was upset with me. I let go of the Peke; he stepped gingerly away, glanced over his shoulder at me then his ears went up, he gave an excited yip, and launched himself back into the snow. He wasn't mad at me at all; he just wanted to play!

For the next five minutes Han had me laughing at his comic antics, but as abruptly as he'd erupted into playfulness, he decided he'd had enough. That was fine with me. I still had to drop my three dogs off at home and get to the stores, but His Regalness had lifted my spirits beyond measure. *It's amazing how a dog can do that.*

Nine

Tyler pulled into the driveway; Vinny, Angel and Coco excitedly rushed to the door. I grabbed the signs I'd made and did my best to calm the dogs while slipping the signs over their heads. As Tyler walked in I sternly told the dogs to sit and stay (no small feat) and stepped aside so he could read the message. He looked a little puzzled

SORRY   REALLY   MOM'S

I glanced at the dogs. *Oh!*

Grabbing Vinny I swapped him with Coco.

MOM'S   REALLY   SORRY

Better.

Tyler said nothing; just drew in a deep breath and let it out slowly. At that point Angel couldn't stand it any longer and had to greet him, and for several moments it was madness as canines and man showered affection on each other. Meanwhile, Tyler still hadn't spoken and my nerves were beginning to get the better of me. When he'd sent a text earlier to suggest dinner I'd thought he wanted to make up; now I wasn't so sure.

"I really am sorry," I said, "you came to rescue me and I behaved like an ass. I mean, I can see why you'd find Britney attractive, she's got a great figure and wears classy clothes and she's so much more sophisticated than I'll ever be and...and..." *Fudge, I'm going to cry.*

"Polly. Sweetheart. I'm the ass, and an insensitive one at that. I laughed at your predicament when Britney showed me the picture..."

"Picture? What picture?"

"Oh...perhaps I shouldn't have mentioned that."

"What picture?"

Tyler pulled out his phone and scrolled to an image, then handed it to me.

That shameless hussy. She'd snapped a picture as I was backside forward wriggling from my sweater and had the nerve to send it to my boyfriend. I felt color rise to my face as I wondered who else she might have shown it to.

"Honey, don't get upset." Tyler reached for my hand. "You know, Britney is one of those women who looks good from afar, but up close she looks far from good. She doesn't hold a Christmas candle to you. Here..." With his other hand he pulled a small box from his pocket. "A peace offering."

Slowly I pulled the lid off. "Ohhh." The most darling pair of earrings were nestled inside; silver mistletoe with pearl berries.

I dashed to the mirror, replaced the earrings I'd been wearing with my new gift and admired how they looked.

"That's better." Tyler came up behind me, putting his arms around my waist. "Now I can do this." And he kissed my neck – *under the mistletoe, get it?* – then spun me around and kissed me the way people in love are meant to kiss.

Ten

Dinner was at the Bombay Indian restaurant, where Tyler and I had our first sort-of date just about a year before. To celebrate, we ordered exactly what we'd had then and didn't talk about anything but us until we'd finished, then I filled Tyler in on my earlier conversation with Mom.

"The social worker turned out to be not so bad. She acted tough because she has to look out for the girls' best interests, but Mom said she softened a lot after she heard their story. Still, it was pretty rough all around when she took them to the police station. Ammi cried and begged to stay; then she wanted to take Dopey with her. Sophie was stoic.

"Mom wanted the girls to come back to *Welcome Home*, but Ms. Harris said that wasn't possible, so they'll be put in foster care for now."

"Why were they going to the police station?" Tyler leaned forward, resting his arms on the table.

"For questioning, though Ms. Harris said they'd also be checked by a doctor."

"You said Linda was with the girls when the social worker questioned them. Didn't she find out anything?"

"She found out that Dopey is named after Ammi's favorite dwarf in Snow White and the Seven Dwarfs."

"I meant anything useful."

"I know what you meant," I grinned. "It turns out the girls got the idea to put the kitten in a box and leave it on my doorstep because that's how Nicole got the bracelet; it was left at the front door for her. Thing is, it couldn't have been a present from their father because he was away. So who gave the bracelet to Nicole? And what does it mean?"

Tyler shook his head. "How did the kids come to pick your doorstep?"

"They'd seen my van in the driveway," My van is covered with decals for the pet-sitting business, "and figured a pet-sitter would know how to take care of a kitten."

"Smart girls." Tyler grinned back at me, and for the umpteenth time I thought to myself I must be one of the luckiest people in the world.

Eleven

I was walking through a beautiful Christmas wonderland. In the distance I heard sleigh bells; the dogs heard them, too. Their ears pricked up, they looked at each other and began singing jingle bells. Then I woke up.

My phone was ringing. To help celebrate the season I'd changed my ringtone to the dogs singing Jingle Bells; or should I say barking? I figured there must be an issue with a pet-sit, maybe one of the overnights, but it was worse.

"Polly, wake up," Mom said. "We need your help; Sophie and Amalie have gone missing."

I sat up as fast as anyone can sit up with three dogs and three cats on the bed with them. "What do you mean, missing?"

"The girls have run away from the foster home." *Aw geez.* "The Sheriff just called to alert us to be on the lookout."

My mood plummeted as I listened to Mom explain someone came to the door, and as the woman stood there holding the door wide the girls pushed past them and ran. "The foster mother didn't even think the girls were up yet. The good news is they'd found their boots and coats, so they won't freeze. They must have been just waiting for an opportunity."

"Where on earth do they think they're going to go?" I sighed. And to make matters even more worrying, they weren't in Mallowapple; they'd been taken to a neighboring town, much larger, where they wouldn't know their way around.

"They're a couple of scared and lonely kids." I could hear the concern in Mom's voice.

"I'm going to free up my schedule and get hold of Tyler; we'll go out looking for them."

"Good. Rooster and Linda are getting ready to do the same. Why don't you talk to Rooster and figure out where you're each going to look, so you don't waste time covering the same area?"

And that's what we did.

Twelve

I was waiting at the end of the driveway when Tyler pulled up in the Subaru. No sooner had I belted myself in than I felt warm breath on my ear.

"Hello, Frank," I said, turning my head so I was nose to nose with Tyler's great dane/bloodhound mix. He gazed mournfully at me and I heard the slow slap of his tail against the back seat. I scratched his ears and kissed him on the nose as he drooled on my shoulder. "Are you here to help?"

"I figured I'd try and put that Nose Work to use," Tyler said.

Now don't get me wrong, I love Frank to pieces, but he's kind of a goofball and doesn't exactly excel in the training department. If you tell him sit or stay he'll probably just stand looking at you, slowly waving his tail. If you say come, he's more likely to turn around and amble away. So when Tyler decided to enroll him in Nose Work classes, I thought he was being a little over-optimistic.

In case you're not familiar with K9 Nose Work, it's a scenting and search activity where the dog searches for specific smells in the way a drug-sniffing dog would. It's not the same as tracking, where a dog actually follows the smell, so I was pretty skeptical of Frank's ability to help our search.

"Great idea," I lied, then I called Rooster to let him know we had a slight change of plan; we were heading to the foster parents' house to get something for Frank to scent, then we'd go from there.

The foster mother, Kaylene, was genuinely distraught about the kids and readily handed us the pillow cases they'd slept on before she showed us in which direction the girls had run. "They took off like a pair of cheetahs," she said. "I went after them, but my old body couldn't get close to catching up."

Tyler bent down and held the pillow cases under Frank's nose. "Search!" Frank lay down and rested his head on his crossed paws. *Oh, boy.*

"Maybe we should start walking and try further down the street," I suggested.

"That should do the trick," Tyler said. *Yeah, right.*

He tugged at Frank's lead, "Come on, Frank. Let's go." With a distinct lack of enthusiasm the dog got to his feet and padded beside us. We reached a crossroad and I looked back to see Kaylene pointing to the right.

"It's this way," I said, raising my arm in farewell to Kaylene. "Shall we try again?"

Once more Tyler offered the pillowcases to Frank, with words of encouragement, "Search, Frank. Come on buddy, you can do this, those girls need your help." I gazed heavenward thinking I was going to have to burst my guy's bubble soon, when a loud baying jolted me back to the present.

Frank's whole posture had changed. His tail was up and his nose down, and he was tugging at his lead. Tyler and

I exchanged startled looks before we took off with the dog. He was moving so fast we practically had to jog.

For half an hour we zig-zagged around. If this was the girls' route it was obvious they didn't know where they were going, but did Frank? The dog stayed determined and I was beginning to think I was going to owe him a special treat for doubting his tracking skills when we rounded another corner to face a row of food trucks.

The scent of hot dogs and hamburgers filled the air and I glared at Frank. We'd wasted time we couldn't afford. Come to think of it, though, I hadn't had breakfast and the smell was making me pretty hungry.

"Sorry this didn't work out, honey," I said to Tyler, "but let's grab a bite while we're here and then get back to the car."

My guy just stared past me and wordlessly pointed to one of the trucks. I followed the direction of his arm, and walking purposefully toward a bright pink truck with pigs painted on the side and a sign proclaiming it to be "The Whole Hog," was a small figure in a pink puffer coat...Ammi.

We moved towards the truck as Ammi reached the window and appeared to call out to whoever was serving. There were only a few people hanging around; it was early yet for the lunch crowd but as we got near, a figure, cloaked in a hoodie, strode up and grabbed Ammi by the arm and began to pull her away. She tried to tug herself free. Tyler and I rushed forward calling Ammi's name and she found her voice, looking back at me and screaming, "Polleeee."

A guy jumped from the back of the pink truck, brandishing a large kitchen knife at the abductor. At the same time a couple of the onlookers sprang into action and the kidnapper let go of Ammi and took off running with several people, including Tyler, giving chase. Ammi ran into my arms and I soothed her, mumbling things like "You're safe, I've got you, it's OK now," while she heaved great, gasping sobs and buried her head in my shoulder. It just wasn't right that at the mere age of six a child should have to go through so much trauma.

Thirteen

How could someone so little consume so much food? By the time Tyler reappeared Ammi was finishing her Pig Mac pork sandwich and getting ready to start on a large piece of buttermilk pie, with hot chocolate to drink of course. *OK, so I was eating the same thing, but I'm a grown up.*

We were seated at one of the small folding tables the vendors had set up, staying close to the heat coming from the trucks. Two more containers were on the table in front of us; one for Tyler, and a double burger, no bun, for Frank.

Tyler shook his head when I gave him a questioning look. "Whoever it was got clean away. We searched the area for a while, but there was no sign of him."

He and Frank wearily flopped down and I pushed the food over to Tyler, then handed one of the burgers to Frank, who suddenly came alive again. "You're a good boy, and I'm sorry I doubted you." He graciously accepted my apology by practically chewing the grease off my fingers, so I gave him the second burger to distract him while I used a handi-wipe.

"Are you OK, Ammi?" Tyler stroked her hair and she looked at him with a mouthful of pie and nodded happily. I guess buttermilk pie can solve a lot of problems.

"Do we know where Sophie is?" Tyler turned his attention to me.

"Ammi said they were pretty lost. When they came across the food trucks she wanted to eat. Sophie objected on the grounds they needed to stay hidden and, besides, they had no money. Young Miss Junk-Food-Enthusiast here," I cocked my head in the little girl's direction, "didn't see that as an obstacle and left her sister hiding in a doorway, and that's where we came in. We were all so focused on Ammi, none of us noticed Sophie. I just hope to God she's OK."

"We need to call the Sheriff."

"Already done," I said and, as if on cue, a police cruiser pulled up beside the trucks and a couple of cops stepped out. Tyler stood and waved at them and they walked our way.

Ammi's face whitened when she spotted them and she scooted closer to me. "Are they going to take me away?" she said. I wrapped a protective arm around her and gave what I hoped was a reassuring smile. In truth, I had no idea what would happen to her.

"Polly Parrett?" The older of the two hiked his belt as he addressed me.

I nodded wordlessly as the officers introduced themselves and asked us to recount what had happened. Tyler and I each gave our own perspectives, then they asked Ammi a few questions but she'd turned into a mute; too scared or confused to say anything except, "It was a dragon." Poor kid, I bet it did seem as if a big, fearful beast was trying to snatch her.

"You know, we can take Ammi back to my mother's house," I said. "She knows us and she'll be well looked after." *And we'll make sure she can't run away.*

"That's something you'll have to talk to Social Services about." It was the younger officer who spoke this time. "Once we report back we'll be joining the search party for the little lady's sister."

I breathed a huge sigh of relief as the cops left us. "Let's get back home before someone has a change of mind." Glancing heavenward at the glowering skies I added, "Or it starts snowing."

Tyler stood. "You girls stay here. I'll go and get the car and pick you up. And you," he winked at Ammi, "can have another hot chocolate."

I realized instantly he was protecting Ammi from having to go back to the foster home. I blew him a kiss. "You're the best," I said.

Fourteen

There were five of us round the table at *Welcome Home* that late afternoon: Mom, Rooster, Linda, Tyler and me. Ammi was fast asleep on the sofa in the room across the hall where we could see her through the open doors. Curled up at her neck, Dopey the kitten was also asleep. A soft glow of multi-colored lights lay over them, reflecting through the window from the Christmas decorations outside and Burl Ives, a favorite of Mom's, was singing a selection of Christmas songs that should have filled us with the joy of the season, but we were caught up in the plight of two little girls.

No-one had let Ms. Harris know that Ammi had been found. In a conversation with Rooster the Sheriff had said he had a "feeling" he might forget to tell her, in which case the child would be best with us for the time being.

It had been decided Ammi and her kitty would sleep in Linda's room tonight. As our only female resident Linda was privileged to be in the house; the barn was just for the guys. Meanwhile, we were having a meeting of the minds to figure out what we could do to find Sophie and help solve this awful murder. Tyler and I had recounted our adventure, now Rooster was speaking.

"Right now our priority is finding Sophie. For all we know the person who tried to grab Ammi could also be after Sophie. And that person could be a killer.

"Feliks," *that's the Sheriff; he and Rooster are pals,* "is working on locating the girls' father. I'll keep bugging him for any news but as Whittier is special ops there's no guarantee the Army will be forthcoming with information.

"There is some good news, though. Feliks confided in me that Sophie is not the killer; she couldn't be. Nicole died from stab wounds, not a head wound."

There was a general sigh of relief around the table before Linda voiced the thought that was in all our heads.

"Then someone must have come to the house after the girls ran off. Do the police know who?"

"You know as much as I do. By rights the Sheriff shouldn't have told me about Sophie, so keep it under your hats."

Rooster gave us all a stern glare, then continued.

"Feliks has also recruited VFW members to help in the search for Sophie. They'll be heading out right about now, and our guys from *Welcome Home* should be setting off soon in the van. Polly, Tyler and I will be joining them shortly. Edwina," *that's my Mom,* "you and Linda will take care of things here."

I have to say something before I go on. Much as I was anxious and afraid for Sophie, I was so darn proud to be part of a group of such selfless people. Members of the military give until it hurts and then some. Many of these volunteers were old, some were broken and some had been forgotten. Yet when help was needed they didn't hesitate to give again, and I was feeling pretty positive that between us we'd find Sophie and keep her safe.

OK, I'll get back to the story now.

Rooster, Tyler and I geared up; it was going to be a very cold night. What's more, snow had begun to fall, and as the temperature fell the flakes fattened and drifts began to form. I hoped to goodness Sophie had stayed in the town.

Fifteen

As it happened we weren't out long before the call came through that Sophie had been found. We'd driven around for a while, stopping a couple of times to get out and patrol the streets and ask the few people we encountered if they'd seen a young girl anywhere. There'd been no good news and my stomach was churning at the thought of the danger Sophie might be in. That changed in an instant when we knew she was safe and all of us were elated, high-fiving and cheering in relief.

Sophie had been taken to the County Sheriff's Department. They were the ones who had been coordinating the search. The desk sergeant there didn't know us from a hole in the ground and we were arguing with him to let us see Sophie when Wisniewski walked in.

"What's going on here?"

"They won't let us see Sophie," I threw up my hands in exasperation.

"Alright, calm down." The Sheriff lifted his hat and ran his hands across his thinning hair. "Let me deal with this; you should go on home, there's nothing you can do here."

"The heck there isn't." All the tension of the last couple of days was about to burst from me when Rooster put a soothing hand on my shoulder and gave a squeeze.

"What Polly means," he said in calm voice, "is that we've all been really anxious about the little lady and we want to be sure she's got someone in her corner in there." He nodded in the direction of the offices where we assumed Sophie had been taken. "In fact, we really want to take her home to her little sister and some people who will care for her properly. And Feliks, we'd really appreciate if you could help us with that... don't we Polly?"

"Sheriff, you know the best place for her is with us. The kid's been through hell. Does she even know she's innocent?"

"That's enough, Miss Parrett." Wisniewski threw up his hand to signal "Stop" and his face tightened as he hissed, "If you want my help, you'll shut up right now. There's a lot of people who want the best for the girls, and I'm one of them. But there are legal procedures I'm duty bound to follow. I've already stepped out on a limb by telling you the girl didn't kill her stepmother and by letting you keep her sister at your Mom's, so I'll tell you again – go home, and leave this to me."

I felt my face burning, partly in indignation but more in shame. The Sheriff was right; he was trying to do the right thing for everyone, and I'd blabbed in public about Sophie being innocent when I wasn't even supposed to know about it. Mumbling apologies I let Tyler take my hand and lead me out.

Rooster hung back and exchanged a few quiet words with his friend before hurrying to join us. "We're good. Feliks will call when he can to let us know what's happening."

"I'm sorry, Rooster, I broke your confidence as well."

"Not to worry, sweetie. We're all emotionally involved in this; it's understandable. But I think it's time we got serious about figuring out who killed Nicole. That's the best way we can help the girls."

"I'm with Rooster," Tyler said. "Meanwhile, it's been a long day. Let's sleep on this and look at it with fresh minds tomorrow."

It hit me then that I was feeling pretty exhausted. We had to get Rooster back to *Welcome Home* and pick up Angel, Vinny and Coco. Knowing I'd be gone a long time I'd taken them over there. Mom would have fed them long before now and, knowing her, she probably had something tasty waiting for us.

Sixteen

Mom had outdone herself. We walked into a full house, the smell of Brunswick Stew drawing us to the dining room.

Normally the *Welcome Home* residents cater to themselves. They have a kitchen in the barn, which allows them to be more independent. Tonight, as thanks for their help, Mom had pulled a few batches of her famous stew from the freezer and invited the men over.

Ammi was holding court as Snow White, and had apparently cast most of the guys as the dwarfs, with Dopey playing the part of, well…Dopey. Batt Vargus was gamely playing the wicked queen, with a paper crown on his head.

Batt had been training as a pararescue specialist in the Air Force when he had a brain aneurysm. During surgery he then had a stroke and it left him with memory loss, daily headaches and partial deafness; he was also prone to dizziness. Not surprisingly he struggled with depression, and attempted suicide.

His life took a turn for the better when a giant-sized black and white Newfoundland mix came into it. Though not a trained therapy dog, Patches acted as Batt's ears, instinctively knew when Batt was having a dizzy spell, and his happy nature was a real tonic. They'd been with us for several months now and were a valued part of our "family."

Tonight, Patches had been allowed to join his person and so had also been roped into Ammi's tableau as the handsome prince, which I thought was a good move as he most likely was the best kisser. For some reason, known only by someone with a six-year-old mind, Linda had been cast as the magic mirror.

Mom greeted us and quietly explained Ammi knew her sister had been found. "But we told her Sophie was staying with a nice lady in town because she had to help the police tomorrow."

It was somewhat close to the truth and the child seemed to have accepted the explanation. I wondered just where Sophie would be tonight. Surely not in a jail cell? And would Ms. Harris trust Kaylene to take charge of her again?

For the next couple of hours, I pushed aside any dismal thoughts. It was nearly Christmas after all and the guys were in great spirits, enjoying the food and knowing the girls were safe. The mood was infectious and soon I was sharing the good cheer.

In the background I heard a phone ring and noticed Rooster get up from the table, putting his hand in his pocket. A few minutes later he came over and whispered in my ear. "The Sheriff is on the way over; says he needs to see us."

"What for?" Alarm bells were going off in my head. Was he coming to take Ammi away?

"Didn't say. Just said to expect him within the hour."

After that my mood soured again. I didn't say anything to Mom; didn't want to spoil her evening. I did tell Tyler, who took the high road to optimism, saying, "It's not necessarily something bad." *I'm not so sure.*

The gathering ended about 10 minutes later when Ammi fell forward, head on plate, fast asleep. Batt gathered her up and climbed the stairs with Linda to put her to bed. The rest of the men cleared the table and cleaned up the kitchen. In no time everything was spotless and the guys left, Batt joining them, with cries of "Thanks," and "Merry Christmas."

The rest of us went back to our usual places in the kitchen, Linda joining us with reassurances that Ammi was out for the count. We made desultory small talk for a while, which dwindled into silence, no-one wanting to voice reasons for the Sheriff's visit. By the time we heard the crunch of tires on the crisp snow outside we were a bundle of nerves.

Tyler got up to open the door. Moments later he came back, a big grin on his face. With him was Wisniewski, his hand on the shoulder of a young girl...Sophie.

Seventeen

Once again it was the dogs who reacted first. My three and Elaine greeted Sophie as if she was the most wonderful person they could ever hope to meet. In moments her bleak expression was transformed and a big smile lit up her face.

One by one the rest of us approached her with hugs and words of welcome. In turn, the first thing she said was, "Where's Ammi?"

"The poor child is worn out." Mom gave Linda a meaningful look, and she responded by guiding Sophie up the stairs to join her sister.

Once we were sure she was out of earshot we bombarded Wisniewski with questions 'til he raised his arms in surrender. "Stop!

"How about a cup of coffee, Edwina, and then we'll talk."

Mom gave him an appraising look. "You look done in, Feliks. Sit yourself down and have a piece of pie with that coffee. The rest of you, give the man some room to breathe."

We backed away – when Mom talks, people listen – and allowed the Sheriff to enjoy his break. Linda returned during that time and filled the void, telling us Sophie conked out in the bed beside her sister within moments. "Ammi didn't even wake. I don't think there's any fear of them running away tonight. Just to be sure, though, I'm going to sleep on a bedroll across the door."

"Gracious, Linda, you don't need to do that. We can put a couple of cots in the room for the girls and you can have the bed back."

"Edwina, I've spent many nights on the hard ground; believe me, a bedroll still seems like luxury, so don't worry. Besides, I'll sleep more soundly knowing there's no way the kids can get past me."

"OK, Sheriff," I was getting impatient. "Spill. Where did you find her?"

"We didn't. She found us." Wisniewski noted our confusion and explained. "She walked up to the same two cops you talked to and announced, 'My name's Sophie Whittier, and it's best for everyone I go with you.' "

"What a funny thing to say." Mom frowned. "Did she say it just like that?"

"Word for word."

"Maybe she'll tell us more in the morning. If she feels more secure she might start to open up."

"Just make sure she doesn't start planning another escape."

"Where's Dopey?" Talking of escape, I had a sudden realization I hadn't seen the kitten for a while and I felt a twinge of concern.

"She's not with the girls," Linda said. Oh, Lord.

With all the activity that had been going on in the house earlier she could have been scared and be hiding somewhere. Even worse, what if she slipped outside? People had been coming in and out all evening; she's so tiny, it would be easy not to notice her.

For the next half hour, we practically ransacked the house and searched around the outside, shining flashlights in every nook and cranny. Linda and I even went up to the bedroom and gently removed the covers from the girls, thinking she might have crawled in bed with them. There was no Dopey...anywhere.

I was in a state of near panic. How could we lose a helpless kitten? How would Ammi react? I dropped onto the sofa in the living room, choking back a sob and burying my face in my hands. I had to get a grip on myself.

Something touched my foot – just barely. Spreading my fingers wide I peered down. A purple glass Christmas ornament rested at my feet. Where had that come from?

Directly across from me, the Christmas tree stood in all its splendor. Actually, splendor is a bit of an exaggeration. To stay pet-friendly we had an artificial tree mostly decorated with paper and silk ornaments. It looked very real and was quite thick. Only the top half had lights because Lief, my gorgeous orange cat who stayed with Mom, had a thing about chewing electrical cords. But we did put a handful of bright shiny things at the top of the tree where they were out of reach of the furry critters. So how had this one ended up on the floor?

As I eyed the tree I saw the top sway a little, and a couple of the branches rustled enough that the ornaments twirled gently one way then back again. I moved closer and parted the moving branches and found myself inches from a white face with splotches of brown and tan, and a pair of startlingly blue eyes. Dopey barely acknowledged me, instead reaching out a paw toward another dangly treasure.

"I found her," I yelled out, laughing in sheer relief, and reached in to pluck her from her hiding place.

The others surged into the room, happy that disaster had been averted, and made a fuss of the kitten who promptly fell asleep.

"It's a good thing the tree didn't come down," Wisniewski was shaking his head.

"We've learned from past experience," Mom explained. "We've had more than one disaster with cats and glittery things, so now the tree gets anchored to the wall."

Glittery things. I was reminded of the bracelet Ammi had put around Dopey's neck. "You know, talking of glitter, we should give some thought to the significance of the bracelet Nicole was given, and the meaning of the inscription."

The Sheriff scowled at me.

Eighteen

Right about now I was feeling fairly warm and fuzzy towards Sheriff Wisniewski. He'd just finished telling us that he'd informed Ms. Harris it wasn't safe for her to be on the roads in her small car with all the ice and snow. That was actually true, but he could just as easily have used his Ford Expedition to take Sophie to another foster as bring her out to us.

Wisniewski drained the last of his coffee and stood. "There's something else I'm going to tell you. Before I do I need to caution you not to go poking around in this investigation." *Why was he looking at me when he said that?* "We're dealing with a murderer, and what I'm going to tell you is because I want you to keep those girls safe...from anyone."

"Spill it already, will you?" Linda yawned, which produced a copycat reaction in all of us.

The Sheriff looked stern. "Neal Whittier has been on leave for the past five days." There was a general gasp of surprise. "And one of the Whittier neighbors thinks they saw him the day before the murder."

"So Ammi's and Sophie's father was in Mallowapple when Nicole was killed?" Mom echoed Wisniewski's words.

"Why wouldn't he have come forward to take care of the girls?" Linda asked.

"Are you saying Whittier killed his own wife? And then abandoned his children?" Tyler was disbelieving.

"I'm saying trust no-one. And keep in mind Whittier is a highly trained and combat seasoned warrior. Don't mess with him." With that, the Sheriff settled his hat firmly on his head and left us digesting the awful possibility the girls' father had murdered their stepmother

Nineteen

I was on a mission. After Sheriff Wisniewski left last night, Mom, Rooster, Linda, Tyler and I sat around the table trying to figure out what we could do about the situation.

I know...you're thinking the Sheriff warned us not to get involved, but what would you do? Two kids were facing the prospect of being without their only parent. And Christmas was almost here. Somehow that made things worse.

We hashed around the meaning of the letters on the bracelet: A V O, or maybe A V D. It seemed most likely they were someone's initials, though none of us could think of anyone who would fit the bill.

"Could it be Nicole had a lover?" Linda asked. "Someone who followed her to Mallowapple?"

"The person most likely to know if there's a stranger in town is Nita," I said (she's the owner of Bennie's Diner, which is the hub of Mallowapple gossip). "I'll stop in there tomorrow and see what I can find out."

So that's where I was headed now, and I was really hoping my time would be productive, 'cause we hadn't come up with anything else of use.

Tyler and I had ended up staying at *Welcome Home* last night. With five bedrooms and only Linda and Rooster in residence there was plenty of room for us. And the roads really were bad; it wasn't worth the risk of driving in the dark.

Mom had fretted she'd have to cancel her hair appointment the next day. She was able to drive herself these days in her compact car, using hand controls. Getting in and out, however, was tricky even on the best of days. It required lifting herself from the wheelchair to the car seat and taking the chair apart to stow it beside her. There was no way it was safe to do that today and, anyway, her car couldn't handle the deep snow. So Tyler volunteered to act as chauffeur. "No one is buying houses at Christmas," he'd said, "so I have all day to help, if you need me."

I was really grateful to him. Tomorrow was Christmas Eve and the *Welcome Home* open house, and I knew Mom wanted to look her best for it. She didn't get much chance to gussy up.

Nita's was pretty full for mid-morning and I had to park a block away. I'd stopped at my house for some quality time with my cats, Ditto, Taz and Amber and to drop the dogs off. Happily everything was going smoothly with my pet-sitting crew, so I was free to delve into the murder mystery.

There was no need to beat around the bush with Nita. Gossip was a way of life and she considered it perfectly normal to want to know another person's business.

"Nita," I leaned against the counter and took a sip from my double shot cappuccino, "do you know who told the Sheriff they saw Neal Whittier a few days ago?"

"Of course I know." She gave me a scornful look. "It was Becky Marchand. She lives across from them and happened to notice a man lurking by the door." *Of course she did.*

"When was this?"

"The night before the murder."

"So it was dark. Then how could she be sure it was Whittier?"

"Ask her yourself. Here she comes." Nita nodded in the direction of the entrance and there came Becky, greeting all the diners as if she were their favorite aunt, while wending her way to us.

"Polly," she beamed, "how nice to see you, dear. Sit down with me and tell me what's going on at *Welcome Home.*"

Yep, these ladies were nothing if not direct.

I treated Becky to a piece of warm apple cider cake with vanilla ice cream. Naturally, I couldn't expect her to eat alone so I had to get some for myself.

Nita sat with us, and I let Becky ramble on, thinking she was more likely to say something of interest if I didn't interrupt. And I admit, I didn't want my ice cream to melt.

"Well, I was sitting at the window with my knitting. You know I can practically knit blindfold so I don't need a light on, and I enjoy looking at the stars. I saw a man walking along the street. Actually, it was more like marching, or no, no...striding. That's it; he was striding." I sighed and Becky chatted on.

"He went right up to the house and tried to look through the windows. The drapes were drawn mind you, so I don't suppose he could really see anything. She, Mrs. Whittier, Nicole that is, got blackout drapes at Pottery Barn. I asked her if I could see how they looked hanging in the house because I was thinking of getting some myself. She had striped ones and I prefer floral…"

Time to interrupt.

"Becky, uh Becky." She looked at me as though surprised I was even there. "How could you know it was Neal Whittier?"

"He was a big man, broad shoulders you know, and had a backpack or some such thing over his shoulder. And in any case, who else would it be?"

Good grief.

Have you ever seen him before?" I asked.

"No, dear. When would I have seen him? He's never been in Mallowapple before."

I grit my teeth and tried again. "Did the man go in the house?"

"Well, he knocked on the door but Nicole wasn't home, was she?"

"Wasn't she?"

"Of course not; she always goes to her yoga class on Wednesday evening. She goes three times a week, actually, Monday and Friday mornings and then Wednesday."

"What about the girls?"

"Ah, that does bother me. They're at school on Monday and Friday, but she leaves them alone on Wednesday and that's not right. The older one is very sensible but I still try and keep my eye out for them."

"If the girls were home when the man knocked, why didn't they open the door?"

"I expect they've been told not to. Honestly, Polly, you do ask some silly questions."

I wondered if I had any aspirin in the van, because I was getting a serious headache.

"One more thing, Becky. Do you know where Nicole went for Yoga?"

"It's that place over in Mud River. Now what's the name?"

"Averil Daine Yoga Studio," Nita injected with an air of triumph. *It must have half killed her to sit so long without saying anything.* "I know because Ginny Hansen takes classes there. Come to think of it, she's never mentioned seeing Nicole Whittier there."

"That's because she took private lessons," said Becky with a nod of finality.

Twenty

I was resting my head on the steering wheel when the phone rang. I'd found an aspirin powder deep in the glove compartment, which I'd had to swallow dry because I'd forgotten to refill my water bottle. The Jingle Bell dogs sounded like a pack of high-pitched poodles and it cut right through my brain. I snatched up the phone, "Yes?"

"Someone's not having a good day." *Mom.*

"Sorry, Mom, I've got a really bad headache. I've been talking to Becky Marchand."

"No need to say anything else," Mom understood right away. "I have some information that might help take your mind off it. Let's meet for an early lunch at the diner and …"

"Not the diner, Mom. Can we do this at my place? It will be private there."

There were murmurings in the background then Mom spoke again. "Tyler said we'll bring lunch. Be there in half an hour."

Bliss is a Shrimp and Shroom pizza. That's what Tyler and Mom arrived with; my favorite combo of shrimp, mushroom and onion from the local pizzeria. There was just one slice left.

"You have it Polly," Tyler shoved the box my way.

"I'm stuffed. You finish it." I was just being polite but Tyler picked the slice up and it was heading for his mouth when he burst out laughing.

189

"You should see your face." Mom was laughing too.

"We'll split it," Tyler said, and he tore it in half, handing the bigger piece to me.

"While you two finish," Mom said, "I'll fill you in on my news.

"Janice Whipple was at Combing Attractions Hair Salon while I was there, and she told me she'd seen Nicole Whittier arguing with Britney Harris about a week ago. Janice was over at the Mud River Mall and was passing Dazzle Diamonds when she heard an uproar. She looked in and there were Nicole and Britney going at it. Actually, she said Britney was doing all the yelling, and was trying to grab something Nicole was holding behind her back.

"The manager was quick to intervene and asked Britney to leave. That didn't go over well and Britney started screaming at him, so they called for security and she was hustled out."

"Phew. That's enough to make Britney murderous."

Mom gave me a cautionary look. "Don't let your personal feelings get in the way of the truth, Polly."

"I'm not. What were they fighting over anyway?"

"A little black and gold frog with diamonds on it. Janice said she pretended to be looking in the case next to Nicole as she bought it, but she couldn't tell if it was a pin or a pendant. I must say, though, it seems a real stretch to think anyone would kill over an item of jewelry."

"Maybe there was already bad blood between them," Tyler suggested. "I think I should have a chat with Britney and see what I can find out."

"Not without me, you don't."

"Oh, Polly," Mom sighed, then continued, "I'm wondering about the connection between Averil Daine and the bracelet. How does her name correspond to A V D? It's very flimsy to me, and we're not even sure the D isn't an O."

She started gathering up the empty pizza box and napkins. "I should get back to the house and help with preparations for tomorrow. Let's sum up what we know for now, and what we can do.

"We have three murder suspects: Britney Harris, because she had an argument with Nicole; the woman from the yoga studio, Averil Daine; and let's not forget Neal Whittier, because he may have been seen at the house before the murder, but has since been missing."

"Perhaps it's time I considered yoga lessons, and I guess it might be best if Tyler speaks with Britney alone," I conceded.

Mom smiled her approval. "And I'll chat with the girls; maybe they know more than they realize."

Twenty One

"Yoga enhances the function of all bodily systems, which may help you lose weight." What was the woman implying? "It calms the mind, enhances muscle strength and flexibility, and helps you face life's challenges and promote self-healing."

I was beginning to wonder if I really should start doing yoga. Instead I asked, "Are you Averil Daine?"

"Gracious, no. Her offices are in New York."

"Oh, so when does she come here?"

The woman gave me a puzzled look. "She's hardly likely to come to Mud River. That's not how it works."

"How what works?"

"If we need assistance or Flavio wants to run a new marketing campaign, they send someone down from corporate."

A penny dropped. "You're a franchise."

"You didn't know? There are Averil Daine studios all over the country."

Instead of responding to that, I asked, "Who's Flavio?"

Behind me a voice replied, "That would be me."

Va Va Voom!

The guy was gorgeous. Everything you could imagine in a Latin lover: dark, Italian looks, alluring eyes, sensual mouth. Oh my.

"Miss Parrett is interested in our beginner classes."

"Miss Parrett? You must have a beautiful first name to match those beautiful eyes."

"It's, uh, Polly."

"I was right, Polly." He practically purred my name. "Has Dalia shown you around?" I could only shake my head dumbly. "Then come this way, please."

He put his hand on the small of my back to guide me along, saying things about stress reduction, deep feelings and love, that pretty much went over my head. *Get a grip, Polly.*

The trance was broken when a door opened and a group of women filtered into the hallway. As they saw Flavio, they bunched around him offering unmitigated adoration and effectively blocking me out. Talk about magnetism.

Eventually, Flavio pulled himself away while the women blew kisses at him and cooed, "Love you." In turn, Flavio kissed his finger tips and blew the kiss back at them, calling out, "Remember ladies, love conquers all."

OK, now I was officially not attracted to the man.

To hide my discomfort, I coughed and mumbled, "You're certainly popular."

"We stress the power of love here, and I encourage the ladies to also express it."

I didn't want to ask exactly what he meant by that, so I trooped along beside him to complete my studio tour. He found every opportunity to brush up against me or take my hand to lead me along. He even stroked my cheek, saying I had lint stuck there, and made a point to remark that my skin was "so soft, like the wings of a butterfly." There was nothing overt in his manner, but it was certainly suggestive, and by the time we were back in the foyer I couldn't get out of there fast enough.

"Uh, thanks. This was very, um, educational. I appreciate you taking the time to show me around."

"I believe in a hands-on approach." *Don't you ever!* "Here, take one of our brochures; it will give you the times of our group classes, or we can always go one on one."

Snatching the pamphlet from his hand I hurried back to the van, locked the door behind me and released the breath I hadn't realized I was holding

Twenty Two

Tomorrow would be Christmas Eve. So far my crew had all the pet-sits under control, and with luck it would stay that way. It was great to have such wonderful people on my team and know I could rely on them.

It had been decided I would stay at *Welcome Home* through Christmas. With the Open House planned for Christmas Eve, Mom and the gang needed all the help they could get. There was one huge problem, though...I still hadn't had a chance to do any shopping.

As I loaded the dogs and cats in the van – yes, Ditto, Taz and Amber were coming for the celebrations, too – I wracked my mind for ideas, but it just kept filling with thoughts of Nicole Whittier and her step-daughters. Oh, well. I'd just have to beg forgiveness from everybody and get their gifts later on.

It was already dark and the roads were still treacherous, and I hoped that didn't stop people from coming tomorrow. Most people had studded tires on their vehicles and were used to the weather, but you never know what might happen. And the guys would be terribly disappointed if their hard work didn't pay off.

My negative thoughts dissipated the instant I reached the farmhouse. Quite simply, it was magical. The lights were on, the little train was running, elves were waving and this time it was Bing Crosby whose voice came over the audio system, singing White Christmas.

I pulled around to the back of the house so the van would be out of the way, and trudged in with my furry dog family.

"Need help?" Tyler was there. He'd been with Mom all day, running errands and helping out. He'd picked up Frank along the way, and both of them would be staying for Christmas. This year Tyler's parents had decided to spend the holidays in Bermuda and had taken his sister along. Tyler elected to stay in Mallowapple. I smiled broadly at him and gave him a big smackaroo on the lips.

"Hey, you can grab the cats in their carriers for me and take them up to my room. Then how about you join me for a little eggnog and tell me what happened with Britney?"

"No time for that," Tyler said over his shoulder as he headed to the van. "Your mother has plans for you in the kitchen, and I'm on loan to Rooster. We're building a stand for the entertainment."

"Entertainment? What entertainment?"

Tyler wouldn't say more on the subject, and I soon forgot about it as Mom, Linda, the girls and I stirred spices into cider, ladled pumpkin and pecan fillings into tartlets, beat together ingredients for sugar cookies and gingerbread men. The aroma was heavenly and none of us could resist sampling a little of our creations.

By the time we were done it was getting late. We'd already packed the girls off to bed and everyone was yawning big time and making mutterings about being ready for bed.

"Hold on, people! We still have a murder to solve." I stood with hands on hips, daring the others to leave, then directed my attention to Tyler. "And I still want to know what happened when you talked to Britney."

"OK, OK." Tyler reached for the coffee pot and poured himself another cup, then eased his frame onto the window bench. "The fight was over a charm, one of those collectible things you buy to put on a bracelet. Apparently this particular charm is scarce and Nicole had just bought the last one. Britney wanted to buy it from her, Nicole refused and you know the rest."

"Then it's possible Britney could have gone to Nicole's house to make another attempt at persuading her to give up the charm," Linda was hypothesizing, "Nicole said, 'No,' Britney lost her temper and stabbed her. She might still have been woozy from the fall when Sophie pushed her, and unable to fight back."

"I thought about that," Tyler said, "but where did she get the knife? If she brought one that makes it premeditated murder, and I don't buy that. And as far as we know, there are no knives missing from the house.

"Britney also insisted she did not contact Nicole again and, anyway, she found another charm online. She was wearing it, so I can vouch for that."

"She might still have gone to Nicole's before she bought online." I sooo wanted a reason for Britney to be the killer.

"She may be conceited but she's not stupid," Mom said. "She'd know it would be easy to check the timeline, so why lie?"

"I suppose," I grumbled. "Besides, she'd never risk breaking a nail or getting blood splatter on her Balmain skinny jeans by gutting someone's insides. She's more the poisonous type."

Mom chose to ignore my comment, instead asking, "I never saw the bracelet; was it the kind to put these charms on?"

Tyler and I exchanged looks. I shrugged. "I suppose so. Are you thinking there's some significance between the bracelet and the charm?"

"Possibly. It struck me Nicole must have gone to buy the charm right after she received the bracelet. Assuming she was buying it for herself, the first charm might well have some special meaning. You saw it on Britney's wrist, Tyler; did anything catch your eye?"

"Not particularly. The frog seemed to be sitting with his arms out."

"For goodness sake, we can easily find out what it looks like. Let me get my iPad." I dashed upstairs and was back and online in minutes. Searching for "black and gold charm bracelet frog" brought up a load of hits, most of them for the Tesoro collection. I opened a link to an image.

Peering over my shoulder, Linda burst out, "Oh my goodness, it's in a Lotus pose."

Wide-eyed we looked at each other. The frog was in a yoga pose. Now surely that had to be significant.

Twenty Three

"What do we know about this Flavio guy?" Rooster asked. "How about A V O is a nickname for him – Avo. He and Nicole have been having an affair, she dumps him, he kills her."

"Hmm," I was doubtful. "He's the kind of guy to be the dumper, not the dumpee. He oozes sex appeal." Tyler frowned at me. "You should have seen the women playing up to him, like moths around the flame."

"Yea," Linda joined in, "but what if he did fall for her? A guy like that wouldn't be used to rejection; he'd likely take it hard."

"He could also have been the guy lurking round the Whittier house." Mom decided to add her two cents to the mix. "It was dark, and Becky Marchand doesn't have the best eye sight. She just saw a man with a backpack. And I suppose Flavio could be the one who tried to grab Ammi. I wonder why, though? Did he think the children had seen something?"

"We're just shooting in the dark here." Rooster spoke. "We're coming up with theories but we need hard evidence. I know we all wanted to clear this up before Christmas but it looks like we'll have to set it aside for now. First thing in the morning I'll call Feliks and tell him what we're thinking. Meanwhile, we could all use a good night's sleep; tomorrow will be a busy day."

Twenty Four

There was a crushing weight on my chest and a foul smell assaulted my nostrils. I opened my eyes and Ditto, my fat cat, stared ambivalently into my eyes as he lay on top of me. Turning my head to the right, Vinny was resting his head on the pillow facing me, sound asleep and snorting. *Eww. Buzzard breath.* I'd have to get his teeth cleaned soon.

I could hear quite a bit of activity downstairs. Grabbing my phone I checked the time: nearly eight. I'd meant to be up at seven.

"What happened?" I addressed my fur-kids. "You used to get me up at five." They were all getting older, and slower, and I wasn't so sure I liked it.

I threw on an old robe and slippers and headed downstairs with the dogs to let them out. "Morning gorgeous," I heard. Turning to Tyler I caught a glimpse of my reflection in one of the windows; spiked hair, squash face and baggy eyes. Nothing gorgeous about it.

"And don't you forget it," I said.

He rumpled my hair, kissed the tip of my nose and we both laughed.

"I've got the dogs. Frank's already outside and then I'll feed them. You go and get dressed and I'll bring the cats' breakfast up when you're ready."

"You're a prince among men."

"Oh, and coffee's ready in the kitchen."

"I take it back, you're a king of kings." *I am **so** lucky.*

Actually, I hadn't got out of the kitchen by the time Tyler and the dogs returned. Mom was telling me she had decided not to charge an entrance fee to the open house. Though it was hoped visitors would show their generosity through donations, the event was more about sharing what *Welcome Home* was about – offering a safe haven for veterans and their pets.

"Did Rooster talk to the Sheriff?"

"First thing," Mom replied, "and Wisniewski is going to Mud River to talk to Flavio today. Which reminds me, I put your brochure in the napkin drawer so it wouldn't get lost."

Obviously I was far short of my caffeine quota because it took me a few moments to realize she was talking about the Averil Daine Yoga Studio brochure. I pulled it from the drawer and leafed through it as I sipped my java, casting my eyes over bulleted points touting the benefits of yoga, from balance and endurance to mindfulness.

"Yikes! Listen to this." The activity around me stopped and everyone looked my way as I recited from the page.

"Improve your love life and increase your appetite for sex. Yoga doesn't have to stay in the studio. Learn poses you can use in the bedroom to delight and excite your partner.

"Stimulating yoga poses will increase circulation to your pelvic area, lighting up your sexual awareness; and special breathing techniques release chemicals in the brain that will increase your sexual desire.

"Join Flavio in his weekly class, Better Sex, and you can learn to achieve whole-body orgasm.

"Private instruction available."

I could feel my face heating up as I read. "It gives a whole new meaning to his motto: Love Conquers All."

"Omnia vincit amor," Tyler said.

"What did you say?" Mom had a startled expression on her face.

"Love conquers all. It's Latin. And I seem to recall there's a very racy, full-frontal painting of a naked cupid by some famous Italian artist, titled Amor Vincit Omnia. It's based on something Virgil wrote. Um, let me think...yes, 'Love conquers all; let us all yield to love!' My old Latin teacher would be proud of me." Tyler grinned, then the smile slowly faded. His brow wrinkled and he glanced in my direction. "Amor vincit omnia." He drew the words out slowly. "A V O. Don't you get it? The initials on the bracelet."

"Um, no I don't. What does Amor Winkit Omni-whatever have to do with the initials?"

"In Latin the letter V is pronounced as W, so although the phrase is pronounced Amor Winkit Omnia, the first letters of each word are A, V and O."

I had enough trouble with the English language at times, so it took a few moments before the penny dropped. "Now I get it," I said, and in the next instance had a startling revelation. "Oh, my stars. It must be Flavio. He's the killer." My mind was racing as I pieced together what must have happened.

"We were right to think he and Nicole were having an affair and she dumped him. Perhaps the bracelet was a peace-offering."

"No," Mom interrupted, "it doesn't make sense for her to buy a yoga-themed charm if she'd already dumped Flavio."

Tyler was skeptical. "She could have been making a point; a metaphorical slap in the face."

"It doesn't matter," I said. "The fact is everything fits. It was Flavio who Becky Marchand saw at the house. He could have been obsessed with her; maybe that's why she broke it off.

"It was Flavio who went to the house after the girls ran off. We don't know if Nicole let him in, or if the girls left a door unlocked. He must have had a knife with him, they argued and he killed her."

"Why would he try and kidnap the kids?" Mom asked.

"He must have thought they saw or knew something." I shuddered. "Which means he probably intended to kill them."

"I'm calling Wisniewski," Tyler said. "Now!"

Twenty Five

We were a huge success. I think all of Mallowapple showed up for the Open House, along with bunches of people from neighboring towns. We'd handed donation envelopes out as folk arrived, and most of them had been handed back with something in them. The baked goods had sold so fast that Mom grabbed some backup gingerbread and cookie dough from the freezer, and we rushed to get more goodies on the table.

Compliments were flowing, laughter was in the air, kids were having a blast, and Flavio was safely out of the way. Sheriff Wisniewski had taken him in for questioning and I was sure he'd get a confession. All in all, I was definitely feeling the Christmas spirit.

"Ladies and gentlemen. Your attention please. The Christmas pageant is about to begin."

That was Tyler's voice. He was on the makeshift stage, and visitors were beginning to form a semi-circle around it as he continued his announcement.

"The residents of Welcome Home are proud to present...The Story of Jesus."

I scooted back to the front porch to get a better view as three of the guys, dressed as the Wise Men, stepped on to the stage singing We Three Kings. A couple of them had really good voices. *Who knew?*

Tucked in the back I noted Rooster was handling audio. Tyler seemed to be in charge of props, holding a star on the end of a pole high over the kings, and a tarpaulin was being used as a screen behind which the players waited their turns on-stage.

The Kings exited the stage, their voices fading, and Batt Vargus stepped out to narrate, closely followed by Linda and a resident named Fozzie - a Chief Warrant Officer, U. S. Army - in the guise of Mary and Joseph. Playing the part of the baby Jesus was Fozzie's really cute Jack Russell mix, Dandy, which brought cries of "Awww," and "How sweet," from the audience.

As the show went on we were introduced to the shepherds, and to Sophie and Ammi as angels, while Rooster jumped on to do a stint as the innkeeper. Batt's dog Patches, along with Frank, were supposed to be cattle in the stable and Vinny and Coco looked perfect as little white sheep. Problem was, none of the dogs had their parts down very well. Dandy just didn't want to stay in the manger, which worked out well because Patches sat his large frame down and leaned against it, sending manger and baby off the stage. Vinny kept trying to climb on Mary's lap, Frank was utterly bored; only Coco was quite happy to be held in a shepherd's arms.

Still, the onlookers clapped and cheered, and when Batt invited them to join in singing Christmas carols at the end, people linked arms, swayed from side to side and lifted their voices in joy.

Someone tapped my shoulder. I looked behind me. "Sheriff. I didn't expect to see you here."

"I wanted to tell you in person. We had to let him go."

I frowned my confusion.

"Flavio. It's not him."

"But...but it has to be!" I could hardly believe what I was hearing. "The bracelet, the inscription; he and Nicole…"

Wisniewski shook his head. "He admits the affair but insists there was no break-up. In fact, according to him Nicole was going to get a divorce and they were going to run the yoga studio together. He says they even had plans to expand."

"So the bracelet…?"

"He admits to leaving the bracelet on the doorstep and that A V O stands for love conquers all. Apparently Nicole was nervous about breaking up her marriage and Flavio claims the bracelet was to give her courage."

"Then who was outside Nicole's house the night before she was killed?"

"Flavio insists he was with Nicole at the studio that evening, and he has alibis for the time of the murder and for the kidnapping attempt on Amalie."

My heart thudded in my chest. "Then Amalie and Sophie are still in danger."

I looked over at the stage. There was Sophie singing Joy to the World. But where was Ammi?

"I don't see Ammi." I clutched at the Sheriff's arm. "She should be on the stage."

"Alright," Wisniewski started scanning the crowd. "What's she wearing?"

"A white angel costume."

He nodded. "You go and check with Rooster; I'll round up some people and we'll start looking."

I raced toward the stage and tugged on Rooster's shirt to get his attention. "Where's Ammi?"

He gave me a startled look. "She had to go to the bathroom."

We'd set up a couple of porta-potties; would she go there or in the house? In the house, I decided and was about to take off when someone firmly gripped my arm. "What the heck is going on?" Rooster hissed.

"Flavio is not the killer. The Sheriff is here, he just told me."

Rooster understood immediately. "Where are you going to look?"

"In the house."

"I'll get Tyler; we'll check the parking area and make sure nobody leaves.

Twenty Six

I hurtled through the front door and went straight for the bathroom. The door was locked so I began pounding on it, yelling, "Open up!"

Moments later the door swung wide and Mom was there in her wheelchair. "Really, Polly, you can't be that desperate."

"We've got to find Ammi. The killer could be here; it's not Flavio."

Mom has such a cool head, she didn't flinch, merely said, "Do we know who it is?"

I shook my head miserably.

"Then you check upstairs; leave me to look down here."

I took the stairs three at a time, calling "Ammi, Ammi," as I went. I threw open the first door – nothing. The second and the third – still nothing. The fourth, and I stopped in complete shock. I took in the arm pinning Ammi close, the knife held against her neck, the look of complete terror on her face, and the dragon tattoo on the neck of her assailant. *How had it not registered before?*

"Just let her go, Dalia," I said to Flavio's assistant from the yoga studio. "How can she possibly be a threat to you?"

"She saw me. Her and her sister, when I was trying to get in the house. I didn't think the brats would be there. I was going to wait for Nicole inside and get her when she came back from her Wednesday evening lover's tryst."

Her face contorted as she spoke Nicole's name. "You were in love with Flavio," I said.

Dalia started waving the knife around. "I helped him start the business; I helped him make it a success. I even put up with his womanizing because he promised we'd always be together. Then *She* came along and suddenly it was, 'I can't come over tonight, Dalia,' 'You have so much potential Dalia, you should be in a big city,' 'I think we need some fresh blood in the business.' He wanted me to leave so that witch could take my place."

"I get that, I really do, and I sympathize," *Lord, what are you supposed to say in situations like this?* "but it's nothing to do with Ammi, she can't hurt you. Please just let her go."

"What, so you can try and stop me? Here's what's going to happen. You're going to help me get out of here, and if you try any funny business, the kid gets cut."

My heart was hammering so hard I was afraid I might hyperventilate. I drew in a deep breath. *Think of something, Polly.*

It was then a miracle happened. A fluffy little white and tan miracle named Dopey. She darted from under the bed and clawed her way up Dalia's leg. As those needle sharp nails dug into Dalia's flesh she gasped in pain and dropped the knife. Instinctively I pulled Ammi from her grasp and ran from the room and down the stairs, screaming for help at the top of my lungs.

As I reached the bottom the Sheriff, followed by a couple of men, rushed upwards.

Hours later, Dalia was in custody and we were slumped in the living room, exhausted, but reluctant to part and go to our separate rooms.

The girls were curled up on either side of Linda, Dopey on her lap. Mom was in her favorite easy chair with Rooster opposite, and Tyler and I were sharing the oversized armchair.

Dalia had been caught trying to escape through the window. "I can't believe I missed it so completely," I said for perhaps the twentieth time.

"Stop beating yourself up," said Tyler.

"But the dragon tattoo was so unusual. I noticed it but was distracted by Flavio "Casanova," and it never so much as registered when Ammi said the kidnapper at the food truck was a dragon."

"That's because you don't have children," Mom gave me and Tyler one of those looks. "When you do, you'll begin to understand how their minds work."

Tyler coughed and changed the subject. "The whole thing came down to simple jealousy."

"Son," Rooster looked over with hooded eyes, "there's nothing simple about jealousy. A woman lost her life and two children were terrorized and nearly killed, all because of jealousy."

We lapsed into silence again, probably thinking the same thought, that we were going to try really hard to make Christmas day special for the girls, and wondering what had happened to their father.

"We should do something special for Dopey," I was watching the rhythmic rising and falling of her chest as she lay, one paw over her nose, the other holding her tail. "She's the real hero here, even if she was just doing what kittens often do." I'd been a climbing post for many a kitten over the years, and I can tell you, it really does hurt.

"I wonder what made her do that at just the right time," Linda said.

"I think it was the knife." Everyone looked at me in surprise. "It was catching the Christmas lights from outside as she waved it around. And as we've said before: cats and bright shiny things. I think Dopey was climbing after the glittery object the way she did on the Christmas tree."

"Well, we're all very thankful she did." Mom stretched her arms above her head. "And now I think we'll all be thankful for a good night's sleep."

Twenty Seven

"Can I tell you something?" We'd just finished opening the presents and Ammi was next to me, cradling Dopey in her arms. I nodded. "This would be the best Christmas ever if my daddy was here."

What do you say? I put my arms around the little girl and hugged her, careful not to crush the kitten. She sniffled a bit then pulled away. "Could I have a sugar cookie?"

"Of course you can."

"I think Angel wants one as well."

I looked over at my mutt, currently enjoying the attention of my brother Seb. "Angel doesn't eat sugar cookies, sweetie."

"Not that Angel," Ammi sniffed. "My Angel." And when I still didn't know what to say she held up Dopey and firmly stated, "Angel."

"Oh, you changed her name."

"Of course."

I resisted the urge to roll my eyes. "And why did you do that?"

"Because Linda said she's like my guardian angel. And anyway, it's prettier than Dopey." *Amen to that.*

I left Ammi with her Angel and crossed the room to chat with my brothers, Seb and Keene, and their wives. They'd arrived early in the morning to spend the day. I had a new niece I needed to get to know as well, and looking down on her I understood how Sophie had so much love for her sister.

"Are we expecting someone else?" Linda was looking out the window as a truck pulled up. "Oh, it's the Sheriff."

I felt a little apprehension. I couldn't think of any reason for the Sheriff to drive out here on Christmas day. Surely something bad couldn't have happened. Not today of all days.

I listened as Wisniewski climbed the porch steps. It sounded as if someone was with him. Rooster was by the door and opened it before there was a knock. The Sheriff was in civilian clothes. He stepped inside, taking Rooster's outstretched hand and saying, "Merry Christmas," before addressing the room and adding, "I've brought something for the girls."

A man stepped around him; he looked vaguely familiar. I realized why when I heard a squeal and Sophie burst toward him, throwing herself into his arms crying, "Daddy." A fraction of a second later Ammi was also in his embrace, and within moments we were all wiping tears away.

I was close enough to Rooster to hear him whisper to Wisniewski, "I hope there's no reason you're with Whittier other than doing him a favor by bringing him out here."

"Only hoping you might offer me some of Edwina's eggnog."

"I think we can do better than that." Rooster slapped him on the back. "Stay and eat with us."

Twenty Eight

So, as you can imagine, it really was a wonderful Christmas. There were seventeen of us round the table; all the guys came over from the barn and we chowed down on turkey, ham and all the fixin's.

Neal Whittier, it turned out, had not been on leave all this time. He'd been in debriefing but would be home for at least a month to take care of Nicole's funeral and make arrangements for the girls. That turned out to be much easier than anticipated. Mom did that gentle, suggestive thing she does so well and in no time it was agreed that Linda would move in with the girls. Sophie and Ammi were delighted, and we were able to assure their father they couldn't have a more caring or capable guardian in his absence.

As for that, Neal said he still had a couple of years to go, but perhaps it was time to think about retirement. His girls needed him, and he missed them. He knew Nicole was unhappy, he told us, and almost welcomed a break-up, though not like this.

My gift–giving ended up being IOUs. I promised Rooster a trip to Home Depot with a gift card. I was sending Mom for a day at the spa. Tyler said he'd take a year of daily kisses. "You already get that," I said. "Good deal," he replied.

Then there was Coco, who had lost her "baby" to the girls. "We're going to the pet store, and you can pick out any cuddly toy you want," I promised.

Oh, and if you're wondering, all the pets got a little turkey as well, though I did have to stop Ammi from giving Dopey, I mean Angel, a piece of pumpkin pie. "But she wants it," Ammi said.

The end

Go here to get a FREE short story from Liz, and become part of the In Crowd:

http://lizdodwell.com/signup/

Bird Brain

A Polly Parrett Pet-Sitter Cozy Murder Mystery
Book 3

Liz Dodwell

One

"You must be joking!"

"I assure you, Miss Parrett, I don't joke."

Looking at the impassive countenance of Newton Alden, Esquire, I believed him.

We were seated across from each other at Alden's desk. A couple of days earlier I'd received an urgent written request from the firm of Shilito, Draper, Crouch and Alden, Attorneys at Law, to contact them regarding a legal matter. Honestly, my first reaction was that it was a spam letter. I tore it in half, crumpled up the pieces and tossed them in the trash. Of course, Amber immediately pounced, knocking over the trash can with all its contents, and started batting the pieces of paper around the floor as if they were the greatest cat toys ever.

I didn't think anything more of it until later in the day when the phone rang. Assuming it might be a client I answered in my perky voice, "Pets and People, Too. This is Polly, can I help a pet or a person today?"

"My name is Sadie, I'm calling on behalf of Newton Alden, Esquire. Am I speaking with Miss Pauline Parrett?"

I almost said she must have the wrong number. Pauline is my given name but nobody calls me that. I've gone by Polly for as long as I can remember. Then it hit me: Newton Alden, Esquire, the name on the letter I'd shredded earlier.

"This is Pauline, but please call me Polly."

"Miss Parrett," *so much for that,* "you should have received a letter from Mr. Alden. I'm calling to see if we can arrange a time for you to meet."

"What is this about?" My scam meter was still running.

"You have been named a beneficiary in an estate and Mr. Alden would like to discuss disbursement of the assets as soon as possible."

What? "Who died?"

"The lady's name is Naomi Ledbetter."

"I don't know anybody with that name. Why would she leave anything to me? This must be some mistake."

"There's no mistake, Miss Parrett. I'm sure Mr. Alden will explain everything when you come in."

Well, I was too curious to ignore the summons, so said I could come in the following week. Sadie would have none of that and insisted it would be too late but, when I asked why, she just gave me the runaround. Finally, I gave up and settled on a time the next day. It was really inconvenient for me as I was preparing to exhibit at a pet show over the weekend. I couldn't deny, though, I was a little excited about my mystery benefactor, so I crawled around on the floor looking for the letter. I found half of it under the credenza along with a dozen or so hair-covered glitter poms, a plastic pen top and a tampon wrapper. The second half remained elusive until I headed into the kitchen for another cup of coffee and noticed something in the pets' water dish. Yep! It was the letter, pretty much disintegrated. Sighing, I dumped the water, cleaned out the dish and accepted I'd learn nothing until my meeting.

Now here I was with Newton Alden, Esquire, wondering what on earth I was getting myself into.

"Why me?"

"Miss Ledbetter had you thoroughly vetted and believed you to be the ideal person to take care of this."

"I was investigated?" That sucked a lemon. "That's a bit much."

Alden pursed thin, dry lips. "A person could simply read your facebook page and know more about you than they want to, including your opinion that Bugs Bunny is the greatest cartoon character of all time." He had a point there.

"What if I refuse to take it, whatever it is?"

The man tilted his head back and peered down his nose at me. He had a slight gap between his front teeth and when he spoke it was with a faint, and irritating, whistling noise. "Against my advice, Miss Ledbetter refused to include any provisional arrangements, which means it would become a matter for the court."

For pity's sake. "I suppose I could take a look then."

With no hesitation, Alden hit the intercom button. "Would you come in please, Sadie?"

Just as quickly, the assistant entered. "Yes, sir?"

"Miss Parrett would like to see her bequest now."

"Of course, would you come this way, Miss Parrett?"

"It's here?" I wasn't expecting that but I obediently trotted after Sadie 'til she reached the ladies' room and walked right in.

"Um, I'll just wait for you out here," I said.

"No, this is where we've been keeping it." *Whaaat?*

I pushed past her and found myself facing a blue and gold macaw sitting atop a stainless steel perch to which one leg was chained. These striking birds have vivid blue plumage with a yellow or butterscotch underside and green on top of the head, but this one was a sorry specimen. Macaws are among the most sociable of birds but the poor animal had its head down and was absorbed in plucking at its pin feathers and had created a large bald patch on its chest. The feathers had none of the usual healthy iridescent sheen you should expect to see and, though I'm no expert, to me the creature looked much too thin.

Appalled, I looked around. There was no window, the bird had no toys, no distractions of any kind, only food pellets to eat and, obviously, no company. I reached out to stroke the macaw's head and it promptly bit me, drawing blood.

"Oh, it does that," Sadie said. "It's not very nice."

"Nice!" I seethed. "If I'd been shoved in here like this I'd be ready to claw your eyes out. How long has she been in here?"

When Sadie didn't respond I spun round and marched back to Alden's office, flinging open the door. "I'll take it, you miserable, mean man. You should be ashamed of what you've done to that poor bird. And that goes for you, too," I said, glaring at the assistant who'd been dogging my footsteps.

"We did the best we could," she snapped. "This isn't a zoo."

"Really? Then how come I'm in a room with an ass and an ape?"

"That's enough." Alden, eternally impassive, whistled through his teeth. "Sadie, put the bird in its cage and get it ready for Miss Parrett to take."

"Me? But it will bite. I can't…"

"Just find a way, Sadie." Then to me he said, "And we have some other business to conclude before you leave, Miss Parrett."

I gave him my most contemptuous look. "I have nothing more to say."

"There is more to the bequest, which I think you will find quite agreeable."

Oh, lord. Not more birds. I sat.

"Miss Ledbetter added a clause to her will. It is conditional on your acceptance of her pet's welfare for the rest of its life. You will receive the balance of Miss Ledbetter's estate, after legal fees and expenses have been satisfied, of course."

Well, I wasn't expecting that. "Um…uh, I…I'm not sure I understand."

"Having agreed to care for Polly, you will receive…"

"Whoa, hold up just a minute. Polly? The parrot's name is Polly?"

For the first time, Alden looked a little uncomfortable. "I believe your name was part of the reason Miss Ledbetter chose you as her beneficiary."

"This just gets better and better." I flung my hands up. "Polly Parrett and Polly Parrot. What a farce. Miss L must have had quite the sense of humor."

Alden cleared his throat. "As I was saying, you are also the recipient of a residential home with all contents, valued at $94,000. There is a certificate of deposit and a bank account with a combined total of $4,058. Fees will be in the region of $3,000 to $4,000. Probate should be quite straightforward. The estate is small and I've handled Miss Ledbetter's affairs for many years, so I anticipate we will be able to wrap this up within no more than ninety days."

I couldn't speak. I'd pretty much stopped listening at $94,000. To me that was a fortune. Alden rattled on about probates and appraisals and such, then handed me forms that I signed in a daze. He had Sadie make copies and the next thing I was really aware of was standing outside the offices of Messrs. Shilito, Draper, Crouch and Alden with a bird in a cage in one hand, a wad of papers in the other and a bunch of bird paraphernalia beside me.

My van was parked on the street so I shuttled everything to it. Moving any bird is incredibly stressful for them and this one was already a mess. Thankfully, I always keep a spare cat carrier or five with me and, using a towel, I carefully extricated Polly from her cage and secured her in the carrier. By now, she was so traumatized, she didn't even object.

It was an easy decision to head to my mother's rather than my own home. There were people there who could help and Polly Parrot desperately needed help. "Hang in there, pretty girl," I crooned. "Everything will be alright." But would it?

Two

The weekend

The poodle, a standard white, was wearing a princess costume with a tiara on her head. By her side, a little toy poodle, black, was dressed up to look like a frog prince. At their owner's command, both dogs stood on their hind legs and paraded across the field. The crowd roared approval.

"It's amazing the lengths people will go to for a fancy dress dog contest," Tina said.

We were both standing on our chairs watching the action. It was the second annual state pet-sitters' association jamboree. Vendors' booths were arranged in a circle facing each other across the open field where all the activities took place – agility contests, demonstrations, fancy dress contest – and attendees milled around, browsing the merchandise and watching the shows.

The little town of Mallowapple, where I live, had been chosen as the site for the event, mostly because it was fairly central in the state. Proceeds went to charity. This year, a group had been chosen that rescued shelter dogs and trained them as service dogs for military veterans. It was something dear to my heart because my mother and I had conceived and were running our own 501c for homeless vets and their pets. Well, actually Mom did pretty much everything.

I probably should back up a bit and explain.

A couple of Christmases ago I got involved in a murder where a homeless Vietnam veteran and his dog were wrongly accused of murder. Happily, they were exonerated and when my mom met Rooster, the ex-army guy, and his pit bull, Elaine, she came up with the idea to turn her big old farmhouse into a sort of half-way house for homeless vets and their pets.

Rooster had moved in and between the three of us – and any other volunteers we could find – we'd fixed up the place and waded through mountains of paperwork to apply for non-tax status, which I can tell you is a major headache. We'd decided on a simple name: Welcome Home. Members of the local VFW (Veterans of Foreign Wars) had provided legal and accounting assistance free of charge and my brother, Seb, who was the techie of the family, set up a website.

Our attorney, an ex-navy man named Orvil Gilroy, instructed we should have an advisory board even though we intended to keep our charity local, and preferably, someone with fund-raising experience. Callisto Padovano, known as Cal, a retired CPA, recommended we develop a five-year budget and operating plan and begin the fund-raising efforts immediately.

So, here I was at the jamboree with a booth to promote my pet-care business and raise awareness for Welcome Home. In a wave of optimism, I'd printed a bunch of flyers explaining what Welcome Home was about, and had set a big glass fishbowl on the table hoping for a few donations. Surprisingly, people had been quite generous and I was happily anticipating the look on Mom's face when I handed her the loot.

"Polly, look at this one." Tina, who is part of my pet-sitting crew, yanked my sleeve. I turned as the announcer's voice came over the speakers. "And here is Yogi."

Yogi, a cute little bichon frise, was masquerading as a racehorse with a stuffed jockey on his back, while his guardian, Sherry, who also happened to be a client, paraded him in front of the crowd. I waved at her and cheered for Yogi when a blur of movement right in front of me drew my attention. Stunned, I realized someone had snatched up my donation jar and was racing off behind the booth.

"Stop thief," I shrieked, thrusting myself from the folding chair, which promptly collapsed, dumping me face first onto the ground that was still muddy from an early morning shower. Helplessly, I watched as my precious funds were carried away. Fudge!

Then from the line of vendor booths a dog appeared, running toward the thief with long, effortless strides. In seconds he closed the gap and as he reached the thief, lunged at him, grabbing hold of the man's arm. The thief howled and jerked to a halt but managed to maintain his footing, at the same time swinging his other arm back with the jar in hand. *He's going to smash the dog's head.*

I think I stopped breathing, then I heard a forceful voice. "Aus!" Instantly the dog released his hold and backed away, which caused the guy to lose his footing and his hold on my money. Down they went. The thief stayed in one piece but the jar shattered and a light breeze began to gently carry the bills away.

I thought I heard someone yell "giblets," though what chicken parts had to do with anything was beyond me, and by now I was more focused on the fact that a horde of people had realized what was happening and converged on the area, snatching at the loose money. Hauling myself to my feet I hobbled toward the activity trying to snag a stray dollar or two along the way.

My knee was throbbing like crazy, which was really a pity because I wanted to kick the scumbag thief in the you-know-whats. How could anyone steal from people in need?

The dog was standing over the thief, barking like crazy. He was a powerful-looking German shepherd, black and tan with dark muzzle and dark ears. As I got close, he broke away and heeled beautifully next to a muscular-looking guy with a high and tight haircut. Someone caught hold of my arm; it was one of the event organizers, Tom, I think. "Security is on the way," he said, and I watched as they arrived, seized the robber and marched him away.

In moments, the whole thing was over. The crowd had dispersed along with the money; even the dog and his master were nowhere in sight. I wanted to cry but that would make me look like a wuss and I still had a little pride, so instead, I limped back to my booth.

Three

How quickly moods can change. The day had begun with so much promise. For a May day in Maine it was expected to be sunny and in the 60s. I'd splurged and bought one of those pop-up canopies and had a banner made with my company name, Pets and People, Too, which was strung above the table where my information and give-a-ways were displayed. To make the set-up even more appealing I'd had the brilliant idea to create a backdrop using a photo of all my own "fur-kids." OK, it really wasn't such a brilliant idea; the using my kids part, anyway. After two hours of trying to get my three dogs and six cats to pose prettily together, I gave up and bought a stock picture where all the animals looked perfect.

Now, all I could focus on was the empty space where my jar had been.

"Here," Tina said, "sit down."

She drew me towards a chair but I glared at it suspiciously. "Is that the one that tossed me?"

"It's fine." She shook it to prove the point and it seemed reasonably stable, so I sat, wincing as my knee bent.

"You need to get that iced," Tina said. "I'm going over to the medical tent to see if they can help. Will you be OK for a few minutes?"

"I think I'd feel much better if you would stop at the ice-cream van and bring me a double dip of pistachio." I gave my best "pitiful me" impression and Tina headed off, shaking her head.

"Polly!" It was Tom, or whatever his name was. I really should try harder to remember people's names. Pets are easy; people – not so much.

"Hey, uh, you." Well, what else was I going to say?

"I think we rounded up most of it, and we're going to make an announcement before the next event begins."

"Huh?" Not the most astute comment, I grant you, but I had no idea what he was talking about.

"I didn't have another jar to put it in, so I had to make do with a bag." He held out a white plastic bag with the words, "Thank You" printed in red on the side. "Well go on. Take it!"

Uncertainly, I took the bag and sat it on my lap then peered inside. *Holy cow.* For once I didn't know what to say. The bag was full of money. Mostly one dollar bills, some fives, and here and there a ten and even twenty. "But, I…."

"Some people added a little extra when they found out what it was for. We're all really impressed with what you and your family are doing for needy military vets. And their pets, of course. Anyway, I must dash, it's almost time for Tootsie and her Dancing Dog to do their number."

"Wait. How can I thank everybody for their generosity? This is so wonderful."

"I'll pass along your words, but the best thanks would be to keep doing what you're already doing. Make us proud, Polly."

What was I saying earlier about moods changing quickly? 'Cause right now, I was on top of the world. "I'll certainly do my best," I said. "Oh, one more thing. Who is the guy with the German shepherd who brought the thief down? I really want to talk to him in person."

"You'll find him at the K9 Security booth. Now I really must go."

Whatshisname took off at a swift pace leaving me to contemplate the kindness of my fellow man, and woman, of course. Tina returned with an ice pack and ice cream, which boosted my good humor even more. And a little later, when I tried to stand, the pain in my knee had reduced to a dull ache.

"I'm going to see if I can find the guy with the dog," I announced to Tina. "Can you hold down the fort?"

We'd been doing some brisk business; signed on several new clients and gathered a bunch of leads. Meanwhile, donations had been pouring in along with offers to help with Welcome Home. Now the show was winding down and I was looking forward to getting home, but I really wanted to thank the hero and his dog.

"No problem," Tina said.

I found K9 Security just a few booths away but it was empty. There were stacks of leaflets on the table so I picked one up and read:

K9 SECURITY GUARD DOG SERVICES
Effective
Dependable
Inexpensive

Underneath was a picture of a snarling shepherd.

"Hi, there. Can we help you?"

Startled, I turned to see two of the most hunky guys I'd ever dreamed of. It was obvious they both spent a lot of time in the gym by the way their t-shirts were stretched tight over their torsos. At heel next to them were two German shepherds.

"Hey, you must be the gal who had her money stolen. We were told it was someone from Pets and People, Too."

I must have looked blank because the one who spoke nodded at my breasts. I looked down. Oh, right. My logo was embroidered on the polo shirt I was wearing. Awkward.

"Um, yes. I'm Polly Parrett." I held out my hand.

A large hand covered mine but its owner was careful not to give a crushing shake.

"Mat Abaroa, and this is my partner, Jake Sinasohn."

In his turn Jake shook hands, then after the formal introductions were over I looked at the dogs. "And who are these guys?"

"Larry and Moe."

I laughed. "Don't tell me there's a Curly somewhere?"

Both men grinned and Jake replied. "As a matter of fact, we're training Curly right now."

For those of you who don't know, Larry, Moe and Curly were the names of The Three Stooges, a trio of vaudeville players famous for their slapstick comedy routines in the mid-1900s.

"Listen," I got serious, "I really want to thank whichever one of you saved my day."

"That would be Mat and Larry." Jake cocked his head toward his partner.

"It's all in a day's work for us," Mat said, "And good practice for Larry."

"Can I pet him?"

"Sure."

I gave the dog a good scruff behind the ears. "You're a really good boy."

Larry slowly waved his tail and gave me a happy dog grin.

I chatted with the guys for a little while, asking about their business and training methods. Jake explained they used German commands. Turned out he was of German origin as well; his first name was actually Jakob.

"That explains why I didn't understand the commands you used," I said to Mat. "But what was it that sounded like 'giblets?' "

The men looked at each with raised eyebrows, then understanding dawned and they burst out laughing.

"That was 'Gib Laut.' It's the command for bark."

I laughed as well, though a little self-consciously, then figured it was time to take my leave.

"I'm going to take some of your leaflets to hand out and if I can ever help you guys, let me know. It seems so inadequate to just say thanks."

"We'll take a hug and call it quits," Jake said and he put his arms round me and gave a squeeze. When Mat grabbed me he lifted me off my feet. All that manhood was making me a little giddy and I laughed self-consciously, which was when I heard a voice say, "Hello, Polly."

It was Tyler – my boyfriend.

Four

"They're really good guys," Tyler said. He was referring to Mat and Jake. We were in my van on the way to Welcome Home. Tyler had insisted on driving when he saw the state of my knee. I'd used the drive time to tell him everything that had happened. He just might be the most amazing guy ever. Not only was he totally caring and concerned about me, he wasn't at all bothered when he found me in the embrace of another guy. Just a minute, maybe I should be pissed he wasn't jealous.

"So it doesn't bother you if other men find me attractive?"

"Certainly not when they're gay."

I felt heat begin to rise in my face and knew it must be turning red as Tyler glanced over at me.

"Seriously?" He grinned. "You didn't know?"

"They said they were partners. I figured they just meant business partners." I was feeling a bit defensive, and let down. I'd never been confident about my looks so I'd been enjoying the thought that a couple of great-looking guys might think I was cute. Tyler read my thoughts immediately, though.

"Oh, honey, guys look at you all the time. Believe me, I've seen them, and it makes me proud that you're with me." Wow. I am one lucky lady to have this guy.

Changing the subject, Tyler continued. "You've had quite an exciting few days. Now you'll have to decide what to do about your inheritance."

"You're going to help me deal with the house." Tyler's a realtor; I looked pointedly at him. "As for my alter ego, Polly Parrot, apparently the new guy has taken charge of her."

We had taken in a new resident very recently. He didn't arrive with a pet but Welcome Home wasn't going to exclude any veteran who needed housing; it's just that we would also welcome their pets when they had them, while most shelters would not.

"What do you know about him?"

"His name's Mike something, he lost a leg in Iraq, though he seems to do well with his prosthetic, and that's about it. I only met him briefly last week."

"Well, I guess I can find out for myself," Tyler said as we pulled up in front of the old homestead.

The dogs must have alerted the household to our arrival. The front door opened and my three, Angel, Vinny and Coco, burst through, followed by an equally happy, though less bouncy, Elaine. You know, one of the greatest things in the world is to be greeted by a dog. It's as if you just made her whole life worth living.

Rooster and Mike came out to help Tyler unload my stuff. There wasn't space to store it at my little house in town so the huge basement in the farmhouse was a blessing. As the men worked I limped inside and found Mom in the kitchen. She spun her wheelchair and smiled.

"I thought you'd probably be hungry by the time you got here. There's oxtail stew ready to go and I made a lemon meringue pie."

I gazed fondly at my mother. A couple of years ago she'd been a bitter, miserable woman. A horse-riding accident had crippled her, and her constant, self-indulgent pity had driven my dad away. But the Welcome Home project had brought back the vital, resourceful woman I loved. Her wheelchair was no longer a handicap but a tool she used to great effect. And since Rooster had been in residence he'd made a lot of improvements for Mom. In the kitchen, countertops had been lowered, cupboards now had pull-out and drop-down shelves, the microwave was at chair height and both the stove top and sink were open underneath so Mom could wheel right up. It was brilliant.

Between us Mom and I set the table, by which time the men were done and we all sat. With the exception of Rooster, the residents usually cooked for themselves in the kitchen of the converted barn. Tonight, though, Mike was joining us at the house to update us on the macaw's condition.

It was an enjoyable meal. Once again I recounted my story and Rooster told us he'd counted the donations and we had more than three hundred dollars! We discussed what to do about the house I now owned. Mom wanted me to keep the inheritance for myself; I argued it would be better used toward rehabbing the farm property for Welcome Home. Finally, Tyler stepped in and suggested we assess the house first, then make a decision, and we all agreed that was best.

"So, Mike. How's Po..." I just couldn't quite bring myself to say the name. "How's the bird?"

The young man had barely spoken throughout the meal. When I addressed him he visibly tensed and snatched at his glass, sloshing water on the table. His eyes dilated and he dropped his chin to his chest, mumbling rapid apologies. Taken aback, I looked helplessly at him 'til Rooster, the seasoned veteran, put out a calming hand and squeezed his shoulder.

"It's alright, son. You're with friends. Nobody minds a little spill. Why don't you tell Polly what you were telling me earlier, about why you think the parrot's been pulling its feathers out?"

Mike looked up and Rooster gave him an encouraging nod. He turned to me, though didn't quite make eye contact and spoke haltingly.

"She's depressed. And frightened. And lonely."

That didn't surprise me, and I told Mike how the macaw had been kept in the bathroom after her owner died. As I talked, he began to relax and paid close attention to my words, nodding in understanding.

"Parrots are very sociable; they like company. Polly, uh, that's the parrot not, uh...you..."

"I get it, Mike. Go on."

"Well, she would have been very attached to the old lady. Imagine if your Mom died and then you were shut away in a bathroom for days or weeks with no company and nothing to do."

"Uh, yes," I said, because I just didn't know how else to respond.

Rooster leaned forward resting his arms on the table. "Mike has already developed a bond with the macaw, haven't you son? Tell us what you do to help her."

"I talk to her. At first she didn't listen but after a while she started to pay attention, especially when I told her we are from the same part of the world, and I described the beautiful rainforests with their colorful fruits and flowers."

"What part of the world is that, Mike?" Tyler asked.

"I was born in Colombia, but my family came here to America soon after. That's why I am called Mike. They wanted me to be American, to have an American name. I am Mike Martinez."

"And where are your family?"

It seemed a natural enough question for Mom to ask, but it had a bizarre effect on Mike who shot to his feet. "I have to go." And he rushed from the room leaving us all wondering what had just happened. Well, all of us but Rooster.

"He lost a leg to an IED in Iraq. Worse still, he lost his best friend in the blast."

"Survivor's guilt?" Tyler asked.

"I'm sure, and PTSD. He needs help but he's resisting it. I had a hard time persuading him to stay at Welcome Home so I don't want to push too hard. Believe it or not, tonight was progress. It was a big step for him to sit at a table with a group of near strangers and actually make conversation."

"But what about his family?" I asked. "Surely they can help."

"He hasn't spoken of them and, like I said, it's best not to push. We don't even know how he found us. He turned up at the door and asked if there was any work he could do in exchange for a bed for a night. Turns out he's a pretty fair hand at fixing things so we've got plenty to keep him busy but, until he took charge of your macaw, I had to coax him to spend each day with us."

"He's not dangerous, is he? He's awfully moody and I'd hate to think of Mom being here alone with him."

"Nonsense!" Mom was emphatic. "He's a nice boy who's lived through a really bad time. He needs a place where he feels accepted and that's what Rooster and I intend to give him. Besides, the animals all took to him right away. Cappy was on his lap the first night and even Ollie has been snuggling up to him. And I don't know how we would have coped with Polly without him. The bird has given him purpose; something that needs him and doesn't criticize."

Three of my cats, Cappy and Ollie, along with Leif, live with my mother. Ollie had been mauled as a baby when a neighbor found him and brought him to me. It took months for him to recover, physically that is, but even eight years later he's still very timid, so I was surprised at his rapid acceptance of Mike. The guy must certainly have something going for him. To reinforce that thought, Mike walked back into the room at that moment with Ms. Parrot on his arm. He held his arm close to his chest and the bird sat facing him.

"I thought you might like to see her," he said, and held out his arm to reveal her.

"I'll be a monkey's uncle. She's beginning to look better already." Seriously, I did think she'd gained a wee bit of weight and I swear there was a little glimmer in her eyes.

"Will she bite if I stroke her?"

"I'll tell her it's OK." He put his mouth close to her head and made soft tutting noises while I reached out and ran my fingers over her feathers. She arched her neck and made kissing sounds. I was thrilled.

"Mike, you're a bird whisperer."

He looked shyly pleased. "I've been keeping her in my bedroom and feeding her fresh fruit with her pellets. She really likes grapes. And some of her pin feathers are beginning to grow back in."

I peered at her chest. "Well, so they are." *Who'da thought it?*

"We need to do something about her name, though. It's not going to work having two Polly Parretts - or Parrots - in the house."

"But she's used to that name." So am I. Mike's expression was rather plaintive, then an idea seemed to dawn on him. "Do you know how old she is?"

"As a matter of fact, it was on the paperwork I got from the lawyer's office. She's 38."

"And how old are you?"

"Weeell…"

"She's 28," my mother chimed in, trying not to laugh at my discomfort.

"Then it's settled. She's the oldest, she's had the name longest; she should keep it."

There's no arguing with that kind of logic.

Soon after, Tyler and I were heading home. He was going to take the van after dropping me off. In the morning his sister, Suzette, would help him pick up his car, which was still at the site of the jubilee, and bring the van back to me. I was just keeping my fingers crossed there'd be no early morning pet-care emergencies. As things looked right now my morning was open, so Tyler and I planned to take a look at Naomi Ledbetter's house.

When we got to my place, Tyler jumped from the van and escorted me inside with the dogs, then immediately began to check around. I shook my head.

"It's time you stopped doing that. The boogie man is not going to jump out at me."

"As long as I'm here, it doesn't hurt to be sure."

Remember I told you I'd been involved in a murder a couple of Christmases ago? Well, the killer attacked me in my driveway one night. In fact, that's the singular incident that really brought Tyler and me together. Then, the following Christmas, I was involved in another murder. Anyway, because of that, whenever Tyler is at my house he can't help but look for errant criminals. It's rather sweet, really.

"Alright," Tyler said, pulling me to him, "it's time I left."

I wrapped my arms around his neck while Vinny, my bossy miniature poodle, did his damndest to push between us. We ignored him.

"You could stay," I said, causing Tyler to draw in a quick breath, "on the couch."

He groaned. "I can't be that close to you all night and guarantee my behavior."

He didn't know it, but I'm not sure I could guarantee mine, either. It's not that I'm a prude, but as sure as Newton's apple fell to the ground, I was crazy in love with this guy and it was scaring the dickens out of me.

"I'm sorry, Tyler. I'm just not ready...."

"Ready, yet. I know." He sighed. "I can wait. Especially for someone really worth waiting for."

He lowered his head and placed a long, soft kiss on my lips while we gazed into each other's eyes. As he pulled away he gave a rueful grin and abruptly changed the subject. "You know, maybe I'll call you Iris from now on, seeing as Polly Parrot is the winner in the name sweepstakes."

I pulled a face. By calling me Iris he was referring to my heterochromia iridum, which is a fancy way of saying

I have different colored eyes: one iris was brown, the other green.

"You're right," Tyler noted my grimace, "you need an exotic name to match the mystique your eyes give you. I'll have to think about it."

"You do that." And I shoved him out the door.

Five

Stale air enveloped us as we stepped through the front door of my inheritance and into the living room.

"Ewww. Let's leave the door open," I said, "and air the place out a bit."

Tyler flicked the light switch; nothing happened, so I stepped to the window and pulled back the vintage floral drapes. As I turned to see what the light revealed, a scratching noise further inside made me freeze and my heart skipped a few beats. I looked at Tyler.

"Did you hear that?"

He nodded while putting his finger to his lips. We stood still and silent and there was the noise again.

"What is it?" I hissed.

"Go to the car and lock yourself in while I check it out."

"I'm not going anywhere. There's safety in numbers. Wait! Was that a dog whining?"

Unsure of ourselves we hesitated then tentatively I called out, "Here puppy. Come here."

There was a whining and scrabbling before a brown dog came dashing into the room, all wriggly excitement and nervous apology.

"Oh, you're just a puppy." I dropped to my knees and the delighted youngster rolled onto his back, exposing his belly for me to rub. "You're so thin, you poor boy. How did you get in here?"

"He's with me."

My head snapped up at the sound of a strange voice, while Tyler jumped between me and the man standing in the doorway. "Who the heck are you?"

The man's clothes were garbage chic, like maybe fifty years ago they'd been considered quality. His face was masked behind a scruffy beard and he wore an old cap, which he pulled from his head and twisted nervously in his hands. "I didn't break in. I knocked on the door to ask if there was work I could do and it was open, so I came inside..." His voice trailed off uncertainly and he turned away from us, unable to make eye contact.

"And you expect us to believe that?" Tyler said. "I'm calling the police."

"No, please don't. I didn't mean any harm. I just wanted some food for me and my dog. If you call the police they'll take him away. He's the only friend I've got, please just let us go."

I was having a definite déjà vu moment. Glancing at Tyler it was apparent he was experiencing the same thing. It wasn't so long ago we'd met Rooster and Elaine in an equally bizarre way. Except that this time there wasn't a body. At least, I hope there's no body.

For reassurance I tucked my hand into Tyler's. "Alright, we won't call the cops - yet. But who are you and why should we let you go?"

"Ma'am, I'm Delbert Forlong and this is Jack. We've been on the road together since I found him with his head stuck in a mayonnaise jar. That was back maybe a couple hundred miles ago. I figured he probably had a home nearby but he decided to come along with me instead. I guess I shoulda gone south, but I figured not many of us would come this way and I'd have more chance of work. That hasn't happened. Fact is, it's been real hard."

"You said 'not many of us.' Who'd you mean by that?"

"Well, ma'am, I mean people who don't have a real home to go to every night, so they wander from place to place."

"And why are you on the road?"

Forlong hesitated, nervously running his hands over his thighs before telling his story.

"I was twenty years in the air force, married, with beautiful twin daughters. My wife had been griping for years she'd had enough of the military lifestyle, so I let her persuade me to retire. Problem was, my background in military intelligence didn't relate to anything in the civilian world. My wife's job had been to take care of the home and kids and she didn't think that should change, even though the girls were off to college. And that's another thing, college fees will eat through your savings faster than you can believe.

"So anyways, after a year, there was no money except my pension and whatever I could make odd-jobbing. We couldn't meet the rent. I was forty-four and started smoking to calm my nerves, and the more my wife bitched about that the more I smoked. My girls wouldn't speak to me 'cause it looked like they'd have to drop out of school and they thought I'd let them down. They were right, of course. I had." At this, the sadness emanating from him was almost palpable. It depressed the heck out of me.

"What happened?"

He sighed a deep shaking breath. "My wife went to live with her parents and they took over the college fees for the twins. I'm really grateful to them for that, though they completely shut me out of my girls' lives. My pension goes to them; I just hope they know it.

"For a while I stayed with different friends, 'til I wore the friendship out. Then there was nothing left for me but to hit the road."

Tyler's face was etched with concern as we exchanged glances.

"Look," Forlong went on in a pleading tone, "maybe you've got some work I can do for you. I don't want anything for me, just a meal for Jack. I'll do anything. Just don't take him away."

Jack was leaning against me - you know the way some dogs do – and nudged my hand to remind me it was OK to scratch his ears. At any rate, it made my decision easy.

"Delbert, it's your lucky day."

It was decided that I would zip over to a nearby burger place to get some food (Tyler was still wary enough not to want me to be alone with our new acquaintance) while Delbert helped take room measurements. As I headed out to the car, Jack bounded along beside me.

"No, puppy. You have to stay."

"It's OK," Delbert said. "He's seems to have taken a shine to you."

I'm always happy to be in the company of a dog so I opened the back door of Tyler's Subaru and lifted Jack in. Of course, as soon as I sat in the driver's seat he clawed his way to the front and onto my lap.

"Ah, ah!" Firmly I set him in the passenger seat and gave him "the look," the one that means, "I'm in charge and you'd better stay right there." He wagged his tail happily and did just that. "Well, I'll be. You're a pretty smart little guy." And off we went.

"I'll take a double quarter pounder, plain, and three Big Mac meals with coffee."

"Ju..yun..dream..that?" Huh? I hate these drive-through speaker systems but after several repeat attempts figured out I was being asked if I needed cream for the coffees.

"Better give me a few, please."

I drove round to the pick-up window. Jack could barely contain himself as his nose picked up the scent of grilling beef, and his boney little body was shaking in anticipation. I held out some money as the cashier opened the window. "That was a double Quarter Pounder, three Big Mac meals and three coffees with two creams," she said.

Two creams? "No, I said a few creams."

"Hold on." The woman turned away to grab the order, at which time the excitement was just too much for Jack. He launched himself across my body and through the open windows. The cashier shrieked like a banshee. Whoever was on the receiving end of the speaker probably burst an eardrum. Instinctively I grabbed for Jack and got a hold of his tail so that he ended up with his head and shoulders in the drive-through window, his rear end in the car, and legs scrabbling frantically for leverage to keep going. I was losing my grip on him when a muscular arm reached around the pup's middle and pulled him, squirming, to safety. A voice I recognized said, "Pfui!" and immediately Jack was still.

From a car behind me a voice called out, "Hey, thanks lady. I'll be putting this on youtube," and I saw a cell phone pointed in my direction. Great.

Inside the restaurant the cashier was still in hysterics and being supported by a couple of her co-workers.

"Sorry, sorry," I said before looking up into the laughing face of Mat Abaroa.

"Why don't you pull over so these other people can get their orders." He waved vaguely at the line of cars and curious onlookers building up behind me. Hurriedly, I found a parking space and wondered how much trouble I was in.

The passenger door opened and Mat set Jack down beside me.

"Mat, you must think I'm a terminal idiot. Things just seem to happen to me. Do you think they'll call the police?"

"Lock the dog in the car for just a couple minutes and let's go find out."

He was still grinning and his solid presence helped put me a little at ease, especially when he put his arm round my shoulders. None-the-less, I was pretty worried.

"Why am I not surprised that you have something to do with this?" The woman who spoke had directed her words to Mat and she stood, arms akimbo, hip hiked and head tilted questioningly.

"Hey, Sky, this is Polly Parrett. Polly, meet Skyler Abaroa, who just happens to be my wonderful sister-in-law," and he gave me a sideways wink.

Back at the house – I suppose I should say my house – I related my tale of woe while we ate our food sitting on an ugly old yellow-checked sofa. I'd let Jack have a burger before we left the restaurant parking lot; the pooch was half-starved after all. Unfortunately, there was now a rather ugly grease stain on the car seat – the car that Tyler drove his clients in! I hadn't broken that news to him yet.

"You're sure there won't be any trouble?" Delbert wasn't convinced that Mat had smoothed everything over. In fact, Sky had laughed herself silly about it, commenting she hoped the restaurant would be mentioned in the youtube video. Even the cashier, Maude, once she calmed down went out to meet Jack and pronounced him "Adorable."

"How lucky was it that Mat happened to be there?" Tyler said.

"And that the owners happen to be Mat's brother and sister-in-law."

"We should invite him and Jake out to dinner sometime."

I lifted the corner of my lip in a little smile. "Mat would certainly like that. He did ask me to give his best to 'that really cute boyfriend' of mine."

I wasn't sure, but it looked as if Tyler began to blush. He covered it by jumping up and announcing that it was time we took our new friends to Welcome Home. We'd thoroughly looked over the house and gathered all the information needed, so we piled into the car - me first, plopping my butt on the stain – and joined the traffic heading to Mallowapple.

Six

Several weeks had passed since Delbert, or Del, as he preferred, had taken up residence at Welcome Home. The guys were making progress on converting the second of two old stable buildings to a bunkhouse; Polly (the parrot, that is) was thriving under Mike's care; and Jack had taken to eating the catnip-filled socks I made for the cats. Twice he'd had to be rushed to the vet and Mom was putting pressure on Del to make more effort to train him.

"Honestly, Polly, he's a nice man but he doesn't seem to have much connection with the dog." Through the phone Mom's frustration was evident in her voice. "As for house-training, Jack's definitely all boy and I'm tired of picking up his messes."

"I'm sorry, Mom. I'll talk to Del. That's his responsibility." I'd noticed, too that Jack didn't seem as bonded to Del as I would have expected.

"Something definitely needs to be done before he turns into a complete terror. Can't you spend some time training him?"

"I'll try and get out there more, Mom, but it's Del who really needs training. He's got to learn to be more attentive and consistent. Anyway, enough of that for now, I want to talk to you about the furniture from the house.

"The estate sale company aren't interested in it. They said no-one will buy it because it's so dated and I should just have it hauled away. Tyler got a call from a company who clear out homes for a fee. He said he'd get back to them but they've been pretty aggressive, said they'd waive the fee, and finally even offered to pay him something for the stuff. But here's my thought. How about we use it for the bunkhouse? It's all really solid and I bet with a bit of paint and some fixing up Rooster could work his magic on it."

"That's a great idea, honey, and we can store it in the horse barn for now."

The third barn on the property was a working horse barn, with three rescued horses in residence. Mom gave riding lessons, which she loved, and it brought in enough income to cover the cost of caring for the animals.

Anyway, it was arranged that Rooster, Mike and Del would use a rental truck to pick up everything a couple of days later and transport it to the barn. I'd intended to throw my weight into the mix but, of course, life got in the way and I had to fill in for a crew member with a sick baby and take over her pet sits. Amazingly, the move went well without me (OK, I'm being sarcastic) and, talking to Rooster on the phone the next morning, I was heartened at his enthusiasm for our "treasure."

"You know, the old lady invested in some real quality items. It's a shame people don't appreciate it these days. Some of that furniture will be around long after your grandchildren."

"I'm a long way off from having grandchildren."

"Exactly."

Ignoring the dig I told Rooster I would be at the home in another day or two. "I'm swamped with work right now but you and I should take an inventory of everything as soon as we can. And I promised Mom I'd talk to Del sometime soon."

"Good luck with that. We don't know where he is."

"What do you mean?"

"Jack was barking like crazy in Del's room early this morning. I looked in, thinking something might be wrong, and Del was gone. Looked like his bed hadn't been slept in."

"That's pretty strange."

"Maybe not. For people like us," he meant homeless people, "transitioning to a more normal life, especially with any sort of family, isn't always easy. You get used to open spaces and being alone and sometimes the urge to get away can be really powerful."

"But surely he wouldn't leave Jack?"

"That's one of the things that does puzzle me."

"One of the things! What else is on your mind?"

"Well, he left a pack of smokes on the nightstand. A lot of homeless people smoke; maybe most of them. And though you might think it's crazy to burn money up that way when you can't even afford to eat, the fact is that sometimes a cigarette can seem like your only friend. I can't see Del going off and leaving his smokes."

Now I was feeling a nagging concern. "So Del left both his friends – his dog and his cigarettes. What do you think we should do?"

"Mike and I took a look around the property and I don't think there's anything else we can do just yet except wait. Your mom said if he doesn't show by this evening we'll call the sheriff."

There was really nothing I could add to that and if I didn't get going I'd be late for my first appointment. So we said our farewells and I dashed off to walk a little charmer of a dog, a black and white fluffball named Boo. But I couldn't quite get rid of that troubling feeling in the pit of my stomach.

Seven

Paperwork was strewn across the table. I was immersed in updating the time sheets when the first shot "popped" and something flew by me just nicking my ear. I threw myself to the floor as I heard more popping sounds. Amber streaked past while the dogs all jumped up in excitement at the new game I was playing. "Down," I shrieked, terrified one of them would be seriously hurt.

In moments it was over but I lay still trying to get my mind around what had just happened and to allow my frantically beating heart to slow down. Then something white and squishy plopped onto the floor beside me. I jerked back. Oh my God. Had one of the cats been hit?

I couldn't seem to get my brain to work until I smelled burning and jolted into action. Grabbing the fire extinguisher from its hook in the kitchen I hosed down the torched pan in which I'd been boiling eggs. Oh, boy! This was embarrassing. My intent had been to make deviled eggs for Tyler – one of his favorites – but I'd forgotten the pot was on the range. The popping sound was the eggs exploding as they boiled dry. The detritus of the explosion had been launched around the kitchen and was now stuck to the walls and even the ceiling.

Of course, that was when Tyler walked in. His jaw dropped. The dogs did their best to give him a warm greeting but they were pretty busy eating bits of egg off the floor.

"Deviled eggs," I said in a whisper, and burst into tears.

Realization showed on Tyler's face and he took two quick steps to me and swept me into his arms. I would have felt much better except he couldn't stop laughing.

"Honey, nobody could ever say life is boring around you."

The pizza was delicious. Tyler had even ordered it with anchovies for me and helped clean up while we waited for delivery. I was going to have to do a little touching up with paint on the walls and ceiling, and suffice it to say I wouldn't be cooking anything in the immediate future, though Tyler thought the range could be saved to work another day.

Mom had phoned to let us know there was still no sign of Del, and Rooster had been in touch with Sheriff Wisniewski.

"The Sheriff said we could stop by the office tomorrow to file a report if he doesn't show up by then."

She went on to say Jack was driving her nuts with his bad behavior so I promised to pick him up in the morning and keep him with me for the day.

"Come for breakfast," Mom said.

"You won't be having boiled eggs, will you?"

"We can, dear, if you want them."

"No, no," I said hastily. "I prefer mine fried."

After we'd finished eating, Tyler was all business. He opened his laptop and pulled up a spreadsheet.

"Come and take a look. I want you to see where we are with your house."

Obediently I flopped onto the sofa, leaning into him, and peered at the screen.

"I went ahead and had a home inspection done. This is the report. You'll see there are no major problems. A few light fixtures need to be changed and some of the plumbing should be updated, otherwise this is really good and the house is solid."

I read through everything line by line even though some of it meant nothing to me. Ridge and fascia boards were not in my vocabulary, and muntins and mullions were a mystery. Still, if Tyler was happy then I was happy and I said so.

"It gets better," he said. "The inspector owes me a few favors so he did it for no charge."

"Yes!" I said and we high-fived.

"Moving on," Tyler switched to another screen. "We already talked about the house needing paint inside and out, and replacing the carpeting. Now, I know your thought was to have Rooster, Mike and Del do as much of the work as possible, but hear me out. The guys already have a lot on their plates at Welcome Home. Bringing them over here will take them away from that work, which I'm not sure you want to do. Also, who knows how long they'd need to get everything done?

"My suggestion is to bring in professionals. The painting can be done in two to three days and everything else in a day. We can have the property on the market by the weekend; maybe do an open house soon after."

"This is sounding expensive."

"Not really. Professionals have the equipment, tools and experience needed to do the best job. Do you know what it would cost to rent equipment for Rooster and the guys to use? Do any of them even have a clue how to lay carpet wall to wall?"

"Uh…" There was more to this than I'd realized.

"Besides, I've already negotiated discounts on your behalf. You're looking at a total bill of about $4,500. Maybe a bit more."

I choked. Concerned, Tyler went to the sink and poured a glass of water for me.

"I don't understand how spending nearly $5,000 – that I don't have, I might point out – is going to help me with this."

"It's going to bring you 10 to 15 thousand dollars more on the sale." Patiently Tyler explained. "Home buyers want move-in-ready properties. Most of them can't see potential or simply don't want to bother with fixing things up themselves. So they'll pay considerably more for something that's in perfect condition.

"As for paying the pros, I'll handle that for now. We can reconcile the costs when you sell. And with all honesty, if you had to buy paint, carpet and fixtures at retail, and rent tools, you'd probably still be looking at a $4,000 bill."

Yowser. I was really out of touch. When I'd bought my little house (where I actually live), Mom had given me several large throw rugs that she wasn't using to cover the old flooring, and I'd repainted bit by bit. Not that it took much, the place only had one bedroom and an open living and kitchen area.

"Sweetheart. Don't worry. It will all turn out for the best. I wouldn't steer you wrong."

Tyler's voice echoed his apprehension and I realized he must be taking my silence as a bad sign. With the back of my hand I gently stroked his cheek and smiled at him. "You," I paused for effect, "are amazing. If I had to deal with all this on my own I would make a complete mess of it."

"That would never happen. You're one of the most capable people I've ever known. And one of the sexiest." He pulled me to him. "Maybe the sexiest." Our lips met. Lucky me.

Eight

At seven the next morning I was tucking into fried eggs, bacon and cheesy grits at Mom's kitchen table. Life is good. I'd brought the dogs along for a ride and Angel and Vinny were now outside playing with Jack. They played rough and it was too much for Coco, so she stayed with me. Elaine just wasn't interested any more. I looked over at her as she lay on her bed, her head on the raised edge using it as a pillow, and thought how much I loved Rooster's sweet old pit bull.

A dog began barking, steadily and insistently. Coco stood up, cocking her head to the side, focused on the sound. Elaine cocked her ears and frowned.

"There's another dog somewhere." I looked questioningly at Mom who gave me a puzzled frown.

"We haven't taken in anyone new. Are you sure it isn't one of ours?"

"It's not."

The barking seemed to be coming closer. Coco and Elaine both stared at the door, my little toy poodle growling softly. The door opened and there stood a red-faced Mike. He had Polly with him, but this time she was on his shoulder and posturing proudly, chest puffed out ... and barking.

"I can't get her to stop. Since we've had her she hasn't so much as squawked but she heard Vinny outside and suddenly found her voice."

Yikes. If she had to imitate one of the dogs, my yappy poodle was not a good choice. That high-pitched yelping could drive you nuts.

"Perhaps you could teach her to say a few words instead. Or sing a song. Preferably a lullaby."

"What? I can't hear you over the noise."

I dismissed the question with a wave and walked over to the coffee pot to pour myself a cup to go. Leaning against the counter I studied the macaw. She really was coming into her own. As annoying as the barking was, it was obvious the bird was having a good time and I was delighted to see her progress. As I passed Mike on my way to collect the dogs I yelled into his ear, "You're doing an amazing job with her." He smiled his gratitude and I made my escape.

I dropped Angel, Vinny and Coco at home. They'd sleep for the next few hours. Young Jack, on the other hand, still had energy but I'd have some time to stop at the park in between calls and run him through some basic commands.

The morning passed quickly enough and I figured I'd grab myself some lunch and enjoy it in the town square with Jack, who was finally slowing down. After I'd secured myself a reuben on focaccia bread I was lucky enough to find an empty bench facing the war memorial. It was a simple tower, etched with the names of Mallowapple residents who'd given their lives in service. Ours is a small town, so the list of names was not long. In fact, there was only one name for World War I but it was especially meaningful for me: Fireman First Class George Parrett, lost at sea 1918. He was my great great grandfather.

"Yo, Polly!"

Startled from my reveries on hearing my name I looked around and saw Dave Cartwright, an old school chum, waving. I raised my arm in return and he headed in my direction.

"Hey, Polly. How's it going? And Jack!" He got down on one knee and scratched the pup behind the ears, talking to him. "What are you doing with Polly?"

"I've got him for the day so ... Wait a minute! How do you know Jack?"

"I never forget one of the dogs we save. Especially when they have as much personality as this one."

No way. Dave works at the County Animal Shelter. He must have confused my Jack with another dog, as improbable as that seemed, so I explained my history with the pup.

"Polly, I'm telling you, this dog was dropped off at the shelter by a family who said they couldn't handle him. It was the same old story of people getting the adorable little puppy only to find out it takes real work and commitment to care for him. He's a quality dog so I knew he wouldn't last long and, sure enough, he was adopted out in a couple of days."

"To Delbert Forlong?"

"Uhhh, Delbert sounds right, but I'm pretty sure his last name wasn't Forlong." Dave shrugged. "You know how it is, I remember the pets but I'm not so good with the people."

"I don't understand. How could a homeless man adopt a dog?"

"Homeless! What are you talking about? The guy had his own business. I remember distinctly because he was a private eye and I thought that was so cool."

Hoo, boy! Things just got really weird.

Nine

There was the usual exuberance from all the dogs as I pulled up at Welcome Home. From inside the house it sounded as if Polly Parrot was getting in on the action.

I yelled out as I walked through the front door, "I'm here!"

"As if we couldn't tell," my mother's disembodied voice replied.

I found her in the office with Rooster going over plans for the barn renovations.

"A group of volunteers from the VA is coming over this weekend to work," Mom explained. "We need to decide how to put them to use and what supplies we'll need. More truthfully, what supplies we can afford."

"Stop worrying about it. Tyler thinks we can expect a quick sale on Miss Ledbetter's house." Briefly, I filled them in on our conversation of the previous evening.

"Enough of that, though," Mom said. "What about Del?"

After my chat with Dave, I'd called Sheriff Wisniewski. He'd been unavailable so I'd left a detailed message, then called Mom to tell her what I'd found out.

"I never heard back from the Sheriff," I said.

"I talked to him." Rooster stood and twisted his torso back and forth to stretch it, commenting, "I can only sit so long before that low back pain starts."

I sympathized, but I wanted to hear what Wisniewski had to say.

"First, I went to the station this morning to report Del missing. I filled out the paperwork but Feliks," that's Sheriff Wisniewski, "said there wasn't much that could be done. No crime had been committed and the man didn't even have an official address."

It had been a rogue cop from Wisniewski's department who tried to frame Rooster for murder. You'd think that might have created tension but both men were better than that. In fact, as an active member of the VFW (Veterans of Foreign Wars), it was Wisniewski who had encouraged Rooster to join and they'd found a bond in service to their country.

"Anyway," Rooster went on, "Feliks called here late this afternoon. With the information from you, he found out that Del's real name is Fannin, not Forlong and he runs a detective agency out of Pittsfield. It's a one-man operation. He uses an answering service company to handle his calls."

"Pittsfield? Then what is he doing in Mallowapple masquerading as a homeless man?"

"He may be close to homeless. It seems he was probably living out of his office. He is state licensed however, which provided some other background details."

"Such as?"

"He actually was in the air force and there is an ex-wife and twin daughters."

"As they say, a good con stays close to the truth."

"But was this a con?" Mom sounded exasperated. "None of this makes sense. Why would anybody want to con themselves into a homeless shelter? This one in particular. We're pretty much broke all the time and we have no ties to anyone or anything of importance."

I shook my head, equally bewildered. "It certainly seems he was targeting Welcome Home or he wouldn't have needed a dog. Poor Jack. It does explain why he hadn't bonded with Del. And that part of Del's story was a total lie. That really ticks me off. He used the puppy and he was using us and I'm gonna make sure I tell him what I think about it."

"Calm down, dear. It doesn't help to get upset." Grr, I hate when my mother uses that placatory tone, even – no, especially – when she's right.

Still, I took a deep breath and managed to ask in a normal tone, "Was there anything else that Feliks could add to the equation?"

"If there was, he wasn't telling me," Rooster said, and the conversation petered out.

I offered to help Mom with dinner but I guess she could see I was still irritable, so she suggested Rooster give me his thoughts on sprucing up the furniture.

We walked in companionable silence to the barn, Rooster throwing wide the doors to allow the fading evening light in. Although the structure was fairly sound, tarpaulins had been laid over the pieces, "Just in case there's a roof leak or two," Rooster said. He caught hold of the corner of a tarp and peeled it back to reveal a solid wood dining set. "This is pecan wood." He rapped his knuckles on the top. "Those scuffs and scratches can all be buffed out and it will look like new. And there's two of these." He showed me a dresser with six curved drawers. "A little elbow grease and some new hardware and they'll be good to go."

With a flourish he tugged at the next cover. "And wait 'til you see this."

A dead body?

My mind couldn't quite wrap around the image of a man face-down and spread-eagled on the floor. Maybe it was because the back of his head was a mess of blood and bone. Rooster's military training kicked right in, though. He darted around me and knelt next to the body, placing his fingers on the neck where there should have been a steady pulse. Looking up, he shook his head.

"Call the police."

My cell phone was in my pocket. I knew I should reach in and dial 911, but my arm didn't seem to want to obey the commands my brain was sending. Instead, I began to shake uncontrollably. Realizing my distress, Rooster yanked the cover back over the man and, holding me firmly by the shoulders, led me outside where I sagged against the wall.

"Where's your phone?"

"Right pocket."

"Are you gonna be OK while I make the call?"

I nodded as he stepped away to talk. I caught snatches of his conversation, "...head wound...old barn...don't know..." and then, "Delbert Forlong."

In the fuzzy recesses of my mind it registered that the body was Del. In some keener part of my brain, however, my thought was, "What about Jack?"

As if he sensed he was on my mind, at that precise moment Jack came loping up, head high, proudly holding a big stick, which he promptly deposited at my feet and waited for me to throw.

"Oh, you poor puppy," I whispered and sank to the ground, taking him in my arms. That was when I noticed blood on the stick, and burst into tears.

Ten

Several hours later I sat at the kitchen table with Tyler holding my hand. Mallowapple is a small community and there's not much that escapes Tyler. As soon as he heard there was a problem at Welcome Home, he rushed out to do what he could to help. I'd spent nearly an hour being interviewed by the police. Sheriff Wisniewski was leading the investigation.

Unsettled by the activity, all the dogs were sticking close to us while Mom made another pot of hot tea. I'd had more than enough already and really needed to go to the bathroom but I wasn't ready yet to relinquish my hold on Tyler.

"I don't know why I'm such a wreck. It's not like this is the first murder I've been involved with."

"It's the first where you've known the victim," Tyler put things in perspective as the Sheriff walked into the room, Rooster at his side.

"The body has been taken away and my men are now sealing the crime scene. Polly, I'll need you at the station as soon as you feel up to it, to read over and sign your witness statement. Meanwhile, if any of you think of anything else, even if it seems trivial, call immediately."

"Do you have any suspects?" Tyler looked worried. "A man has been murdered practically on the doorstep and the killer is still out there."

"Are we safe?" I was particularly concerned for Mom. "Can you leave someone here to keep an eye on things?"

"I don't have the manpower for that. You do need to be very vigilant, though. Keep doors and windows locked, even during the day, and don't go out alone."

"That's not very encouraging." My tone was sour. "Do you at least know if this was a random murder or was Del targeted?"

"I hope to know more tomorrow." With that, Wisniewski turned and left.

"Well that wasn't exactly helpful. For all we know there's a crazed killer on the loose just waiting to take pot shots at us."

Rooster squeezed my shoulder. "Give the man a break, Polly. If he thought we were really in danger he'd figure something out. And I'll keep watch tonight. After this, I'm not sure I could sleep anyway."

"Rooster, I hope you're not staying up for my sake. I can take care of myself," Mom said. "I've ridden 1200 pound horses over five-foot-high fences, given birth to three babies, even hiked the Appalachian Trail. I have a gun and I know how to use it. Don't let these wheels fool you." She patted the wheels on her chair.

"Edwina, I know you're one tough lady," Always the diplomat, that Rooster, "but for my own piece of mind I want to be sure no-one messes up all the good work we've done around here."

"Maybe none of us needs to worry." Tyler reached for his phone. "I have an idea." He walked away from us as he appeared to peruse his contacts then turned, leaning against the counter and holding the phone to his ear.

"Hi, K9 Security, Tyler Breslin here. I know it's getting late but we have something of a crisis at Welcome Home and could really use your services. Call me, please, as soon as you get this message." He left his contact details then hung up, nodding at us with a satisfactory air. "We'll have the professionals take care of safety. And before any of you object because of the cost, it's on me. Consider it a donation to the cause."

Within a couple of hours Jake from K9 Security was at the farm with Moe at his side. We all listened carefully as he talked. "We'll set up a nightly schedule for you with a handler and a dog. It's a small area to patrol so I don't think you need more than that. For tonight, I'll be here, but we have half a dozen other guys we might rotate through.

"First thing I want to do is scope out the area with one of you so Moe and I get familiar with the lay of the land. It's important that when we're on patrol you don't come outside without alerting us first. All our guys carry handguns and the dogs are pretty much lethal weapons so…no surprises, OK?"

Moe didn't exactly look lethal at the moment as he lazily scratched his nose with a paw. Jake noticed the direction of my gaze. "I haven't given him the work command yet."

I put my hands up in a defensive gesture. "No need to explain. I've seen one of your dogs in action, remember, and it was awesome. I'm just really grateful that you're able to help us out."

"I second that," Mom said. "Now, tell me what I can get for you? Coffee? Treats for the dog?"

"No ma'am…"

"Edwina," Mom interjected.

Jake smiled. "That's nice of you, Edwina, but we have everything we need, and the dogs are not allowed treats when on duty. That's something they get from their handlers for a job well done."

"OK, then," Rooster stepped forward. "How about Mike and I show you around?"

The three of them moved off, leaving me with Tyler and Mom.

"Are you going to stay here tonight, Polly?"

"I can't, Mom. I've got to get home to take care of the cats." Amber, Taz and Ditto could be pretty self-sufficient if need be, but I really didn't like leaving them alone for too long.

Mom and Tyler exchanged a look. I knew that look. They thought I was being rash. Before either of them could say a word, though, I made my feelings known.

"There's nothing to suggest I could be in any danger. Everything points to Welcome Home or something personal in Del's life. Besides, I have an attack cat."

The dogs could only be relied upon to kiss someone to pieces but Ditto, my tuxedo cat, was very territorial and could be meaner than a junkyard dog if he felt threatened.

"That is true," Tyler conceded. "But I'm following you home so I can check out the house before I leave you there alone."

Of course you are, my knight in shining armor.

Eleven

Polly the parrot had really come into her own, and as she shed her fear so Mike began to shed his shyness. To distract her from the annoying barking, he'd decided to teach her to talk. Already she was saying "hello" and "pretty girl." Right now she was entertaining the volunteers from the VA who'd come out to help work on the barn conversion. There were also a few who'd responded to our email plea after signing up at the jamboree a few weeks ago. All in all we had about fifteen helpers, which was fabulous.

We were taking a break for lunch. Long ago my dad had built a big old brick grill outside; now Tyler's dad was wielding tongs over hot dogs and sweet sausages that he was dishing out to the helpers. Foil-wrapped potatoes were cooking in the hot coals and Mom had made up a huge batch of her homemade coleslaw along with one of my favorites, oatmeal apple crisp. We may not be able to pay people for the work but we could sure feed them.

"Hey, Polly! Give me a kiss!" How rude.

I looked around to see who was being so forward before it dawned on me the words were not meant for me. Polly Parrot's admirers were throwing kisses at her. In turn she was making kissing sounds back while lifting one leg and waving it. I couldn't deny, she was darn cute.

Mike had her on his shoulder. He must be clipping her wings so she couldn't fly away. I really should chat with him about her care and condition. I was feeling a bit guilty for leaving him to take charge of her. After all, Naomi Ledbetter did specify me as her care-giver.

Noticing me watching, Mike lifted his chin in salutation and headed my way. The day, as well as the work, was quite warm so this was the first time I'd seen him wearing shorts. Because of the artificial limb his gait was just slightly off, but I marveled at the technology and his ability to use it.

"You know," I said as he neared, "with long pants on I doubt anyone would know you had a prosthetic leg."

"Yep. Things aren't always what they seem."

"Not what it seems. Not what it seems," chanted his feathered friend.

"Gracious." I was astonished. "Did she just pick that up?"

Mike shook his head. "I can't take credit for her verbal skills. I think Mrs. Ledbetter must have taught her quite a vocabulary. That's the first time I've heard her say that."

"She's becoming a real chatty Kathy, then. Or, I should say Polly."

Mike chuckled and immediately Polly mimicked him. He reached up to scratch her neck and as he did so I noticed an unusual tattoo on his arm, partly hidden by the sleeve of his t-shirt. It looked like some sort of bird with bared teeth.

"What's the meaning of the tat?"

His face turned hard. "Nothing."

"Sorry. I didn't mean to upset you. It's just unusual and ..."

"I said it's nothing!"

His words were like a verbal slap. I took an involuntary step back and, of course, stepped in one of the holes the dogs had industrially been digging. My already bum knee gave out on me and I crashed down onto my hip.

"Ow!" I sucked air through my teeth as a stinging pain embraced my rear. Mike's mood did another one-eighty as he crouched beside me, evoking nothing but concern.

"Are you OK?" Obviously not. I bit back the words, though, not wanting to trigger "Menacing Mike's" return, and accepted his assistance getting back on my feet. Well, foot actually. I could only put my weight on one leg – again.

You're probably thinking I'm a real klutz. Honestly, I don't know why this stuff keeps happening to me. As a kid I was in Miss Rispin's ballet class for a long time so I'm well-trained in balance and... Oh! Come to think of it, Mom pulled me from the classes when Miss Rispin suggested I might be more suited to clogging.

Mike helped me to the picnic bench where my half-eaten sandwich waited for me. It had become a little chewy but I was hungry so I gnawed on it while wondering what the heck was wrong with the young veteran. There wasn't much time to ponder the question, however. Rooster, who was in charge of operations, called the helpers to order and everyone returned to their duties of sanding, scraping, painting, hammering and whatever else was needed.

Doing my best to ignore my discomfort, I rose to the occasion and, by the end of the day, we had ourselves a pretty nice bunkhouse with six areas blocked out for individual rooms. They weren't actual rooms because the walls didn't go all the way to the roof, but at least they would give the residents some privacy.

It was thrilling to see such improvement and the mood amongst the workers was downright elated, with plenty of back-slapping and high-fiving as they said their good-byes and headed home. For a while, I even forgot about the murder.

An arm came across my shoulder, giving me a squeeze. "I think we deserve a major pat on the back."

"More than that," I said, hugging Tyler's sister, Suzette. "I see a big glass of wine in my future. Care to join me?"

"You're on!"

Suzette is a couple of years younger than Tyler. She's beautiful to look at and has a beautiful personality to go with it and I thought the world of her. She tucked her arm in mine and together we strolled to the house. Well, I sort of stumbled. The dogs all fell in behind us as if we were a pair of pied pipers, including Frank, Tyler's big, goofy bloodhound mix.

"Where were you all day?" I asked. "I hardly saw you."

"Working with Mike cutting wood for framing and sub-flooring."

"Don't you find him a little unsettling?"

"In what way?"

"Let's get our wine and find a quiet place to talk."

So we did, and while we sipped I told Suzette about Mike's reaction when I mentioned the tattoo, and his reluctance to talk about his family.

"Have you talked to Rooster about this?"

"Sure. He says to give Mike more time, but his mood swings really worry me. We know he has PTSD and it scares me that he could have an episode and harm Mom in some way. In fact," I leaned in close and dropped my voice to a whisper, "I can't help but wonder if he had anything to do with Del's death."

"Polly, that's a shocking thing to say. Do you have any evidence?"

"No, and I feel guilty for saying it. But you hear stories of people who have been hurt by someone with post-traumatic stress syndrome. There was that young war veteran not long ago who beat his girlfriend to death. He said she just set him off but he doesn't remember how."

"You're over-thinking this, Polly. I've seen no evidence of anything but a gentle soul. As I recall, drugs and alcohol were involved in the incident you're talking about and Mike doesn't drink or have access to drugs, at least as far as I know. Seriously, Welcome Home is all about helping people like Mike. Let's find a way to do that before we condemn him."

She was right, of course. I was just about to say that when I glanced up and realized Mike was watching us. We'd settled ourselves on the back patio. Mike's room was on the second floor above us. His window was closed, but I had no idea if he could have heard our conversation. Weakly, I waved a hand at him. He didn't move and his face remained completely impassive. Rats.

Twelve

It had happened again. Someone had disappeared from the farmhouse. This time, it was Mike. Polly, the macaw, was gone, too.

A mid-morning call from Mom alerted me while I was walking Chester, a Newfoundland Rottweiler mix who was one of my new clients from the pet-sitters' jamboree. Technically, Chester was still a puppy – a 130-pound puppy. He may have seemed as big as a grizzly bear but he had the heart of a teddy bear. For nearly an hour he'd been romping round with a high-energy fox terrier who went by the not unlikely name of Pistol.

I'd planned to use the afternoon to spy on my crew. That sounds terrible, I know. Here's the thing, though, my first obligation is to my clients and their pets. To ensure my staff are fulfilling that obligation I make it a point to check on them unexpectedly from time to time. The crew I have now is pretty great, but you can never be too careful. I once called a walker and asked where she was. Blithely she announced she was walking her charges as scheduled. That was a lie. I was sitting in my car down the street, saw her arrive at the client's house and not leave. She was pretty red-faced when I knocked on the door. She was also without a job.

Anyway, the point I was meaning to make is that I was able to free up the rest of my day to help look for Mike.

I just had to get Chester home. Wouldn't you know, however, that wasn't going to be so easy?

Chester was tired and ready for a nap. Problem was, he was ready for his nap now! He flopped down, closed his eyes and was asleep in an instant. I nudged him, shook him, called his name and he unconsciously rolled onto his back exposing his belly for a rub.

I bobbed around acting excited and shouting in a high-pitched voice, "Walkies! Treats! Cats! Good boy! Come on!" None of it had any effect, but the dog park contingent was highly amused. Unfortunately, they consisted of two elderly ladies and a wizened old man. At this time of day during the week all the young muscle was at work.

Crouching down I tested the feasibility of carrying Chester to the car. *Holy smokes!* Even without my knee and hip problems, there was no way. I was going to have to call in the cavalry.

You're thinking I'm referring to Tyler, aren't you? Wrong! I scrolled through my contacts list and found K9 Security. "Um, Jake? Do you think I could hire you for just half an hour or so?"

"Polly, don't ever change," Mat Abaroa said. "Who else would give us so much to smile about?" He and Jake had both come to my rescue and between them, lifting Chester had been a breeze. The dog park oldsters had cheered as they carried him to my car, still firmly in the land of slumber. The guys had then followed me to

Chester's home and reversed the procedure, depositing the pup on his bed in the laundry room, which was his pseudo crate. I tucked his favorite toy between his front paws, made sure the door was closed and locked up the house, meeting Mat and Jake outside.

Putting on a business air to hide my embarrassment I asked how much I owed for their services.

"We don't want anything. We had the time to spare and it's always fun when we see you." Did I detect a hint of sarcasm there? I decided to ignore it.

"I can't tell you how much I appreciate this. I really need to get to the farmhouse – Mike has gone missing."

Of course, then I had to tell them what happened.

"Who did we have on patrol there last night?" Mat asked of his partner.

"It was Samson, with Delilah." *For real?*

Both men looked concerned.

"They're a good team," Jake assured me while Mat stepped away from us, his phone to his ear, dialing Samson.

"I don't doubt it."

Mat was pacing as he talked. Snatches of words floated our way but they were no more than dust in the wind. After a few moments he strode back to us.

"Samson is adamant no-one left the house before his shift ended at seven. He says Rooster came out with coffee just before he and Delilah headed home, and that's it." Looking back and forth between Jake and me he added, "I think we should consider extending the patrols."

Mat's words made feel a bit panicky. When Del disappeared he ended up dead, and I was beginning to have visions of Mike with a bloody head and Polly Parrot stiff and cold beside him.

"Let's not panic," I said, pretending to be cool-headed and reasonable. "Before anything is decided I need to speak with Mom and Tyler. Besides, Mike could have left of his own accord. The word is out he's missing and, let's face it, how hard should it be to find a one-legged man with a parrot on his shoulder?"

Mat bit his lip and looked at Jake who dead-panned, "Aargh, we be lookin' fer Long John Silver." At which they both burst into laughter.

"This is hardly a laughing matter!"

"Don't you realize what you just said? A one-legged man with a parrot on his shoulder. It sounds like a pirate."

"Oh, my." Indeed it did, and I recognized the silliness and joined in the laughter and felt much better for it.

A little later, hysteria aside, we became serious again.

"Honestly, I'm just so confused right now. The most important thing is finding Mike, but I'm also responsible for the bird. Then there's a murder to solve, a killer is still on the loose, I'm worried about Mom and I need to figure out what to do with Jack."

"Anything we can do to help, anything at all, just name it," Jake said.

"Have I told you how glad I am to have met you two?"

"Aw shucks," Mat quipped. So I slapped him on the arm. It was like hitting steel tubing; my hand stung and my fingers wouldn't bend. So when my phone rang an instant later I had to contort my body to try and reach into my right jeans pocket with my left arm. Mat offered to help but I figured it was time I showed I could be independent. It wasn't easy but I managed to retrieve the device. By then it had stopped ringing and gone to voicemail but I saw that it was Mom and hit redial.

"Thank goodness," was Mom's urgent greeting. "There's been a sighting on the Old South Road. Mamie Soames called the sheriff's office and said she'd seen an alien creature walking there. Ruby Peach took the call and was going to hang up when Mamie said something about the alien giving birth to a multicolored babe. That got Ruby's attention and she got from Mamie that the alien was carrying something brightly colored in its arms. She figured it might be the parrot and called here."

"How did Ruby know about Mike and Polly being missing?"

"I called the hair salon."

That explained it. Drop a word at Combing Attractions Salon and it would become a tsunami in no time at all. The whole of Mallowapple would know about Mike by now.

"Right. I'll get going and see if I can spot them."

"Should you be doing this alone?"

"I think I'm covered," I said, smiling at Mat and Jake.

Thirteen

The K9 Security duo were more than willing to provide backup for me but one of them needed to get back to their own business. So it was decided Mat would ride along and I'd drop him off later, which gave me an opportunity to tell him about Mamie Soames.

"No-one knows just how old she is, including Mamie. She's as nutty as a fruitcake and pretty much blind as a bat. In her whole life she'd never been to the movies, so several decades ago she upped and decided to go. The movie happened to be Alien, and it changed Mamie's life. Since then, she sees people birthing bioforms about once a month."

Mat gave me one of those "you've got to be kidding" looks.

"Honestly. It's a real problem when kids knock on her door at Halloween holding baskets of candy in front of them."

We were on the Old South Road now and Mat was silent. I wasn't sure if it was because he was concentrating on looking for Mike or if he just didn't know what to say after the Mamie revelation.

The road was pretty typical for this part of Maine; narrow and winding, uninhabited for miles at a time and flanked by pines with a few broadleaf trees mixed in. If you followed it long enough you'd eventually get to a major highway that would take you all the way south to Florida. Mamie would have been driving it because she was going to pick up a bottle of Pop Stegall's herbal remedy, which was really corn liquor flavored with wild horseradish. Whatever. It seemed to be working for her.

We'd passed the turn-off to Pop's property now and I slowed down so we could eyeball through the tree line in case Mike was trying to hide from traffic. Somehow I didn't think he'd try and flag down any passing vehicles.

Mat pulled the sunglasses from his face and pressed his head against the side window.

"See something?"

He grunted and sat back again. "I guess not." Then he shook his head. "It doesn't make sense that Mike would just up and leave like this. What could possibly have caused him to run off?"

"Uh, dunno." Except he might have heard me suggest he was a potential murderer.

We lapsed into silence, me dwelling on my guilt for being suspicious of Mike and worrying what might become of him and Polly.

"There!" Mat's shout jerked me from my absorption. "Straight ahead; it looks like someone on the side of the road."

Sure enough, as we drew closer, the vague shape morphed into a human being. A little closer still and we saw it was Mike, sitting cross-legged on the berm. I say cross-legged but that wasn't strictly true as his prosthetic leg was bent at a crazy angle.

I pulled off the road and parked. Mike didn't even look our way; his whole posture was of defeat. Mat reached for the door handle but I tugged on his arm. "Let me do this." He must have seen the determination in my expression so gave a brief nod and let me go.

As I closed the van door I realized I was trembling, and it occurred to me the demon I was about to face was the fear of rejection by this young man who I'd rejected when he needed all the friends he could get. And where was Polly? Please, Lord, don't let something have happened to her.

"Hello, hello!"

I laughed in relief. There she was tucked inside Mike's shirt.

"Polly, you beautiful girl. I am so happy to see you." I softened my voice. "And Mike, I'm even happier to see you."

Finally, he looked at me. His face wore a mask of pain and betrayal.

"Can I sit down?... Please?"

He gave a slight lift of his shoulders, so I eased myself onto the ground in front of him.

"Mike, I've been a complete ass. It's not the first time but it's certainly one of the worst. I should never have talked behind your back; I should have come to you to talk about my concerns. Please give me a chance to make it up to you."

He began chewing on his lower lip, obviously unsure what to say or do.

"I'm so sorry, Mike. Please tell me what I can do to make things better?"

"Give me a kiss, give me a kiss." Polly Parrot spoke with impeccable timing.

This time, it was Mike who began to laugh, then I joined in and we just couldn't seem to stop until Mat stood beside us. "What on earth is going on?"

Fourteen

There'd been a lot of back-slapping and hugging at Welcome Home when we returned with Mike. Turned out he had nearly been hit by an eighteen-wheeler hurtling round a bend. The driver probably never saw him, but he'd leapt away and fallen into a stony ditch that ran alongside the road, breaking his prosthetic leg and smashing his hip. He managed to drag himself back up to the road, hoping to thumb a lift somewhere because he certainly couldn't walk. The thing that really tore him up, though, was that Polly, who was secured in his shirt, could have been crushed when he fell.

Once again, I was more than a little thankful for Mat's presence. He got Mike into the van and we drove straight to the hospital to get him checked out. While Mat waited with him I took the parrot to Doctor Jim, our local vet, who gave her a thorough going over before pronouncing her a little stressed, but otherwise fine.

Mike had X-rays taken, which showed a lot of bruising and the need for a chiropractor. Thankfully, nothing was broken and he was released with pain killers and instructions to alternate ice and heat and be careful. He and Polly had now been reunited and sent to rest, while Rooster worked on the damaged prosthetic.

"Think you can fix it?"

Rooster peered at me over the top of his glasses. "Nothing actually broke. These things are made really strong; the material didn't even bend, it just went out of alignment. All I have to do is undo a couple parts, realign it and put it back together. Mike could easily do it himself if he had a few tools with him. I'm gonna put together a small pack he can carry in a pocket, in case anything happens again."

"Maybe you shouldn't give it to him 'til we're sure he's going to stay."

"That's not really our call to make, is it?"

"Then I'm going to do everything I can to persuade him this is the best place to be."

"Atta girl," Rooster grinned.

Fifteen

Suzette and I were tucking into grilled bacon and pimento cheese sandwiches with crunchy fries. We were lunching at Bennie's Diner, Mallowapple's favorite eating place and gossip hub. When she wasn't helping at the halfway house, Suzette worked in her family's real estate firm, and we tried to get together for lunch every couple of weeks or so.

Today we were discussing the murder of Del Forlong, or Fannin, I should call him.

"And Rooster hasn't been able to get anything out of the Sheriff?"

I shook my head. "If Wisniewski has any idea why Del was posing as a homeless vet he's not telling anyone, not even Rooster, which makes me think he just doesn't know."

"Do you girls need more coffee?" Nita, the diner's owner and gossip-in-chief hovered beside us.

"Not me," I said, while Suzette shook her head. Nita promptly put the pot on the table and settled herself into an empty chair.

"I heard you mention the murder. What's the latest?" Elbows on the table and chin on her clasped hands, Nita leaned towards us.

"There's nothing," I said.

"Oh, come on. I know Sheriff Wisniewski talks to Rooster. You must know something."

"Really," I shrugged, "we haven't heard a thing."

Nita sat back with a grunt. "Unless I come up with something soon people will begin to think I'm losing my edge to Combing Attractions."

There was a bit of an ongoing feud between the diner and the hair salon as to who got the best gossip. It could be really annoying at times, but right now an idea was forming in my mind.

"Nita, how about we start a rumor and catch a killer?"

Suzette raised her eyebrows at me. "Is this something I might regret being a part of?" But Nita was instantly hooked.

"Tell me what you want?"

Sixteen

Being a pet-sitter is not always easy, but then there are times it's just plain fun.

Tina was spending a week with a bulldog by the name of Otis, while his pet parents romped around Cozumel. It happened that it was Otis's birthday today, and we'd been asked to give him a "pawty" and video the happy event. The preparation had all been done by Tina; my job was to run the video and take pictures.

Otis was already in his pawty hat when I got there. As I used my phone to film, Tina brought out a pupcake she'd made using a recipe from a book called The BARKtender's Guide. She'd shaped it and decorated it with peanut butter frosting to look like a dog's face. In it were three lit candles and she sang Happy Birthday as she presented the pupcake to Otis, whipping the candles out before he devoured them with his cake. The Pawty Animal Pupcake, made with oatmeal and watermelon, was a huge hit and Tina confided there were a couple more for Otis to enjoy another day.

When it came to opening presents, no dog could have been more excited. Otis snorted and whuffled as he ripped the paper off the hide-a-squirrel from his parents – a soft tree trunk with holes in which plush squirrel toys were hidden. He poked his head in the holes as Tina played peek-a-boo with the squirrels, and carried them off proudly when she let him have one.

From Pets and People, Too he received an organic elk antler that he promptly began to chew and drool over. All in all, it was a great success and I left soon after, giving Otis a generous scratch on the rump.

Tyler's car was in my driveway as I pulled in. It wasn't like him to turn up unannounced, so my first feelings of pleasure turned to concern that something was wrong.

The dogs gave me their usual ecstatic greeting as I went in the house, but Tyler stood with his arms crossed and his expression stern. Uh oh.

"I hear something's been found at the farmhouse."

"Hi, honey." I tried to sound normal but my voice came out as a squeak. How had he heard so soon? Surely Suzette didn't rat me out?

In answer to my unasked questions he continued. "I stopped into the diner for lunch right after you and Suzette left." Yep, that would do it. "Nita told me it was something valuable. In fact, she told everybody in the place that an item of great value had been discovered out at Welcome Home and you have it in your possession. Of course, I tried to call you," Oh, yeah, I'd turned my ringer off while I was filming Otis, "but you didn't answer. So I called Suzette."

Not even Tyler's sister could resist him when he was determined to get the truth. She would have caved and told him everything. I didn't blame her; I would have done the same.

I swallowed and took a deep breath. "Nothing was happening about finding Del's killer or why he was pretending to be someone he wasn't. So I..."

"So you what? So you invented a story that would put you right in the killer's crosshairs. What kind of lame-brained idea was that? And how do you know nothing's happening? Did it never occur to you that this is a police investigation and there's no reason they would include you in it? Maybe Sheriff Wisniewski deliberately kept you in the dark because he knows you just can't stop meddling where you don't belong."

By now my face was burning and my emotions had run the gamut from shock to hurt, to anger. "It's not meddling; I was trying to help." Damn, I was going to cry.

"How the heck is it helping when you put yourself in danger? And maybe others, too?" Tyler wasn't backing down. Worst thing was, I was beginning to realize he was right, but I couldn't bring myself to admit it. Instead, I stamped my foot – jeez, how juvenile was that? – and yelled back.

"Someone had to make a move. You just don't have the guts to do it."

As soon as the words were out of my mouth, I regretted them. Tyler's eyes went wide then his lips tightened. He gave a curt nod and strode past me, and out the door. I heard his car start up followed by a piercing wail, which happened to be me. My chest felt tight and it was hard to breath. I sank to my knees, dropped my head back and moaned Heavenward. How could I have been so stupid? How could I have said something so mean?

Upset, the dogs crowded round me, whining, and I buried my face in their necks, sobbing loudly. Had I just destroyed the best thing in my life?

I didn't hear the door open, but strong arms came around me, drawing me close. A hand pulled my head into a shoulder, and over and over a voice said, "I'm sorry, I'm sorry," as I was rocked gently. Tyler. He'd come back.

"Yum buk," I mumbled into his collar.

"What?" He released his hold on my head and stroked the hair away from my face.

I sniffed and took a steadying breath. "You came back."

"How can I leave when I'm so in love with you?"

Wow. There aren't many things that can shut me up, but that was one of them. He kissed me softly on the lips and of course I burst into tears all over again.

Seventeen

At Tyler's insistence I'd had to come clean with Mom and Rooster about starting the rumor. Concerned for my safety they'd insisted I come and stay at the farmhouse where there were lots of people to keep an eye on me. Meekly I'd agreed, knowing it would make Tyler happy.

Business was running smoothly right now and I'd put Tina in charge for a couple of days, thinking this might be a good opportunity to go through the furniture and furnishings from my inheritance. So Rooster and I were doing inventory to decide which things to keep and which to donate or dump.

"Most of the soft furnishings aren't worth keeping." Rooster gestured to the ugly yellow sofa, "but these," he placed his hands on a pair of wing back chairs, "will clean up real good."

Rooster read the doubt on my face as I looked at the pukey-mustard chairs.

"You buy these new today, you'd probably be looking at upwards of $2,000 each."

My mouth dropped. "Then how come we couldn't sell them?"

"I guess most folk don't look beyond the dirty fabric, but they don't even need new padding. In fact, they don't look like they were ever sat in much. If we can pick up some cheap upholstery fabric I can have them good as new. It just takes a little time and patience."

"Who's going to do all the sewing?"

"There's not much to do, most of it's stapling. Besides, your mom's pretty handy with the sewing machine."

OK, who was I to disagree?

"What else do you think we can use?"

"Pretty much all the wood furniture. I showed you some pieces when we, er, found, er..."

Rooster's voice trailed off as we both remembered finding Del's body. There was an awkward moment of silence, broken when Mike walked in with Polly the parrot on his arm. "I wondered if I could help at all," he said.

"Help, help," the bird shrieked, dancing a jig and bobbing up and down, causing us all to laugh.

"Yeah, Mike," Rooster waved him over. "Help me move some of these boxes out of the way so we can get a look at the furniture behind."

Mike stepped forward, then stopped uncertainly. "Polly," he looked at me, "would you hold Polly for a while?"

I sighed. This name thing was really irritating me, but I smiled and held out my arm, "Come here, pretty girl."

Mike dug his hand into a pocket and pulled out some nuts for me to use as encouragement and Polly stepped onto my arm. I kept her occupied while the guys cleared the way, then we all eyed a dark-stained credenza.

It looked pretty out of place among Naomi Ledbetter's rather ornate things; this was square-cornered and plain.

"Isn't that art-deco style?" I asked.

"It's the kind of thing that was popular in the 1950s," Rooster said. "Does seem out of place with everything else, I agree." He ran his hands over the wood. "Teak, I think."

"Aunty pan, aunty pan," Polly said. At least, that's what it sounded like.

I raised my eyes at Mike and he held out his hands in a "who knows" gesture.

"Oh well, let's look at some other stuff," I said, but Polly had something else in mind. She hopped from my arm onto the credenza, yelling her aunty pan thing followed by "Don't tell," over and over.

Mike reached for her, making soothing sounds, but she avoided him while keeping up the chatter and then began pecking at the back of the credenza. It was made of that cheap fiber board, and her powerful beak was more than a match for it; a macaw's bite is as strong as a large dog.

"Hey!" Mike tapped her on the head to get her attention. She stopped ripping at the board, puffed out her chest and gave one last, "Aunty pan. Don't tell," before going back to her perch on Mike's arm.

"What was that all about?" I shook my head.

"It sounded to me like she was saying panel, not pan," Mike said.

"Aunty panel? That still doesn't make sense."

"Well, she's a bird," Mike gave a look that said, "duh."

"You're right. Why should I expect her to make sense? She's just making noise."

"Maybe not." Rooster was bending over the back of the credenza, Swiss army knife in hand. He straightened his back. "I think she might have been saying, 'Antique panel.' "

I gave him a questioning look and he held up a finger, indicating I should wait. He turned to Mike, "Son, help me turn this thing around.

"See here." Rooster pulled back more of the board where Polly had loosened it. "There's a piece of carved wood underneath, and it looks real old to me."

Together, Rooster and Mike carefully peeled away the fiber board and we were presented with a panel, made up of sections decorated with an intricate pattern of stars. At any rate, to me they looked like stars; Rooster and Mike started talking about polygons and geometric rays. *Huh?* So I interrupted.

"Basically, you're saying this is an antique panel?"

"Antique panel. Don't tell," Polly squawked, looking pleased with herself.

"I'm saying," Rooster spoke slowly, "we might have found the reason Del was in here."

Eighteen

Paul Schroeder looked more like an aging hippie than an antiques dealer; a tie-dye bandana holding down long hair, and a droopy mustache framing his mouth. He'd pulled up in a new Mercedes though. I wasn't quite sure how that fit with the whole "free spirit" thing but the guy was donating his time and expertise, so I wasn't going to question it.

After finding the panel yesterday we decided the smart thing would be to get it looked at by an expert. Of course, we didn't know any, but the VFW came through again when Rooster put out a call for help. Schroeder was a member in Greenville, but he'd driven over to Mallowapple to help us out.

"Well, what's the verdict?" Sheriff Wisniewski was getting impatient. We'd contacted him as soon as we figured we might have found something of relevance to Del's murder. He'd been pacing up and down for the last fifteen minutes, but Schroeder wasn't going to be rushed.

Actually, most of the Welcome Home family had crowded in to the barn and there was an air of excitement between us. Even Mom had wheeled herself over and Tyler had brought Suzette to join in the spectacle. I suspected Schroeder was enjoying the notoriety and he had spent a lot of time on his knees inspecting the panel while emitting a steady stream of "ahs" and "hmms." When he finally tried to stand his knee gave out on him, and he was about to clutch the credenza when Tyler grabbed him and helped him up.

Clearing his throat, he gazed slowly around at his audience then directed his attention to Wisniewski. "The verdict, Sheriff, is that you have a late fifteenth or early sixteenth century Spanish or Moroccan door panel. This particular style of paneling originated in Maghribi, North Africa and spread to Spain in the fourteenth century. There's a strikingly similar panel in the Museo de la Alhambra and a comparable pair of doors in the David collection in Denmark."

Schroeder sucked in a deep breath but I figured I'd better butt in before he continued his Antiques Road Show parody.

"That's all very interesting. I think we all want to know the same thing, though. What's it worth?"

Schroeder looked a little miffed at being cut off mid-monologue. "It's impossible to say for sure without more detailed examination, and carbon dating to confirm the age."

"Then you're not sure it is genuine?" Mom sounded disappointed.

"I am sure," Schroeder was emphatic, "but the rest of the world requires proof. I expect you understand that Sheriff, more than most."

In the background someone said, "We still don't know if it's valuable."

"Just give us your best estimate." The Sheriff fixed an unwavering stare on the antiques dealer.

"Keeping in mind that it does have some small nail holes where it's been attached to the credenza, and I haven't been able to examine it closely..."

Wisniewski made a low growling noise and Schroeder gave him a nervous glance. "Uh, yes. Well, I can tell you a similar panel sold at auction a few years ago for $75,000."

There was a collective gasp. I clutched at Tyler's arm and we exchanged shocked looks. "You're saying this thing is worth that much money?" My voice was actually quavering.

"Perhaps more, or you might get less. Selling at auction is very volatile. I should think you'd certainly get $50,000 though."

Nineteen

Everyone was on tenterhooks. At one and the same time I think we were all elated over our found treasure, and really nervous we were no closer to finding the killer.

Schroeder was making arrangements for the credenza to be picked up the next day and taken to a secure place for examination. Meanwhile, it had been brought into the house where Rooster and Tyler planned to watch over it through the night. K9 Securities were doubling their guard outside and the rest of us were hoping to get some sleep.

Polly the parrot had been showing off all evening by talking up a storm. No-one complained, though. After all, she was the one who'd directed our attention to the door panel.

"Old Miss Ledbetter must have taught her to say 'Antique panel. Don't tell,' and shown her where the panel was hidden," Mike said.

"Oh, come on," I rolled my eyes, "I doubt she could associate the credenza with a few words she learned to mimic."

Mike looked offended as he handed Polly one of her favorite pine nut treats. "Birds are a lot smarter than people think, and macaws are among the most intelligent."

"I'll take your word for it. And no matter what, she's the greatest bird in the world as far as I'm concerned. I would have dumped that credenza with hardly a second look."

Mike's expression softened as I scratched the bird's head. We were the last two in the kitchen, finishing up the dishes before heading to bed. It felt good that Mike and I could chat like old friends; the tension of a few days ago now behind us.

"How about a hot chocolate to take with you?"

Mike nodded his appreciation and sat at the table as I put water in the kettle and grabbed the chocolate from the cupboard before plopping down opposite him to wait for the water to boil. He was wearing a short-sleeved t-shirt that exposed the bird tattoo on his arm. I couldn't help but look at it for a moment, then quickly glanced away. Mike caught the look, however, and I bit my lips, feeling awkward.

"Sorry, I'm not prying. You don't have to tell me anything."

He dropped his head and began to drum his fingers on the table and I thought I'd just messed up again. Then he surprised me when he began to speak.

"I always loved birds, even when I was really young, but my family was so poor they couldn't even afford a bird as a pet. There was a bird store in the town; it started as a place for people to buy bird feed and cages and such. Then customers began asking the owner if he would watch their pets when they went away, and so he started a boarding business alongside his store.

"Mr. Votaw was his name, but everyone called him Mr. V. He had a gray parrot of his own, Biggles, that hung out in the shop with him. I'd go in just to see Biggles and Mr. V. He was really a good man, started to let me help out with the birds he was looking after. He'd give me a quarter here and there; I thought I was rich."

The kettle whistled and I jumped up to fix the hot chocolate. Mike went silent 'til I set a mug in front of him.

"One day, a guy came into the store while I was there. He had this tattoo on his arm and I just couldn't get my eyes off it. He saw me watching and came to talk with me. I thought he was being nice but Mr. V. later told me to stay away from him, that he was bad news.

"A few days later I came across the guy again. He recognized me, told me he had racing pigeons and did I want to see them? Of course, I didn't give a thought to Mr. V.'s words of warning and off I went. That was the beginning."

Mike wrapped his hands around his mug and sipped at the drink; I kept quiet, waiting for him to go on.

"The tattoo on Raptor's arm – that was his name, Raptor – was for the Catbird Brotherhood. Raptor started calling me Little Big and drew me into his gang. Before long, I was running drugs for him. I felt important, and as if I belonged. But what did I know; I was a kid, just thirteen.

"Raptor would toss money at me from time to time and I would stash it away. When I had two hundred dollars I handed it to my parents, thinking they would be proud of me." Here Mike paused and his eyes began to tear up.

"They were angry. So angry. They'd had no idea what I'd been doing.

"A few months after that, Raptor took me into Mr. V.'s with him. The old man refused to serve him; said he was corrupt. Then he told me if ever I needed help, he would be there for me. Raptor was furious, swept his arm across the counter, shoving things aside, and grabbed Mr. V. He told him he'd better watch his back, 'cause he would be coming for him.

"I was scared. Then a few days later I was even more scared when I found out Mr. V.'s store had been trashed and the old man was in hospital."

Mike sipped at his chocolate again, and I noticed his hand shake.

"Anyway, it took me five years to break from the Brotherhood, and this," he raised his tattooed arm, "is all I have left to remind me what a fool I was."

"But what about your parents?" I asked.

He shook his head. "I was too ashamed of the life I'd been living to approach them. I joined the Marines and started fresh."

"Surely now is different?"

"My dad told me then that I was no longer his son. I doubt that has changed."

I was about to say something more when Mike rose and announced he was tired. Biting the words back I jumped up and put my arms round him. At first he stiffened, then relaxed and gave me a brotherly pat on the back.

"Goodnight, Polly."

"'Night, Mike."

Twenty

It felt good to get back to my little home. I opened the door and the dogs barreled past me, rushing around and sniffing at everything to make sure all was in order. While they did their doggie thing I lugged the cats inside in their carriers, and released them from incarceration. Leif and Ollie immediately rushed away, but Ditto's attention went to the dogs who were whining and pawing at the pantry door.

Uh oh. Did something go bad in there?

I pulled the door outward. There was something bad in there alright. It was Sadie, attorney Newton Alden's assistant – and she was holding a gun, pointed right at me.

Of course, the dogs rushed right in, tails wagging, excited to find a friend in the pantry of all places. But Sadie was no dog lover. She turned her gun toward Angel.

"Get them off me or they're dead."

"Angel, Vinny, Coco!" I used my sternest voice and clapped my hands. As expected, none of them paid the slightest bit of attention to me.

Horrified, I watched as Sadie's finger appeared to tighten on the trigger, when she let out a shriek and her face took on a wide-eyed look of fear. Her hands jerked upwards and at that moment the gun went off, blasting a hole through the roof of my pantry. Angel whipped around, her paws frantically scrabbling for a hold on the tile floor. With Vinny and Coco close behind, she tore through the pet door into the back yard and to safety.

"What kind of freak place is this?" Sadie screamed and kicked out viciously at Ditto. I realized instantly what had happened. Wanting attention as much as the dogs, Ditto had rubbed himself around Sadie's legs. Obviously, she didn't like cats any more than dogs.

Fortunately for my chubby feline, he was still very light on his paws and dodged the kick with impressive ease. Not one to take a threat lightly, though, he managed to shred his claws down the offending leg before he, too, vanished with speed.

That left me alone, facing a dangerously freaked-out woman with a loaded gun. I held my hands up and tried to appear non-threatening. "Sadie," I said, hoping my tone was soothing. "What do you want? How can I help you?"

"Help? You?" Her voice seemed to have gone up an octave or so. "Look what your disgusting creatures have done to me?"

She held out her bleeding limb.

"I'm so sorry, Sadie. Let me put something on that for you." If I could work my way to the kitchen, I might at least be able to grab a knife to defend myself with.

"Forget it," her lip curled in an ugly snarl. "Just get me the papers."

What? "What papers would that be, Sadie?"

"You know, the papers from Naomi Ledbetter."

"You have all the papers I have. In fact, you gave me all the papers I have."

"Stop procrastinating. Just give me the stock certificates or bonds the old witch left. I know she had money; she kept hinting about it but would never tell me where she'd hidden it, but I heard the other day you'd found it. So hand it over."

"Sadie, there are no stocks and bonds. The money is in the value of the door panel."

"What are you talking about?" She was waving that wretched gun all over the place and I could see a vein pulsing in her neck. Her eyes narrowed. "You're trying to confuse me because I've been awake for more than twenty-four hours. Well, it won't work."

My brain suddenly jerked into life. "Is that how long you've been here?"

"Of course it is, you idiot, and I've waited long enough."

Good grief. She must have heard the rumor I originally started and assumed the money was in paper. Then she'd been lying in wait for me and hadn't heard about the antique panel.

"Sadie, an antique door panel was attached to the back of a credenza. It's been valued at fifty to seventy-five thousand dollars and has already been taken away. Even if I could get to it, it's not something you can easily hide, or sell for that matter."

Sadie's color turned from an ugly red to paper white. Her body went rigid except for the arm with the gun, which began to rise in my direction. I dove for the floor, sliding under the table, and had a moment of déjà vu

Liz Dodwell

about exploding eggs before I heard a shot and everything
went black.

Twenty-One

It was an evening of celebration. Earlier in the day the antique panel had sold at auction for a whopping eighty-three thousand dollars. When the auction house heard what the money was to be used for, they had waived their fee, so Welcome Home would receive the full amount. All the residents and a lot of friends were crowded into the farmhouse enjoying a big feast with much laughing and back-slapping and hugging.

I was over the moon, even though my head still hurt a little from whacking the table leg and knocking myself out as I slid across my kitchen floor. The shot I'd heard hadn't been from Sadie's gun, but was Tyler.

I'd left Angel's favorite squeaky toy, Itt - so named because it reminded me of Cousin Itt in the Addams Family - behind when I headed home. Tyler, who left soon after me, had seen it and decided to drop by my place so Angel wouldn't fuss. He'd pulled in as Sadie's gun went off in the pantry. Fortunately, *he's* able to recognize the difference between actual gunfire and exploding eggs, and crept up to the window to see what was going on.

Not wanting to spook Sadie, he grabbed the gun he keeps in his car, climbed the fence into the backyard, and peeked in through the pet door in time to see Sadie lose her cool. As she lifted her gun arm, he got a shot off and into her butt; a fairly substantial target, I might add. By the time

I came around a few minutes later, the cops and medics were arriving. Tyler had my head cradled in his arm. "The one time I don't check your house is when you get yourself in trouble." That's my knight in shining armor.

"Where's Tyler?" Mike parked himself on the arm of the chair in which I was sitting.

"He called a few minutes ago to say he's almost here."

At that moment the man of my dreams appeared in the doorway. With all the chatter I hadn't heard his car pull up. I waved to get his attention and said to Mike, "Talk of the devil."

Mike stood. "I'll leave you two alone."

I grabbed his sleeve. "No, you need to stay."

His brows drew together in puzzlement, then we both watched as Tyler made his way across the room, closely followed by a Latino man and woman. As they got close, Tyler stepped aside. The man stopped and stood stiffly, but the woman barely hesitated. Crying out in her native tongue she rushed at Mike, throwing her arms around him and sobbing on his shoulder.

Quietly, I eased myself from the chair and, joining Tyler, we left them to it. When we looked back, Mike's dad – you guessed it was his parents, right? – had inserted himself into the mix and the three of them looked like they would be a family again.

Twenty-Two

Tyler and I were sitting on the front porch in the swing as the last of the guests headed home. We were staying to help clean up but decided first to take a little time to ourselves.

"I enjoyed spending time with Mat and Jake as friends," I said. "They're so serious when they're working."

"You didn't get jealous when they both hugged me, did you?"

I looked at the grin on Tyler's face and slapped him on the chest. "Ha ha."

He wrapped his hand around mine and we sat in companiable silence for a while 'til he spoke. "I didn't get a chance to talk to the Sheriff at all. Did you find out anything?"

"Yeah. Sadie pretty much fessed up to everything. Whenever Miss Ledbetter needed to sign anything or have something notarized, Sadie would go to her house, where the old woman would drop hints about having hidden wealth.

"Remember that company that tried to get you to let them clear the furniture out of the house after Miss L. died? Sadie hired them. She thought there would be a secret drawer or some such thing where the clue to the money would be hidden. When that didn't work out she found

Delbert Fannin, private investigator, and hired him to search for the money."

"I don't get it. Why would she kill him, then?"

"She spun Del a yarn about the money being rightfully hers. Said she was related to Miss L., and that I'd coerced her into changing her will. Whether Del really believed her story or not, at the end he turned out to be a good guy and told Sadie he was going to find the money and then figure out who it really belonged to.

"Sadie hightailed it out to the farmhouse that night to conduct her search and just happened upon Del. They had an argument and she grabbed a stick and clobbered him over the head, then dragged the body under the tarp."

Tyler sighed heavily. "Del didn't deserve this. Sadie is greedy and vicious. She would have been making decent money as a legal assistant; apparently it just wasn't enough. I hope she goes away for life, especially after she tried to kill you."

"She was a shopaholic, according to Wisniewski."

Tyler guffawed.

"No, seriously," I went on. "She had a serious shopping addiction; there were piles of unopened boxes in her home, from Amazon and other online stores, and she had a mountain of debt."

"How does this happen to people?"

"Couldn't tell you. Just be glad I'm not like that; your money is safe with me." I poked Tyler playfully in the ribs. "Oh, there is some great news!"

Tyler looked at me expectantly.

"Mat and Jake are adopting Jack. They think he has great potential as a guard dog."

"That crazy pup?"

"He just needs a chance. And if anyone can give it to him, the K-9 Security guys can."

Tyler smiled. "Yep, that is good news."

It was time to head inside and do our part in the cleaning. Entering the kitchen, we bumped into Mike, Polly on his arm.

"There you are. I was looking for you," he coughed and shuffled a little. "Uh, listen. I really want to thank you both. My parents told me how you tracked them down and persuaded them to come here."

"Persuasion wasn't needed," Tyler said. "They were over-joyed to know you were safe."

"We've got a lot to make up for, and I'm going to try really hard to make them proud of me again."

I smiled. "Will you move back with them?"

Mike hesitated. "I don't know yet. Actually, I'd like to talk to you about Polly before I make any decisions."

I understood immediately. "You don't want to leave her. Well, I can tell you right now it's obvious she belongs with you, whatever you decide. She wouldn't be happy anywhere else."

A big grin spread across Mike's face, and scratching the bird's neck I said to her, "Would you, pretty girl?"

"Pretty boy, pretty boy," Polly responded, bobbing her head up and down.

"Wait a minute," Tyler frowned. "She said 'boy.' 'Pretty boy.' Is she a he?"

We all looked at each other.

Oh my gosh. "That would make sense; males are generally better talkers than females."

"But why would Naomi Ledbetter call a male parrot Polly?" Tyler asked.

"There's no way to sex a macaw by external examination," Mike chimed in. "Most people do DNA testing."

"So perhaps Miss L. thought she had a girl at first, hence the name. By the time she discovered her parrot was a boy, the name had stuck." This was exciting news to me. "Then Polly should really be Paulie, or Pally, or Phillie, or oh, oh, how about this? Polo?"

Tyler put his arm around my waist and steered me into the kitchen. Calling goodnight to Mike, to me he said, "Come on, there's work to do." But I didn't hear him. My head was still full of happy possibilities for renaming Polly the parrot.

I just love happy endings. Don't you?

Go here to get a FREE short story from Liz, and become part of the In Crowd:

http://lizdodwell.com/signup/

Seeing Red

A Polly Parrett Pet-Sitter Cozy Murder Mystery

Book 4

Liz Dodwell

One

At long last Chester was walking beautifully by my side. Actually, *Chester* was walking, I was sort of loping; after all, Chester *is* a 150-pound Rottweiler Newfoundland mix with a looong stride. Still, this was a big improvement for the boisterous one-year-old, so I was rather proud of my training skills as we moved along the wooded trail. And with dappled sunlight dancing over my face through the autumn leaves and the hushed sounds of the woodland surrounding me, I was becoming quite Zen.

Abruptly that changed. A large reddish-brown creature hurtled around the bend ahead of us. It stopped when it saw us, then began a deep-throated barking while jumping in circles.

Chester, who had never met another dog he didn't love, bounded forward to greet this new friend. Unfortunately, we were still joined by the leash, which I had wrapped around my wrist, and as Chester went forward, I went down - hard.

You may not realize it, but large, powerful dogs are not unlike large, powerful trucks: once they are in motion they take a little while to stop. And so it was with Chester; he dragged me several feet along the dirt trail before grinding to a halt and looking back at me with a puzzled tilt of the head.

My arm felt as if it had been yanked from its socket, my t-shirt was torn, and I dreaded to think what cuts and bruises were now adorning my body. Dragging myself to my knees I was distracted by an urgent whimpering and looked up to see the Red Setter – yep, it was a setter – gazing intently at me. As soon as our eyes met, he bounded backwards, then turned and ran forward a few paces, looking over his shoulder at me. When I didn't respond, he repeated the exercise, giving me a few anxious woofs.

Chester tugged at the lead, wanting to get in on the action. "Don't you dare," I snarled, giving him "the look." It worked, because his expression immediately said, "Whoa," and he parked his butt promptly on the ground. Meanwhile, the setter was almost frantic.

"Okay, buddy, I'm coming," I said, gingerly getting to my feet and taking a few careful steps. There were no breaks or sprains, thank goodness, but I had a feeling I was going to be pretty sore before long. Putting that aside I did my best to hurry after the dog, whose long legs were sprinting him away.

I figured the setter had most likely run away from his owner. They have a strong hunting instinct and will take off after a bird in a heartbeat if not leashed. This guy was wearing a collar and was certainly well cared for; some poor person was probably worried sick right about now to find him, though that didn't explain why the dog so obviously wanted me to follow him. What I saw next did.

The pup darted left onto an intersecting deer trail. I cursed as I turned after him. The trail was pretty overgrown and thorny branches reached out snatching at my clothes. Carefully pushing the branches aside, I looked ahead and froze. Sprawled across the rough path was the body of a woman. She was face down, legs straight out and long red hair splayed around her head.

Somehow, dead bodies keep cropping up in my life but I really wasn't ready for another one.

Get a grip, Polly. I scolded myself and forced my legs to take me closer, this time with no regard for the thorns scratching my face and arms. The dog, who was nuzzling the woman's neck, looked up at me and began talking in a pleading rurr, rurr voice, the way dogs do. It took several moments before I realized there was another sound…moaning. *Oh my gosh.* The woman was alive!

Two

"For a while there I was pretty freaked out." I was recounting my adventure to Mom and Rooster in the kitchen at Welcome Home, the shelter we run for homeless military veterans and their pets. Mom had guided her wheelchair next to me at the table, while Rooster set a mug of hot, sweet tea in front of me. I smiled gratefully at him as he settled opposite me. "Go on," he said.

"Well, I pulled the hair away from her face and checked her pulse in her neck. It was pretty strong and there were no obvious injuries, at least no bleeding, but she was out cold, so I called 911."

"You did the right thing," Mom patted my hand. "She could have had a stroke, or concussion…any number of things."

"Stroke? She's a bit young for that; she looked to be about my age."

"Young people have strokes. Remember little Timmy Fenmore? He stepped up to do his saxophone solo with the school marching band and lost his balance and threw up right into the bell of his sax. Everyone thought he must have the flu. You were playing piccolo at the time. You were quite good…"

"Yeah," Rooster grinned. "I heard you were the only one who could keep in step."

"Ha ha, very funny." I laced my voice with sarcasm then turned back to Mom. "So Timmy was having a stroke? I never knew that."

"That's why the family moved away. They wanted to be close to the best medical facilities."

"Huh." I sipped my tea. "Alright, let me get on with the story.

"It must have taken twenty minutes for the medics to arrive. They had to run down the trail to find us. By then the woman had started to come around, though she was really groggy. She managed to tell me her name, Heather, and her dog's name, Erik."

At that we turned our heads as one and looked into the corner of the kitchen where Erik lay with Elaine, Rooster's sweet old pit bull. Elaine responded with raised eyebrows and a single soft slap of her tail, but Erik jumped up and came to me, resting his noble head on my lap. He gave me a sorrowful look and a tentative tail wag, and I scratched his ears and told him everything would be alright.

Heather had been unable to give a coherent account of what had happened to her, and she kept rambling about Erik. When the EMTs said she needed to be in the hospital she all but panicked about what would happen to him, and so I promised to keep him with me until she was OK.

"Poor thing." Mom reached over and ran her hand over his silky coat. He gave her a grateful lick as she fingered his collar. "What's this on his tags?"

Not surprisingly he had a rabies tag; the other was worn almost smooth. Twisting it around I peered at the letters on it. "Erik Haggerty. And there's a phone number."

Rooster came around and looked over my shoulder. "Haggerty," he said. "That's probably Heather's last name."

"Do you think we should tell someone?" Mom wondered out loud. "Or try calling the number? Did she have a wallet or a purse with her?"

"I expect it's her own cell number," I said, "and she might have had a wallet but I wasn't going to grope through her pockets. Besides, what was the point?"

"To identify her, of course."

Sometimes my mother could be quite exasperating. "She was awake, Mom! She could just tell the EMTs who she is."

"What if she passed out again?"

I sucked in a slow breath through gritted teeth. "Mom…"

"Tell you what," Rooster, ever the peacemaker, butted in, "I'll call the hospital and see what I can find out. Maybe her family's already been notified."

He pulled out his phone and at the same time a duck started laughing in my back pocket. I drew my own phone out and my mother rolled her eyes at my new ringtone. "It's Tyler," I said, and darted into the living room where I could speak in private.

"Hey, hon."

"Are you OK?" Anxiety was evident in his voice. "I heard there was an accident."

The Mallowapple gossip train was obviously in full swing. Nothing stays secret in this town, it does, however, tend to get exaggerated.

"I'm fine. I found a woman who'd fallen on the trail when I was walking Chester this morning. I wasn't sure how badly she was hurt, so I called the EMTs. They took her to the hospital and Rooster is just now on the phone trying to find out what's going on."

Tyler exhaled loudly. "You had me worried. Talk was that someone was attacked."

"Well this time it wasn't me, so you can relax. Besides, as far as I know, it was just an accident."

On more than one occasion I'd found myself in a threatening situation. OK, to be honest, I might have put myself in dangerous situations a time or two, but always with good cause. Tyler was my self-appointed knight in shining armor, for which I loved him, but I didn't want him to have to keep rescuing me.

I recounted my story again and told Tyler about Erik. "Funny," he said, "When I was a kid I used to know a girl who had a setter she called Erik; actually, he was Erik the Red, after a famous Viking."

"A girl who was into Vikings?"

"It was my fault. She got the puppy for her birthday and brought him over to show me. I hadn't known it was her birthday and I wanted to give her something. I had rather a crush on her." He chuckled softly. "Anyway, I ended up giving her my prize possession – a book about Vikings. On the cover was a picture of Erik the Red, perhaps the most famous Viking of all, and as soon as my friend saw it, that was that. The dog had a name."

A call-waiting signal interrupted his tale. "Oh, sorry sweetie, gotta take this, it's a client. I'll see you tonight. Will you be at your mom's?"

"No, I'll be back home."

"OK, bye." And he was gone.

Three

The aroma of Hunan Beef and General Tso's Chicken was making my mouth water. Apparently, it had a similar effect on my dogs, who were grouped near the table in hopeful anticipation.

"Sorry, Kids," I said as I opened the boxes Tyler had brought. "This is much too spicy and salty for you."

Coco's brows went up a half inch and she gave her best sorrowful look. She's spent her whole twelve years practicing that look, so she's really good at it. Fortunately, I'm immune and besides, I'd never risk my pets' wellbeing for an unhealthy treat.

"Do you still have some of that Tsingtao beer?" Tyler asked while setting plates and forks on the table.

"In the fridge."

He reached in, grabbed a couple of bottles, popped the caps and we were good to go.

"So," he said, "are you going to fill me in on what happened today?"

I nodded, because my mouth was too full of beef to speak, and held up my finger to signal he wait a moment, took a swallow of beer and began to detail everything up to the point where Rooster called the hospital.

"Turns out Mom's instincts were right, of course, and Heather passed out again before giving her full name, so the authorities were glad to have the information from us. Rooster was also going to talk with Sheriff Wisniewski later on. They have their poker game at the VFW tonight."

"I know; my dad will be there."

The Veterans of Foreign Wars organization had a strong presence in our small town, for which I was extremely grateful. They'd given a lot of help to Mom and me when we were setting up Welcome Home. In fact, we might not have managed it without them, and they continued to be supportive.

"What about the dog?" Tyler pushed away from the table and grabbed the fortune cookies from the kitchen counter.

"I left him with Mom. He seems to have bonded with Elaine, and setters are high energy; I don't have the time to exercise him properly or the space for him to run. At Welcome Home there are plenty of people to help with that."

"Yeah, you're right. Your Mom will spoil him rotten as well."

I laughed, and in my mind's eye I could see my mother preparing special meals for Erik and wrapping him in soft, fluffy blankets.

At that moment the ducks started laughing again. This time it was Tyler who looked heavenward as I eyed the caller's name on my cell. "It's Rooster."

I thumbed the phone open. "Hey, Rooster. Any news?"

While I chatted, Tyler cleared the table, then poured himself a glass of water and headed to the couch, holding up the fortune cookies to indicate I should join him there.

"Good news!" I tossed my phone onto the table and jumped to the couch, bouncing on my backside and accidentally jabbing my elbow hard into Tyler's ribs.

"Ooph." Air exhaled from his lungs and his face reddened as his eyes went wide. "I'm beginning to think I need hazard insurance to come here," he complained.

"Stop being such a grouse," I said. "It should cheer you up to know that Rooster called to let us know Heather is doing well and her father has been found. Apparently, her name *is* Haggerty and her dad lives in Corkeep."

"So she's local?"

"I'm not sure, but that's all the information Rooster had. We'll find out more when she comes to get Erik."

Tyler grunted acknowledgement then held out his clenched hands with a fortune cookie in each. "Pick one."

I tapped his left fist and he opened his hand to reveal the cookie, which I hurriedly broke open and eyed the note inside.

"Life is like a dogsled team. If you're not the leader, the scenery never changes."

Tyler guffawed. "That's hard to dispute."

I grinned back, "Open yours."

He crumbled the cookie and held the slip of paper so that I couldn't read it.

"A sexy woman is about to kiss you," he said.

"It does not say that!" I tried to snatch the paper from him but he held it away.

"Sure it does," he laughed. "And it's going to come true."

His features softened as he held my gaze and pulled me close.

Well what do you know? He's right.

Four

Across the field I could see guys working on the roof of the old barn. This was to be our second conversion at Welcome Home and would give us room for six more residents, but it was a much tougher job than we'd tackled before. We had to lift the frame to put in new footers, straighten the building and now we were working on roofing. Once that was done we'd be on to the interior framing and insulation. Luckily, we had a wealth of knowledge and skill to call on between the current ex-military residents and members of the VFW, who also graciously donated their time. Even so, the project would have been a non-starter if not for an influx of money from the sale of a small house and an antique panel I'd inherited not long ago. Best of all, there was still some money in the bank. At long last things were looking really good.

"This must be them," I called out to Mom as my attention was drawn to a car heading toward the farmhouse.

We'd had a call earlier in the day from Dennis Haggerty, Heather's father, to say she was to be released from the hospital that afternoon and would it be OK if they came to get Erik. I'd had to rearrange my schedule to be there, but I didn't want to miss the reunion between owner and dog.

As the car came to a stop I went to the front door, calling for Erik. "Your mommy's here, Erik. Come on."

He came, but with little enthusiasm. He'd been pretty unhappy since he'd been with us. After all, his world had been turned upside down.

I opened the door just as Heather stepped from the car. A huge smile lit up her face as she saw Erik behind me.

"Erik, Erik. Come here baby!"

The pup's head snapped up, his tail began to whip from side to side and he hurtled down the porch steps, jumping at Heather with high-pitched cries. Laughing, she sat on the ground and gathered him to her, but he was just too excited and wriggled loose to run madly back and forth, 'til he flopped, panting, across her lap.

Mr. Haggerty fussed around his daughter. "Take it easy, kiddo, you just got out of the hospital."

"I'm fine, Dad. Better than fine now I've got my beautiful boy back."

Mom had followed me down the ramp in her wheelchair and we'd stayed off to the side watching the joyful reunion. Now she steered herself close to the Haggertys and held out her hand. "Welcome. I'm Edwina Parrett," she inclined her head toward me, "and this is my daughter Polly."

"Dennis Haggerty," Heather's dad said, taking Mom's hand in his, "but please call me Dennis. And you, young lady," he turned to me, "I will be forever in your debt. If you hadn't come along I don't know what might have happened to my little girl."

His voice began to break and I shuffled awkwardly, not knowing where to look or what to say. Happily, I was saved by Heather who got to her feet saying, "I'm not a little girl any more, Dad, but I am more than grateful to Polly for saving me and taking care of Erik." She put her hands together and gave a slight bow.

"Actually," I said, "it's Chester and Erik who are the heroes. Erik was determined to find help and Chester was determined to follow him."

"Who's Chester?" Dennis Haggerty asked.

"Why don't we all go inside," Mom interrupted, "and we can talk over a cold glass of lemonade."

To universal murmurings of agreement, we followed Mom up the wheelchair ramp and into the living room rather than the kitchen. We weren't usually that formal but when I entered the kitchen after volunteering to get the refreshments, I realized why. Two of our residents, Scott Hamm and Lou Berger, had taken over and were washing piles of fiddleheads in the sink. Pots of water were heating on the range and Kilner jars lined the counters.

"Uh, hi guys. What's going on?"

Scott looked over his shoulder at me. "We took Apache and Neo walking this morning" – that's the guys' dogs - "and came across some fiddleheads, so we decided to go foraging and this is what we got."

For those of you who have no idea what a fiddlehead is, they are ferns before they become ferns. You know, that curled-up shoot that pushes through the ground in spring and early summer. And they're delicious.

"We're gonna can them in cider vinegar with mustard seed and allspice," Lou chimed in. "Scott's teaching me some of the tricks of the trade."

"That's right, you were a Navy Mess Specialist, weren't you?" I said.

"Until I ended up like this." Scott held up his hands. One was missing three fingers, the other was pretty much mangled.

"An explosion?"

"Yeah, but not in action; it was a grease fire in the galley." He shook his head. "I'll tell you about it some other time."

"How about when we open our restaurant?" Lou said. "The Hamm Berger Joint. What do you think?"

I laughed at the use of their last names. "It's a match made in heaven. Are you serious, though? You really want to open a restaurant?"

Scott shrugged. "I hate to waste the culinary arts degree I earned at Le Cordon Bleu in Boston before I joined up. Though I can't do all the physical work, I still have the knowledge and Lou is willing to be my hands."

"Well, I'll definitely be one of your first customers," I said and left them to it, busying myself setting up a tray of lemonade and cookies. As I carried the refreshments back to our guests the front door opened and Tyler walked in.

"Here," he hurried over and took the tray, "let me carry that." Leaning close he gave me a quick kiss. "Where are we going?"

I nodded at the open living room door and stepped aside to let Tyler go first. He walked through the doorway and abruptly stopped, causing me to bump into him as I followed.

"Cassie?" I heard him blurt, and pushed my way past him.

His face was white, his mouth hung open and his gaze was fixed on Heather.

"Cassie, is that you?"

Five

The lemonade was finished, the cookies eaten, and father and daughter Haggerty were getting ready to leave. Tyler had glossed over his awkward moment, explaining that Heather could have been a double for someone he used to know. We then spent an hour chatting, with Heather telling us she'd recently been laid off from her IT job in Boston.

"I got a pretty good severance package," she told us, "so I decided to take some time and visit Dad now that he's retired here, and consider what I want to do next. I'm thinking of setting myself up as an independent contractor. I can also do web development and Photoshop work, and I know people who are killing it as independents working through sites like fiverr."

"What's fiverr?" Mom asked.

"It's an online marketplace where freelancers offer their services – anything from graphic design to video creation, um... writing resumes or even books; lots of things. And everything starts at five bucks."

"It sounds interesting," Mom murmured, though she still looked puzzled.

Tyler hardly said a word. Instead, he leaned back on the sofa, elbow on the arm and chin resting in his hand while he sent covert looks in Heather's direction. At one point I tried prodding him to divert his attention. He made an attempt to contribute to the conversation but soon lapsed back into his contemplative mood.

I was trying to think of a polite way to ask Heather how she came to fall when Mom spoke.

"You know for someone who had such a bad fall you look remarkably well. What actually happened? Did Erik pull you over?"

"Oh no, he was off-leash." Heather gave me a rather guilty look. "I know that's against the rules but he so loves to run. I should have anticipated he would give chase if he saw a bird or a small critter."

"You were following him, then?" Mom prompted Heather to continue.

"I was worried he'd get lost, after all Mallowapple is new to us." Heather glanced away briefly. "Actually, I'd been feeling a bit dizzy and nauseous, thinking maybe I'd better head back to Dad's, and wasn't really paying attention to Erik. When I noticed he was gone I panicked and took off running, calling for him. I heard his bark and turned onto the deer trail, and that's when the dizziness really caught up with me."

"Perhaps you had a panic attack," Mom suggested.

"Possibly. The real damage was that I stumbled into a patch of poison ivy, to which I am deathly allergic. And I'd left my epi-pen at home."

"Which you'll never do again." Dennis gave his daughter a stern look, then turned to me. "If you hadn't come along when you did, it could have been all over for my girl. You're a hero, Polly."

I squirmed. "Hero is such an over-used word. All I did was follow Erik, then call for help."

"You're a hero to me, young lady," Dennis spoke with an emphatic nod of his head.

"I'll second that." Heather smiled at me and I got all tingly and warm and allowed myself to enjoy being in the limelight for a few moments.

After that, conversation returned to every day topics and soon Heather and Dennis prepared to leave. We all promised to stay in touch, including Tyler.

"Bring Erik over any time," I said to Heather. "We'll miss him."

"I'd love to." She smiled at me. "And I'm sure Erik the Red will, too."

Beside me Tyler stiffened. "What did you say?" His voice was gruff and Heather's brows lifted slightly.

"That I'd love to come over sometime." She spoke slowly.

"No, something about the dog's name."

"Oh, Erik the Red." Heather laughed. "I call him that because we're both redheads. Only I'll let you into a secret – mine's not natural."

I laughed with her and she gave me a sisterly hug, saying, "Maybe we can get together for a girls' night glass of wine or two sometime?"

"That would be great," I said.

We waved as they drove away and I closed the door, leaning back against it as the latch clicked and giving Tyler an intense look.

355

"Are you going to tell me what's going on in your mind?"

Before he could speak, Mom wheeled her chair around. "I'll leave you to it. I have other things to do." And she headed back to her kitchen domain.

Tyler took my hand. "Let's sit on the porch."

He led me to the swing where I sat with legs tucked under so I could face him.

"Remember I told you I had a friend with a dog named Erik?" I nodded, but kept quiet. "I have a story you should hear." Taking a deep breath, he began.

"There was a family with two girls. Shelly was the older one and she was my best friend. The parents were Runyon and Neve Reed.

"Shelly was eight when Cassie was born and, as you might imagine, after all those years of having her parent's full attention, she was a little put out when her baby sister came along. That's why, on her ninth birthday, she got the puppy she'd always wanted: Erik the Red." He drew the name out slowly and gave me a meaningful look. Still I said nothing, and he went on.

"When Cassie was just two, the family went on vacation and chartered a yacht in Florida. They were docked in Miami one evening and Neve and Runyon decided to go out on the town. They hired a baby sitter to stay with the girls; when they got back, Cassie was missing. She was never found.

"There was speculation the nanny or one of the crew might have taken her, or she could have fallen overboard or just wandered off."

"So a body was never found?" I interrupted.

"No. I was only eleven at the time, though, so I'm not clear on all the details, but I do remember how awful it was. The Reeds were never the same, including Shelly. We stayed friends, of course, but I suspect she felt guilty because she never really liked her little sister."

"You don't suppose she might have done something to her? Pushed her overboard maybe?"

Tyler looked off into the distance and sighed. "I can't deny it crossed my mind."

"So when you saw Heather, you thought of Cassie? How? She was hardly more than a baby when she disappeared."

"Because she looks exactly like Shelly and her mother, Neve Reed. She's also about the right age for Cassie...and she has a setter she named Erik the Red. I mean, what kind of a coincidence is that?"

Tyler pushed himself abruptly off the swing, leaving me swaying jerkily back and forth.

"It probably is just coincidence," I said, hanging on to my seat. "Heather has a father after all, and they do say we all have a doppelganger."

"Yeah," Tyler ran his hand through his hair. "I expect you're right, but I've gotta say it really threw me to see her sitting there. She even sat the way Shelly used to sit, with one leg tucked under the other. That could be a family trait."

"Well, why don't you contact Shelly and tell her about Heather? Let her decide whether to do anything."

Seating himself back on the swing, Tyler took my hand. "I can't. Shelly was killed in a car crash during her first year of college. She'd been out drinking with a bunch of friends and lost control of her car. No other vehicle was involved but she drove straight into a brick wall. There were four other kids in the car; three of them walked away, the fourth was left paralyzed."

"Oh, God, what a terrible story. It must have destroyed Mr. and Mrs. Reed."

"They pretty much dropped out of site for a long time. These days they sometimes show up at VFW affairs; Mr. R is an ex-navy man."

I really didn't know what to say. Besides, I was late to cover a visit so I suggested Tyler join me.

"I'd better not," he said. "I'm expecting a counter-offer on a house." Tyler's in real estate, which I've learned is pretty much a twenty-four-hour job.

I felt bad leaving him, he was clearly depressed, but Brownie was waiting for her dinner. So I kissed his cheek and let duty call me away.

Six

Brownie's given name is Audrey Henburn, which suggests a rather elegant bird. She looks the part; a beautiful Partridge Plymouth Rock hen with deep brown plumage and black penciling outlining her feathers, and she's the newest member of the Weevleduntz family.

You might remember Mrs. W. is the doting parent of Lefty, a one-legged rooster. She took Audrey in a couple of weeks ago from a battery cage hen rescue. I was there when Audrey arrived. It was a joy to see her walk on earth and stretch her wings to the full for the first time in her life. She was also very scrawny and, consequently, very food driven. Unfortunately, a few days later, she got into a pan of brownies that Mrs. W. had left cooling on the open window ledge.

Chocolate and sugar are not good for chickens. *For that matter, Mrs. W's cooking isn't good for any living creature.* Audrey had to be rushed to the vet. Thankfully, Doctor Jim saved her, and in a nod to her coloring, jokingly kept referring to her as the brownie who ate the brownies. The nickname stuck, and now Audrey is known as Brownie.

It's not often that Mrs. Weevleduntz asks for my help, but today she was on a mission with a group of activists who were lobbying for poultry slaughterhouses to have glass walls, on the premise no-one would eat chicken if they saw how cruelly they were treated. I can't say I didn't sympathize.

Putting aside all gruesome thoughts I let myself into the house and walked through to the kitchen. I was to feed Lefty and Brownie, and Tallulah Beaky, known as Lulu, a gorgeous Rhode Island Red who had been the sole survivor when a skunk got into someone's chicken coop. It suddenly struck me that a lot of fowl have a pretty foul life.

Mrs. W. had said Lefty would be in the kitchen – he pretty much is a house pet – and the girls would be outside.

The kitchen was empty, and I noticed the pet door to the yard was unlatched. *Oh, rats.* Looking through the window, I spied Lefty hopping around and puffing out his chest, showing off to Lulu. Now, I don't know much about chickens, but I'm pretty sure it's not a good idea for a rooster to be with the hens.

I rushed outside and quickly got hold of Lefty - it wasn't too difficult seeing as he couldn't exactly run away – popped him inside, securing the pet door and firmly closing the kitchen door.

Lulu came hurrying over, cackling a greeting. Or she might have been demanding food; I wasn't sure which. I stroked her back briefly then stood, looking around for Brownie.

"Brownie! Here chicky," I called out. I didn't expect her to come dashing right up to me, she'd had a pretty rough time of it and probably wasn't too trusting yet. Still, the yard wasn't that big, so where was she?

The coop was in the middle so I looked inside – nothing. I was beginning to get a sour feeling in my stomach. "Brownie! Where are you chicky, chicky?" Still nothing.

With Lulu pecking at my heels and my concerns mounting I searched and called in every direction, praying I would see her pecking for worms in the soft ground somewhere, or perched in the low branches of a tree. There were so many things that could have happened, so many places she might be. And spotting a brown bird in a vista of brown and green was simply not that easy.

Fighting down a rush of panic I headed back to the house. Mrs. W. didn't have a cell phone so there was no way to contact her. I decided I'd better feed Lefty and Lulu to keep them happy, then I'd have to keep trying to find Brownie.

Oh, no! Lefty was out again! I must not have latched the door properly. I scooped him up for the second time and deposited him on the kitchen floor, and fastened the latch on the pet door flap. It was as I straightened up I noticed a note on one of the counters. I snatched at it, hoping it would tell me Brownie was somewhere safe. Not so, there was just a single line to tell me spaghetti – a favorite chicken food - was in the fridge.

By now I was truly sick with worry. A scrabbling sound distracted me. I glanced down and there was Lefty prodding with his beak at the latch on the pet door. "Why you little Houdini," I said. Grabbing a step stool from a corner I shoved it against the door and very firmly pushed the latch down. Behind me I heard scrabbling again. "Lefty," I swore under my breath.

But it wasn't Lefty.

The door to the cabinet under the sink swung open and out stepped Brownie. Open-mouthed I watched as she strutted around the kitchen, head bobbing back and forth and clucking proudly. Pulling my gaze back to the cabinet I could see a bunch of clean rags piled inside, and in the middle of the pile lay a big beautiful brown egg.

It kind of gave a whole new meaning to not counting your chickens.

An hour later the girls were safely locked in their coop and Lefty was secure in the kitchen. Brownie's egg sat in a bowl by the sink. Tomorrow I'd call Mrs. W. and tell her the whole story.

I'd learned a lot about chickens today. They're very smart, very determined and really affectionate; all three birds were ready to climb into my lap to be petted. Oh, and chickens can jump. At least, Brownie could. When I held out the strands of spaghetti for her she jumped a good six inches, straight up, to grab the dangling treat. What an athlete. *I wonder if chickens can be trained to run an obstacle course?*

Seven

"It's outrageous!"

Mom crumpled up the paper in her hand and hurled it away. If she'd had the use of her legs she would have been stomping around. Instead, she drove her wheelchair in tight circles around the kitchen table. I jumped aside as she narrowly missed my feet.

"Now, Edwina, it doesn't help to lose your temper." Rooster's tone was soothing as he bent to retrieve the offending note.

"Right now I don't care," Mom snapped.

"Can I see?" I held out my hand to Rooster and he passed me the paper. It was a white form with a red sticker on it, something called a notice of non-compliance, and said the Welcome Home barn was not to code and so housing benefits currently paid for the residents would be stopped, which meant we wouldn't be getting paid for housing them. It was signed by Ward Nesmith of the Department of Veterans Affairs.

I should explain that when a new resident came along, we immediately had them apply to the VA for housing benefits. If approved, those benefits were payed directly to Welcome Home. Of course, it was nowhere near enough to run the place; we still relied heavily on fundraising and the generosity of others. And sometimes, a resident was turned down, but we never turned them away.

"I don't get it," I said, looking to Rooster for an explanation. "Who is this guy? Can he just do this? What's not to code?"

"He's an inspector with the VA. Yes, he probably can stop the payments. The code violation is that there should be two means of egress from the upper level of the barn."

"You're saying we need two exits?"

"Right. As of now, the only way down from the top floor of the barns is via the interior stairway. Apparently there has to be another exit at the end of the corridor upstairs."

"But everything was inspected and approved when we converted the first barn. Did the rules change or something?"

Rooster sighed. "No. I think the original inspector was just more sympathetic to our cause and let things slide."

I was steaming as much as Mom now. "So this guy doesn't care about people who have lost their limbs, their families, their peace of mind, in service to men like him! Where does he expect the residents to go? Back on the streets?"

"It's not as bad as that." Rooster held out his hands in a placating gesture. "No-one's getting thrown out." He turned to Mom, "Are they Edwina?"

Mom had brought her chair to a halt, for which my toes were grateful, and slumped back. "No, of course not. We'll think of something." She paused. "I'm just not sure how."

"Let's get ahold of Zill Granger and run this by him," Rooster said.

"His background is criminal law," I said. "How can he be of help?"

"He knows a lot of people in other areas of the law, and he's certainly been a good friend to us."

Indeed, that was true. It was Granger who'd taken on Rooster's case when he'd been accused of murder. And frankly, I didn't have any other suggestions, so Rooster went off to make the call and I flopped into a chair and buried my head between my arms on the table.

There was a shaky breath nearby. I turned my head to eye my mother, lips quivering and silent tears creasing her cheeks. She noticed me watching as she pulled a box of tissues close and blew her nose. "Oh, Polly, this can't be happening. After all we've done."

Moving quickly to her I hugged her tight. Not so long ago Mom's world had been miserably unhappy. Welcome Home had been her salvation and she'd put all her resources and everything of herself into it. The outcome was that we'd helped a number of homeless veterans and their pets regain fulfilling lives. I'd even go so far as to say we'd saved a life or two, and I was immensely proud of our halfway house, and especially proud of my mother.

"Mom," I pulled away from her, "we're not going to let this happen."

She drew a tissue across her eyes then dropped her hands into her lap. I watched as she filled her lungs with a calming breath and allowed her features to relax. Looking me dead in the eye she gave a curt nod. "You're right. We're not."

I would have stayed with Mom but, once again, business came first. I had a couple of visits to make, then my evening was spent on payroll. Not one of my favorite duties, but necessary if I didn't want my crew to rebel.

Of course, I'd called Tyler earlier to fill him in on all that had happened. Now I was ready to crash in bed, so I hit speed dial again to wish him goodnight.

"Hi, hon," he answered.

"I'm ready to fall asleep, so I'm just calling to say I love you."

"It's only just past nine," he said.

"I know, but I'm really tired. Let's plan on breakfast at the diner; we can talk then."

"OK, sweetheart. Sleep tight. Love you," and we hung up.

Carefully I inserted myself into bed between all my furkids, reached out to turn off the light and settled down with a sigh. Oh, it felt good to lay my head on the pillow.

That's when the phone rang.

"What d'you forget?" I mumbled, assuming it was Tyler.

"Polly? Polly, it's Heather. Something's happened and I really could use a friend."

Eight

"Just bring me a gallon of coffee." I turned bleary eyes on Nita as she poured me a cup.

"Wow, and good morning to you too," she said with more than a hint of sarcasm, then hiked her hip and gave me a meaningful look. "OK, what's up?"

Nita is the owner of Bennie's Diner, where I sat waiting for Tyler, and prides herself on knowing more about everybody's business than they know themselves.

"Sorry. I was up very late talking to a friend on the phone. I'm just more than a little tired." I didn't dare say more or Nita would never go away. She had no qualms about putting gossip before customer service. Surprisingly, that didn't seem to deter people from coming in. Maybe because Nita was as willing to dispense the gossip as obtain it.

"Hmph," she grunted, then glanced toward the diner's entrance. "Well, here comes that gorgeous guy of yours. I'll bet he's a lot more fun than you this morning. I'll go get another cup."

Actually, Tyler's face was tense. He sat abruptly next to me and spoke without preamble.

"Polly, something happened last night."

"Was it anything to do with Neve Reed passing out at the VFW when she saw Heather Haggerty?"

Tyler's head jerked and his eyes went wide. "How did you know that?"

"Heather called me last night. But how did *you* hear about it?"

"My mom called first thing. She wanted to tell me about it in case I ran into Neve or Runyon. According to her, Neve was very shaken and Mom felt rather guilty. The Reeds used to be regulars at the VFW but they stopped going after Shelly died. It was Mom who persuaded them to attend the benefit last night."

I was about to ask a question when Nita appeared with coffee for Tyler.

"I've ordered today's breakfast special for you both. It's peanut butter and chocolate pancakes with chocolate sauce." *Great, a sugar rush to go with the caffeine.* "You kids look like you could use a pick-me-up. Wanna tell me what's going on?"

Before I could respond with a snippy remark, Tyler spoke up, giving Nita's arm a quick squeeze.

"You're a wonder. Pancakes sound delicious."

Nita grunted, knowing she'd been shut down for now, and went off, no doubt to see what other conversations she could butt into.

I took a sip of my coffee then set the mug on the table, wrapping my hands around it. "OK," I said to Tyler, "tell me your version of events, then I'll tell you what Heather said."

"Alright," Tyler began. "The mood was light-hearted. In fact, Mom said it's the most relaxed she'd seen

Neve in a long time. Then Dennis Haggerty showed up. You may not know, he's just recently retired up this way and it was his first time at the VFW. One of the regulars introduced him around and, when he met Neve, Mom said he looked quite taken-aback and commented that his daughter looked like her. Of course, none of them took it seriously, but Haggerty said to them, 'You'll see. She's joining me soon.'

"Sure enough, a short time later he came back to them with Heather in tow. They were all shocked at the resemblance but Neve went white. Mom said she got off the bar stool, held an arm out to Heather, then simply crumpled to the floor. Runyon carried her into one of the offices. Doc Crocker happened to be there and went with them while the Haggertys hung around with my parents. They were both really upset and Dennis Haggerty kept blaming himself, though of course there was no way he could know how Neve would react."

"Well," I said, drawing out the word, "that's not necessarily true."

Before I could go on, one of the waitresses appeared and set our plates on the table. I guess Nita had given up on us.

The smell of warm chocolate and maple syrup was divine, and I grabbed my fork with enthusiasm. "Why don't we eat and then continue talking?"

"Oh no you don't." Tyler snatched my plate away and put it out of reach on the far corner of the table.

"Hey," I said.

He glared at me. "You can't make a statement like that without explaining it."

"I can explain after I've had my pancakes."

Tyler's eyes narrowed and his lips formed a thin line and I knew he wasn't going to budge.

"Oh, all right," I grumbled. "Heather is adopted."

Tyler jerked upright in his chair and his jaw dropped. I took advantage of the moment to stand and stretch across the table to retrieve my plate, and fork in a mouthful of sweet, fluffy delight.

"You'd better back up a bit," he said, "and tell me everything."

"Only if you promise not to take my plate away again."

He gave a curt nod, then leaned forward on his elbows to listen as I gave my narrative, in between bites.

"Heather and her dad were waiting with your parents to be sure Neve was OK. Of course, they'd asked about the Reed's daughter but your parents simply said she'd disappeared as a child and they didn't feel it was their place to comment further.

"When Runyon came out of the office he told them Neve had come round and was asking to see Heather. He explained Neve was convincing herself that somehow Heather was her long lost child and asked Heather to gently let her know it wasn't possible.

"So Heather went off with Runyon, her dad saying he'll wait for her, that he doesn't want to stress Neve with too many people hanging about. Heather said she thought he was just being considerate."

"But he didn't want to tell the truth," Tyler interrupted.

"Not then, anyway," I said and sighed. "Heather was genuinely upset about what happened. She said it was heartbreaking to watch the hope fade from Neve's eyes when she insisted she couldn't be related to her in any way. She described Neve as 'crumpling in on herself.' Imagine Heather's shock when, back at home, her dad confessed there *was* a possibility she could be the Reed's daughter...because she was adopted."

"What did she do?"

"She got angry. Furious was the word she used; said she felt betrayed, and stormed out of the house and went over to the C'mon Inn where she got a room for the night. That's when she called me."

"What exactly did Dennis Haggerty tell her?"

"We didn't get that far. She spent most of the time crying, then her cell phone battery started to run down and she'd left the charger at her dad's. So we agreed to meet up later today. Wanna come?"

"Maybe." Tyler drained his coffee and held up the mug to signal he needed more. "I have a couple of showings, so it depends how long they last. What time are you getting together?"

"I'm going to pick Heather and Erik up at four at the Inn. Probably I'll take them out to Welcome Home; that way I can also get the latest on what's happening with the inspector and the VA benefits."

"Whoa! Erik is at the C'mon Inn? I can hardly believe it."

Hattie Pan, the owner of Mallowapple's most illustrious lodgings – which didn't take much because there was almost no competition – was definitely not a dog person. In fact, as far as I knew, she'd never before allowed a dog on the premises, especially as she had two Siamese cats, Chatty and Kathy, who reigned over the Inn in the manner to which they no doubt believed they were born.

"This I have to see," Tyler chuckled. "I'll find a way to join you."

Nine

"But we had plans to meet here at this time."

Behind the reception desk, Hattie Pan pursed her thin lips and shrugged a boney shoulder. "I don't know anything about that. She left with the dog about an hour ago and I saw them hurry off in the direction of the Puttyroot Trail. I reckoned she needed to walk him."

"Perhaps she forgot you were coming," Tyler said to me.

"I hardly think that's likely, considering she was so insistent on getting together." I knew I sounded waspish, but I was puzzled and irritated by Heather's behavior.

Tyler had managed to clear his schedule and so we'd driven together to the C'mon Inn, expecting to find Heather waiting for us in the lobby but it was empty. The bell over the door alerted Hattie to our entry and she came out of the office, obviously disappointed when she saw we were not prospective customers. We asked her to call Heather's room to let her know we were waiting, and that's when Hattie announced Heather had left.

"She could have lost track of time," Tyler said to me, still looking for a logical explanation, "and be running late. Just give her a call on the cell."

I pulled out my phone and hit her number, then shook my head as the call went into voicemail. "Heather, it's Polly. I'm at the Inn; did you forget our appointment? Please call me and let me know what's going on."

Maybe I was overreacting, but this just didn't feel right.

Tyler put an arm around my waist. "We can wait a while. I'm sure Hattie won't mind if we sit here." He glanced in her direction and she gave a slight incline of her head.

"Or," I said, "we can follow the Puttyroot Trail and see if we can catch up to her."

Tyler looked down into my face. No doubt he could read the anxiety there. "Let's do that," he agreed, and took my hand and led me away.

The Puttyroot Trail is an easy walking and biking path that follows the route of an old narrow-gauge railroad that once supported the now defunct logging industry. Wildflowers bloomed in profusion along the way and picnic areas dotted the trail. It's quite popular with locals and visitors alike in the early mornings; right now, though, it was deserted and I would have enjoyed the walk if not for the nagging tension in my gut.

"Is that someone sitting on a bench?" Tyler pointed ahead where a bench lined the trail. We were looking into the sun and I didn't have my sunglasses with me so I shaded my eyes with a hand and squinted.

"Looks like a lump to me; maybe a bag?"

"No," Tyler said, "it's a woman slumped over," and he started running.

I scrunched my eyes up tighter, but it still looked like a bag to me - *Maybe I need glasses* - then dashed after Tyler. He closed in on the woman and put a hand out to shake a shoulder. In an instant she jumped up, screaming, and back-pedaled away from him, arms swinging wildly. "Get away from me. I have pepper spray."

I saw her dig into a pocket and yelled at the top of my voice, "No, no. Stop. We thought you needed help. Don't spray; we won't hurt you."

She hesitated and Tyler took the moment to move away, hands up in surrender. I came up beside him and we stood facing the woman 'til she gave a shaky laugh and relaxed her stance. "Oh, geez. I'm sorry, but you really startled me. I heard someone was attacked around here recently and when you touched me I immediately thought the worst. I was actually just taking a minute to stretch out my low back, but I guess it must have looked a bit odd."

"We should be apologizing to you," Tyler said.

"As a matter of fact," I took over, "the woman you're referring to is a friend of ours. She wasn't attacked, though, she fell in a patch of poison ivy and had a severe allergic reaction, so you don't have to worry about using the trail. I'm sure it's quite safe - unless you also have allergy problems."

"Well, that's good to know and no, poison ivy is not a problem for me." The woman gave a crooked smile. "I guess I can enjoy the rest of my walk then."

"Oh," I said quickly, "you haven't seen a young lady with long, red hair, have you? That's the friend we just mentioned and we're trying to catch up with her."

"I did see someone with long red hair but it wasn't a woman, it was a dog."

Tyler and I exchanged troubled looks; the woman frowned, noting our reaction.

"It was a big dog," she said. "I tried to get it to come to me but it ran off."

"Which way?" Tyler swiveled his head as he asked, eyes scanning the distance.

"Perhaps a quarter mile down the trail. Where the boardwalk starts. Is everything OK?"

Ignoring the woman's question, Tyler and I took off running, yelling thanks over our shoulders.

The boardwalk covered a short stretch of the trail that went over a deep gulch. As we neared, Tyler began to call Heather's name; I figured it made more sense to call for Erik.

"Erik! Eeerik!" I cupped my hands over my mouth and directed my calls from left to right, pausing to listen every few moments. Sure enough, after a couple of minutes, there was an answering bark and moments later the dog appeared, clawing his way up the side of the gulch. He rushed to us, barking and whining, then did his backward jog and turn.

"He wants us to follow," I said to Tyler. "That's how he behaved when he took me to Heather before."

"Right," Tyler said, striding after Erik. But the dog disappeared over the side of the boardwalk and slithered down into the ravine. Tyler and I hesitated and leaned over the side. *Oh no!* Heather lay on her back in the shallow and swiftly moving stream, one arm flung outward and her head at an impossible-looking angle.

"Call for help," Tyler spoke urgently then jumped off the boardwalk and slid down on heels and butt. With trembling fingers I tugged my phone from my back pocket and hit 911. As the operator answered I watched my guy touch his fingers to Heather's neck, then he lifted her, placed her on a narrow strip of dirt just above the water level and began vigorously to pump the center of her chest. I went cold; I couldn't quite wrap my head around what I was seeing.

"What is your emergency?" The operator repeated. *Pull yourself together, Polly.* I scolded myself and found my voice, shaky though it was.

"I need an ambulance…and the police."

Ten

"Miss Parrett... Miss Parrett, did you hear what I said?" I shook my head and brought myself back to the middle-aged couple on the sofa in front of me. The wife glowered through vintage-style round glasses, while a sleek black cat lay stretched across her lap. Beside her, her husband sat with a coal black Labrador retriever leaning against his legs.

Garrett and Wendy Gurfinkel were potential customers, and if I didn't get my act together they'd be taking their business elsewhere.

"I'm so sorry. I was struck by how sleek and glossy your pets' coats are," I lied, while in truth my mind had wandered back to thoughts of Heather. "You obviously take wonderful care of them."

A look of pride crossed Wendy's face as she ran her fingers down the cat's back. "Pavlova's made that easy. She's very fastidious, you know? She's also very athletic; that's how she got her name."

In my mind I conjured up an image of a fruit and cream-filled meringue, which was the only pavlova I knew, and wondered what that had to do with an athletic cat. My confused look triggered Wendy to explain. "She's named after the ballet dancer, Anna Pavlova; probably the greatest female dancer of all time. You're probably familiar with a dessert named after her." *Ah. Now it made sense.*

"And Jelly Roll," she scratched the dog's head, "is named after Jelly Roll Morton."

"Uh, is he a dancer?"

Wendy gave an exasperated little sigh, "No dear, he was a famous jazz pianist in the early 1900s."

I wondered if that meant the dog also played the piano. As if reading my mind Wendy turned her head to her husband. "Garrett loves the music from that era, and Jelly Roll is his dog so he came up with the name."

Leaning forward I rubbed the dog's chest lightly with my knuckles; he ran a wet tongue over my arm. "Nice to meet you Jelly Roll," I said, then turned my attention back to the Gurfinkels, forcing a smile on my face. "Well, why don't you tell me how I can help you?"

An hour or so later I left the Gurfinkel family, having salvaged the meeting. The sitter I planned to assign to them was Tina, my second in command, and before finalizing a contract I'd arranged to bring her over for a meet and greet. Tina was great and I had no qualms that she'd be a hit, so I gave myself a mental pat on the back and allowed my thoughts to return to the previous day.

Tyler had continued CPR on Heather until the emergency unit arrived, while Erik hovered anxiously over his owner and I paced on the boardwalk above so I could alert the EMTs to our location. It was all to no avail, though. Tyler was so exhausted from his effort to save her that he had to be helped up the side of the ravine to the boardwalk, where he sank to his knees.

"If only we'd got to her a few minutes earlier," he gasped in between ragged breaths, "I might have saved her."

"There's no way to know that," I sank down beside him and cradled his head against my chest. I wanted to say more but, in truth, I was trying too hard to maintain some composure, and so we hung on to each other until someone applied gentle pressure to my shoulder.

"Polly, can you help us with the dog?"

I looked up through watery eyes. Officer Wayde Frellick was standing over me – I hadn't even noticed the police arrive. "We need to get down to the body," I flinched at the word, "but the dog is being aggressive and won't let us get near."

Shrill barking pierced my brain. I jumped up and once again peered into the ravine. Erik had positioned himself between Heather and two of the emergency personnel. Whenever one of the EMTs tried to approach, Erik would assume a protective stance and bare his teeth.

"He's scared and confused," I said.

"I get that," Frellick nodded, "but I need to take a look around and then we've got to bring the body back up here. Do you think you can get the dog out of the way?"

"Erik," I said, "his name's Erik."

Frellick narrowed his eyes at me. "OK...Erik." Then with more urgency in his voice added, "I have to get down there."

"Sorry," I said. "This has been a shock. Of course I'll help."

In my most soothing voice I tried to coax Erik to me. He responded by yipping fretfully, but when one of the EMTs tried again to approach, his stance stiffened and his lips curled back over his teeth in warning.

"I'll have to go down there." I looked at the steep drop and Heather's lifeless form and began to feel queasy. *Suck it up*, I scolded myself.

The men had rigged a rope to facilitate the climb and gingerly I stepped off the boardwalk onto the edge of the ravine, reaching for the rope. The soft earth immediately gave way, my knees buckled and I began to tip forward when a strong arm came around my waist and hauled me back. *Tyler*.

"I'll go." His voice was gruff. "One body is enough."

With that he grabbed the rope and swung over the side and, this time, half-rappelled to the bottom. I watched as man and dog eyed each other. Tyler crouched, his lips were moving but I couldn't hear what he said. A minute or so went by before Erik's body relaxed and he took a few tentative steps forward. Tyler kneaded his neck and shoulders then reached backward for a length of rope one of the EMTs was offering. Efficiently he fashioned a makeshift harness around the hound's chest and attached it to his collar. With his free hand he took hold of the rope still hanging down the side of the ravine and began to haul himself up, pulling at Erik's harness.

The dog looked over at Heather's lifeless form and began to resist. From above I called him again and, this time, he responded with a yowl of misery and suddenly bounded upward. Tyler released his hold and Erik scaled the ravine with the ease of a mountain goat and ran right to me. Squatting before him I ran my hands gently along his back. He bent his head in supplication and tucked it under my arm, leaving a little streak of blood on my sleeve. Concerned he might be bleeding I checked his mouth, but he looked OK and I figured the blood must Heather's. Massaging his neck I whispered to him. "I'm sorry puppy, but your Mom's not coming back."

Officer Frellick had made a cursory examination of the area and asked a few questions of Tyler and me – had we seen anyone else in the area, did we have Heather's phone - and now the EMTs were bringing Heather, in a body bag, up to the trail. They strapped it to a gurney and began to wheel it to the end of the trail where the ambulance was parked. In solemn step we followed, me hanging tightly onto Erik with one hand, the other firmly in Tyler's grasp.

A few onlookers had gathered nearby, prevented from stepping on the trail by another officer. One of them was the woman we'd talked to earlier. She looked at us and mouthed, "I'm sorry." I acknowledged her sentiment with a slight nod but couldn't bring myself to speak.

The ambulance doors closed with a firm thwack. Tyler and I turned away and I gave a slight tug on Erik's lead. "Come on, puppy. Time to go."

The dog's face immediately registered alarm; he stiffened and pushed his rear firmly to the floor. *Oh, dear, am I'm gonna have to lift him?* It was still at least a quarter mile back to the C'mon Inn and I didn't relish carrying 70 pounds of dog that far.

"I'll do that." I swiveled my head at Tyler's words and gave him a crooked smile. *My guy. Always there for me.*

"Are you OK?" I asked, registering the pallor of his skin.

He let his fingers brush my cheek. "Sure."

His voice wasn't too convincing but I stepped aside to allow him room to gather the dog up. Erik gave one long mournful howl that faded into little whimpers but, thankfully, he didn't struggle. Instead, he went limp like a rag doll and together Tyler and I trudged away.

Eleven

I ran my fingers through Taz's black hair and she rolled over to expose her tummy for rubbing. She's a funny cat, completely secure with me but will rarely let anyone else get near her. She's never been ill-treated - I rescued her as a kitten – she's just never liked anyone else.

"What a sorry few days we've had, monkey face," I sighed, allowing my body to sink deeper into the couch and my thoughts to wander back over recent events.

Two days had passed since Heather's body had been recovered. Though there was still an ongoing investigation it seemed more than likely that the death would be ruled accidental. Dennis Haggerty had gone to ground, distraught with grief. When I called him with condolences and to arrange to bring Erik to him, his response shocked me rigid.

"If I ever see that animal again I might put a bullet in his head. He killed my girl."

"Wh..what, n..no," I stammered. "He didn't do anything."

"Twice Heather fell and both times she was walking that, that creature. I should have known after the first time it was the dog that pulled her over. I'll never forgive myself for not insisting she get rid of him. He's a danger to anyone near him, and you can take that as a warning."

"Look, Mr Haggerty. Dennis," I softened my voice though my emotions were reeling, "I can't imagine what you're going through right now, and I get that you want to blame someone, but I don't think Erik…"

"Don't you make excuses," Haggerty interrupted, his voice brittle and cold. "I know you want to help, but I've said what I mean and the only thing that matters now is that I'll never see my beautiful girl again. So keep your thoughts and your intentions to yourself and leave me alone."

With that the phone went dead and I sat, stupefied, looking at it as if it could explain to me what had just happened.

Now, with the passing of time, I was wondering whether Dennis would be more reasonable. Not that there was any urgency for Erik's sake; he was at Welcome Home where Scott Hamm and Lou Berger had appointed themselves as his guardian. Their dogs were both young and easy-going, and the thought was they would likely be a positive influence on the grieving Erik.

A soft rap on the door got my attention and I looked that way as Tyler walked in.

"Hi, sweetheart," he said, coming to me and kissing my forehead, then tickling Taz under the chin. She completely ignored him, instead wrapping her paws around my hand to indicate I should keep petting her tummy.

"Sorry, Tazzie." I gave her one last rub. "I have to go."

It was Tyler's dad's birthday, and we were joining his parents and sister for dinner at Beers and Steers, his dad's favorite steakhouse, which was a good half hour drive. The restaurant was new to me and normally I would have been excited about going, but I was struggling to get my spirits up.

"Suzette has arranged for a birthday cake and the restaurant staff will sing Happy Birthday," Tyler said, trying to make conversation.

"Your dad won't like that." I'd learned last year that Mr. Breslin didn't much care to be reminded of his advancing years, but Tyler glanced my way and gave a sly grin, "Yeah, but the rest of us will."

"You're bad," I grinned in response and we fell silent again. My thoughts immediately reverted to events of the last few days and I twisted in my seat to face Tyler.

"I know you probably won't want to hear this," I spoke slowly and watched the corner of Tyler's mouth tense up, "but I can't help but wonder if Heather's death *was* an accident."

When Tyler didn't respond, I took a deep breath and pushed on. "Seriously, it just seems so coincidental that she would fall twice in such a short period of time. And the second time it was right above the ravine?"

I waited for Tyler to tell me I was letting my thoughts get the better of me; then he surprised me.

"It's more than likely a coincidence, but I can't deny being a little troubled by what happened."

I slapped my hand on the dashboard. "I knew it."

"Alright, don't get carried away." Tyler tried to dampen my rush of excitement. "The odds are the fall was accidental, but it's not that big a drop into the ravine and as I was climbing up and down the side I did see some of the vegetation was damaged."

I frowned. "What do you mean?"

"Some of the shrubs down the side of the ravine had broken branches and were a bit flattened, which suggests Heather landed on them and rolled on down to the bottom. It strikes me that would have softened the fall, so a broken arm or ribs would be more likely than cracking open the skull."

"You have to tell the sheriff."

"Let's not stir up a hornet's nest; at least not before the coroner's verdict. And don't forget, when Heather fell the first time she said she blacked out. Maybe she had a medical condition that we don't know about and she passed out again."

"Right above the ravine?" I repeated, my voice laced with sarcasm.

"OK. How about we agree to keep our thoughts to ourselves until the coroner is finished? It's not the subject for a birthday celebration anyway."

As it turned out, that wasn't our call to make.

Twelve

"Neve's insisting on a DNA test. Dennis Haggerty is refusing point blank and even threatening to take out a restraining order against Neve if she doesn't leave him alone."

Franny Breslin, Tyler's mom, ran her finger lightly around the rim of her wine glass as she told us of Neve Reed's determination to prove Heather was her long lost child.

"She's become quite manic," Franny went on. "When Runyon called and asked me to talk to her I wasn't prepared for what I would find. She babbled non-stop but never looked me in the eye; just sort of gazed over my shoulder and kept repeating the same things. And she looked terrible, I thought her eyes were bruised 'til I realized they're just so puffy and dark from lack of sleep. I couldn't get through to her at all."

"How is Runyon handling it?" Suzette, Tyler's sister, put her elbows on the table and locked her hands together.

Franny looked at her husband and he picked up the narrative.

"At the very least he has to bring in a nurse or caretaker of some sort to look after Neve, and she may even have to be committed, so how do you think he feels? He lost both his daughters and now he's watching his wife fall apart – again."

We all fell silent until guilt forced me to speak up.

"This is my fault. I'm the only one Heather told about being adopted. Someone at the diner must have overhead me talking to Tyler about it and then told Neve. If I'd kept my mouth shut, Neve could have gone on believing Dennis was Heather's real father, and couldn't possibly be her child. It was finding out Heather was adopted that gave her hope she'd found her long lost Cassie."

Franny clasped her hand over mine and gave a squeeze. "That's ridiculous. Neve has always been desperate to believe her daughter was alive."

"Besides," Suzette added, "you don't know for sure whether Heather told anyone else."

I flashed her a grateful smile, though I thought it unlikely Heather had talked to anyone else.

It was at that moment we were startled from our dismal mood by loud, energetic clapping and watched as a group of restaurant workers surged our way. One guy held a cake aloft, which he deftly set on the table as they reached us and burst into a loud rendition of Happy Birthday that ended with other diners cheering and clapping.

Roland's face was a deep crimson and he rubbed the back of his neck as he shook his head at each of us. Then he looked at the cake and gave a loud guffaw. It was baby blue and covered with frosting-molded false teeth, pill organizer, Bengay and things that signify old age.

"That's brilliant, Sis," Tyler said to Suzette. "How did you come up with that idea?"

"Oh, you know how Dad's always complaining about getting old."

Roland wagged his finger at us, "Just you wait, you youngsters. Growing old is not for the faint of heart."

"Age may have slowed you down, Dad," Tyler quipped, "but it hasn't shut you up."

And that was the beginning of a lot of age-related banter. The mood was lightened considerably more when Franny cut into the cake and passed the slices around. Red velvet chocolate cake. *Oh yeah.*

Thirteen

I said goodbye to Cooper, a boisterous, fun-loving Australian shepherd. I was filling in for his usual sitter who had an emergency dental appointment with her eight-year old son. Aussies are extremely energetic and intelligent, and I'd enjoyed the two hours I'd spent at the dog park watching Cooper trying to herd all the other dogs together. There were several owners there that I knew and it had given me a much-needed change of pace, so I was feeling pretty perky as I got into my van and the phone rang.

"Rooster," I said, registering his name on my cell. "What's new?"

"Nothing you're going to like to hear," he said in a sour tone.

My bubble of bonhomie immediately burst. "What's wrong?"

"It's the VA inspector."

"I thought you and Mom had that covered with the attorney Zill Granger recommended."

"We do," Rooster said. "Plans have already been submitted for the exterior stairways of both barns and there's no reason to think there will be a problem with approval. And there's a lumber yard all the way over in Millinocket that heard about us, who are donating the wood. We have to go pick it up but one of the VFW members has volunteered his truck."

"This sounds great," I said, "so what's the problem?"

"We've been told we don't have adequate care for Scott Hamm. The inspector reported he thought Scott should be in a facility that provides nursing care. A woman came out this morning from the VA, looked around and talked to Scott and agreed Welcome Home is not the right place for him."

You may remember Scott is the guy with damaged hands who likes to cook. There's no doubt it's difficult for him, but he's still able to deal with most everyday things; you know, like getting dressed.

"What does Scott say?"

"He's seriously ticked off. He's been trying to get a prosthetic for a long time for his one hand and feels if he goes into nursing care that will be an excuse not to give him one at all. He's even more annoyed that this means Welcome Home won't get any benefits for him as long as he stays here."

"Well that doesn't matter much at the moment because we're not getting benefits for anyone right now." A throbbing pain was building at the base of my skull. I drew a deep breath, held it, then let it out slowly, willing myself to calm down.

"You there, Polly?" Rooster's voice came from the phone.

"Trying to get my zen back," I said. *It wasn't working.* "Listen, I'm gonna come over. Let's you, me and Mom sit down with Scott and see what we can work out."

"Good thinking. See you soon."

"OK," I said, and turned the van in the direction of my old home.

Fourteen

"The worst of it, Mrs. P., is that I'm causing you a heap of trouble. But I'll not be a burden much longer, I'm going to find another place to stay..."

"You just stop right there, Scott Hamm." Mom positively bristled with indignation. "Having you and the other vets here at Welcome Home is a privilege for us." Her gaze swept to me and Rooster sitting at the kitchen table. "Yes, we're having a bit of a tough time right now, but we can get through this if we all stick together."

"Edwina's right," Rooster injected. "We'll have the second set of stairs finished by the weekend and the attorney will immediately request a re-inspection. As soon as we get approval we can re-apply for benefits, and there's a good chance we'll get them retroactively."

"Meanwhile," Mom took over again, "thanks to Polly's inheritance, we've got the money to fund operations. So don't you let me hear another word out of you, either of you." She glared at Scott and his buddy Lou, who had pushed his chair back from the table as if to get out of Mom's verbal firing range.

"No, ma'am," both guys responded smartly.

"Good." Mom gave a curt nod. "Now, don't you two have chores to do?"

This time they grinned as they spoke, "Yes, ma'am," and in a much happier mood they left us.

I directed my attention to Rooster. "Do you have any idea exactly how long the process of reinstating the benefits will take?"

He shrugged. "Not a clue. The inspector will be able to sign off on the work right away, but we're dealing with bureaucrats. Exactly how long it will take the inspector to get here and then how long before we see any money is anybody's guess."

I sighed in resignation, then something registered. "Where's Erik?"

"The guys left him with the other dogs. And before you ask," Rooster said, "he's still pretty down. He's eating, though not much, so we've been making sure he gets supplements to give him a boost."

"Rats, I was really hoping for better news." I began to drum my fingers on the table and Mom looked at me, her brows raising in question.

"Um, there's something else I want to talk to you about," I said. "Tyler and I," I figured using his name would give me more credibility, "suspect Heather's death may not be accidental."

"This I have to hear." Rooster, who'd got up to get a refill of coffee, sat back down next to Mom, so I told them what Tyler and I had discussed, then filled them in on Neve Reed's desire for a DNA test.

"That's not going to happen," Rooster said. "I didn't get a chance to tell you earlier, I saw Feliks at the VFW last night." Feliks is Sheriff Wisniewski; he and Rooster are good friends. "The coroner pronounced accidental death.

As soon as Dennis Haggerty was informed, he arranged for Heather's body to be collected by the funeral home for cremation. To put it bluntly, she's already a pile of ash in an urn."

"Why such a rush?" I asked. "And no funeral?"

"Maybe he'll have a memorial," Mom suggested.

"That still doesn't explain his actions."

Mom gave me a meaningful look. "There's no accounting for the behavior of people who are grieving. Not everyone feels the need for a formal farewell. It could be that he just wanted to get things over with as quickly as possible."

"Or he wanted to prevent Neve Reed from getting any DNA," I said, "which seems pretty suspicious to me."

"Oh, Polly," Mom sighed, "you think everything is suspicious or a conspiracy. It's always possible Dennis wanted to spare Neve's feelings by forcing things to a close."

"And there are other ways to get DNA," Rooster said. "so Dennis would have to deal with a lot more than cremation."

"That's right," I perked up. "There must be items of clothing, or a hairbrush we could use."

Mom tutted. "*We* are not going to use anything. Just leave it alone, Polly."

Annoyed, I shoved my hands in my pocket. "I'm going to check on Erik," and I stomped out the door.

Fifteen

"Don't you let Angel, Vinny or Coco know about this," I admonished Erik as he lay in the front seat of the van, "or they'll expect the same privilege."

I'd decided to bring the dog with me on my rounds, hoping it would spark some interest in him. Normally I don't allow pets in the front seat, but today I was making an exception. So far it wasn't helping. Still, I chattered on in an upbeat voice. "Look, there's Ben Mallone with Butch. He's a German shepherd mix, Butch that is, not Ben. You'd like him, he loves to run. I'll see if I can arrange a play date for you sometime."

Erik momentarily raised his head, then seemed to decide my words weren't worth listening to and laid his chin back on his front paws. *Oh dear.*

We were driving through the center of town. I was a little early for my next appointment and my eyes just happened to be drawn to a sign that read The Drippity Cone, on which was a picture of a double dip of chocolate ice cream in a waffle cone. And wouldn't you know? There was a parking space right in front of the shop.

I pulled hard to the right and bumped onto the curb before bringing the van to a stop as the motorist behind me honked his horn and yelled something rude about women drivers.

403

"You shouldn't follow so closely," I yelled back. *Really, some people.*

I climbed out of the van and opened the passenger door, grabbing Erik's lead.

"Come on, you'll feel better if you have a little dish of vanilla. It works for me."

And I know what some of you are thinking right now. You're thinking ice cream is bad for dogs. Well, hah! You're right. But The Drippity Cone makes a special lactose-free canine concoction, so that man's, and woman's, best friend can enjoy a treat now and then.

I dropped my change into the tip jar at the walk-up window, and with Erik's lead looped over my arm, stepped away. I was holding his dish in one hand and my double-dip pistachio in the other when Erik suddenly came to life. He lunged to the side giving my arm a violent jerk. I hung on to my waffle cone but the scoops of ice cream shot forth into an arcing lob and landed on the sidewalk with a soft splat.

I would have tried to save some of it but Erik was out of control, barking and growling as he strained at the lead. It needed both hands to hold him, and without further thought I tossed aside the doggie dish and hung on.

"Enough!" I tried to step in front of him to force him to break his eye contact with whatever, or whoever, had him riled, but he was intent on getting past me, to what I didn't even know. People were grabbing their kids and keeping their distance, and I heard someone say something about vicious animals needing to be muzzled. Then a voice I recognized spoke up.

"I told you that dog should be shot."

Dennis Haggerty.

With an effort I dragged Erik to the back of the van. With his line of sight broken his frenzy began to subside. Hurriedly I opened the door and lifted him inside, slamming the door shut and falling back against it, realizing I was actually shaking. A second later there was a full-throated yowl and I felt the van move as Erik threw himself against the window.

I shot round the side to see Dennis standing with a young man, both staring at the dog. I grabbed each of them by an arm and pushed them forward.

"Get away. What the heck do you think you're doing?" I kept pushing 'til I'd forced the two men around the side of the ice cream shop where Erik couldn't see them.

It was then that a police cruiser pulled into the lot and Officer Frellick stepped out. Immediately after, Howie, who runs the Drippity Cone, joined us, a grim look on his face. He and Frellick acknowledged each other with curt nods.

"Wanna tell me what's going on, Howie?" Frellick asked.

There's no need for me to tell you word for word all that was said. Suffice it to say we pretty much all agreed Erik went nuts when he saw Dennis and the young guy. I couldn't deny I'd lost control of the situation, and Howie was ticked off, saying the incident had damaged his business.

"I like you, Polly," said Howie. "And you and your mom do good things out at that old farmhouse of yours, but this kind of thing is likely to send my customers over to Franco's Gelato, and I can't afford to lose any business." His face drooped longer than a bloodhound's as he added, "I'm not the kind to sue, but well..."

He left the sentence hanging and I forced myself not to scowl, because he was talking absolute hogwash. Franco's is in another town, for Pete's sake, and none of the people who had witnessed Erik's meltdown had left. In fact, more people had gathered around us, eager to hear what was going on.

I raised my voice. "What if I buy everyone here an ice cream cone?" There was a universal cheer and a few people clapped. Howie's face began to take on the look of a Boston terrier as the corners of his mouth turned upward. Fortunately for me he was willing to take a cheap payoff, though my credit card was still going to take a bit of a hit.

"And it wasn't entirely my fault, I'll have you know." I flicked my wrist at Dennis and his friend. "They made things worse by antagonizing Erik."

The young guy took a step toward me, shoulders tense and hands fisted. *Uh oh.*

Frellick stepped between us. "Just stop right there, sir."

For a moment the man hesitated, as if he was deciding whether to step round the officer. Then his shoulders went slack.

"I'm sorry," he said in a grudging tone. "I saw the dog, and after everything Dennis has told me, I saw red."

"So you're saying you did threaten the dog?" Frellick asked.

"I know how much Heather loved him, but he's the reason she's dead, and for that I could kill him myself."

What the heck? Who was this guy?

Frellick obviously wondered the same thing. "Let's back up a bit, sir. Why don't you give me your name?"

"It's Sturges. Kent Sturges."

"And the Heather you're referring to is Mr. Haggerty's daughter?"

Sturges nodded mute assent.

"Now why would you have any interest in Miss Haggerty?" Frellick wanted to know.

Sturges's eyes narrowed and he looked first at Frellick, then at me before saying, "She wasn't Miss Haggerty, she was Mrs. Sturges. My wife."

I stopped breathing. Whatever I might have expected, it wasn't that. Feeling dizzy I fumbled behind me for something to grab onto and my hand found some sort of course strap. I twisted to look. It was Howie. I'd caught hold of one of his suspenders, and I continued to hang on as if it was a lifesaver. He didn't seem to notice. Instead, he said to me, "I need your credit card, Polly."

Sixteen

What a glorious day. Once again I was out with Chester, but this time I'd chosen to bring him to Barton Pond where there was a grassy area for him to run, and access to the water so he could swim. No wooded trails for us today. It meant I'd have to give Chester a vigorous towel dry and then brush him out, but it was worth it to watch his antics as he dove into the pond after the sticks I threw and proudly brought them back to lay at my feet.

"I had a feeling I'd find you here."

Startled I jumped a one-eighty, and there was Tyler.

"And what feeling was that?" I held out my hand. He took it and gently drew circles in my palm with his thumb.

"You wouldn't want to be reminded of Heather by walking in the woods."

I gave a rueful smile. This man completely understands me.

"Sit down," Tyler said, pulling me to the ground beside him and putting an arm across my shoulders. I wrapped an arm around his waist and let my head rest against his neck. It felt good and we stayed that way, not needing to talk, 'til a soaking wet Chester came romping back and shook himself with great energy right next to us.

"Eek." I crab-walked backwards but too late; I was soaked. Taking my behavior as an invitation to play,

Chester bounded forward and stuck his great big slobbery face into mine. *Ah the joys of a pet-sitter.* I could hear Tyler laughing as I put my arms over my face and rolled onto my hands and knees. I glared at him and he hurried over to help me to my feet. I shrugged off the hand he put under my arm and struggled to my feet.

Slobber was running down my face, but as I swiped at it with the back of my hand I realized it was tears. The shock of all that had been happening suddenly caught up with me. Heather's death, the shock of finding she had a husband, the VA inspector making life difficult, Scott Hamm struggling to live a normal life, Neve Reed falling apart, Runyon Reed carrying the burden of caring for his wife, Dennis Haggerty turning on Erik, and Erik grieving for Heather. Why it hit me at that precise moment in time, I have no idea, unless being laughed at was the last straw. I began to shake.

"Honey, what's the matter?" Tyler said.

"Nobody believes Heather was murdered and… and everyone wants to k_k_kill Erik, and I l_look a mess…and I don't know why I'm crying."

"Oh, sweetheart." Tyler's arms were around me, strong and sure, and I let myself melt into his embrace.

"You're crying because you care. And we won't let anyone hurt Erik." He looked down into my eyes. "And we'll find out what happened to Heather."

Back at my house after dropping Chester at his home, I stepped from the shower to be greeted by the aroma of Earl Grey tea. Quickly I dried off, donned jeans and a t-shirt, and headed for the kitchen.

At the counter, Tyler was gently shaking the teapot. "Here you are," he said. He poured a little milk in two teacups then added the tea and set both cups on the table. With a grateful look I took a sip.

"Feeling better?" he asked.

"Much," I said, before noting his own expression.

"Why so serious?"

"Let's sit."

This didn't sound so good.

"There was a reason I came looking for you at the pond. I heard some news today and I wanted to tell you what happened."

"Go on."

"Runyon Reed stopped by to see my dad. He's taking Neve away for a while. Immediately."

"Well, that's probably not a bad idea. Give her a chance to rest and all that." I wasn't sure where this was going.

"He's afraid for her mental state. It seems Sheriff Wisniewski contacted Runyon to let him know Kent Sturges is claiming he can prove Heather really *was* the Reed's daughter."

Whoa.

"Neve doesn't know about this yet, and Runyon thinks it might just put her over the edge. He's convinced

411

Sturges is playing some sick game and wants no part of it. His lawyer will act as his proxy, but he wanted to know if Dad would keep his eyes and ears open as well, and let the lawyer know if he heard anything relevant."

"Back up a bit." I lifted my hand in a stop gesture. "How could Sturges prove Heather is Cassie unless he has a sample of her DNA? How is that possible? More to the point, *why* would he have it?"

"The how is obvious, assuming he really is Heather's husband," Tyler toyed with his spoon, "but it does seem awfully convenient." He smacked the spoon on the table to emphasize his next words. "Why *would* someone get a DNA sample?"

"We need to be more methodical about this." I began to rummage through the papers stacked on the table – it doubles as my desk – and pulled out a notepad. I skimmed through the first pages, pausing a couple of times to wonder what I'd meant when I wrote "N – dck CC gray" and "RM + cherry = 349." *Too late to worry about it now.* Turning to a blank page I began to write.

"Don't use any of your weird hyroglyphics," Tyler said. I pulled a face at him and continued.

Why would Heather get her DNA taken?
Possible answers:
1. Heather knew she was adopted, wanted to find her birth parents
2. She had health problems
3. ID in event of a catastrophe

Looking over my shoulder Tyler spoke, "OK, I can understand someone wanting DNA to confirm their parentage, and to find out about risk factors they may have inherited, like cancer, but I don't get the last one."

"Some people get DNA samples in case their remains need to be identified after an explosion or such."

"That's pretty paranoid. It's hardly likely Heather would die in an explosion."

"Stop interrupting." I flapped my arm at Tyler to shoo him away. "I'm putting down any possibilities I can think of. If you don't have anything helpful to contribute then just be quiet."

With thumb and forefinger Tyler "zipped" his lips, then parked his butt on the table and crossed his arms, waiting for me to continue. I thought for a moment, then bent my head over the paper.

What we know
Heather looks just like Neve Reed
She is adopted
She's about the same age as Cassie would be
Heather has a setter named Erik the Red, just as Cassie's older sister Shelly did years ago
Cassie went missing in FL when she was 2 and has never been found
Dennis Haggerty lied about Heather's birth
Erik hates Kent Sturges

"How do you know that?" Tyler put his finger on the last entry.

"Because Erik tried to attack him." *Duh.*

I made a new heading.

Questions

Does Sturges have Cassie's DNA (see above)?

Is Heather the missing Cassie?

Why did Dennis Haggerty lie about Heather being his own daughter?

Just who is Kent Sturges?

Why does Erik hate Kent?

"Can you think of anything else?" I chewed on the end of my pen, a bad habit I've had since I was a kid.

Tyler cast his eyes over the list. "On a completely different tack, maybe we should consider the possibility that someone we haven't thought of before could have it in for Heather. Or even the Reeds, for that matter."

"The Reeds might have it in for Heather?" That didn't make sense.

"No, no. That's not what I mean. I'm saying someone might kill Heather in order to spite the Reeds. I know it's far-fetched, but what if the guy who was paralyzed in the car accident when Shelly was driving has a burning hatred for her family and wants revenge."

I gave him a blank stare. "You're right. That's completely far-fetched. First off, how would someone who is paralyzed be able to shove a healthy, energetic young woman over a railing and into a ravine? Second, why would he kill Heather when it's not even sure she is in fact Cassie? And third, would he even know what's going on in Mallowapple? He could be in Timbucktoo for all we know.

"Honestly, it's usually me who comes up with the lame ideas, not you."

Looking suitably chastened Tyler said, "I guess you're right. We'd better put that idea on the back burner for now, but we still need to keep an open mind about someone who might have targeted Heather for her own sake, and not because of the possible connections with Runyon and Neve."

"I'll concede that," I said, and at the bottom of the list added:

Unknown suspect targeting Heather

"OK, are we done?"

"For now, but I think we should send this to your mom and my parents and ask them for any ideas."

"You know my mother will say we should leave it to the experts, and I'm guessing your parents will have the same reaction."

"Hmm." Tyler stroked his chin. "You may be right."

In the end we agreed we'd only enlist help from Rooster and Suzette. We couldn't be certain they'd keep things quiet, but we needed their skills. Suzette was great at online research and Rooster was thoughtful, intuitive and persistant. Between us I hoped we could find at least enough evidence to convince the Sheriff to do some serious digging into Heather's death.

Seventeen

My morning was free so I was on the way to Welcome Home to tackle Rooster and ask for his help. I thought it best to approach him face to face. And to get out of Mom's hearing range I planned to ask him to show me the progress on the barn renovations.

Though I loved my little house in Mallowapple, the old farm still felt like home, and my heart swelled as I passed through the gates and took in the gabled building surrounded by its fenced acres and restored barns. Several of the residents' dogs were outside and Angel, Vinny and Coco all perked up at the same time, knowing they too were at a place they loved.

Rooster was walking toward me and raised an arm in greeting. I honked the horn in response before allowing my trio to burst forth from the van and rush straight for the other dogs. Tails wagged in greeting before they all took off in a game of chase.

"Hey, Rooster," I called out, "thought I'd come take a look at the work."

"Let's walk over," he said. "Or do you want to say hi to your mom first?"

I glanced at the house. "Uh, no." Mom can read me like a book and I was afraid she'd sense something was up. "I'm really anxious to see how much progress has been made; and I want to talk to you as well."

"I get it. You don't want Edwina to know."

"How did you..?" I began.

Rooster's look was scornful. "As if that glance at the house wasn't enough, when you're not telling the truth you get all dithery."

"I do not get dithery." Hands on hips I took a defiant stance. Rooster merely rolled his eyes and after a slight pause I dropped my arms and sighed. "That bad, huh?"

"That bad," he nodded, then continued. "We'll look the barns over first, then you can tell me what it is you want."

The original eight-bed barn was completed with a single simple, yet sturdy, stairway and wood railing running up the outside to a heavy-looking door. I placed my foot on the first step but Rooster caught my arm and drew me away.

"We can't get in that way. It has an emergency bar for exit only."

"Will that pass inspection?"

"Sure," Rooster replied. "We needed another way for people to get out in the event of fire, but without allowing any Tom, Dick or Harry to get in any time."

So we trooped into the barn, up the inside stairs and along the corridor where I admired the sturdy door with the Exit light above it.

"Here's what you didn't know." Rooster knocked on one of the bedroom doors, and when there was no answer he turned the handle and peered in. Satisfying himself that no-one was there, he widened the door and pointed along the wall. Looking past him, I saw a small fire-extinguisher mounted just inside.

"We got a donation of them," Rooster explained. "Enough to put one in each room. We were already up to code, of course, but it should help keep the bureaucrats happy."

"And our residents safe," I smiled.

By the time we'd looked over the second barn I was feeling truly pleased. Along with our veterans in residence, the volunteers had really come through, and work would be completed within the week. Rooster had already requested the inspection and, with luck, we'd be back on track and ready to accept new people very soon.

My elation soon turned to awkwardness as I wondered how to approach the subject of investigating Heather's death. Rooster nodded in the direction of a cooler nearby. "We can grab a lemonade and sit at one of the picnic tables."

There was an area we'd created for the guys to barbeque or just hang out. Right now it was empty, so we sat in a shady spot and I showed Rooster my list and told him what Tyler and I thought. He listened with expected intent, leaning forward slightly and occasionally tapping the tip of his nose – something he subconsciously did when concentrating.

When I finished, he sat straight and grunted. "Hrmph."

There was a long silence as he thought things over and I fidgeted, not daring to interrupt.

"There you go getting all dithery again," Rooster said.

"Now you're accusing me of dithering when I'm silent," I protested.

"You make it hard to think."

I was about to speak when Rooster held up his hand. "But," he said, "I believe you and Tyler might be on to something. The Sheriff is convinced this was nothing but an accidental fall..."

"That's ridiculous," I said, "he has the same information we have. Why can't he see what we see?"

"Take it easy, Polly." Rooster took back the conversation. "From Feliks' point of view, there's no evidence to suggest anything else, that's why we need to come up with new evidence to substantiate a claim of murder."

"*We* need new evidence? So you *are* going to help!" I jumped up, threw my arms around Roosters neck and kissed him on the cheek.

"Wait up now, young lady." His voice was stern as he released himself from my grip. "There's one condition."

Uh oh.

"You have to tell your mother."

"Rooster, you know she'll have a fit. She'll get all paranoid something will happen to me."

He said nothing. I tried again.

"She'll try and talk us out of it." I hesitated. "No, she won't – she'll *demand* we *stay* out of it."

Still nothing.

"I wouldn't put it past her to call the Sheriff and try and get me arrested."

This time Rooster sighed and looked Heavenward.

"Oh all right." And I sighed, too. "I suppose I am exaggerating a bit." Then I glared at him. "But you have to come with me."

"That I can do."

Eighteen

Things went better than I'd expected with Mom. Turns out we weren't the only ones feeling skeptical about the accidental death ruling.

Suzette had proclaimed herself "all in" after Tyler explained our suspicions, and now we each had a role to play in our investigation.

Because there was a lot of online research to do, Tyler was going to coordinate with Suzette to find out all they could about DNA, Cassie's disappearance, Dennis Haggerty and, most of all, try and find out just who is Kent Sturges.

With his Welcome Home duties, Rooster didn't have a lot of time to spare, but we agreed he would be best used to ascertain what he could from Sheriff Wisniewski. With that end in mind, he'd already made plans to meet the Sheriff that evening at the VFW.

My part was to work on possible reasons why Kent hated Erik, and vice versa. I honestly had no idea how I was supposed to do that, or what it would gain us. I also suspected I was being given "busy" work; I'd intercepted a strange look between Mom and Rooster when duties were being assigned and it rankled that they were trying to sideline me. For now, though, there wasn't much I could do about it. And as things happened, a panicked phone call from one of my crew had me racing back to Mallowapple to try and find a missing ball python.

The door flew open before I had a chance to ring the bell.

"Thank goodness you're here," Desandra said, pulling me hurriedly inside. "I've been looking everywhere and I'm at my wit's end. Jeremy will be devastated if he loses Squeezy."

Desandra is a newer member of my crew. She was a stay-at-home mom. After her kids started school she wanted a chance to earn a little money and be done in time to pick her boys up at the end of the day. Jeremy is her 10-year-old's best friend, which is how we got the job of looking after the python when his parents decided to combine a business trip to Paris with some fun time.

"I got here and found the top of Squeezy's cage loose," Desandra said. "Jeremy was probably so excited about going away he didn't make sure it was properly locked. The worst of it is the snake could have been gone for hours, even a day. The family left yesterday morning."

Oh, fudge. My stomach clenched. This wasn't good. Snakes are amazing escape artists. I took a deep breath.

"OK. Let's not panic yet. Was Squeezy confined to one room?"

"His cage is in Jeremy's bedroom but the door was open, as were most of the doors in the house. I did check to

Seeing Red

be sure all the windows and exterior doors were closed, though."

"Well done," I said, then looking up added, "The heating vents are in the ceiling, so that's good. Ball pythons tend to like low, dark places and ductwork is often how they escape. Are there any vents you know of where he might have found access?"

Desandra shook her head. "Only the dryer vent in the laundry room and that was fine."

"OK, then there's a good chance he's still in the house. We just need to be methodical and search every inch of space." My mind suddenly flashed back to Brownie the chicken. "Did you look in the kitchen cupboards?"

"No, the doors were all shut."

"A door might have closed on him after he was inside, so let's assume he could be anywhere and start searching."

It's a good thing this wasn't a big house, because it took us more than two hours to go over every inch. We found plenty of dust bunnies, a few odd socks and 97 cents in small change, but no Squeezy.

Dejected, we sat on the kitchen stools and Desandra lay her head on her arms. "What am I going to do?"

"It's not your fault," I said, "and I'm not going to let you take the fall for it. Meanwhile, we can set up a trap with some food and hope it might entice him in, and we'll

425

keep looking. I'll get some flyers made and we'll put the word out; it's just possible someone will see him."

"Thanks, Polly. I really appreciate you sticking by me. I feel awful about this."

"Come on," I stood. "We can't do anything else here, and I guess I'll have to call Jeremy's parents. What time is it in Paris anyway?"

"It's on my notes. I left them in the garage when I went to get Squeezy's food from the freezer."

"Hold on. Did you look in the garage?"

"The door was only open for a few seconds."

"Let's look anyway," I pulled a face. "At least we'll know we've done everything possible."

The garage was a typical repository for boxes, old tools and all the stuff we tend to hang on to, thinking it will come in useful someday. I had a slight surge of hope that our errant reptile would be lurking in a box of toys or behind a pile of magazines, but no such luck.

The only thing left was an older two-door hatchback. I pulled on the passenger door handle; it was locked. I tried the driver's side – locked. Desandra and I both pressed our faces to the glass and peered inside.

"I don't see anything," she said.

"Me neither," I mumbled, stepping away and eyeing the vehicle. "You know, I've heard of snakes getting into car engines. I suppose I should try and take a look."

"How are you going to open the hood?" Desandra asked.

"I'm not," I sighed. "I'll have to crawl under and look."

We pulled apart an old cardboard box so I'd have something to lie on and I eased myself beneath the engine. It took a few moments for my eyes to adjust then I began to poke around, but the only thing I accomplished was loosening a lot of oily dirt over me. *Yuk.*

Pissed off by now I lay back and closed my eyes for a moment, imagining how good a hot shower and a chill glass of white wine were going to feel, when something dry and scaly touched my outstretched hand. Instinctively I squealed and jerked away.

"What is it? Are you OK?" I heard Desandra call out, then I burst out laughing.

"He's here," I yelled back. And sure enough he was; curled up in the wheel but curious to see what I was doing. Carefully I eased him from the hiding place. He gave no resistance, obviously used to being handled, and I passed him on to Desandra who carried him back to his cage, which we made sure was locked tight.

Squeezy seemed none the worse for wear after his adventure, which was more than I could say for myself, so it was with great relief that I said my goodbye to Desandra, climbed in my van and headed home.

Nineteen

"You're a regular Indiana Jane, you know that?" Tyler grinned at me across the table as we waited for our beef vindaloo and malai kofta – that's beef curry and veggie balls in curry sauce – to arrive, at our favorite Indian restaurant.

"Hey, Mr and Mrs Parrett didn't raise their daughter to be a sissy, and I had brothers, remember? I'd never have survived if I freaked out every time Seb and Keene put a milk snake in my bed. A python isn't so different."

"Well, I'm still impressed," Tyler said. "You're one tough lady."

"And don't you forget it," I smiled back at him.

The day had been long for both of us and we decided to catch up over dinner. I sipped at a cup of chai masala tea as I finished telling of my adventure with Squeezy.

"Now you know everything about my day, other than that I've tried to think how I can find out why Erik was so aggressive toward Kent Sturges but, honestly, I think I'm wasting my time. What does it matter, anyway?"

"It matters, I suppose, if Erik *used* to like Kent and this is a change of behavior. It suggests something bad happened – like killing Heather, perhaps? That would certainly cause him to go after Kent."

"Yeah, but assuming Erik is that protective, surely he would have attacked her killer at the time he shoved her into the ravine."

Tyler stroked his chin and lifted his eyes in thought. "That's worth considering. The murderer *could* have been bitten. We should keep in mind, though, that Erik might have been off chasing birds or rabbits – remember, Heather used to let him off-leash – or didn't understand what was going on. We're only guessing at what happened, so there's no evidence to suggest an argument took place. Heather could have been taken completely by surprise, not even cried out, then gone over the edge of the ravine and Erik would have chased after her."

"You make it sound very plausible. But I don't remember if I told you I found a little blood on Erik's mouth. Of course, it could have been from Heather or even a bird he caught, but then again, it could be he bit someone. So let's keep a dog bite in mind. Is there any way we can check whether someone has been treated for a bite wound?"

"I think that's something the Sheriff would have to do. As far as I know, it's not a requirement in Maine for hospitals and doctors to report dog bites, but there must be a way for law enforcement to check hospital records for bite victims."

"But the killer could have gone to any of a thousand private doctors and there's no way to check that," I sighed.

Taking hold of my hand Tyler smiled. "Cheer up, I do have some news. This is what Suzette found."

He pulled a couple of papers from his back pocket and handed them to me. I flattened them out on the table and saw they were copies of newspaper articles about the disappearance of two-year-old Cassie Reed. I began to read while Tyler quietly finished his tea.

There were three articles from a Miami paper, and two from our local county newspaper, the Weekly Post, which was produced in Corkeep. The gist of most of the articles was the lack of evidence and the inability of the police to find any trace of the child. I wasn't particularly surprised by this. After Tyler told me the story of Cassie going missing I'd done a little research, and the terrible truth is that more than 800,000 children go missing in the USA every year. That's more than 2000 a day! Of course, a lot of those are runaways, but there's really no way to know for sure how many are lost, or abducted or killed. The only reason Cassie's story gained a little notoriety was because her parents were well-known in some circles, and had wealth.

The articles did name the baby sitter as 23-year-old Isabel Cisneros, and went into some detail that she had been hired through a local agency who insisted their employees were thoroughly vetted, and stated Miss Cisneros had an exemplary record for the six months she'd been with them. According to the reports, she'd been interviewed extensively by the police and claimed she'd gone to check on the sleeping toddler and found her missing from her bed.

There was nothing else about the investigation, just some general information about the Reeds, and a brief follow-up piece in the Mallowapple section of the Weekly Post saying a memorial service had been held at Holy Cross Church.

"Well," I said looking up, "it's good to get some background but, other than knowing the baby sitter's name, this hardly moves us further on."

"It's another piece of the puzzle," Tyler said. "Suzette tried to track the baby sitter down, but do you know how many Isabel Cisneros's there are in Miami alone?"

I pulled a face. I had no idea but guessed it must be a lot.

Tyler continued. "She also searched for background information on Dennis Haggerty and Kent Sturges. Kent is on several social media sites that show his occupation as Investigative Journalist. Not that he lists an employer, presumably he's an "independent." There were also pictures of him with 'the love of my life,' Heather, including one from their civil wedding ceremony, three months ago. Oddly, Suzette couldn't find anything on any social site for Heather Haggerty, or Heather Sturges."

I frowned. "Don't you find it odd that Heather never mentioned a husband?"

Tyler just grunted.

"Did Suzette find out anything about Dennis?"

"Nothing on the social networks, so we decided it was time to turn to a professional."

"Oh? Isn't that expensive?"

"Well, we did think about using some of the online search tools, but they're still quite limiting. There's a group my company has used to vet potential commercial tenants or track down delinquent ones, so I called Phil Doherty, the owner. He owes me a favor or two so he said he'll get someone on it and get back to me tomorrow."

"You always seem to have people who owe you favors."

Tyler laughed. "Between my dad and I, we've sent Phil quite a bit of business. Besides, dad taught me a long time ago it's good to go the extra yard for people because you never know when you might need something in return."

"It seems then, that there's nothing else we can do for now," I said.

The corners of Tyler's mouth pulled up in a sly grin. "Oh, I can think of a few things."

Actually, so could I.

Twenty

With my back up against the brick wall of the building I chanced a peek around the corner. There was no sign of my target so I checked my watch. Four minutes to go. If something didn't happen soon there would be trouble.

"Hi, there Polly. Checking up on one of your sitters, are you?"

I jumped and aimed my best "Be quiet and get lost" glare at Willard Bartles, who happened to be the owner of Bartles Antiques, the store I was hiding beside.

"You'll blow my cover," I hissed.

"Not likely," he said. "Everyone knows you sneak around watching what your sitters do."

"I do not sneak." I stood straight and pulled my shoulders back, and was about to give Willard an earful when I heard, "Hello, Polly. Are you here to check on me?"

It was Emma, the new sitter.

"Wha..?" I sputtered. "No, no, of course not. I, uh, was here to see Willard, Mr. Bartles, about an antique."

"It's OK, Polly." Emma gave my arm a little shake. "Everyone knows you do that but I don't mind."

Everyone knows?

I pulled myself together. "I have complete faith in you, Emma." I pointed to an apartment above a book shop.

"That's Bark Twain's home. He's very low key for a cairn terrier; I'm sure he'll love you."

Willard and I watched her walk away. "See, that worked out alright," he said.

I bit my lip and did my best to maintain a modicum of dignity as I headed back to my van.

Now that I'd assured myself of Emma's reliability, I had a quiet day ahead of me. I was anxious to get Phil Doherty's report but I knew Tyler would be in touch as soon as he heard anything. Not knowing what to do with myself I decided to gather up the dogs and go out to the farm.

As usual, I experienced that warm sense of belonging as I pulled up to the house, which was enhanced further when I opened the door and was met with an abundance of heady aromas coming from the kitchen.

Apache, Nero and Erik were barred from the kitchen by a pet gate across the door. All three heads turned at my arrival and I was accorded a few wags of greeting, then the dogs returned their attention to whatever was going on. I peered in to see Mom, Scott and Lou with a table full of cupcakes in front of them.

"Looks like I'm missing out on something good," I said, leaving my dogs with the others and stepping over the pet gate. And before anyone had a chance to say a word I snatched up a warm cupcake and took a big bite.

"Ugh." Instinctively I spat the stuff into my hand. "What the heck kind of cupcake is this?"

The others burst into laughter.

"It's not a cupcake," Mom said, "it's a *Pup*cake."

"Huh?"

"A cupcake for a dog," Lou explained. "Sooo...*pup*cake."

I cocked a finger in acknowledgement but couldn't speak for a moment because I was busy rinsing my mouth out at the sink. Then I poured myself a cup of coffee with plenty of sugar and cream and took a healthy swallow.

"Better?" Mom asked, still smirking at me.

"Much," I said. "Mind telling me why you're baking *pup*cakes?"

Scott and Lou exchanged glances, then Scott spoke. "We've come up with an idea to produce Welcome Home food products and sell them to cover my expenses and, we hope, bring in some extra revenue for the Home. We can do bottled goods like the fiddleheads we had the other day, vinegars and meads, jam... the list goes on and on."

"It also occurred to us that we could do cupcakes," Lou took over. "We'd create them with military themes – camouflage cupcakes, or with badges, boots, the flag, you name it. That got us talking about dog-themed cupcakes, since most of us here have dogs. Then Scott got really inspired and said, 'How about cupcakes *for* dogs?' We found some recipes online but figured we could do better."

Now Mom chimed in. "The boys came to me with the idea and I thought it was brilliant, so we've been

437

experimenting and these," she waved her arm over the table, "are the results."

"That is positively an awesome idea. But what did I just eat? Obviously, it's not for human consumption. Will the dogs like it?"

Lou pushed a pupcake into my hand. "Here, why don't you find out?"

I broke it into pieces and the dogs, realizing they were getting a treat, went wild. Well, Erik didn't exactly go wild, but he showed interest and that was a huge step forward. All six woofed their piece down and looked expectantly for more.

"This is great. When do we start selling?"

"Slow down," Mom said. "This is in the early planning stages right now."

"Well, you're definitely on to something, but you still didn't tell me what's in the pupcake I ate."

"Tuna, cottage cheese and peas," Scott said.

"Huh." Tentatively, I pulled a small piece off another pupcake, popped it in my mouth and chewed. "You know, it's not that bad. I was taken by surprise before because I was expecting something sweet."

"Have another, if you want," said Scott.

"Uh, no." I put my hands up. "I'll leave them for the dogs.

Twenty-One

I was frustrated, and irritable. Four o' clock had come around and still no word from Tyler. There was plenty of work to keep me occupied at the farm, but I wanted answers and I was tired of waiting for them, so I made a spur-of-the-moment decision to go and see Dennis Haggerty. I didn't have the guts to tell Rooster or my mother. Instead, I grabbed one of the residents and asked him to give them a message that I'd been called away for work and that I'd pick the dogs up later. *OK, so I lied; it seemed easier at the time.*

The Haggerty house was on the far side of town. Not exactly remote, but certainly private. Not being sure of my reception I parked on the road where the van wouldn't be seen and crept to the door in stealth mode, figuring that Dennis would not then have a chance to barricade himself in. Pressing the doorbell I steeled myself for a hostile reception. Was I ever surprised?

Haggerty looked, well, haggard. The man who eventually opened the door had great dark circles under his eyes, the lines on his face deeply etched, the look he gave me blank.

Taken aback I hesitated, then recognition dawned on him.

"Polly. Why am I not surprised?"

Though the words were not welcoming, his tone was flat. I pushed on.

"Dennis, could I talk to you, please?"

He stepped back, a little unsteady on his feet, and gestured me in with a wave of his arm. It was only as I passed him I got a whiff of whisky on his breath and realized he was drunk.

We sat in the living room, me perched on the edge of my chair while Dennis dropped into his like a sack of potatoes. A half-full glass sat on a table beside him with a bottle next to it. Lifting the bottle he looked at me, "Drink?" I shook my head, "No," and he topped his glass up with a shaky hand then carefully put the bottle back down and waited for me to begin.

Now that we were facing each other I stumbled for words to say, and experienced a pang of guilt knowing I'd done exactly what Mom and Tyler would have told me not to do. I hadn't thought things through.

I swallowed hard. "Uh, Dennis. There's no easy way to say this, but I think... um that is... *several* of us think Heather's death was not an accident."

The man showed no emotion, merely stared at me through bleary eyes then took a slug of his whisky. Was he too drunk to understand?

I leaned forward. "Look. The day I found Heather, she admitted later that she'd become dizzy before she ran into the poison ivy. Did she get dizzy often?"

"'S my fault," Dennis slurred.

"What's your fault? Is it your fault that she fell, or got dizzy?"

"Should never have come here."

"Why should I not have come?"

Dennis creased his brow. "Not you. Me. Should never have come..."

His chin started to sag onto his chest. I stood and put my hands on his shoulders and gave him a rough shake.

"Stay awake, Dennis."

He blinked a few times and made a visible effort to pull himself together.

"Are you saying it was wrong to come to Mallowapple? Why?"

"Heather. She'd still be alive."

"I don't think you can blame yourself for Heather's death. Unless *you* pushed her into the ravine." I narrowed my eyes and spoke slowly. "Did you push her into the ravine?"

"Not me."

"Then you know that someone did. Who was it?"

A wary look crossed his face. "It's none of your business what happened. You keep your nose out of it. That dog killed her."

"Oh come on, Dennis. You know as well as I do that Erik no more knocked her down than the Easter Bunny. You were about to name someone. Who was it? Was it Kent Sturges?"

With a speed that took me completely by surprise, Haggerty caught hold of my arm and yanked me close. "I told you to leave it. Stop messing in things that aren't your business, before it's too late."

"Too late for what?" Another voice said behind me.

Kent Sturges had come in and placed himself squarely in the doorway. Something about his stance and the way he drew out his words struck me as menacing, and I wasn't sure whether to be thankful or more concerned for his presence.

I twisted my arm away from Dennis and stood, rubbing where it hurt. I was going to have bruises to show for my escapade, that much was certain.

"Hi, Kent." I laughed awkwardly; it came out more like a cat choking on a hairball. "Dennis and I were just having a chat. About Heather and what happened."

"We know what happened, so what's to chat about."

Think of something, Polly. I urged my brain to come up with a good reason for being there.

"Um. Oh. Some of us wanted to have a little remembrance service for her. Though we didn't know her well we felt it would be a way to pay our respects. So I thought, um…" This wasn't going so well by the mocking look Sturges was directing at me. But I was in too deep now; I couldn't stop. "I thought I'd see if I could get some background on her to say a few words."

"And what sort of background would that be?"

"The usual sort of stuff. You know, her likes and dislikes, where you two met, something about her adoption…" Sturges began to scowl but I blurted out, "and why did she call her dog Erik the Red?"

Kent pulled his lips back over his teeth and practically snarled. *Uh oh. I think I've overdone it.*

"Well, I guess I'd better get going."

I tried to ease past Sturges but he stood his ground.

"My boyfriend will be wondering why I'm late. I told him I was coming here and he'll get worried if I don't call in the next couple of minutes. Probably will drive right over here to look for me." I wondered if I sounded as desperate as I was beginning to feel, not that it made any difference, Kent still didn't move.

Then Dennis spoke with a surprising sharpness to his tone. "Let her go, son."

I looked over my shoulder. Dennis had pushed himself to his feet, and for several moments the two men glared at each other until Kent gave way and moved aside, allowing just enough room for me to squeeze through. It felt like pulling myself from the jaws of a snake.

At the road I looked back to see both men at the front door watching me. I chanced one more question and called out, "Why did you cremate Heather so quickly?"

Kent took a step toward me. I didn't wait to find out what might happen. I ran.

Twenty-Two

"Alright, already. I made a mistake and I'm sorry." I turned on my heels and flounced into the living room, throwing myself into an armchair where I sat, arms crossed and feeling like a chastened child.

Mom, Tyler and Rooster left me alone. It was Erik who found me. Sensing my need for comfort he climbed into the chair and squeezed down beside me, laying his head under my chin and a leg across my chest. With the tips of my fingers I caressed his chest.

"You are the sweetest boy. I'm trying to help. I can't bring your mom back but I want to find who did such a terrible thing to her."

Erik made little murmuring noises in the back of his throat and turned his head to lick the hand I was using to scratch his nose.

I'd had to come back to Welcome Home to collect my three pooches and, of course, phoned Tyler on the way. He beat me out here and by the time I arrived Mom and Rooster were waiting with him to give me the third degree.

"Are you done sulking?" Mom wheeled into the room and gave me the "you're not a little girl anymore" look that mothers do so well.

"I guess," I mumbled into Erik's ear.

"Good, because Tyler just told us what he's found out from his friend – Phil Doherty, I think his name is - and you're going to find it very interesting."

"Really." I perked up a bit. "What is it?"

Mom ticked off on her fingers.

"One. Heather Haggerty doesn't exist."

"What?" That floored me.

"The woman who called herself Heather Haggerty is actually Heather Maloy. Or was until she married Kent Sturges and became Heather Sturges."

"So the marriage was real," I said.

Mom nodded and held up her second finger.

"Two. Heather was studying acting at Florida International University in Miami.

"Three. At the time of Cassie Reed's disappearance, Dennis Haggerty was living in Miami and has convictions for petty theft *and* assault..." Mom delivered a significant glare as she said that last word "...and has done jail time."

I decided to ignore the barb and asked, "Did Doherty find any connection between Dennis and the baby sitter? What's her name?"

"Um," Mom glanced at some notes she held in her hand, "Isabel Cisneros. She turned out to be a dead end, and the agency that the Reeds hired her through has long since gone out of business."

"Nothing about Kent Sturges?"

"Nothing new. On paper he's squeaky clean. Not even a parking ticket. Doherty says he can continue to dig but it will require putting a man on the ground, so to speak. What we have so far was dug up on the internet."

I sighed. "We need to think all this over before committing to anything more. Use our little gray cells, as Hercule Poirot would say." Looking down at Erik I said, "I wish you could talk. I bet you would clear this mystery up in a heartbeat."

In answer, Erik rolled on to his back and presented his tummy to be rubbed.

Mom smiled, "It's so good to see him begin to be a normal dog again. And I think he's becoming quite attached to you."

"You're the one who's been spoiling him. If he's getting attached I expect it's to you."

"It's a mutual thing," Mom laughed. "I've become quite fond of him."

"Where are the guys?" I said, realizing Rooster and Tyler had disappeared.

"They figured there might be enough now to persuade Sheriff Wisniewski to take another look at the situation. Rooster tried to get hold of him on the phone but couldn't get a reply, so they decided to go on down to the VFW and see if he might be there."

"They went without me? Is Tyler that mad at me?"

Mom hesitated. "You give that boy a fair bit of grief; always getting yourself in trouble. It may be he's going to get tired of always coming to your rescue."

I gulped and started to chew my lip. "Perhaps *I* should head to the VFW."

"I think you should leave things well enough alone for now. Go home and let the guys deal with this." Mom was stern, so I gathered up my furry clan and drove away.

Twenty-Three

The ducks started quacking and the dogs all snapped to noisy alertness, jumping around on the bed, and on me, trying to focus in on what woke us.

"Quiet, guys. It's just the phone." *I guess it's time I changed that ringtone.*

"This is Pets and People, Too." I tried to sound chipper even though it was – I glanced at the clock on the phone – *Good Grief*, just past six. Why can't people let me sleep in?

"Honey wake up!" Tyler. "I'm sorry to cut your beauty sleep short but something major has happened. Kent Sturges has been killed."

Suddenly I was wide awake.

"Tell me."

"The only thing I know is that an anonymous call came in to the police during the night to say a body was in the forest. The caller was probably someone illegally trapping raccoons, and they'll never be found. Anyway, apparently the Sheriff heard Rooster and I were looking for him last night and he's called us in this morning to find out what information we have."

I told Tyler my suspicion about Kent being Dennis's son. "You should mention that to the Sheriff," I said.

We exchanged a few more words and Tyler agreed to stop by once he was done.

"I have to get going," he said.

"Uh, Tyler." I stopped him. "Are you angry with me?"

I heard his sigh over the phone. "There isn't time to discuss this now. We can talk later."

A sour feeling began to seep into the pit of my stomach, but I merely said, "OK," and hung up.

The wait was excruciating. It was lunchtime before I heard Tyler's car pull into the driveway. I flung the door wide.

"You must have been getting the third degree."

"No. The Sheriff had to break away so we talked to Officer Frellick. Afterwards we hung around hoping to pick up some information."

"Did you?"

"A bit." He waved a bag in the air. "I'll tell you while we have lunch. I stopped by the diner for some Corn Chowder."

I loved Nita's chowder. She made it with just enough bacon to give it a hint of smoky maple flavoring, then served it with her homemade buttermilk biscuits.

While I organized the table, Tyler spoke.

"Sturges was shot, though it seems the body was moved to the woods after the fact, presumably to hide it. It was sheer luck someone stumbled on it so quickly and that someone was willing to risk calling it in."

Tyler was right. A lot of poachers would have ignored the body for fear of getting caught for their own illegal activities.

"But here's the really big news."

I put down the spoon I was about to use and waited for Tyler to go on.

"Dennis Haggerty has disappeared."

"No! Then he must be the killer; he's on the run."

"I suspect," Tyler said, "that's the theory the police are working on."

"You did tell them about the possibility of Kent being Dennis's son?"

Tyler nodded.

"If he is," I said, "that's really cold of Haggerty, to kill his own son."

"We need to keep in mind this is still conjecture. We have very little hard evidence of anything."

"I've been thinking about that all morning, trying to make some sense of what we have, and in light of Kent's murder I don't think anyone could say Heather's death wasn't deliberate."

"Go on."

"Let's look at the clues we have, then consider what theory we can come up with to satisfy all of them.

"We start with me finding Heather in the woods. We're told she is Heather Haggerty, daughter of Dennis Haggerty who has recently retired to Mallowapple. Heather is the spitting image of Neve Reed, a woman whose daughter, Cassie, disappeared in Miami at the age of two and who has never been found. Heather is also the age that Cassie would be, assuming she is alive. Neve Reed meets Heather and is convinced she is her daughter. On top of that, Heather has a red setter she calls Erik the Red. The same breed and name of a dog Cassie's older sister used to own. With me so far?"

Tyler grunted.

"Now the waters get even muddier. Right after Neve declares Heather is her long lost daughter, Heather tells me the man she believed to be her father – Dennis – has confessed she is adopted, so it's possible she really is Cassie Reed. Before I have a chance to talk in detail to Heather, she is killed. Later we find out she is not even Dennis's adopted daughter. Heather, in fact, is Heather Maloy, a wannabe actress.

"Enter Kent Sturges who claims to be Heather's husband, and who turns out, indeed, to be Heather's husband of just a few months. Sturges is an investigative reporter. At least, that's what he calls himself. Oh, and Erik hates him." I put my finger to my lips. "Have I forgotten anything?"

"Hmm. We know the name of the baby sitter who watched Cassie on the night she disappeared, but have no idea where she is now. And, of course, Dennis Haggerty has disappeared."

"That's pretty damning by itself," I said. "But what was the original motivation for Dennis, Heather and Kent to come together in Mallowapple?"

Tyler scooped up the last of his chowder. Since I'd been doing all the talking I'd barely started mine, so I let him take over.

"It has to be money. The Reeds are filthy rich. Somehow this revolves around passing Heather off as Cassie Reed, though that begs the question of how they knew about Cassie."

"As an investigative reporter it wouldn't have been difficult for Sturges to find out."

"Yeah, but he had to know more than we do. Somebody had to tell him about Erik the Red for instance. That wasn't in any newspaper articles."

"About that," I said. "it strikes me as unlikely a two-year-old would remember her sister's dog, even subliminally."

"I have to say I agree with that, but frankly, this whole thing is implausible. Surely no-one with half a brain would expect to get away with passing Heather off as Cassie, when a simple DNA test would prove or disprove it."

"I suppose there's always the chance that Heather really was Cassie."

"Then why not just come forward and make that claim? Why go through this elaborate charade?"

"Talking of that, there's one thing we haven't considered at all. If they're using Erik as part of the scam, when did Heather get him? He's at least 18 months old and he and Heather had a definite bond."

"You know better than anyone that a bond can be formed almost immediately, but if you're suggesting a lot of planning went into this, then I agree."

"I think we're both theorizing the same thing. Kent found the information and probably he and Dennis plotted together to get money from the Reeds. Either they hired Heather or she willingly agreed to get involved. She was an actress and looked enough like Neve to pass as Cassie." I looked at Tyler and blew out a deep breath. "But we still come back to the same problem. How could they possibly hope to get away with it?"

Tyler shook his head. "We're going to drive ourselves nuts if we don't drop this for a while. Besides, it's up to the Sheriff to deal with it now, and I have something to say to you before I leave."

Oh, dear, here it comes. I looked down at the fingers twined in my lap, too nervous to face Tyler eye to eye.

"I was very angry last night," he said, and once again I was aware of that sour feeling.

"Polly, look at me."

I raised my chin and gave a rueful smile as Tyler leaned toward me on his elbows.

"I was angry because you didn't give me a chance to keep you safe. It's not that you aren't capable; you're more capable than any woman I've ever known. But that doesn't make you invincible, and you get these ideas and go rushing off into the lion's den and leave me terrified and helpless.

"Maybe it's a guy thing. I feel it's my role to be your protector. I *want* to protect you, I don't ever want anything bad to happen to you, but you have to help me. Before you decide to visit any other potential killers on your own, please call me. Talk to me. Let's figure out together what will be the best thing to do."

This was going better than I'd expected. "So that's it?" I said. "You're not delivering an ultimatum?"

Tyler let his shoulders droop and pushed himself back in his chair. "You think I was going to tell you 'do this or else?' Sweetheart, we're in this together and I'm asking you to remember that. So the next time you have an idea to visit someone when a murderer is on the loose, call me first. Would you please do that?"

Slowly I nodded. "I will." And for several minutes we gazed at each other across the kitchen table, 'til Tyler said, "I must go. I've an appointment at the office."

We stood, and I stepped into his arms, and by the time we were done I was pretty sure everything was alright. The door closed behind Tyler and I turned to Ditto, who had been watching the whole exchange from the top of the hutch, front paws hanging over the side. I reached up and scratched the top of his head.

"I think I dodged a bullet there," I said.

Twenty-Four

It was business as usual for the next couple of days. I took care of a few pet visits and ordered some new T-shirts for my crew. Of course, my mind was also constantly filtering details of the case. Was there something I'd missed?

I was working on the timesheets at home with only half a mind, while rethinking my confrontation with Dennis and Kent, and it struck me that I'd not mentioned to the police that Dennis had called Kent "son." Sure it was a minor detail, but it gave me an excuse to go to the station and see if there was any progress. Besides, I hated doing the timesheets.

Once at the station I was told Wisniewski was unavailable, but after insisting I had important evidence Officer Frellick appeared and took me to his desk. He set a notepad in front of him and looked at me expectantly.

I explained to him what had happened at Haggerty's house, then said, "You know, when Dennis told Kent to leave me alone he called him 'son.' It didn't register at the time. I mean, I thought then that Heather was Dennis's daughter and it seemed perfectly normal for him to refer to his son-in-law that way, but I wonder if it's possible Kent actually *is* his son."

Frellick continued to look at me as if waiting for more. When I stayed mute he said, "That's it?"

"It could be pretty significant." I tapped my finger on the desk. "Do you really think Haggerty would kill his own son? And why would Kent use Sturges as his name instead of Haggerty if he is Dennis's son?"

"We already know that. We haven't been sitting around doing nothing as some people seem to think." His tone struck me as just a little snarky. "Kent's mother is Susan Sturges. She had an affair with Haggerty and Kent was the result of it. After the boy was born Haggerty took off, and to cover her indiscretion Susan told people she'd been married to a guy named Sturges who'd died in a car crash."

I gasped. "Then how did Kent and Dennis reconnect?"

"Look, I'm the one supposed to be asking questions."

"Come on, Frellick. I helped you with Erik at the ravine."

The officer hesitated a moment then shook his head. "Alright. We're assuming Kent tracked his father down, but the boy left home in his teens and his mother has had no contact with him since."

"Like father like son," I mused. "I wonder how they found Heather."

"With luck we'll have some answers soon," Frellick said. "I don't suppose it hurts to tell you this, it will be all over the news in the next few hours. Dennis Haggarty has been seen in Bar Harbor. That's where Sheriff Wisniewski is, he's gone to help track him down and bring him back here."

I left the police station in a bit of a daze. Was that it? Was Haggerty the killer and it would all soon be over? Something still didn't add up, though. What was the ultimate game plan? I needed to think.

Across the square I saw the sign for The Drippity Cone. You know, I never did get my pistachio ice cream the day that Erik freaked out, and now seemed like a good time to make up for that. For once there was no-one waiting at the window so I ordered my double-dip and watched as the kid at the counter started to scoop. From the corner of my eye I caught movement and realized Howie had sidled up behind him.

"Howie," I acknowledged him. He shuffled a bit and coughed.

"Hi there, Polly. Listen, that cone is on the house, and a few more besides."

I narrowed my eyes in suspicion and watched as color rose from his throat 'til his face was an ugly pink.

"And why is that, Howie?"

"You see, uh…never let it be said I'm not an honest man."

"Why *would* I ever say that?"

"It was quite unintentional, you understand?"

"For pity's sake, spit it out. What are you trying to say?"

"Well, I accidentally charged you for the full gallon of raspberry chocolate chip Mr. Reed bought, when I should only have added in the cost of a scoop. I'm sorry, but it was a confusing day and…"

"Wait a bit. You're saying Runyon Reed was here that day?"

"Mrs. R loves the raspberry chocolate chip, so they usually get a gallon to go."

"I didn't see him here." I wasn't really listening to Howie, I was a little taken aback I hadn't noticed Runyon.

"Not surprising. You were rather occupied, but he was right behind that Haggerty guy and the other young fella."

Something started gnawing at my gut, and it wasn't the ice cream. I'd always assumed Erik was trying to get to Sturges, but was it possible he'd been after Runyon?

That's ridiculous, I told myself. What earthly reason could Runyon have for killing Heather? For all he knew Heather was his daughter Cassie. Though he had seemed very certain that she wasn't.

I pulled out my phone and hit speed dial for Tyler. I needed to talk this out but the call went into voicemail. Frustrated, I decided to head for Welcome Home. Mom and Rooster would help me make sense of things.

As I drove I ran a lot of "What if's" through my head. What if Runyon Reed knew for sure that Heather couldn't be Cassie because *he'd* killed her? Perhaps it had been an accident but in that case, why hide it? Either way, if Haggerty and Sturges somehow found out, then it would give Reed reason to get rid of them, and Heather. The whole charade still struck me as overkill – *ooh, bad pun* – because, surely, they could have simply demanded blackmail money. *Unless* – now I was really reaching – they wanted more.

It struck me like a ton of bricks. They wanted everything! If Heather was acknowledged to be Reed's daughter, that would also make her their heir. Kent, as Heather's husband would benefit and so would Kent's father, Dennis.

I was so excited by my deductions I could hardly wait to share them, but by the time I reached the farm I'd rethought everything again, and it seemed preposterous.

Twenty-Five

"Mom," I called out as I ran in the house. Erik and Elaine both came to greet me and I scruffed their necks. "Mom," I called again and went in the kitchen. It was empty. Back outside I headed over to the barns where a couple of the guys were stacking wood ready for the cooler months that were coming soon. They told me Rooster and Mom had left earlier for Corkeep, to pick up supplies at the warehouse club. *Drat!* That meant they wouldn't be back for a few hours.

I tried Tyler again, and again got his voicemail, so I called the office. It was Suzette who answered.

"He's in a closing, Polly. It's dragged on a lot longer than expected, that's why he couldn't answer his phone. They should be through pretty soon, though."

I made a snap decision. "Tell him I'm going out to Runyon and Neve Reeds' place, and ask him to meet me there."

You're thinking I'm breaking my promise, aren't you? But I wasn't planning to do anything 'til Tyler got there. He'd drive faster than me, anyway, so I figured I'd have only a few minutes to wait and then we'd approach the house together.

I'd tossed my car keys on the kitchen counter when I arrived. As I dashed back in to grab them Erik jumped up and gave me a hopeful look.

"OK, sweet boy. You can come for a ride."

This time Erik sat up and looked out of the window as I drove, and whenever I spoke to him he would flick his tail in acknowledgement or bend his head and give me a quick lick on the arm.

The ride out to the Reed's estate would normally have been enjoyable, rolling along the winding road, passing recently harvested potato fields, then turning onto a narrow tree-lined lane where branches met overhead to form an arch and showcase the leaves in their gorgeous fall colors. I'd never been to the Reed home and nearly missed the entryway, which was nothing more than a small pillar on either side of the driveway, with a mailbox and no gate.

My big old van took up most of the road when I stopped, and there was no way for me to pull over because both sides were furrowed with deep ditches. Deciding it was safer to park in the drive, I turned in. If someone needed to get past I'd just have to back up.

It was still heavily wooded inside the entrance and I realized with some surprise that dusk was coming on; in another half hour it would be dark.

The drive ahead curved to the right, so I couldn't see the house. *The Reeds must have a lot of acreage,* I thought, and curious to see more I jumped from the van, shutting Erik in, and walked to the curve.

The view was the same - this time with the drive bending left – except for a woman moving hurriedly along, hugging the trees and giving furtive glances back over her shoulder.

My first instinct was to dash back to the van, after all I was trespassing, but the woman's manner struck me as decidedly fearful and I couldn't bring myself to ignore someone who might be in need of help. In a low voice I hissed, "Hello! Hello!"

The woman's head jerked around and her hands flew to her throat. Locking eyes with me she froze.

"It's alright." I held my hands up in a gesture of surrender. "I won't hurt you."

Tentatively I took a step closer. "Don't be afraid; you can trust me."

I realized I was speaking to her in the exact way I would speak to a frightened dog, but it seemed to be working. She continued to glance back down the drive then suddenly hurried to me. Clutching at my clothes with fluttering fingers she brought her face close to mine. "Help me," she said.

I put my hands over hers and held them together. It felt like holding a bunch of thin twigs, her fingers were so boney. Looking into her face the skin appeared paper thin and blue veins riddled her cheeks. In contrast, her eyes were overly bright, the pupils fixed, and her head shook from side to side in a rhythmic tremor. She was terrified.

"You're Neve, aren't you?" I said.

"I have to get away," she whispered. "They'll lock me up."

"Who will lock you up?" I whispered back. "Is it Runyon?" *What the heck was going on here?*

Liz Dodwell

Neve didn't answer, just pulled away from me. I couldn't let her stagger off on her own, so I wrapped an arm around her waist to support her.

"My van is right around the bend. I'll take you somewhere safe."

I hurried her along. There was Erik, standing now in the seat and watching for my return. I saw his mouth drop open in a happy grin. Moments later his lips pulled taught over his teeth and I knew he was growling, even though I couldn't yet hear him. I whipped my head around, expecting to see Runyon hot on our heels, but there was no-one in sight.

Erik's behavior escalated to frenzied barking and he began hurling himself at the windshield. Next to me Neve stiffened and pulled away again. I caught hold of her forearm and she winced.

"It's alright," I said, "he must sense something is wrong, but he won't hurt you."

She snatched her arm away and distanced herself several paces.

"He already has," she said, and in that moment realization dawned. The wincing when I touched her arm was because Erik had bitten her there. He was going crazy now to get at her because she must be the one who had killed Heather. How could I have thought her eyes reflected terror? Looking at them now I saw the eyes of a mad woman.

The shock of it made me dizzy. I gulped air into my lungs and told myself to stay calm. Neve looked as if she might weigh 80 pounds soaking wet, and she was more than twice my age. No match for me, if she wasn't holding a gun!

A gun! *Where did that come from?* It looked enormous in her small hand, and that hand was as steady as a rock.

"Neve..."

"Don't move," she said. "I grew up hunting so don't think I don't know how to use this. As a matter of fact, I'm an excellent shot."

Wow! The frail, frightened woman had transformed into a lethal predator. This was certainly no even match; the only weapon I had was my words. If only I knew how to use them wisely.

"Are you going to kill me?"

"I'm going to kill that barking brute, then you're going to drive me away from here."

"No! I'll keep him quiet. He'll listen to me." *I hope.*

"He bit me! And then he tried to get me at the ice cream shop."

"*You* were there? I thought..."

"You thought he was trying to get at those two crooks, but it was me he saw. Me he wanted to sink his teeth into again. He doesn't deserve to live." And smoothly she adjusted her aim and fired straight into the windshield at the dog. There was a high-pitched yelp and I swung around to see the glass shattered, and no sign of Erik.

"You...you! He didn't deserve that. No more than Heather! You're mad. Completely mad!"

"Don't you say that," Neve shrieked. "That's what *she* said. She thought she could pretend to be my daughter. What a shock it was when I saw her at the VFW. She called me afterwards to ask if we could meet. I suggested the trail, by the ravine, but I never thought she'd bring that dog with her. She confessed the whole scheme. And do you know what else she said?"

Numbly I shook my head.

"She said she was sorry, sorry that she'd given me false hope and she wished that someday the real Cassie would turn up. What a joke that is. Do you know why?" Neve didn't wait for my answer. "Because Cassie is dead!"

Twenty-Six

My jaw went slack but I managed to find my voice. "How can you be so sure?"

Neve gave a snort of derision. "She was always a whiney baby. Cry, cry, cry. We were going out to dinner at The Forge and I'd spent hours getting ready. The baby sitter was late and Cassie wouldn't stop crying, so I picked her up and she threw up on my new Helmut Lang dress. It was a gorgeous red brocade and she ruined it. So I shook her. I just wanted her to shut up, and it worked all right." She smiled a pleased smile and I felt sick.

"Now get moving." She gestured toward the van but my feet were rooted in place while my mind was racing. Could I get round the side of the van and make a run for it? Where was Tyler? Right now I wasn't so sure I wanted him to turn up for fear of him being shot. And wouldn't you know as that thought flitted through my mind a pair of bright headlights lit up the scene. Neve swung round and began firing; simultaneously I dove down beside the van and heard tires screeching and the roar of an engine as the light receded.

Please get away, Tyler.

Hardly daring to breath I lay on the ground and twisted my head to peer under the van into the half-darkness, seeing nothing, and listening for any sound that might suggest where Neve was. Still nothing. But she'd said she was a hunter, she would be used to waiting out her prey.

Bit by bit I eased myself onto my hands and knees, and crawled slowly to the front of the vehicle. There I crouched and tried to screw up enough courage to poke my head out to take a look.

A hand clamped over my mouth. I froze. Seconds later I went limp with relief as a voice whispered in my ear, "It's me." Tyler had found me. He took his hand away and immediately put a finger over his lips to indicate I should stay quiet. I nodded to let him know I understood and he began to guide me back.

At the door I reached for the handle. Tyler knocked my arm away and hissed, "The light," and I understood his fear. The interior light would come on if the door was opened.

"I called the police, but we need to get under cover 'til they get here," Tyler went on. "I'm going to cause a distraction then we'll dash for the trees."

He felt around on the ground and found a rock. "Ready?" he mouthed. I gave a single brief nod and he hurled the stone into the trees. We raced in the opposite direction and in moments we hit the understory, the dense layer of shrubs and bushes beneath the tree canopy. The good news was a lot of leaves had already fallen, making it a little easier to push our way through. The bad news was it had been a very dry fall, and those leaves crackled beneath our feet, and twigs snapped off and branches rustled and I wondered how animals were able to move through the forest with such stealth.

After a few minutes Tyler stopped. There was a slight hollow and we lay down in it.

"Keep completely still," Tyler warned, and as quietly as possible he used his hands to rake leaves on top of us. As camouflage it probably wasn't much help, but the thickening darkness was our friend and, hardly daring to breath, we clutched each other and prayed help would arrive soon.

Twenty-Seven

"What fools you are."

I flinched and Tyler tightened his hold on me. Neve's voice floated above us but I couldn't tell where she was, I only knew it was close.

"You sounded like a pair of elephants crashing through the forest. Any fool could follow you." In a sing-song voice she added, "I know you're near."

My face was buried in the dusty leaves and a dry tickle in the back of my throat was driving me nuts. I chewed my cheeks trying to create some saliva and swallowed. It felt as if I might choke. Panic was beginning to take hold and I knew Tyler was aware of it as his muscles tensed. He was getting ready to charge at Neve, I was sure. But where was she?

"Ah, there you are."

Simultaneously we raised our heads. Neve stood several feet away, the gun fixed in our direction. I couldn't make out her features, but I was pretty certain she must be gloating.

Tyler spoke. "The police will be here any minute. You need to get away. I'll drive you anywhere; just let Polly go."

"I have a better idea," Neve said, "hand over the keys and I'll let you both go."

"No you won't," I croaked. "You'll kill us both."

Neve laughed. "You'll find out soon enough won't you? Now," she directed her words at Tyler, "give me the keys or she dies."

"OK, OK. I'm reaching into my pocket for them." Tyler slipped his hand into his jeans and slowly began to pull out the keychain, then with a rapid twist of his wrist he tossed them away.

Distracted for a moment Neve turned her head trying to follow the trajectory of the keys. At the same time Tyler coiled ready to propel himself at her, but already she was focusing back in on us and I knew it was too late for us. We were going to die.

That's when the miracle happened, and its name was Erik the Red. I didn't know at first it was Erik who saved us, I was only vaguely aware of a dark shape hurtling from the darkness and knocking Neve from her feet. The gun went off and I think I screamed Tyler's name. Neve's screams mingled with mine and with the guttural, fierce growling of the dog.

"Get him off!" I heard Neve's desperate cry. Then Tyler called to me. "Polly, get the dog!"

I sprang to my feet and that's when I knew what had happened. Erik hadn't been killed. He must have climbed through the broken windshield and found us…just in time to avenge Heather and keep me and Tyler alive.

"Erik! Enough!" I commanded, and grabbed his tail, pulling him steadily away from Neve. It got his attention and he looked back at me ready to snap, then realizing who it was a look of confusion crossed his face and I was able to step between him and Neve and take control.

Tyler had a firm grasp on Neve, who again had reverted to a seemingly frail, helpless woman.

"Are you OK?" he asked, looking at me.

"I think so." In truth I was too numb to be sure. "What happened to the gun?"

"Erik must have knocked it from Neve's grasp. As long as she doesn't have it, I don't care where it is."

Ain't that the truth.

I realized I was starting to shake and my legs were feeling weak. I slipped my fingers through the hair on Erik's neck and took comfort in its softness and the warmth of his body.

"Do you know which way it is to the house?" I was completely disoriented.

"Perhaps Erik can lead us," Tyler said. But it didn't matter, because that's when we heard the sirens and knew our ordeal was over.

Twenty-Eight

"I like this one." I held up the shot glass of golden liquid. "Which is it?"

"That," Lou Berger said, "is the pear, cinnamon and ginger mead. We were given a couple of crates of Bosc pear windfalls and were going to bottle them, then we decided to experiment with the mead."

"Good call," I said. "What are the other samples."

This time Scott Hamm answered. "The rosy-colored one is wildflower honey and the darker one is blueberry mead. Keep in mind they've just gone through the first fermentation. It will take up to four more months to complete the aging process and then the flavors will be much fuller."

"Hooey," Rooster said, "you're starting to sound like a regular vintner."

"A vintner is a winemaker. The proper term for someone who makes mead is a mazer," Scott said.

Rooster clapped Scott on the shoulder. "Then all I can say is you're an amazing mazer."

We all laughed. It felt good. Two weeks after the scare in the woods I was still having flashbacks to Neve Reed, her manic stare and the gun aimed at my chest. I caught Tyler's eye and he winked. I grinned back.

"Hey," Lou said. "What's going to happen with Erik?"

We all looked at Mom in her wheelchair. Erik sat beside her, leaning against her legs. A big soft collar was around his neck to prevent him from chewing his right front leg, which was heavily bandaged where Neve's bullet had clipped the bone just above his knee.

"Yeah, Mrs. P." Scott took an empty glass from Mom's hand and placed it in the sink. "We'd hate to see him go."

"He's not going anywhere." Mom wrapped a protective arm over his shoulders. "He saved my daughter's life. You think I'd let him go to someone else?"

There was a chorus of cheers and "Way to go, Erik," and "Good job" as we all expressed our pleasure. Wanting to get in on the excitement Erik stood, then winced and gave a little whimper.

"Easy, big guy." Rooster crouched beside the dog and ran his hand gently down his back. "The vet says it will be a while yet before he can put his weight on the leg."

"It's amazing he was able to chase Neve down with an injury like that," Lou said. "I wonder if he was determined to avenge Heather or save you, Polly."

"Maybe a bit of both," I said. "I'm just glad it's all over. Especially now that Dennis Haggerty is in custody…"

"…and your suspicions have been proven right," Mom added.

"What I still don't know," said Scott, "is who killed that Sturges guy."

"Runyon," Rooster and I said together.

"But why?"

I shared a look with Rooster, and between us we told the whole story.

It began with the killing of two-year-old Cassie. Runyon and the babysitter, Isabel Cisneros, found Neve with the dead child. Isabel, as it turned out, was not above covering up the incident for a very generous payout from Runyon. She got Neve into a clean dress and Runyon hustled his wife off to be seen at dinner while Isabel disposed of the body.

To control Neve's manic tendencies, Runyon for years has been taking her to doctors out of state and kept her medicated.

Dennis Haggerty came on the scene when he met Isabel. They lived together for a while, during which time she told him about the Reeds. Later, when Kent Sturges appeared and hooked up with his father, Dennis, it was Kent who researched the Reeds and came up with the idea to run the scam, not that Dennis took much persuading, especially when he realized a girl Kent knew, Heather, looked remarkably like Neve Reed.

Blackmail was always the ultimate plan. But they wanted Heather to inherit all the Reed wealth and so they needed it to look as if the Reeds accepted her as their daughter.

"We know from Dennis," I said, "that they never told Heather the full story. For her it began as a way to make some extra money to pay for school. She adopted Erik from a setter rescue group, and it just happened that she quickly came to love him. Things changed as she began to realize the extent of the deception and she hated what the men were doing to Neve."

"Poor Heather. There was no way she could guess what kind of woman Neve was."

"Did Runyon Reed know his wife had murdered Heather?" Lou asked.

Rooster spoke up. "He certainly suspected it. That's why he took her away."

"Then how did he come to kill Sturges?"

"Without Heather, Kent's plan was unraveling, so he decided to go for straight blackmail. He texted Reed and said he wanted to meet. Reed picked the time and place and secretly drove back to Mallowapple in the night, leaving Neve in care of the doctors. He killed Kent, dragged the body into the forest and high-tailed it back to his wife, and nobody knew he'd even gone."

"Then I assume Haggerty took off because he feared for his own life," Scott said.

"Exactly," Rooster replied.

Lou whistled and shook his head. "What a mess."

"It's a horrible story, isn't it?" Mom said. "The Reeds were considered pillars of the community. Everyone was so sorry for them when Cassie disappeared, and all the time they were responsible."

"There's one thing that still puzzles me," Lou said. "How did they know about Erik the Red?"

"From the baby sitter," I said. "Remember, she was there to look after Cassie *and* her older sister Shelly, who had a dog called Erik the Red."

"I wonder if he hated Neve as much as our Erik does?"

None of us had a reply to that, so it was a relief when the front door opened and Tyler walked in.

"Did I miss the mead tasting?"

"There's plenty left," Lou said. "Come on over here."

"Just a minute. I've got something for the hero dog." From behind his back he drew a large soft duck toy. "Listen to this." He squeezed it and it honked just like a real duck.

Erik's tail was going a mile a minute as he took the toy from Tyler.

"It's good to see you didn't break his tail when you tugged him off Neve." Tyler gave me an impish grin.

"Hey. I wouldn't recommend anyone do that to a dog unless the alternative is sticking your hand in front of one in a vicious frenzy."

"Absolutely right," Tyler said and swept me into a big bear hug as Erik discovered his toy made wonderful quacking noises, and the phone in my pocket began to quack and everyone groaned and laughed and said, "Turn it off." And I knew that everything was alright again.

Liz Dodwell

Go here to get a FREE short story from Liz, and become part of the In Crowd to receive insider news, previews and specials:

http://lizdodwell.com/signup/

The Christmas Puppy

A Polly Parrett Pet-Sitter Cozy Murder Mystery

Book 5

Liz Dodwell

One

"Tom, as soon as the Mayor finishes his speech the lights will come on. That's your cue to drive round to the front of the house."

"So what time should I be out there?" Tom Ouelette looked at Rooster. "Do we even know how long the Mayor will talk?"

Rooster shrugged and turned to Mom. "Any thoughts, Edwina?"

Mom shook her head while she backed her chair away from the desk and wheeled herself across the room where she could face us all.

"Mayor Dinkins is scheduled to speak at six-forty-five – it will be quite dark by then - and has been given a suggested time of no more than 10 minutes. Unfortunately, he does tend to like the sound of his own voice so expect him to go on for 20. If he exceeds that we may have to implement plan B."

"What's plan B?" Diego spoke up.

"Rooster could suddenly have problems with the sound system." Mom winked and we all laughed.

It was the final meeting of the Welcome Home Christmas Festival committee. It was also Thanksgiving morning and we were all in great good humor, looking forward to a grand dinner with all our residents and then to the Grand Opening of our Christmas Festival the following evening.

I should explain, Welcome Home is the place my mom and I established to provide housing for homeless military veterans and their pets. The property is made up of the farmhouse – our old family home – a couple of converted barns, and various other outbuildings. We had the capacity to house 17 residents, and we were full. We didn't have medical facilities or anything like that; I suppose you could say we were more of a halfway house. Our goal was to provide a temporary home until the vets could re-establish themselves back into a normal life. And, very importantly, we welcomed pets.

It's amazing how many veterans and other homeless people will refuse to enter shelters because their best friends are not allowed. We're trying to change that. And here in Maine, where the winters are long and very cold, we didn't want anyone or their pets to suffer without shelter.

I tuned back in to the conversation, where we were tweaking the details of our annual Christmas Open House. This was our third year and, with the help of all the residents, it was going to be a doozy.

"Polly!"

"Uh, yes Mom."

"I hope you're ready with the dogs."

Just because I have a pet-sitting business everyone seems to assume I can train animals to do anything. I mean, I can teach a dog to sit, stay and roll over – most of the time

– but getting them to perform in a pageant is a totally different thing. None-the-less, I'd been designated to come up with an act to include at the Opening, and when my mother tells you you're going to do something well, let's just say there's no point in arguing.

"Yep, we're good to go," I lied.

"What are you going to do?" It was Tom, our designated Santa who asked.

"The dogs will be dressed as elves and working in Santa's toy shop. Except Angel," she's my pit bull mix, "who is playing the part of Rudolf." That's if I could get her to keep the red nose and antlers on.

"Are they going to make toys?" grinned Carl, a marine combat veteran who'd served in Vietnam.

I gave an airy wave of my hand and replied vaguely, "That will be a surprise," because based on my lack of success in our "rehearsals" what happened on stage was likely to be as big a surprise to me as it was to anyone else.

We talked a little longer, discussing refreshments, the raffle, other entertainment, 'til Rooster called a halt and gave a quick summation.

"Tom, you will get into your Santa suit and be out back at least 15 minutes before the Mayor begins speaking at six-forty-five. The packages will have been loaded into the carts and the train ready to go by six-thirty. Carl will be out there to help you until then, but if you're late you'll be on your own because Carl," Rooster cocked a finger at the man, "you'll have to hustle to the stage and make sure the choir is in position behind the curtain."

Some of the guys had built a little trolley train in which Santa was going to make his appearance, driving out of the trees to the front of the house. It would be pulling a couple of carts filled with packages that we were going to raffle. Oh, I should have told you, the aim of the event was to raise money for Welcome Home; running a shelter was a very expensive business and we relied heavily on the kindness of our community. The event was also designed to showcase what we were doing and, perhaps most importantly, spread the joy of the season to one and all. I know that sounds sappy, but that's how we all felt.

Rooster pointed at Diego, who had been with the Army Corps of Engineers as an interior electrician. "You'll need to be running a final check on the Christmas lights. We don't want any problems when the Mayor flicks the switch to turn them on."

Glancing at his notes Rooster continued. "Back to you, Carl. As soon as the mayor finishes, the curtains will open and that will cue your music.

"Tyler," Rooster said to my boyfriend who, so far, had been very quiet, "you're in charge of props, so be sure everything is ready."

"Yes sir," Tyler gave a mock salute, then blew a kiss my way. I caught it and pressed it to my lips and there was a general groan amongst the others and murmurings of "Yuk," and "Get a room." We just grinned at each other.

"OK, everyone," Rooster called the meeting back to order. "We're nearly done. Edwina," he addressed Mom, "you'll be at the food booth with Scott and Lou. Hayley," she's our only female resident, "is in charge of selling raffle tickets. The Mayor will finish speaking and turn on the lights, Santa will appear driving the train as the choir sings. We'll have about an hour for folk to buy tickets and food, kids to sit on Santa's lap, and for everyone to admire the display. Polly, you and I will be floaters, helping out wherever needed, just give yourself time to get ready for your own entrance on stage. The pageant will begin promptly at eight. Are we all clear?"

There was a chorus of "Yes" before everyone gathered up their notes and hurried away.

My nose drew me straight to the kitchen where Scott Hamm and Lou Berger were prepping for the Thanksgiving dinner. There would be more than 20 of us sitting down to eat, so tables had been pushed together in the bigger of our two dormer barns as we could no longer fit everyone into the house.

"It smells absolutely wonderful in here. Any chance you're in need of a taste tester?"

Scott rolled his eyes at me as Mom wheeled her way in behind me. "The only way you get to stay here is if you pitch in and help," she said.

"Anything." I held my hands palms out. "I'll even peel potatoes as long as we can listen to Christmas music."

"Deal," Lou said. He pulled an ipod from his apron pocket and in moments we were listening to Rockin' Around the Christmas Tree.

"Alright," I said, "just hand me the peeler and I'll get cracking."

489

"Actually, Polly," Scott looked over his shoulder from the range where he was stirring something in a big pot, "I'm about ready to fill the pie crusts. Would you grab them from the pantry? I set six of them in there to cool."

"Sure thing." I rocked my way across the kitchen floor, singing along with Brenda Lee (she's the one who first recorded the song, in case you didn't know) and opened the pantry door.

The people who built these old farm homes understood the importance of a pantry, and ours was huge. Right now, it was also packed with jars of jams and relishes that Lou and Scott had prepared to sell at our event, along with the usual stuff Mom kept in there. I gazed around looking for the pie crusts. *Ah!* Of course they were on the highest shelf. Not to worry, though, we kept a small step ladder handy. It was a bit shaky but it did the job. I climbed to the top, still bopping around to the music.

Oh, no!

You're thinking I fell, aren't you? Well, for once I wasn't a klutz. No, I was looking at the six pie shells, neatly lined up to cool, and in one of them my little orange and white cat, Amber, was curled up fast asleep.

"How did you get in here?" I hissed, lifting her from the shell. She wriggled and swatted at me, annoyed to be taken from her warm, cozy bed. I shoved her inside my sweater and tucked the sweater into my jeans. I looked as if I was about to give birth to some strange alien life form, but I knew Amber would soon settle down and go back to sleep.

Pulling the pie shell from the shelf I studied the hairs lining the inside. Tentatively I blew on them. Several of them rose lazily into the air then drifted down onto boxes of pasta and rice. *Oops.* That wouldn't go over well with Mom.

I tried picking the hairs out one by one, but it was really hard to see them. *I know, I know.* You're grossing out now, but I didn't want to be the one responsible for messing up Thanksgiving dessert and having to beg everyone's forgiveness. *Maybe if I shook the shell?*

Flipping the pie dish over I gave it a quick shake and, for good measure, a hearty slap on the bottom, which is when the shell slipped out and fell to the floor in a crumpled heap.

"What on earth are you doing?"

Mom was in the doorway. Startled, I nearly did tumble off the steps but saved myself by grabbing at a handle. It gave me enough leverage to find my balance and jump to the floor. Unfortunately, the handle was attached to a drawer that came with me, spilling its contents of neatly folded aprons and kitchen towels beside me. Under my sweater Amber dug her claws into my stomach in an effort to hang on, and growled in protest at the jerky ride. I sucked in a harsh breath of pain.

"Hi, Mom."

My mother did what she usually does in these situations: looked Heavenward and probably said a silent prayer. Lou came rushing in when he heard the kerfuffle, closely followed by Scott. They tried extremely hard not to laugh too hard as I endeavored to explain myself. Nobly, I took the blame for everything on myself so Amber wouldn't be in trouble. Mom pointed out that Amber was my responsibility and I should have made sure she was kept away from the kitchen, so *of course* I *was* to blame.

Anyway, in the end I was banished from the kitchen while the other pie shells were examined for evidence of sleeping cats, and new shells were baked. The good thing was the story provided for much laughter at dinner; the meal, including all the pies, was delicious and by the time I was heading for bed I'd got over feeling like a scolded child and was very thankful for it.

Two

The puppy waddled into the clearing on chubby little legs. At eight weeks old he was quite fearless, but he was also tired and getting cold. He had no concept of time, of course, and didn't know he'd only been away from his mother for about half an hour. Still, darkness had now descended and the temperature was below 40F and dropping rapidly.

It was the lights at the back of the farmhouse that had drawn him there and he was happy to see a human sitting in a box thing. Obviously, he couldn't understand it was Santa sitting in the train, but humans were nice to him, they picked him up and cuddled him, and he was ready for some serious snuggling.

He broke into an unsteady jog, his ears bouncing up and down as he went. At the train he skidded to a stop and yipped for attention. *Hmm.* The human apparently didn't hear him so he tried to jump into the train, but his stocky body wasn't built for athletics and he plopped back on the ground. He yipped again. Still no response.

Undeterred, the pup tried again and again, and at last was able to hook one of his back legs over the running board. Scrabbling furiously he hauled himself aboard. Pleased with his success he swatted at the human's leg, making gurgly growling noises and whining. This behavior, he'd learned very quickly, always elicited immediate sympathy from humans and he would be picked up and talked to in that sing-song voice that made him feel warm and happy.

It wasn't working! What was wrong? The puppy had never been ignored like this before. He redoubled his efforts and bounced up and down, trying to claw his way onto the human's lap; all to no avail.

Puzzled that he was being ignored, the pup sat on the floor and looked up into the human's face. Not that he could actually see the face, because it was so hairy. He shivered, and awareness of being cold began to make him quite cross. He gathered himself for another leap, his little butt wiggled and he launched himself upward.

He almost made it. His front paws latched onto the seat and he tried to claw his way up. As he did so, one back paw hit a little switch tucked under the seat. It didn't even register in his brain but, in fact, the puppy had just put the vehicle in gear. Then he lost his tentative hold and tumbled backwards onto the foot pedal. All he knew was that something gave way beneath him and the train jerked, then he rolled to the side. That jerk was enough to cause the human to slump forward and his knee to come down on the pedal, holding it there, and the train began to move.

The puppy didn't budge. He didn't want to, because the folds of Santa's coat had fallen over him and at last there was something to keep him warm.

Three

Mayor Dinkins was five minutes into his speech when I felt someone tugging at my arm and twisted around to look into the anxious face of Dorcas Phipps.

"Polly, Mule has gone," she said.

I must have missed something in the planning because I had no recollection of a mule being involved. And why would Dorcas, the head of a local bulldog rescue group, have anything to do with a mule?

Reading my confusion, Dorcas hurriedly explained.

"Mule is one of the puppies. So many people have been looking at them and picking them up, I lost track. Mule is a stubborn little guy - you probably guessed that already from his name - and I should have been more careful. It's just like him to go exploring if he got the chance, but I'm scared. We've got to find him soon; he'll never survive the night and it's already dark."

Dorcas's words were beginning to run together and tears were welling in her eyes. Mule was one of five puppies born to a bulldog, Charlotte, owned by a well-meaning but decidedly stupid pet owner who thought she could mate her female and just leave the dog to get on with giving birth.

A little research would have taught her that the puppies' large heads can make whelping difficult, and sometimes a C-section is necessary. This was one of those cases, and by the time the owner realized there was a major problem and got the dog to a vet, it was too late for two of the puppies and Charlotte nearly died.

Traumatized by what had happened, the woman gave her dog up to Dorcas in whose care the mother had recovered and the pups were thriving. To introduce the one male and two female puppies to potential adopters, Dorcas had asked if she could bring the family to our Open House. She'd set up a tent with heating and had welcomed a steady stream of admirers, but now another one of the pups was in danger of his life.

It took me only a few moments to process the situation and decide immediate action was called for.

"I'm going to interrupt the mayor and start a search. Probably half the people here are ex-military and they know how to handle an emergency."

I made to push my way through the crowd to get to the stage when I became aware of a stirring in the people behind me. A young voice cried out, "It's Santa," while an older voice immediately followed with "Watch out!"

Standing on tiptoe I peered over the heads to see Tom in the train, heading for the crowds. It registered almost simultaneously that he was too early, was going in the wrong direction and was slumped over. I bolted toward him, yelling out "Move! Let me through!" The crowd milled in confusion and one guy roughly pushed me aside so that I almost fell. Recovering, I pressed on and caught a glimpse of someone else rushing in from the opposite direction.

It was Rooster. He got to the train first, reached in and flipped the switch. The train came to an abrupt halt, Santa wobbled then flopped to the side and a high-pitched wail came from beneath him. Rooster bent and pulled off the Santa hat as I bent and lifted his cloak.

"It's not Tom," Rooster said.

"Mule!" I cried.

"Hey, that's my Santa suit." I swiveled my head to see who had shouted. A figure was stalking in our direction. It was Tom.

Four

"His name is Chandler Slattery, he's a real estate developer."

Officer Wayde Frellick stood in the living room and addressed us - "Us" being Mom, Rooster, Tyler and me - as he gave up the identity of the dead man, and we all gasped.

"But he's the man who wanted to buy us out," Mom said.

"Buy you out? You mean he wanted to take over your charity?"

"Hardly," Tyler sneered. "He approached me months ago to act as his representative and make an offer to buy the Welcome Home property, but there was nothing altruistic about it. He wanted to put in a single-family home development. I turned him down flat and told him Edwina and Polly would never consider it."

"And that's exactly what we did tell him when he came to us directly," Mom said. "He got very pushy, very rude, so I told him to leave and never come back."

I chuckled. "Actually, what you said was 'Don't you get ugly with me, you jo-jeezly dub.'" (For those who don't know, that translates loosely as "Don't you get nasty with me, you overblown idiot.").

"That's beside the point," Mom picked up again. "We didn't hear any more from him and forgot about it. Besides, we had other things on our minds. It was when we were having trouble with that nasty little man from the VA."

"What trouble would that be?" Frellick asked.

"Oh, he was giving us a hard time about the barn conversions. Made us jump through hoops to get them licensed for use as living quarters for veterans."

"You know, I think I saw him here," Rooster suddenly said.

"Saw who?" I swiveled to face Rooster. "Ward Nesmith?"

Rooster nodded.

"What the heck would he be doing here?" I wondered.

"He should be ashamed to show his face," Mom said.

"This Ward Nesmith," Frellick interrupted, "he's the one from the VA?"

"He was the inspector assigned to oversee the construction on the barns," Rooster said. "But I can't be certain it was him. Coulda been someone who looked like him."

"OK, that's enough!" Frellick held his hand up in a "stop" gesture. "You can explain all this later. Meanwhile, the Sheriff wants you to stay put until he's ready to talk to you himself."

Mom wheeled herself practically toe to toe with the officer and pinned him with a flinty gaze.

"You're telling me Sheriff Wisniewski wants to keep me incarcerated in my own home?"

Frellick shuffled awkwardly. "Uh, no ma'am, he's requesting you remain here and not impede his investigation..."

"Impede his investigation?" Mom's voice was getting a little shrill. The rest of us knew the warning signs, but poor Frellick was out of his depth.

"Impede his investigation?" Mom repeated. "A man has been killed on *my* property. Our Open House has been shut down, which means a lot of people have been disappointed, our fund-raising efforts have been sunk and who knows how it will affect our reputation? A lot of good people who have served their country well, and then been abandoned by it, are relying on the Welcome Home organization for help, and you're telling me to butt out!"

"Well, I, I didn't exactly mean to put it that way."

"And what's more," Mom went on relentlessly, "there's a killer who may still be here. What are you doing about that?"

Frellick was saved at that moment when the door opened and there was Sheriff Wisniewski. He looked around the room, taking stock of the situation before directly speaking to Mom.

"We're conducting a murder investigation, and based on past experience," he looked pointedly at me, "I deemed it wise that we have a cautionary little chat about not interfering with police business."

Of all the nerve. I'd been caught up in a murder mystery or four in the past, but that didn't make me a liability. In fact, I think it safe to say my "interfering" had helped solve those crimes. Still, I crossed my arms and parked myself on the edge of one of the easy chairs and waited to see what else Wisniewski had to say.

"Reinforcements are on the way from County. There are a lot of people to interview and I'd like to set up in one of your barns so we can get people out of the cold while they wait."

Mom nodded assent then asked, "And what about us?"

"Frellick here will take your preliminary statements. I'll talk to you myself when I can."

With that he turned on his heel and walked smartly away.

We all looked at Frellick. "Well?" I said.

"I, uh, I'll need to talk to you each separately." No-one moved or spoke. "And privately," he added.

It was Rooster who took pity on him. "Come on. I'll go first. We can use the den."

"I need to let the dogs out," I said. My three – Angel, Vinny and Coco – were in a bedroom upstairs with Erik, the setter Mom had taken in recently, and Rooster's old pit bull, Elaine.

"You can't leave until I've got your statement," Frellick said.

"Don't be ridiculous. I'm not leaving town, I just want to give the dogs a breather. They've been shut up for hours now."

"You'll get me in trouble."

As always, it was Rooster who poured oil on the troubled waters.

"Don't worry, officer. When we're done, I'll bring the others to you," and he clapped a hand on the man's shoulder and guided him away.

"I'll come give you a hand with the dogs," Tyler said to me.

"Before you go..." Mom narrowed her eyes at us and jerked her head at the door. "Shut that."

Tyler stepped around me and pushed it firmly closed. "What's on your mind, Edwina?"

She took in a deep breath through her nose then exhaled loudly from her mouth. "I can hardly believe I'm saying this, but I don't care what the Sheriff says, I want us to do some investigating of our own."

My jaw went slack and I actually didn't know what to say. It's true in the past Mom had been in favor of leaving things to the authorities, so it was hard to accept her change of heart.

"Sheriff Wisniewski is a good man, and a good policeman...as far as it goes." Tyler and I exchanged bewildered glances at Mom's words. "But he's not a great investigator. He lacks imagination, and that's something that you, Polly, have in abundance.

"I meant what I said earlier; people are relying on us. The longer it takes to resolve this murder, the more it could damage everything we've worked so hard to achieve. What if this somehow jeopardizes our standing with the VA? We don't need funds being denied again."

We'd been through a rough patch not so long ago, when Veteran's Affairs had denied assistance to the Welcome Home residents. It had taken months to resolve and been very costly. I'd been so looking forward to this Christmas because we'd finally be able to put it all behind us. Now this!

"You've got my support," Tyler emphasized his words with a nod. "Do you have a game plan?"

"Well, I think we need to talk to Tom first. Or should we start by pooling whatever information we already have? You two are the ones with experience in this sort of thing. What do you think?"

"I think we'd better start writing things down," I said, "before we forget them. Let's each make notes of our own and have Rooster do the same, then we'll compare. After that, we can decide who else we should talk to."

"That makes sense. I'll get started while I wait for Frellick to come back. And Polly," Mom directed a stern look my way, "I want your promise that you won't go off on your own and do something silly."

I returned her look with a "Who, me?" one of my own.

"Polly..."

"Oh, alright, Mom. I promise."

"Tyler," Mom wasn't finished yet, "I expect you to make sure she keeps that promise."

He grimaced, "I'll do the best I can."

"I guess that will have to do," Mom said. "Go on and see to the dogs, then. We'll get together later."

Five

Tyler and I had to put the dogs on leads, which did not please them, but with much of the area around the house roped off, and cops everywhere, we didn't dare let them run loose. Welcome Home was on a little over 10 acres of land, so we walked as far from the hubbub as we could, only to discover some of our residents had had the same idea, including Scott and Lou.

"Hi, guys," one of the men greeted us. "Any idea how long this is going to take?" He gestured with his arm to take in the scene at the house, and in an instant questions were being thrown at us by everyone. I threw up my hands in mock surrender.

"Whoa, there. Give me room to breathe and I'll fill you in." And I told as much as I knew.

"What's the story with Tom?" The guy who asked was called Gerry. I couldn't remember his last name but I knew he was an ex-Army Corporal and his dog was called Andie, after a bomb-sniffing dog who'd saved his life in Iraq, then later lost her own.

"Yeah, what gives?" Scott queried. "Tom wouldn't hurt anyone but I saw him being taken away. We ought to do something about it."

"Was he in handcuffs?" Tyler asked.

"No, but a couple cops put him in the back of a cruiser and drove away."

Tyler and I looked at each other. The concern of the men was palpable, so much so it was affecting the dogs. Andie, who was a German shepherd mix, sat leaning against Gerry's leg and nosed at his hand for reassurance.

"Shall we?" Tyler asked me in a low voice.

I gave a brief nod of assent and turned to the men.

"Guys! Listen up! We agree something needs to be done, and so does my mom. Here's the thing, the Sheriff has already warned us not to interfere, but I promise you we won't let Tom take the fall for something he didn't do. For now, though, I'm going to ask you to hang tight 'til we have a better grasp of the situation."

"What does the Old Man say?" It was Gerry, again, and "Old Man" was the name the vets gave to Rooster, who was looked upon as a commander of sorts in our little community and was highly respected.

"He's being interviewed now, so we haven't had a chance to talk, which is all the more reason to be patient."

"Polly's right." Scott spoke up. "Let's see what the morning brings. You'll keep us up-to-date, right?"

"Me or Rooster," I said.

Tyler gripped my arm. "We'd better get back in case Frellick is looking for us."

I nodded agreement and again assured the others they wouldn't be left out, then we hurried away.

As we approached the house we saw a group of people outside the big barn. Voices were raised, though we couldn't make out what was being said, but it was apparent tensions were high.

"We'd better find out what's going on," I said, and veered toward them.

"Quiet down," I heard as I neared and realized the speaker was one of the county police who'd been called in to help. Not that anyone paid any attention to him, they just kept talking at once.

"Hey," I called out.

Either no-one heard or I was deliberately being ignored. I looked to Tyler for help and quickly he pulled out his phone and tapped the screen and a loud siren blasted out. It shut everyone up in an instant as I gave Tyler a questioning look.

"It's an anti-theft alarm," he said, returning the phone to his pocket.

"Polly, thank goodness you're here." Dorcas Phipps stepped from the group. "It's Mule. He's disappeared again." And she burst into tears.

Six

Softly, in the background, Pentatonix were singing "It's the most wonderful time of the year," which definitely didn't reflect the mood in the room. It was three in the morning and Sheriff Wisniewski was on a tirade.

"I should lock you all up. A man has been murdered and you lead a horde of people on a search for a dog!"

I gave him a sullen look. "A puppy. A very small and helpless puppy."

"Dog. Puppy. It makes no difference. You trampled all over a crime scene and probably destroyed vital evidence. And for what? Nothing!"

Next to me Dorcas began to sniffle and I rubbed her back; it was true, there had been no sign of Mule.

Mom, Tyler and Rooster were in the room with us but none of us responded to the Sheriff, we were too depressed to bother.

Wisniewski paced up and down as he ranted on, but all I heard was "blah, blah, blah." My mind was on the events of the evening, trying to make some sense of what happened. It wasn't working, I just kept coming up with more questions.

At last the Sheriff stopped moving and I realized he'd said something to me. "Uh...I, uh..." I fumbled for something to say.

"Is that clear?" Wisniewski snarled at me.

"Oh, absolutely," I said, hoping I looked as though I knew what he'd been talking about.

He held my gaze and I could feel my face heating up. *Stay cool, Polly.* It was only when he finally looked away that I realized I'd been holding my breath.

"OK, now that I've got your attention," the Sheriff ran a hand through his hair, "I have a couple of questions. There's a headless garden gnome on your back porch. What can you tell me about it?"

Huh? I pulled a face at Tyler, in return he gave me a helpless shrug. Then Rooster spoke.

"A couple of the residents got hold of some old gnomes and decided to repaint them as Christmas elves. One of them got dropped and the head broke off." He looked around at us. "They're concrete," he added, then turned his attention back to the Sheriff. "You'll see several of them out front as part of the display."

"You said 'headless gnome,'" Tyler frowned. "Does that mean you can't find the head? What's the significance of that?"

"It's the murder weapon," I said with dawning realization. "Chandler Slattery had his head bashed in by a gnome – in a manner of speaking."

"As usual you're jumping to conclusions Miss Parrett. I didn't say anything about how the victim was killed."

"You didn't have to, I was there, remember? So were Rooster and Tom; when Rooster took off the Santa hat we all saw the man's head was bashed in and bloody. If he was hit first and the hat put on him later, there will be blood all over the gnome's head."

I heard Dorcas moan and glanced at her. She looked awfully pale. I guess she wasn't used to murders like the rest of us. Still, I prattled on.

"If you didn't find the head perhaps the killer took it with him to get rid of later. He might have thought his fingerprints were on it." A thought struck me. "Had the head been painted? Surely you can't get fingerprints off concrete, but a heavy coat or two of paint would be a different story. The smart thing, of course, would be for the killer to have crushed the head and completely obliterate any evidence."

The Sheriff's hand smacked down on the old mirrored sideboard against the wall that had originally belonged to my grandparents.

"What part of 'absolutely' did you mean when I asked if you were clear about keeping your nose out of this?".

So that's what he'd been saying.

"Sorry, Sheriff. I tend to have an active imagination." I threw a furtive glance at Mom and saw a corner of her mouth turn up. "It won't happen again."

He drew himself up tall. "Make sure it doesn't. Now, can anyone tell me if you know of any relationship between the deceased Mr. Slattery, and Ward Nesmith who works for the Veterans Administration?"

Well, this was unexpected.

There was complete silence and blank looks.

"What sort of relationship?" Mom asked.

"Do you know if they were acquainted? Did any of you see them talking before Mr. Slattery's body was found?"

My jaw dropped. "You were right, Rooster. Nesmith was here."

Wisniewski pinned his sights on Rooster. "You saw the man?"

"I *think* I did," Rooster affirmed.

"Come with me!" Wisniewski commanded. To the rest of us he said, "You can all leave now. I'll deal with you in the morning, so be sure you can make yourselves available."

Tyler and I stood, Dorcas remained limp in the chair.

I crouched in front of her. "There's nothing more we can do for Mule tonight. I promise as soon as it's light we'll get search parties going again. Don't give up hope yet."

Her look was forlorn but she pushed herself to her feet. "I know you'll do your best Polly, I just..." Her lip trembled and the words were lost.

Mom wheeled herself over. "Dorcas, perhaps Tyler could drive you home," Tyler gave a brief nod. "Get some rest and come back in the morning."

"If you don't mind, I think I'd rather stay. My van is a camper, so I can be comfortable in there with Charlotte and her other two pups."

"We can do better than that," Mom was emphatic. "You can stay in the house."

"That's sweet of you, but I'd rather be in the van. The dogs are used to it and maybe a miracle will happen and Mule will find us there."

I forced my features to stay blank, not wanting to show my thoughts that a miracle was all Mule had left.

"Let me walk you out." Tyler took Dorcas's arm and she leaned heavily on him. I noticed Tyler brace himself. Dorcas was a big woman; not fat, but big-boned and tall.

I moved to the window, pulling back the drapes and peering into the dismal dark, thinking how much I'd been looking forward to the lights, the laughter, the good cheer.

"It's so depressing." I turned back to Mom and crossed my arms.

"Do you remember," Mom said, "when you and your brothers were quite small we had a chimney fire shortly before Christmas, and you were so worried that Santa wouldn't be able to bring your present because he couldn't get down the chimney?"

"Yeah, I do." In my mind I saw the four-year-old me struggling to stay awake to see Santa when he landed on the roof. I was planning to open the window for him to climb in, but things didn't work out as expected.

"We were never sure exactly what happened, but when your dad went to check on you before we went to bed, he found you hanging halfway out the window. It was 20 degrees and you were ice cold."

"I thought I heard reindeer on the roof. I was looking up to see Santa; I don't know what happened then."

"Well, something else you didn't know was the Pound Puppy toy you wanted so badly hadn't arrived in the mail. We didn't have the money, or the time, to order you another one. Of course, that didn't matter when we had to rush you to the hospital in Corkeep.

"We sat by your bed all night and all morning, with your brothers, and prayed you'd be alright. It was just about noon when you woke up, and the first thing you asked was..."

"Did Santa come?" I said. "And he did! He arrived right then."

Mom laughed. "He walked right to your bedside. 'Polly Parrett,' he said, 'I've been looking for you. I have a special present with your name on it because you've been a good little girl.' And he handed you a box..."

"It had paper with angels on it. I remember," I interrupted again. "It was my Pound Puppy. But, you know, I've never known who that Santa was."

"It was old Mr. Gregory, the post master. Your toy came in on a late Christmas Eve delivery. Mr. Gregory decided to bring it over himself on Christmas day, after he played Santa at the children's hospital in Corkeep. He hadn't known we were there but the nurses told him. His wife had wrapped the toy and he came looking for you after he said goodbye to the other kids. The timing was perfect, and you had no idea how close you came to missing Christmas altogether.

"But the point I'm making," Mom continued, "is that we prayed for a miracle and we got one. You were thrilled to meet Santa, and Dad and I were thankful you survived with no long-term problems."

"I'm not so sure about the long-term problems," Tyler quipped as he leaned against the door frame. I grabbed a cushion, which he ducked handily. "It was a good story, though, especially the bit about miracles."

"And now it's time we all got some rest," Mom said. "We need to be bright-eyed and bushy-tailed in the morning. We have a murderer to catch."

Seven

"Order! Let's have some order." Rooster stood on a makeshift dais of wooden pallets that we'd stacked in the horse barn. We'd lifted Mom up in her chair beside him. It was the morning after the ill-fated Open House. We were tired and tension was palpable among all who were present, which was about a dozen of the Welcome Home residents, plus Mom, Rooster and me. The other few had been deployed to run interference if any of the police – there were a couple still here – came near the barn. This was a secret meeting to jump start our murder investigation.

Military training tends to stick with a person and, instinctively, our veterans turned their attention to Rooster.

"You've all given statements to the police, but we don't have access to those, of course, so we're gonna ask you to repeat what you said, then maybe we'll have a round table – even though you're all standing in straight lines," there were a few chuckles here, "and see if we can make some sense of what happened. First, though, Edwina wants to say a few words."

Mom let her gaze roam over the group. "Rooster called you together because I insisted, so I think I owe it to you to explain my thinking. We all have a vested interest in Welcome Home, and every day the Sheriff keeps the lights turned off costs us money in lost donations. There's also a concern that we'll come under scrutiny from the VA again. But it's more than that.

"Christmas was when it all started. When Rooster and Elaine came into our lives." She caught hold of my arm and shook it gently, and smiled up at Rooster. I smiled too. "It was Christmas two years ago when the idea of Welcome Home was born. At that time we had nothing but the farmhouse, a couple of old barns and absolutely no money. What we did have in abundance was the heart to open our home, to give whatever comfort and encouragement we could, to men and women who had given so much to us, to our country, and then been forgotten or turned away when they needed help.

"You might say we were filled with the spirit of Christmas and I would agree with you, for I truly believe as the bible says, it's a time of great joy for **all** people. And Christmas reminds me how making that decision has brought me more joy than I can ever explain. Just look at what we've accomplished – together.

"I know it's trite to say we're all family, but no matter where you end up in this world, and what you may think of your time here, I want you to know you are always family to me, and you will always be welcome home."

Cheers erupted from those gathered and I heard calls of "Love you." Mom swallowed hard and snatched a tissue from the bag she hangs on the arm of her chair, and blew her nose loudly. When she regained her voice she went on.

"In a convoluted sort of way, I'm trying to tell you why Christmas means so much to me, and why it's so important to find Chandler Slattery's killer so we can get back to celebrating the wonderful things about this time of year. And rather than having a round table," she gave Rooster an apologetic look, "I think it would be most helpful if you would each write down your movements and anything you saw or heard, and hand it to one of us. After we've gone through them, we'll talk to you individually if need be."

"That's it," Rooster called out. "Find a quiet corner and start writing. When you're done, come over to the house and we'll chat."

"Just a minute!" I waved my hands above my head. "Mule, the bulldog puppy, still has not been found. Would you please all keep an eye out for him? It's possible he found a place to shelter and is still alive."

Almost all our residents had a pet, most of them dogs, and understood the risk to a small pup. They would also never give up looking, even though the odds were very much against Mule.

Tyler put his arm across my shoulders and gave a squeeze. "Just keep praying for a miracle," he said.

Eight

I bit the head off my gingerbread man. Some people start at the hands or arms and eat the head last, but it always seems a bit macabre to me to see the little fellow's smiling face as I devour his extremities and body.

"You know," Tyler said, "you could lick his facial features off. That would accomplish the same thing." (He knows my little idiosyncrasies).

I merely grunted. Not that it mattered right now. I could have stuffed the whole thing in my mouth at once and not enjoyed it much; I was too frustrated.

The two of us, with Mom, had been going through the resident's notes, but we weren't getting very far. There were no great revelations, nobody had confessed and no obvious answers to the mystery.

"Let's start with what we know," Mom said. "For one thing, the train was out back all day; I could see it from the kitchen window. I saw the trolleys being loaded up and Diego worked on something for a while, but nothing looked at all suspicious."

"I don't think any of that matters," I said, "unless you saw someone put the body in the train and hit the starter."

"I'd drawn the drapes long before there was a chance of that happening. From about four o' clock on anyone could have done anything and I wouldn't know."

"It's also conceivable that Mule somehow hit the starter and the body shifted on to the peddle," Tyler said.

"Do you think someone put the puppy in the train?" Mom asked.

I shrugged. "No idea. I can't imagine someone who's just murdered a man taking the time to rescue a puppy."

"You would," Tyler gave me a meaningful look.

I scowled at him. "So you think I'm capable of murder?"

"If someone was going to do cruel and terrible things to a helpless pet, or old person, or small child..."

I thought about that for a few moments. *Yeah, he was probably right.*

"Enough of that," Mom chided. She'd been sifting through the notes and pulled out a couple of pieces of paper. "Based on these," she waved the papers in the air, "no-one saw Tom after he'd helped Scott and Lou finish setting up the food table. That was around five-thirty. He told them he had to get into his Santa costume."

"Which he didn't." Tyler stroked his chin. "And that begs the question of where he was and what was he doing from that time until we discovered Slattery in the train."

"By the way," I said, "who had access to the Santa costume?"

Mom exhaled loudly. "Anyone who used the bathroom by the back door. That's where Tom was going to change. I hung the suit in there first thing in the morning and I'm sure at least a few people went in, but I couldn't say who."

"Hmm. We should probably ask if anyone noticed who used those facilities."

"That's really a longshot." Tyler reached past me to grab a gingerbread man. "Edwina, you said you couldn't see anything from four on. But Carl was out back later than that. So that narrows the window of opportunity for the killer from six-thirty to what? Six-fifty or so when the train appeared?"

"Ah," Mom shuffled papers again. "Carl was called away 10 minutes early, some confusion about sheet music, so the window widens from six-twenty to six-fifty, about half an hour. Plenty of time to do mischief."

"We really need to talk to Tom," I grumbled.

"With luck we'll be able to soon."

Tyler and I gave Mom a surprised look.

"Rooster talked to the Sheriff earlier. Tom hasn't been charged with anything and they're letting him go. Rooster's on the way to pick him up."

"Yes!" I raised a fist in the air. "What did he say? Why did they keep him so long?"

"Calm down, Polly. We'll find out when he gets here. Meanwhile, let's get back to what we know."

It was at that moment a couple of large dogs started barking to the tune, "We Wish You a Merry Christmas," while a chorus of small dogs and cats provided back-up. I pulled out my phone and saw it was one of my sitters.

"What's up, Jenn?"

"Oh, Polly, something's wrong with Little Bit. He hasn't had a bowel movement since I got here yesterday and he's been throwing up. You can tell he's very uncomfortable. I'm on my way to the vet, figured I'd better let you know."

"Good thinking, Jenn. I'll meet you there as soon as I can. Did you call Miss Teasdale yet?"

"No."

"Then I will. You've got your hands full already. You're doing the right thing."

"Everything alright?" Tyler asked.

"Cat emergency," I said. "I've got to run."

"Good luck," I heard as I dashed to my van.

Constipation is not unusual in cats, especially as they get older, but it can have lots of causes, some of them serious. And when the kitty is also throwing up and is in fact quite young – Little Bit, I knew, was five - a trip to the vet is the best course of action, especially when the cat is not your own.

Ardith Teasdale is an exceedingly sensible woman, I'm happy to say, and one who doesn't take chances with her pet's care. She was away for a few days on business but readily agreed her darling Little Bit should get whatever treatment Dr. Jim, our local veterinarian, recommended, cost be damned. So it was with a modicum of relief I arrived at the vet's office.

"Hi, Polly," the receptionist said. *They know me well here.* "They're in room three; just go on back."

I found Jenn with the doctor, looking over some x-rays.

"There you are," Dr. Jim gave me a nod of greeting. "I was just explaining to Jenn..."

My sitter began to speak at the same time. "He has to have an operation."

"Whoa." I squeezed Jenn's arm. "Let the doctor explain."

"Sorry, doc," Jenn said.

"It's fine, Jenn. Now Polly, take a look here..."

The doctor proceeded to explain to me that Little Bit had ingested something that was now causing a serious obstruction and pointed to a section of the intestinal tract where the blockage could clearly be seen.

"What do you think it is?"

"There's no telling from the x-ray. But I was able to palpate it and there's no way it's going to move. He's also severely dehydrated. I would say this happened at least two or three days ago. At this point the best thing is for me to go in and cut out the obstruction."

"Whatever you think best Dr. Jim. Miss Teasdale has already given me the go-ahead to do what's necessary."

"Good. Then I'm going to get him on some fluids right now, and start prepping him for the operation."

"How long will it take?" Jenn asked.

The doctor shook his head. "Depends what's in there, how badly it's stuck, has it perforated the intestinal wall.... We could be done in an hour or so, or it could be several hours. There's no need for you to wait. I'll call you as soon as I'm done."

Jenn and I looked at each other. "I'd rather stay," she said.

"Me, too," I agreed.

I made a quick call to Tyler and explained what had happened.

"Take your time, honey," he said. "Rooster's back with Tom but has sent him to rest. He's had a bad time and needs peace and quiet for a while, so there's nothing earth-shattering going on."

Relieved I wasn't being left out of anything important I reminded myself I had an obligation to my client. And I truly was worried about Little Bit. He was such a sweet cat. You could cradle him like a baby and he'd lay in your arms all day, purring like crazy. I resolved to concentrate on sending positive vibes into the Universe for his recovery.

"Polly, you guys can go back to room three. Dr. Jim will be with you in a few minutes."

The receptionist smiled at us encouragingly. I took that as a good sign. We'd been waiting a couple of hours for word of Little Bit. I'd spent that time alternating between visualizing the cat as well and happy, and rethinking the events at Welcome Home.

Doctor Jim looked serious as he entered. "Well, ladies, I have to say this is a first for me."

"Is he OK?" Jenn blurted out.

The doctor's expression relaxed. "He came through with flying colors. I'm going to keep him overnight to be on the safe side but you should be able to take him home in the morning."

"Then what do you mean by it's a first?" I asked.

From behind his back the doctor revealed a soggy, stringy thing. With finger and thumb from both hands he shook it out and held up a teeny, weeny lace thong.

"I'm not sure which one of you two this belongs to, but you might want to be a bit more careful where you leave such things." By now he was grinning broadly.

"It's not mine," Jenn said.

"And it's certainly not mine," I added.

"Well it surely can't belong to…" Dr. Jim began, looking aghast.

We all three gazed at the tiny undergarment, and a vision of the fifty-something Ardith Teasdale wearing it flashed into my mind; all five foot nothing and 300 pounds of her. It wasn't pretty.

Nine

"You haven't missed much," Rooster was reassuring me as he cut himself a hefty slice of pumpkin bread.

"If you cut another piece of that I'll get coffee," I said, pulling a couple of mugs from the cupboard. "And plenty of butter for me."

We sat across the table from each other and for several minutes munched and sipped quietly 'til Rooster broke the silence.

"Tom was jittery as a junebug and getting pretty angry when I picked him up. I figured he might be about to start getting flashbacks, so I had him take some meds and go lie down as soon as we got here."

"I'm not surprised, poor guy. An experience like this must be rife with triggers." PTSD, which nearly all our residents suffered with, is a cascade of symptoms — anxiety, anger, withdrawal among others, leading to flashbacks. It's a terrible thing to go through, in many ways because it's an invisible wound. Rooster was a rock at times like these and I felt a wave of gratitude that he'd come into our lives.

I bit into my pumpkin bread. "Was Tom able to tell you anything?"

"I let him be for now. I did get to have a few words with Felicks, though, and Tom is no longer at the top of the suspect list, though is still a person of interest."

"He still could have been the intended victim," I reminded Rooster.

"Could be, but I believe Felicks is concentrating now on the possibility that something was going on between Slattery and Ward Nesmith."

That was good to know. Rooster and Sheriff Wisniewski were good buddies and the top cop would sometimes drop inside information on Rooster. But why would he suspect there was link between the two men? I asked Rooster the question and he gave me a "Dunno."

I dunked my last piece of buttered bread in my coffee. Did you know butter stirred into coffee tastes delicious? Seriously, you should try it sometime. Grass-fed butter is best.

"By the way," I said, "where are Mom and Tyler?"

"Your mother's also taking a nap. She's hardly slept since the murder took place. And Tyler figured he'd check in at his office, said something about a new listing."

"How are we supposed to catch a killer if everyone disappears?"

Rooster gave me a "cut the nonsense look" and picked up a sheet of paper from the table.

"They went through the notes the residents wrote up and made a summary of relevant facts."

"Great. That's what we were working on when I got called away. Let me take a look." I snatched the paper and here's what I read:

- Early morning: Mom put the Santa outfit in the bathroom by the back door of the farmhouse. *Anyone who had access to the house could have known it was there. The general public did not have access.*

- The train was at the back of the farmhouse all day. *Various people worked on it throughout the day, and loaded the gifts in the carts. As far as we know, there was no-one with the train after Carl left at 6.20.*

- No-one recalls seeing Tom after about 5.30 when he said he was going to get ready for his Santa appearance. He reappeared when the body was found in the train at about 6.50. *Where was Tom during that time? Was Tom the intended victim? Who would have a motive to kill Tom?*

- Ward Nesmith was seen by several residents. Having been here a few times he was easily recognizable to them. No-one spoke to him or noticed if he was with anyone, except for Rooster who saw him with Slattery. (At that time, Rooster didn't know who Slattery was). *Why was Nesmith here? He must know he's not popular with any of us. What did he and Slattery have to talk about?*

- Chandler Slattery was unknown to all of us except Tyler, who did not notice him at the Open House. Several months ago Slattery made known his interest in buying Welcome Home but his offer was refused. *Was Slattery here merely to enjoy the festivities (unlikely) or to scope out the property (more likely). Why does the Sheriff have an interest in Slattery and Nesmith? Could they have been colluding to force us to sell?*

- From 6.20 on, all the residents, except Tom, claim to have been at their posts and are able to alibi each other. *Where was Tom? It's possible more than one person was involved in the murder, in which case some of the alibis could be suspect.*

"Jeez, the only thing this does is reinforce that we don't know anything!" I tossed the paper aside. "As I've said before, we need to find out from Tom what he was up to. And we should to talk to Nesmith; ask him about his relationship with the victim."

"And how do you propose to do that? You'd better not be thinking of approaching him on your own. He could be a killer."

"For goodness sakes, does nobody trust my judgement?"

Rooster's brows raised in quizzical fashion.

I huffed loudly. "Oh, alright. Maybe I have been a little hasty in the past, and maybe it did get me in a bit of trouble..."

A slight cough came from Rooster and he pursed his lips. *The man has a knack of getting his point across without saying a word.*

"OK, OK. I'll be a good girl. I'll ask Tyler to come with me."

"Not good enough. I want your pledge."

I grit my teeth and glared. Of course, it didn't make any difference. Once he set his mind to something Rooster was immovable, and I knew when I was beaten. So, meekly I raised my right hand and intoned, "I swear on the lives of all my furbabies that I will not approach Ward Nesmith alone. Satisfied?"

In response Rooster gave a barely perceptible nod.

"Well, if it meets with your approval," my voice was laced with sarcasm, "I'm off to see Dorcas."

Again with the slight nod so, feeling exasperated, I spun around and marched off.

Ten

Dorcas Phipps had moved her van to the side of the house where she'd hooked up to an electric outlet. Now that the yellow police tape had been removed I assumed Mom had told her it was OK to do so, but it made me wonder just how long she planned to hang around. I mean, if Mule's mother, Charlotte, combined with the full complement of Welcome Home's residents, hadn't found the pup by now, then I had to conclude this was a story with a sad ending.

It made me sick to think of all the dreadful things that might have happened so I shoved my thoughts aside and banged on the camper's door. Squeaky yips answered the noise – the two remaining puppies - though the door did not open.

"Over here!" As I was about to knock again I heard Dorcas call. She came from the back of the house with Charlotte on one of those extendable leads, and I could tell by the bits of twigs and leaves stuck on them that they must have been searching in the trees.

"We were raking about in case Mule got caught in some underbrush. If he dug down a bit it's possible he created a warm spot ..."

The look on my face must have said all I was thinking. Dorcas shut up and dropped her gaze to the dog.

"I feel so guilty." A sob cracked her voice and in a wave of sympathy I put my arms around her.

Her reaction wasn't quite what I expected. She stiffened and pulled away.

"Sorry," she whispered. "Sorry. I, uh..." She shivered – not from the cold, I'm sure – before pulling herself together and giving me a thin smile. "I think the reality is setting in. He's gone isn't he?"

I pictured Mule's wrinkled bulldog puppy face. The black-rimmed eyes, the smudge above his mouth and the little brown spot perfectly placed on top of his head. I remembered how he reacted when I found him in the train; completely unruffled yet glad for attention. So young and already with so much personality. I wanted to lie to Dorcas and tell her there was still hope, but I figured that would be delaying the inevitable.

"I wish I could tell you everything will turn out fine. Truth is, it doesn't look that way." I paused, waiting for Dorcas to speak. When she didn't, I continued, gently. "Don't you think it's time for you to go home?"

In an instant, Dorcas's face tightened and her tone became waspish. "You're telling me to leave?"

"Well, no. I, uh, just thought you'd be happier in your own home." I glanced at the dog. "And it can't be easy living out of your van with Charlotte and the pups."

"So now you're telling me how to take care of my bulldogs?"

Duh? Aren't you the one who lost Mule? I didn't say that, of course, but my hackles were rising. We'd done nothing but try and help the woman and now she was turning on us.

Perhaps sensing my ire, Dorcas suddenly deflated. *Good grief, the woman was a chameleon.*

"Polly, forgive me. Your family have been wonderful. And you're right, I should go home, at least then I'd probably get a good night's sleep; I'm not feeling very well at the moment."

I studied her face and noticed the sunken eyes and gray pallor to her skin.

"Look, Dorcas, you're no good to anybody if you don't take care of yourself."

She hesitated. "You're right. Do you mind, though, if I wait 'til the morning to leave? For now I just need to lie down."

"Sure. Is there anything I can get you?"

"No thanks. I'll be fine."

I watched her enter the van. The puppies tumbled excitedly around their mother, the show of happiness lifting my spirits. The feeling didn't last but a minute. As soon as I turned and took in the sight of the decorations around the house my good humor left me. So much effort had been put into creating our Christmas realm, and not a light had been turned on.

I wanted Christmas back. That meant I needed answers. Tom Ouelette might have some of those answers, so I squared my shoulders and strode to the barn to confront him.

The lower level of the barn was one large room with a kitchenette at the far side. Gerry and another guy were leaning against the counter, sodas in hand as they talked.

"What number is Tom's room?" I asked.

They showed no surprise at my abrupt question and the answer came back promptly, "Four."

I took the stairs two at a time and stopped in front of the door with a 4 on it. That's when I wavered. What if something I said or did sparked a flashback? I couldn't imagine Gerry would have let me come up here if there was any danger. Still, it might be prudent of me to enlist Rooster's help. Come to think of it, Rooster was likely to be pretty pissed if I approached Tom without him.

With hand fisted ready to knock, these thoughts raced through my mind, when the door slowly opened a few inches.

"Hayley?"

She put her finger to her lips and glanced back into the room, then slipped out, closing the door behind her.

"He's sleeping," she said.

"What are you doing here?" I knew I sounded suspicious but as I watched color rise in Hayley's face I knew my feelings were right.

Hayley cocked her head to the side. "Let's go somewhere private."

I followed her out of the barn and wordlessly we went to the farmhouse, where she had a room upstairs. I entered ahead of her and sat on the single chair and waited. Hayley stood, moving her weight from one foot to another then suddenly reached past me, grabbing a photograph from the nightstand and holding it out for me.

"You and Tom?" The picture was a selfie, a head shot of Hayley and Tom, cheek to cheek and grinning like sappy lovers.

"It started about three months ago," Hayley said. "I was an Army medic, and struggled with PTSD myself, so it's not unusual for the guys to talk to me about their problems. With Tom it turned into something different but we agreed it would be best to keep it quiet. On one hand I didn't want the others to feel they shouldn't talk to me, and then there were a few who had come on to me in the past, and I was concerned jealousy would raise its ugly head. I'd made it clear when I came here that I wasn't available to anyone, then Tom just, you know, happened."

Yeah, I could understand that.

"Listen, your relationship is none of my business so long as it doesn't interfere with anything else at Welcome Home."

"That's just the point." Hayley hung her head, then sat on the edge of the bed, hands clasping her knees. "Gerry found out."

"Is he one of the ones who made a pass at you?"

"Yeah. I didn't realize his feelings went so deep. I mean, it's not like I'm a raving beauty or anything, but the male to female ratio is definitely in my favor."

She was wrong about the beauty part. She wasn't one of those typical Hollywood "beauties," who've all been sculpted to look the same, but had soft features, wide-set eyes and a generous mouth. I could see why men would fall for her.

"Did things get nasty with Gerry?"

"He was more hurt than angry. The thing is, it made me realize I should never have allowed the relationship with Tom to get so far. That's why Tom was late for the Open House."

"I don't get it."

Hayley leaned closer. "He was with me. Here, in my room." She took a deep breath and straightened up again.

"Gerry confronted me earlier in the day; he'd seen Tom and I together. So later, when Tom found me alone, I told him it was over. He wouldn't accept that and followed me here when I tried to get away from him. We argued. Neither of us realized how late it was until we thought we heard shrill barking. It must have been the puppy, Mule. We looked out the window in time to see the train moving off. Tom sprinted downstairs, and you know the rest."

"Not quite," I said. "Why were you in his room just now?" I pretty much knew the answer already, but I wanted to hear it from her.

"He needed me."

I lifted my brows and gave my best piercing look.

Hayley returned it with a winsome smile. "And I'm in love with him."

I reassured Hayley everything would work out OK for her and Tom. I'd explain the situation to the others and let Rooster face Sheriff Wisniewski with the news, because it was obvious Tom had not informed him where he was when the murder took place.

Oh. A thought struck me. Was it possible Gerry was angry enough to want to kill Tom? Could he have killed Santa thinking it was his nemesis?

Eleven

Tyler and I were parked across the street from Ward Nesmith's home in a middle-class subdivision of cookie cutter houses. The kind of houses where you could open your bedroom window and shake hands with your neighbor, the places were so close together.

True to my word I was not going it alone with Nesmith. Tyler had suggested we ambush him at home – er, I should say "approach" him at home – rather than his office, on the assumption it would be harder for him to get away from us. We'd easily found his address online and arrived a little before we anticipated he'd get there. The idea was to ring the doorbell before he got settled.

"Shouldn't he be here by now? What if he decided to go out to dinner?" I fidgeted in my seat.

"Stop jumping to conclusions," Tyler said, "like Gerry being the killer."

Oh, yeah. When I told Tyler my fears about Gerry he pointed out that Gerry had been alibied by at least a dozen people because he was part of the choir. They'd been in the small barn doing a final run-through of some of the songs, then walked together to the stage to get in place for the switching on of the lights.

Talking of lights, it was getting very dusky and the street lights were coming on. An old SUV turned into the road and then into the Nesmith driveway. The garage doors opened and the vehicle disappeared inside.

"Here we go," Tyler said.

At the front door, the only nod to Christmas was a tired-looking wreath. The doorbell didn't work so Tyler banged hard with his gloved hand, but it wasn't Ward who stood before us when the door opened. A young boy politely inquired "Can I help you?" He seemed to have a slight speech impediment – it came out more like "Can I hep you?" - but before we had a chance to reply a younger girl pushed in front of him, saying, "Hi, I'm Glory." In her arm she carried a chubby, wrinkly puppy with a smudge on his mouth and a brown splodge on top of his head. "And this is Olaf," said Glory, trying to thrust him forward for our inspection.

My jaw practically dropped to my knees. I knew the little bulldog pup as Mule. What shocked me even more were the braces on the child's legs and the wheeled walker she was hanging on to.

Tyler's ability to recover was much faster than mine. "Hello, Glory," he said and, "Hi, Olaf," scratching the puppy's brown spot.

"Children, who is it?" The woman who came up behind the kids tapped the boy lightly on his shoulder. When he turned his face to her she began to sign and mouthed words to him. In response, he bent down and took the puppy from the girl, saying in his stilted way, "Give me Olaf, Glory." *Good grief. The boy was deaf.*

The woman turned her attention to us and smiled warmly. I liked her instantly, which made me feel awkward about being there. Tyler, thankfully, was still in command of his feelings.

"We're here to see Ward," he said.

"Oh, of course. I didn't know he was expecting anyone. Come in, come in. You'll freeze out there." We stepped inside. "Ward got home only a few minutes ago, he's putting his slippers on. I'll go and tell him you're here. Oh, I don't know your names."

"It's alright, Merry. I'm here."

Ward Nesmith stood on the far side of the room. My first impression was that he looked defeated, but when Glory called out, "Daddy, Daddy," and hurried to him as fast as her braces and walker would take her, his whole being changed. He caught her in his arms and twirled around.

"How is my beautiful princess?"

Glory laughed with glee, and beside me Merry spoke in a low voice. "He gets so tired and he works so hard, but the children always make him feel better."

On the contrary, I was now feeling decidedly glum. Had we walked onto the set of "A Christmas Carol?" The Nesmith's were beginning to look like Bob Cratchit and his wife, with Glory playing the part of Tiny Tim. Did that make me Scrooge?

Cratchit, uh, I mean Nesmith, hugged his son then turned to his wife. "I think a little hot chocolate would be nice, my dear. The children can help you."

She understood his veiled request for privacy and ushered the kids away with promises of extra marshmallows.

Nesmith's expression turned suspicious. "What are you doing here?"

Again, Tyler took the lead. "I'm truly sorry we burst in on your family this way. I hope you understand we're here on behalf of the veterans at Welcome Home. This murder is jeopardizing their welfare. We heard recently that you knew Chandler Slattery and are hoping you can answer a few questions."

Delicately put, my wonderful guy.

"Like did I kill the man?" Nesmith wasn't being at all delicate.

I finally found my voice. "Did you?"

He sighed heavily. "You'd better sit down."

We dropped onto a small loveseat and waited while Nesmith appeared to gather his thoughts. I took the time to look around at the worn furniture and fraying carpet. In spite of the furnishings having seen better days, the room had a cozy, welcoming feel. Homemade Christmas ornaments decked the mantel where a fire was burning. In the corner a live spruce tree was hung with glass balls and strings of popcorn, and fresh cut holly had been arranged in vases.

Something touched my foot. I looked down and there was Mule – or should I say, Olaf – attacking my bootlaces. I picked him up and hugged him, reveling in his warmth and his puppy breath, and ridiculously grateful he was alive.

"Perhaps we could start with him," I said to Nesmith.

"Let me tell it my way," he said. And he did.

"Chandler Slattery approached me right after I did the first inspection at Welcome Home. He wanted me to find reasons to stop construction on the barns, and offered me a lot of money to do it."

"So that's why you forced us to make changes. You were trying to get us to give up!"

Keeping his tone even but firm, Nesmith replied. "No. Those changes were to bring the construction up to code, necessary for the safety of the residents. Something the previous inspector should have made sure of. And as it happens, I turned Slattery down flat. Much as the money was tempting, I am a man of principal and never wished to put the veterans at risk of losing their homes."

"Well you did," I snapped.

Nesmith started. "They were still able to live there while changes were made."

"True enough. But their housing benefits were withheld. It was lucky we had enough funds in reserve to keep going."

He looked stricken. "I'm sorry. I guess I could have handled things better."

I wasn't sure how to respond to that, but I didn't have to. Merry Nesmith stepped into the room.

"I need to say something." Directing her attention to her husband she added, "The kids are making the hot chocolate." Then to Tyler and me she said, "I wanted to listen. I know who you are, Polly. Ward talked a lot about your veterans' home and he was very impressed with what you were doing. I also know my husband will never defend himself when it comes to his job..."

"Merry," Ward stopped her. "Don't make excuses."

Tenderly she touched the back of her hand to his cheek. "Alright, no excuses, but I want them to know there was a reason you were struggling with work at that time."

Talking again to us she continued. "Glory was being fitted for her leg braces and it wasn't going well. She has cerebral palsy, caused by her mother violently and repeatedly shaking her as a baby. The leg braces gave her the chance to have some independence and a little normality in her life. Without them she'd be confined to a wheelchair. You can imagine how stressful it was for us.

"The situation with Slattery didn't help. It wasn't as simple as Ward implied. The man kept badgering him, even threatened his job. Honestly, we were scared. Then when I saw that dreadful man at the Christmas event, and he had the nerve to plague Ward again, well, I could have killed him myself." In an aside she added, "I didn't."

"Tell me," Tyler asked, "did either of you see Slattery with anyone else, or did he say anything to suggest he could be in danger?"

"We were there for a fun family night out," Ward said. "After I brushed him off we stayed as far from him as possible."

"I don't know if it helps," Merry absent mindedly toyed with a cross around her neck, "but I did hear a rumor that Slattery's wife was going to divorce him. Apparently, he was something of a ladies' man and she'd had enough."

"You think his wife killed him?" I asked.

"I'm not sure what I think. She's the one who had the money, I'm told, and I don't suppose he'd want to give that up."

"But he had a successful business; money wouldn't be an issue."

"Oh, it was." Ward said. "His company was in trouble, that's why he was so desperate to get your property cheap."

Wow. This visit was turning out to be quite a revelation.

All this time, Mule/Olaf had been dozing on his back in my lap. I tickled his tummy, his legs twitched and he made sleepy squeaking noises. All eyes were drawn to the display of cuteness.

"We have to deal with this," I said.

Merry and Ward exchanged anxious glances. It was Merry who spoke.

"We knew it couldn't last. When Glory saw the pups at the Open House, she instantly fell in love. We tried to explain we couldn't afford a puppy but her heart had been stolen. It wasn't so different to the way Ward and I felt when we first saw Robby and Glory." She looked lovingly at her husband.

"We were devastated when we found out we couldn't have children, and the idea of adoption didn't appeal at all. Then one of our church members who fosters special needs kids brought a young boy to the Christmas Eve service: it was love at first sight. That was five years ago. Same thing with Glory. We've loved her now for a year; and Robby adores his little sister." She bit her lip. "That's why he took the puppy for her."

Once again I was stuck for words, and this time so was Tyler.

Wouldn't you know, it was at that awkward time the children came back with a tray of hot chocolate and cookies. Glory's face lit up at the sight of the puppy and she came over to me and kissed his nose, ever so softly. Robby followed and offered the tray.

"You have to eat a cookie. Me and Robby helped Mommy make them, then we decorated them. You should have that one," Glory nudged a cookie toward me. "I did that one, it's a Christmas tree."

She was so proud of herself. Dutifully I took a bite. "It's delicious." *Really, it was.*

"Children," I heard Merry's voice, "there's something we have to talk about." Her hands flew as she signed to Robby.

"Oh... uh..." I almost choked on my cookie. I knew she was going to say the puppy had to be returned and I wasn't at all sure that was the thing to do. "Why don't we talk about this later? We can work something out."

Ward's brow wrinkled. "The kids have to learn to do the right thing."

"I get that, I do. All I'm saying is, let's take some time to figure out exactly what the right thing is."

"Polly, I appreciate what you're trying to do, but we can't afford to take care…"

"Stop right there." I waved my hand before he said something in front of Glory and Robby. "Please give me a chance to think of something."

He opened his mouth to reply when Merry took his hand. "Ward. Please."

Under his wife's pleading look, Ward caved. But only a little.

"We'll take the puppy to the rescue place in the morning."

"Come to Welcome Home. Dorcas Phipps is still there with the pup's mother. If you can be there about ten I'll make sure she's available."

Glory wrinkled her face in puzzlement. "Is Olaf going to see his mommy?"

"Yes, darling," Merry said.

"Oh, goodie." She beamed. "You'll like that, won't you Olaf?"

A few minutes later Tyler and I crossed the road and got in the car. Glory had insisted we finish our cookies and hot chocolate, then both kids hugged us goodbye as if we were their favorite aunt and uncle.

"Do you feel as humbled as I do?" I asked.

"Probably more," Tyler said.

"We had Ward pegged completely wrong. What a lovely family they are."

Tyler nodded. "What are you going to do about Mule?"

"Olaf," I corrected. "I have absolutely no idea."

Twelve

Something was tickling my nose. In my half-awake state I swatted at it and felt fur. Amber! My little calico. Sometimes she likes to stick her nose in my ear or chew my hair; either way she won't stop 'til I get up. I twisted as best I could with two other cats and three dogs on the bed with me, to look at the clock. Seven.

I pushed my furkids aside. Time to get up. I wanted to be out at the farm to talk to Dorcas before the Nesmiths arrived.

Tyler had driven me back to the farmhouse last night where I'd found Dorcas in her camper. When I told her Mule was safe and would be back at ten in the morning she burst into tears and sank to the floor. Alarmed, I helped her onto the bed. She looked pretty ragged but insisted she was OK.

"I've been so worried, I haven't been sleeping."

"Let me bring you some chamomile tea," I said. "That always helps me."

It wasn't the right time to discuss Mule's future, so I gathered up the dogs and came back to my little house in town. The cats were delighted to have me back as usual. On the few occasions I stay with Mom I take them with me but this time, with all the noise and activity going on, I decided they'd be happier at home. Still, they missed the company so I skipped my morning coffee to give the three of them some extra cuddling before rushing out again with Vinny, Coco and Angel.

A couple of the veterans were walking dogs as I pulled into Welcome Home, and Rooster was leaning against the porch railings, coffee mug in hand, keeping an eye on Elaine as she went about her morning business. I caught a whiff of the strong brew as I went up the steps and decided I'd better fuel myself with some caffeine before I tackled Dorcas.

There was always a pot of coffee on in the kitchen. The rule was whoever poured the last cup started the next pot. Helping myself to a couple of cookies as well I stood munching and nibbling, looking out the back window. A beautiful red cardinal landed on a branch and began preening. How nice, I thought, to have at least one splash of color when everything else seemed so drab.

Not just one, I realized as my attention was drawn to a stirring deeper in the trees where I caught a flash of blue. What was it? One of the dogs?

Setting my nearly empty cup down I went out the back door and headed toward the disturbance. Now I could tell it was someone on hands and knees who appeared to be digging. Or were they hacking at tree roots?

My approach was pretty noisy; I had no reason for stealth. The figure suddenly stiffened and straightened, then Dorcas Phipps turned her head to look at me.

"What on earth are you doing?" I asked, gazing at the butcher's knife in her hand and stupidly wondering if she was cutting greens for Christmas decorations. The look of guilt I then noted on her face dispelled that notion, and in rapid succession other thoughts fired in my brain and I knew I was facing a killer.

Dorcas stood and squared off in front of me, knife pointing my way.

I tried to stay calm and calculate my chances if I ran. We were about the same height, but would my fear give me an edge over her compulsion to fight? *Talk her down*, I told myself. *Isn't that what you're supposed to do?*

"Killing me won't help, Dorcas. You'll never get away with it."

She took a step toward me and I stepped back. "I must say, it was clever of you to dress the body in the Santa suit. That is what you did, isn't it? I can admire that kind of fast-thinking because I'm sure you didn't plan to kill Slattery, did you?"

"He hurt me. He'd said he loved me and wanted to be with me, but it was all a lie. When I confronted him he laughed. Do you believe that? He laughed at me, and what do you think I did? I *begged* him. I made a bigger fool of myself than I already had and I begged him to leave his wife and be with me. Then he laughed even harder and it made me so angry," now she was sobbing.

"I wasn't thinking. I don't even remember picking the stone up but there it was in my hand and I hit him. It made a soft thudding noise and he gave me a look of such surprise, then he crumpled. I looked at the stone and it was a Santa head: red hat, white whiskers and chubby red cheeks. It looked at me as if it was accusing me and I just

555

wanted to get rid of it, so I threw it as far away as I could, into the trees. But it reminded me I'd seen a Santa suit in the bathroom when I'd gone in there earlier, and it gave me an idea."

"You dressed Slattery in the suit. That was a heck of a risk, though. Tom was supposed to be getting ready by then, he could have turned up at any moment."

"Maybe that wasn't the best idea. Believe it or not, you don't think straight when you've just killed your lover." She laughed maniacally. *Oh, Lord, she was losing it.* "I thought I was buying time to distance myself from what happened."

"Did you know then that Mule was missing?" In spite of being in danger I was still trying to piece together all the facts.

Dorcas managed to look contrite. "I didn't realize 'til after. That's when I began to be glad Chandler was dead. Because of him I'd left the dogs unattended, otherwise Mule would be safe."

"He is safe now, Dorcas." I kept my voice low. "He'll be here very soon. Don't you want to see him?"

"Of course I do," she snapped. "But I have to take care of you first," and she held the knife out, taking another step nearer.

OK, the talking thing wasn't working; it was time to run. I spun quickly, only to snag my foot on a tangle of dead vines. I went down on my side, my foot twisting beneath me and a searing pain shot through my ankle. I tried to shake free but the vine might as well have been nylon filament, it wouldn't give.

I looked up. Dorcas was almost on me and from somewhere nearby I heard high-pitched yips and a voice yelling, "Hey." Dorcas hesitated, looking away in confusion, then a body hurled past me and charged into her, knocking her to the ground. The knife flew from her grasp and embedded itself in the trunk of an Eastern White Pine.

You probably think it was Tyler who saved me, seeing as it's usually his role. This time, however, it was Ward Nesmith. Who knew he could move like a linebacker?

The Nesmiths had arrived and parked beside Dorcas's camper van. Ward knocked and the dogs made noise. Mule/Olaf got excited. Realizing Dorcas was not there, Merry suggested they move away so the puppy would calm down and they walked behind the house. It was the pups continued yapping that distracted Dorcas from knifing me, and it was Robby who saw something was wrong. He nudged his dad and Ward sprinted into action.

We were all still behind the farmhouse. Rooster and a couple of the other guys had taken hold of Dorcas, who had completely deflated. Mom was fussing over my ankle, telling me an ambulance was on the way. Merry had sent the children closer to the trees where they were playing with Mule and his siblings, and their mother, who had been released from the camper. Ward was sitting next to me on the back stairs while Merry dabbed peroxide on a couple of scratches he'd got on his face.

"I see my knight in shining armor status has been challenged." Tyler had walked up unnoticed. His gaze went from me to Ward, then he held out his hand. "And all I can say is, thank you."

Ward grasped the hand and both men shook solemnly. Soon after, Sheriff Wisniewski arrived, which gave me the opportunity to say we'd solved his case for him. I have to give him credit, he took it well, but did say he'd learned of the affair between Dorcas and the victim and had been taking a closer look at her.

"When it came to the ladies," the Sheriff said, "Slattery was a busy boy."

"I feel sorry for Dorcas," I said.

"I don't," Mom snapped.

"She's what, fortyish? Never married. Her life has revolved around her beloved bulldogs. She's not someone men pay attention to, then suddenly there's this charismatic guy who sweeps her off her feet. She fell big time and he turned out to be scum."

"What will happen to her dogs now?" Merry asked.

"There are other people involved with the rescue. They'll be taken care of, and I'm quite sure there won't be any problem now with adopting Mule."

"Oh, Polly," Merry sighed. "There's still a problem with the cost."

"We have an idea for that," Mom said. "Polly and I talked last night. We can always use extra help around here and we thought the kids could come over, say a couple of times a month, and do a few chores in exchange for dog food and supplies."

Ward shook his head. "There are still vet bills and other expenses..."

"Come on hon," Merry gave his shoulder a squeeze, "we can work it out. I can help, too, and..."

"Mom! Mom!" Glory's urgent call interrupted. "Look what Olaf found."

Merry hurried to the children and took something from her child. She went quite still, staring at it, then called back to us. "It's a gnome's head."

Olaf, formerly known as Mule, had found the head in a hole under a tree root. We guessed that when Dorcas tossed the thing it must have hit a branch, bounced back and rolled into its hiding place. Remarkably, it hadn't broken. All the time Dorcas claimed to be searching in the trees for the puppy she'd been looking to find the gnome head and destroy it, fearful her fingerprints were on it. After being slobbered on by dogs and handled by the kids, there was little likelihood of that now. Good thing she'd confessed.

I felt kind of stupid that I hadn't suspected Dorcas. Think of it. She was so adamant about staying close to the scene of the crime, but it was to follow the murder investigation, not to find a lost puppy. Then when she fell apart telling me how guilty she felt, she was talking about the murder, and I assumed it was about losing Olaf.

Oh, well. Things turned out alright in the end.

Thirteen

Vinny looked adorable in his elf outfit, only no-one in the audience could see it because he was refusing to come on stage. It had been set up as Santa's workshop and Vinny, followed by Coco (looking equally adorable, I must say), were supposed to enter carrying gifts.

In a low voice I did my best to coax Vinny. It wasn't that he was unwilling, he just got distracted easily and at the moment was showing more interest in the leg of a table holding props. In an effort to spur him on, Tyler tossed the gift onstage and gave Vinny a shove. In return Vinny sniffed his rear and the crowd, finally able to see him, shouted encouragement.

"Vinny," I whispered. "Chicken," and showed him a piece of meat tucked in my hand. I guess he didn't see it, but Coco certainly did. She burst onto the stage and tore around in circles then jumped up and down trying to get my attention. In an attempt to go on with the show I signaled Tyler to let Angel go. She stepped onto the stage and in a couple of deft moves with her paw pulled off her reindeer antlers and harness, then lay on her stomach daring me to try and put them back on.

The good thing is the audience was loving it. And after this fiasco maybe Mom wouldn't make me do anything next year.

While people were still cheering I gathered my mutts and made my escape to the house. At the porch I stopped and looked out at the brightly lit trees, the Santa train, reindeer, snowmen and yes, gnome elves. So many people had come back even after the tragedy of the week before and there were lots of familiar faces, friends old and new.

The Nesmiths were among them, but without Olaf who was safe at home. We'd already put the kids to work, Robby helping Tyler with props for the show, and Glory was designated to add sprinkles to the cookies as Scott and Lou baked them.

This was the part of Christmas I loved best. People embracing the giving spirit. Some, like our veterans and volunteers, gave their time and expertise to create enjoyment and raise funds for our shelter. Others gave their support through donations or showed it just by turning up at our events and making our efforts worthwhile.

For a few moments more I watched the smiling faces and my heart swelled with joy. A voice from the crowd called out, "Merry Christmas, Polly," and was soon joined by a chorus of others. I couldn't tell who it was, but I raised my hand and waved madly, "Merry Christmas everyone," as the choir began to sing, "Joy to the World."

Free short story offer

Go here to get a FREE short story from Liz, and become part of the In Crowd:

http://lizdodwell.com/signup/

Get the next book in the series:

Valentine's Day
https://www.amazon.com/dp/B06VTKF6P8

Find all of Liz's stories here:
http://lizdodwell.com/books/

Look for the audio books on Audible.com

Are you a coloring enthusiast? Here's where you'll find Liz's coloring books:

http://www.mix-booksonline.com/category/coloring-books

Independent authors such as myself rely heavily on your feedback and support. So please leave a review; your words are much appreciated.
Liz

Liz Dodwell

...devotes her time to writing and publishing from the home she shares with husband, Alex and a host of rescued dogs and cats, collectively known as "the kids." She will tell you, "I gladly suffer the luxury of working from home where I'm with my 'kids,' can toss in a load of laundry in between plotting, writing, editing and general office work while still in my PJs. I love what I do and know how lucky I am to be able to do it. Oh, and if you asked me what my hobbies are, I'd probably say reading murder mysteries, drinking champagne, romantic dinners with my husband and yodeling (just joking about that last one)."